Blue Moon

Kevin Bouchard

Cover Art:
Michelle Crocker

http://mlcdesigns4you.weebly.com/

Publisher's Note:

Solstice Publishing - www.solsticepublishing.com

Blue Moon

Kevin Bouchard

Dedication:

To my wife Robin, the love of my life, the sort that comes
along once in a blue moon.

***Super Moon*: a full moon coinciding with the moon's closest proximity to the Earth during its elliptical orbit.**

Chapter One

H olding onto someone is like holding onto moonlight. I've heard that expression many times, but never stopped to consider its true meaning until this moment. I'm sitting on my back porch, watching the full moon carve a path through the summer sky, and all I can think of is that damned expression. It's scary what creeps into your brain when logic and reason have stepped out the back door.

Spooky, my Lhasa Apso, shudders in my lap. Stunned and confused by what has happened, by what she's *seen*, she looks to me with those bottomless black eyes asking questions in a tongue no human can speak, but which are as easy to decipher as a flashing red light at the scene of an accident. She's searching for some indication that her master is still in control. Dogs, like people, need to be reassured that no matter how terrible things get, we are still masters of our universe. But I can offer her no such reassurance; I'm too busy trying to conjure up some for myself.

The reality that had been as indisputable as the moon above has collapsed into a pile of rubble, much like the shattered porch light at my feet, and I find myself in a place where logic and myth intersect and reason falters like the flame of a dying candle. The moon is the one constant in all that has happened. It's a blue moon, the second full moon of the month, and a powerful omen to some. Only it's not blue, it's pink, tending toward red like a great spot of blood in the sky. I sense that it's watching me, has been for days. The Thunder Moon was what the meteorologist on television called it, doubtless a name derived from

Native American lore, an arcane reference to the thunderstorms that accompany the July heat.

Tonight, though, I've assigned a different meaning to the term; tonight I've decided that the moon's thunder is not the sort heard with the senses, but rather with the heart, with the mind. It's a sound that marks the end of one phase of life and the start of another, a change of internal seasons. Perhaps that's what the ancients meant after all. Tonight the moon is signaling the end of the world I knew and the beginning of a new, dark reality, once relegated to legend and superstition, now sentient and alive.

Despite all that has happened, all that is *still* happening, here I sit, my senses numb, my mind broken like the porch light, locked in a spell from which I must break free before it's too late.

Thunder rumbles in the distance, signaling the approach of a storm. The sound stirs me from my dark dream. Precious little time has passed since *they* disappeared into the night. I am hopeful that I am not too late. There are things I must do, things no one else *can* do. Two people are dead and the rampage is not over.

Spooky whines and nuzzles close, transfixed by the spot on the lawn where *they* stood. There is nothing there now, except perhaps an odor only a dog could detect. It's a spot Spooky will avoid for the rest of her days, a cold patch that will forever deny the sun's warmth.

In my brain a desperate plan begins to form. I have no guns, never believed in them, but I have the old baseball bat in the back of my SUV, the one I used as a boy to hit baseballs in the field behind this very house. And of course, there are knives in the kitchen.

I can't believe I am entertaining such thoughts, but drastic times call for drastic measures and deadly times call for deadly ones. To think that it had all been so ordinary, so comfortably routine just a short time ago ... but that wasn't true; things had been skidding off the road to ordinary for days.

It all began Tuesday evening. It was the night the Summer Harvest Fayre came to town, the night I found the first 'deposit'. That night had seen the last tranquil moment in my otherwise normal life. Since then, everything has gone to hell.

***

My name is Jack Graves and I teach high school history and literature in the town of Wickham, Massachusetts. My wife, Joanna, runs the library at the middle school; during the summer she works part time at the town library.

Summer is a relaxing time for us; we spend days at the beaches of Newport, cook out on our patio and vacation in southern Maine or Cape Cod. We take in movies, some at a nearby drive-in, one of the last in New England, and play cards with friends, not to mention the occasional visit to a nearby casino to try our luck, which is mediocre at best. I spend time working in our yard, maintaining the shrubs and lawn as well as servicing our hundred-year-old house, scraping and painting and repairing whatever needs to be scraped or painted or repaired. I occasionally take a course at nearby Bridgton University or tutor students at the town library. And of course there is the Fayre.

The Summer Harvest Fayre is a conglomeration of rides, games, entertainment, and food which provides a means for local schools and charitable organizations to raise needed funds, thereby filling financial shortfalls left by numerous budgetary cuts. Joanna heads the effort for her school, renting a booth, selling food items and using the profits to buy supplies deemed extraneous by the fiscal powers-that-be. Last summer she raised nearly twelve hundred dollars in one week by selling ice cream. She is quite the entrepreneur, though she would never brag about her successes. This year she is selling doughnuts and, as usual, I have volunteered my services.

The Fayre, with its pseudo-Medieval theme, rides and entertainment, serves as the perfect diversion for the summer-time doldrums. Such activities are, however, far cries from the grim task lying before me. Ironically it was one such routine activity that set things in motion. And, like the conflagration started by a careless match, what began so simply is now raging out of control and must run its course.

Someone once said that our choices define who we are and, on Tuesday night, I chose to mow the lawn. If I had waited one more day, perhaps things would have turned out differently. But looking back, I realize that the events that followed were somehow inevitable. I don't know what I would have done if I could have looked into the future and glimpsed what lay ahead. Nothing, I suppose, probably doubting the madness of the vision entirely. But hindsight is twenty-twenty and I suppose some things are simply meant to be.

In any event, the sun was still high in the sky on that beautiful evening as I broke out my mower and went to work. I was making good time listening to U-2's first batch of Greatest Hits on the Ipod Nano Joanna had given me for my birthday. Bono had just reached the final chorus of *All I Want is You* and was reaching for those high notes that screamed of desperate longing when I saw it.

Some years back I'd torn up a strip of earth running along the side of my garage. I'd staked the space off with edging, filled it with peat moss, and planted six carefully chosen white-tipped Hostas. They had taken to the mixture of shade and sun provided by the branches of the big red maple tree that occupied the center of our back yard and had flourished. I'd checked them only yesterday, weeding them and redressing the peat. But now it was clear that something had gotten to them. Some of the leaves on two of the plants, those directly beneath the tree, were burned yellow as if something acidic had been dumped on them. The peat surrounding them had been turned over as if an animal had been burrowing. And the leaves had been defaced by dark, fetid streaks.

Recalling the work I'd put into the project, I silenced the mower and the music, knelt beside the Hosta bed and considered the damaged plants. Flies buzzed busily around the leaves and the smell of smeared excrement was unmistakable. I winced, sitting back on my haunches, covering my mouth and nose. I was fuming. My first thoughts were of Spooky, but it was immediately evident that the damage was too extensive and the amount of urine and feces too copious to have been left by my thirteen-pound Lhasa. Besides, this was not a behavior she had ever exhibited; she usually relegated her business to the back portion of the yard. The peat was also disturbed in such a way that suggested that the intruder was much larger. One culprit came to mind and my blood began to boil. Rufus.

Rufus is the German shepherd that lived in the dilapidated hovel immediately to the north of my property. Once before, Rufus had cleared our fence and torn apart our trash barrels and, at Joanna's insistence, I had spoken to his owner, a slovenly character named Bob Renko.

Renko was a walking lump of apathy who managed to look unshaven but never managed to grow a beard, drank too much and let his house and lot go to hell, dragging down everyone else's property value. Futile was the word I used when Joanna asked me to speak to him. Waste of time was the phrase I offered as a follow-up when she pressed her point, arguing that neighbors deserve our best efforts, at least once.

Resigned to the task, armed with my doubts and Joanna's best intentions, I approached Renko, who, to my surprise, swore that Rufus would not pay us a return visit. No neighborly small talk followed; there was no handshake to seal the deal. But in the end Renko proved to be a man of his word and Rufus had caused no more trouble. That is, until now.

I strode to the chain-link fence that ran the length of my driveway to stare intently at the rotting hulk my neighbor called a house, my anger growing like one of the weeds that ruled his yard. I would gladly have gone over and pounded on the oversized paint chip that served as a door, but Renko's rusted-out pick-up truck was nowhere in sight; he was not at home and I was in no mood to waste my time.

Most people would have taken Renko at face value, but such consideration was beyond my capacity. I'm the sort who follows the rules, cuts my lawn regularly, and pays my taxes. I would be hard-pressed to produce a speeding or parking ticket, and as such, I suppose I had been looking for a fresh reason to dislike my neighbor. Rufus had conveniently provided me with one.

As I shook my head in disgust, another plan crept into my fevered brain, an infinitely more delicious plan. I've often quipped about celebrities who join the self-help circuit, becoming card-carrying members of what I like to call the Church of I-Have-Way-Too-Much-Free-Time-on-My-Hands. But perhaps, in my own way, I am equally guilty. With the summer at my disposal, I sometimes look for diversions, and unfortunately, not all efforts lead to productive ends.

Standing at my fence, fuming over what I presumed to be an affront to my property, I stumbled upon my latest diversion. My plan was simple: using a plastic baggy to transport the filthy offerings, I would return the 'deposit' to its rightful owner. Renko would creep in at two AM after shutting down whichever dank watering hole he frequented, only to stumble upon the urine and fecal-spattered leaves which would be awaiting him like a long-lost friend.

A smile lit on my face as I perceived the simplistic genius of my scheme.

Freshly energized, I returned to the John Deere and finished mowing the lawn in record time, my mental wheels spinning faster with each swath of lawn trimmed. When I finished bagging the clippings, setting them on the far side of the garage to await my weekly trip to the dump, and putting the mower away, I went inside to set my plan in motion.

I found Joanna standing at the kitchen sink, slicing vegetables for supper. She looked as amazing as ever in her bare feet, worn jeans, and black tank top. Sun streaming in through the windows above the sink cascaded down over her shoulders like molten light turning her tanned flesh to gold. Her jet-black hair hung in a pony-tail against the nape of her neck, the tendrils stirring ever-so-slightly, teased by a gentle breeze drifting through the window.

"Done with the lawn?"

"Not quite," I said re-focusing on the task at hand. I went to the bank of drawers beside the refrigerator and withdrew a sandwich-sized baggy, thought better of it and retrieved a gallon-sized one. Then I went to the drawer at the far end of the counter and scooped up a pair of tongs.

"What are you doing?" Joanna asked in the sing-song voice she usually reserved for children during the town library's Saturday Story Time.

"Rufus crapped in the Hosta bed," I said deciding against the tongs and fetching some paper towels from the roll beneath the island instead.

"How do you know it was Rufus?" she asked, switching deftly to her voice of reason mode. "It was probably just Spooky."

Spooky, who had been dozing in the bedroom doorway, raised her shaggy old head at the mention of her name.

"There's too much for Spooky to be the culprit," I countered heading for the door, hoping to make my escape without further interrogation.

"Bad girl," Joanna chided and Spooky uttered an indignant snort before resuming her repose.

11

Counting my lucky stars for my clean getaway, I'd barely set one foot in the service porch, when Joanna started in again.

"So what are you planning to do?"

"I'm going to bag it and return it to Renko," I blurted out, immediately regretting my slip. I must confess that hearing my plan stated aloud actually made some part of my brain cringe. "See how he likes it," I added half-heartedly hoping to drum up support, but sensing defeat before the words left my mouth.

"Wait," she said setting down the knife, but still not turning to confront me. "We spoke to Bob about Rufus knocking over the trash cans, and it hasn't happened since." She glanced back at me, her green eyes winking in the sunlight. "Why can't you let sleeping dogs lie?"

I started to speak, but was overcome by a sense of foolishness. Where do women get the knack for making a man's cleverest notions seem infantile?

"When we see him, we'll ask him if Rufus got loose again," she said picking up the knife and returning to the cutting. "Until then, just let it be."

There was an air of finality in her tone. "Now, these vegetables are almost ready and the steaks are begging to be cooked. Why don't you start the grill so we can eat?"

"All right," I said, studying the baggy in my hand with the enthusiasm of a man heading to the gallows. She was right and, at a cerebral level, I damn well knew it. But my primordial brain stem was still seething.

"Thanks, Hon," she said with a playfully patronizing tone.

Resigned to Joanna's logic, I let myself out and headed to the Hosta bed to clean up the mess. The sound of an old engine rattling like a collection of tin cans shattered the tranquil afternoon and I turned to see Renko, Rufus in tow, bounding down his back steps, and hopping into his idling truck. The man had evidently come home to make a

12

pit stop while I was in the house watching Joanna shoot down my revenge plot.

Fresh anger lit in my brain and I stopped to watch Rufus assume the shotgun position in the truck's cab, peering out the filthy window at me, his tongue lolling out of his mouth like a strip of raw bacon. Renko gunned the old engine and backed out into the street, kicking up a cloud of dirt.

That did it. The image of Rufus mocking me was simply too much.

Seething, I went to the Hosta bed and, using the wad of paper towels I had fetched, snapped off the decimated leaves with their fecal coating, and dropped them into the baggy. Then I stuffed the used paper towels in as well. I sealed the baggy, took two steps toward my gate with every intention of heading over to Renko's back porch to make my own 'deposit', but stopped when I thought of 'Gospel' Tom.

'Gospel' Tom Williams, as he was known, was a high school friend who had received a BS in chemical engineering from UMASS, Amherst, followed by an MS from MIT. He had since evolved into a local science wizard, a Gandalf for suburbia, a man who could decipher any chemical problem with any swimming pool, or analyze a lawn to determine how much of what was needed to bring it up to snuff. If Tom recommended a line of treatment, it was as good as Gospel, hence his nickname, 'Gospel' Tom.

Tom kept a working lab in his basement, much to the dismay of his relatively new wife, Alice, a woman who seemingly found *everything* Tom did to be annoying. I wasn't sure if anyone could determine whether Rufus was the culprit, but if it was possible, 'Gospel' Tom Williams, with his home lab and access to his company's extensive equipment, would be the man for the job.

I found myself grinning uncontrollably at my newly devised scheme and studied the plastic baggy's disgusting contents with sick glee. Scientific proof was something Joanna could not refute.

Tomorrow was Wednesday; Joanna had already made arrangements to go shopping with my sister, Ellen, before heading out to the Fayre. Macy's, it seemed, was having a sale. I could drop the sample off with Tom while she was gone.

I went to the garage, beaming with anticipation, and set the sealed baggy in the way back of my SUV.

I stood for a moment considering my handiwork, basking in the late afternoon sunlight streaming in through the open bay door of the garage. All was once again right with the world.

Supremely satisfied with my efforts, I headed back to the house, flicked on the Weber as I crossed the patio, and went inside to help Joanna.

Chapter Two

Supper went well; it's tough to ruin steaks, baked potatoes, and salads, especially on a beautiful summer evening. After we cleaned up, we returned to the patio, me with my coffee and Joanna with her Earl Grey with lemon and honey to bask in what she liked to call 'the gloaming'.

Relaxing as a Henry James summer afternoon faded into twilight, I found myself gazing out into the acre-sized field that abuts our back yard. An extension of a piece of property situated at the southeast corner of our oversized block, this overgrown stretch of land was, as always at this time of year, rich with an assortment of summer weeds, grasses and a few young trees.

"I used to play baseball in that field," I said, admiring the way the evening breeze caused the sun drenched grasses to undulate like a sea of molten gold.

"Shortstop," Joanna said between sips. The steam from her Best Story-teller, Ever mug caused her eyes to shimmer as a mischievous little grin crept across her lips. "Derek Jeter," she teased, laughing her dirty laugh.

"Now you did it," I said feigning anger, my life-long Red Sox fan pride reeling. "I don't care if he *is* retired, I just ate supper and now I've got to throw up."

"Oh, stop," she said giggling to the point where she had to set her tea down to keep from spilling it. "You know I'm a Sox fan; you wouldn't have married me if I wasn't. Besides, you've told me the 'baseball in the field' story a hundred times. I wish you wouldn't leave out the part where the ghosts of Shoeless Joe and the Black Sox showed up."

"All right," I said in a voice rich with indignation.

"Tell me," she said while desperately trying to squelch a fresh wave of laughter. "Please. Which position

15

did you play?"

"Catcher," I said.

"That's right, catcher." Joanna became thoughtful, folding her legs beneath her, lifting her tea and gazing off into the distance, her eyes filling with twilight. "The Catcher in the Rye," she whispered more to herself than to me. "I'd like to have seen that."

Joanna and I never knew each other as children. She'd grown up out west and later spent time in the UK, (which accounted for the slim trace of an accent that presented itself when she was angry or excited). She'd moved to New England a few months before I met her. That had been more than seven years earlier.

The chance encounter had come to pass at a fireworks display in the nearby town of Bridgton one July Fourth. She caught my eye while walking past the blanket I was sharing with some friends (among them, 'Gospel' Tom). There was something about the way she moved with grace and confidence, her jet-black hair swaying across her shoulders, her sense of humor immediately setting me at ease, (that is, once I got up the nerve to talk to her). The way she looked in her shorts and tank-top didn't hurt either.

After a leisurely year-long romance, we married and moved into my grandparents' house, which we bought from my mother, Elise, a retired grade school teacher, shortly before she moved to Florida to spend her last days far from the biting chill of New England winters. My mother died two years later, comfortable in the knowledge that I'd met the woman of my dreams. My father preceded her to the afterlife by nearly a decade. An associate professor of Sociology at Bridgton University and a one-time high school teacher, Jonathan Graves would have loved Joanna. Like my mother, Joanna was the self-reliant type, independent, stubborn and not afraid to tell you what was on her mind or what she planned to do about it.

"How about some dessert?" Joanna said. "Field's

Bakery is open late for the summer."

I opened my mouth to protest, but caught myself; my brain had started churning.

Field's Bakery is a local establishment that has been providing delicious holiday pies and pastries to the denizens of Wickham since I was a boy. The owners, not ones to miss an opportunity to sell their wares, typically extended their summer hours to accommodate middle-aged softball players, fresh from the playing fields of Bridgton, and summer league soccer moms seeking a chocolate fix to relieve their stress headaches.

Ordinarily, the mere suggestion that I leave my seat after a meal to fetch *anything* would have brought an array of protests from my sun-tired brain. But tonight was different, as I realized that Tom Williams' place was only a few blocks from the bakery! I could drop off my samples this evening and save myself the drive in the morning.

"Sure," I said, eliciting an amazed look from my wife.

"Okay," she said, stunned. "There's some money on the dresser."

I got to my feet, grinning like a schoolboy in June, kissed her on the forehead and ran inside. Spooky, who was lying contentedly at Joanna's feet, raised her eyes as I passed, equally surprised.

I retrieved the cash, went to my car and backed down the driveway, leaving two wide-eyed females in my wake.

I drove west, into the last rays of the vivid July sunset, past the chain link fence that bordered St. Brigid's Cemetery, at the end of our street. The oldest cemetery in town, St. Brigid's winding paths proved to be a tantalizing haven for joggers training for marathons both real and imagined, who at this hour, were peacefully mingling with power walkers with their headphones firmly in place, their fists pumping vigorously. Beyond this healthful exhibition, on the far side of the Elm Street and River Avenue intersection, stretched rows of houses, many of them bustling with Rockwellian images of summer. The air was likewise rich with the lush sounds of the season, lawn mowers humming, heat bugs buzzing, all vainly clinging to the last remnants of a perfect day. All was right with the world.

Wickham Village, referred to simply as Wickham by its inhabitants, is an old mill town that survived the quagmire of the Great Depression by attracting enough land developers who understood its marketable location, nestled equidistantly between Boston, Providence, Newport, and Cape Cod, to keep it afloat. Later, as the late eighties descended, yuppies fleeing the cities for the imagined charm of the suburbs served to ease the sting of supply-side economics making the town a pleasant enough place to live.

Wickham's streets were relatively peaceful, though the town had its fair share of problems. Police and fire engine sirens shrieked on occasion, usually when one of the old mills that peppered the town's skyline caught fire. The revving of engines could sometimes be heard as kids raced cars after dark in the out-of-the-way wooded places. A handful of vagrants were known to set up shanties at the edge of town during the summer months, beyond the old state psychiatric hospital, (a place they had probably once called home) which had been closed down a decade earlier, due to the state's fiscally-motivated push toward privatization. Some of the facility's former residents could still be seen panhandling around the town green or carrying bags of trash-picked cans to the various liquor stores and markets that redeemed them, sad reminders of those in need of services who had fallen through bureaucratic cracks.

Wickham was no Winchester, but it was no downtrodden mill town, the sort that watched its bread and butter head south for the lure of cheaper labor during the thirties. Wickham was Wickham. It had its quirky denizens and petty criminals, but it wasn't a half-bad place to raise kids.

Joanna and I had no children; she couldn't have any. This had never been an issue other than to acquaintances who thought the situation odd. Marriage is step one, people would tell us. Children are step two. Joanna and I ignored them and got by just fine. And with us both in professions charged with enlightening young minds, we found there to be no shortage of children in our lives, even if only peripherally.

I passed Field's Bakery just as several men in matching burgundy-colored tee's reading 'Ajax Plumbing All Stars' exited with bags of desserts and coffees; my plan was to stop there on the way back. I proceeded two more blocks, then turned onto King Phillip Road.

I pulled into Tom's driveway and found him sitting at a makeshift workbench in the bay doorway of his garage. A lawn mower sat disassembled atop a table, looking like a gutted prop from a Star Wars movie. Somewhere in the garage, a radio was playing The Rolling Stones' *Sympathy for the Devil*.

Tom turned, looking perplexed, set his tools down and ambled my way, his lean five-foot ten-inch frame looking ridiculous in his baggy sweats. "Out for a drive?"

More than a few people in Wickham imagined Tom to be a misplaced Brit. But he was in fact as American as apple pie; he'd just grown up on the right side of the tracks, an act of fate that had gifted him with a degree of culture, something bound to confuse any blue-collar town regular.

"Not exactly," I said, retrieving the baggy from the way-back and holding it out for him to see.

Tom grimaced. "You'll never get into my Fruit-of-the-Looms bearing gifts like that," he said, taking the baggy from me and holding it at arm's length. "Do you want me to throw this out for you?"

"It's dog shit," I said. "And piss."

"I can see that," he stated with a twinge of impatience in his voice. "The mystery is why have you brought it here?"

I grinned, shaking my head; Tom's eccentricities had that effect on me. They had the opposite effect on Joanna. Truth to tell, Joanna didn't appreciate Tom at all.

Tom was the sort of fellow women might consider to be annoying, a walking, talking Three Stooges episode, or more precisely, in Tom's case, a Monty Python rerun. It was no wonder his wife, Alice, who, after less than two years of marriage, appeared ready to throw in the towel.

"Did your dog Shithead leave you a gift?"

"Spooky," I corrected. "And no."

Tom sat at the table and tossed the baggy aside, picked up a screw driver and went back to servicing his mower.

"I found that in my yard," I began. "It's too big for Spooky, so I figure my neighbor –"

"The old fart across the way?"

"No, my neighbor to the north."

"Ah, the 'grunge'?"

"The same," I affirmed.

"Dear Lord, spare us from the droppings of the men from the north," Tom said, snickering at his attempt at Viking humor.

"I figure his dog left me a little 'deposit.'"

"What sort of dog does he have?"

"A big shepherd."

Tom sat back in his folding chair and set his screwdriver down. I could almost hear his brain switching gears. He scooped up the baggy and studied it.

"What exactly am I supposed to do with this?" he said with a smear of disgust on his face.

"Joanna thinks I've gone around the bend."

"She's not alone in that assumption."

"She thinks I'm wrong about Renko being responsible. Rufus is the dog's name and I need to determine if *that* came from Rufus' hairy ass."

Tom snorted, swinging his gaze my way.

"You're insane," he said, then after a beat, "but it's an interesting problem. And what will you do if this turns out to be Rufus,' ah, *property* after all?"

I opened my mouth to speak but nothing emerged. It would be too late to leave the thing on Renko's back porch; the timing would be all wrong. But at least I could get Joanna in my court about the whole Renko thing.

"Judging by your gaping mouth, I see you haven't thought that part through yet."

"Not exactly," I said sheepishly.

"But I'm sure it would involve some clever revenge plot costing millions of dollars and hundreds of lives," Tom volunteered.

"Definitely."

Tom sighed and set his eyes on the baggy. My tale had intrigued him, but now it was time to set the hook.

"I couldn't think of anyone who could solve my mystery except 'Gospel' Tom."

The Stones had finished up and the DJ announced that he was going to play an 'oldie but a goody.' The next thing I heard was the opening twang of The Swimming Pool Q's *She's Bringing down the Poison.*

Tom turned to me. "Spare me the patronizing bullshit, will you?"

He could complain all he wanted, but the fact was that Tom's ego would fill a five-yard dump truck and we both knew it.

Tom scooped up the baggy, got to his feet and headed down his driveway toward the bulkhead at the back of his house with me in tow. Without losing step, he swung the metal door open and descended into the basement.

"Who are you with?" It was Alice Williams' voice

booming from above.

"The Pope," Tom shouted as he reached the bottom of the stairs and flipped on the wall switch, activating a bare bulb dangling from the ceiling.

"Hi, Alice," I shouted.

"Oh, hi, Jack," she called, her voice a tad more cordial. "Tell my idiot husband not to leave the garage door open like he did last night. Who knows what's liable to crawl in there after dark."

"Sure," I said. "Hey, idiot husband –"

"I heard," he said, flipping his unseen wife the bird while heading for a doorway at the back of the cellar. "You know my wife?" Tom added. "She's a little like Russia: a mystery, wrapped around an enigma, wrapped around a *bitch*."

"Nice talking to you," Alice shouted from above. "Tell our girl hello."

"Sure thing, Alice."

Our girl was Joanna. Since meeting, Joanna and Alice had taken to each other like fish to water. They would shop together and often behave as if they were in a private club consisting of only two members, but I didn't mind. I suppose Alice provided Joanna with a dose of well-needed female company.

Two years earlier, Tom's short-term steady, a bar fly named Dale Lees, had vanished, seemingly without a trace. Dale had always been a little flighty, and Tom figured she had moved to California to pursue an unrealized acting career. Most folks who knew Dale apparently agreed with Tom, as little concern over her sudden departure ever manifested itself.

Dale had no family of which Tom was aware. No long-lost aunts or cousins emerged from the woodwork to ask what had become of her, so Tom mended his wounds, which were minor as the relationship had consisted of little more than occasional inebriated sex, and got on with it.

Joanna brought Alice home one night after bumping into her at a local church bazaar. They'd begun talking while looking over the used paperbacks. But over the years Alice had grown enigmatic and moody, keeping to herself at cookouts, canceling plans, complaining about her asthma and allergies. It was evident that Alice's ailments were more severe than she wished to let on, and Tom would never divulge anything without her permission, lest we find him floating face-down in the West Wickham River.

In any event, Alice adored Joanna but seemed less enthralled with Tom's bizarre sense of humor, a point that was blatantly obvious, judging by her response to his quip moments earlier. I, as well as more than a few others, found ourselves wondering what Tom and Alice had in common, if anything. Perhaps in the grand scheme of things, Alice was simply the rebound that decided to stay awhile. The only question remaining was when would 'a while' be up?

"Mind the mess," Tom said as we passed from one empty room to a cluttered smaller room in the southeast corner of the house.

The walls surrounding us were lined with stacked sections of sheet rock and two-by-fours, a framing project Tom had never quite started. Like the disemboweled mower, Tom's basement remained unfinished. Doubtless some other intriguing project much like my 'deposit' had presented itself and the sheet rock and wood then passed from Tom's busy mind like a thunder shower on a summer afternoon.

"This way," he said as flatly as if giving a guided tour, in spite of the fact that I'd visited his lab countless times. I said nothing and followed obediently as he passed through another doorway and flicked on a light.

The room in this corner of the basement might have been a storage facility for the set to a Frankenstein movie. There were beakers, test tubes, Bunsen burners and chemical-laden shelves along with several functioning and a few non-functioning computers. The only thing missing was a sheet-draped corpse on a gurney, and, with all the clutter, it was impossible to rule it out.

"Sit," he said, gesturing at a folding chair situated at one of the long worktables. I obeyed.

Tom plopped down in front of a computer terminal, his eyes never leaving the thing in the baggy until he set it down to take hold of the cordless mouse. The screen came alive with the image of an Asian woman in a blue bikini winking and repeating the phrase, "Me so horny!" Tom ignored her and began tapping keys. I leaned closer to watch as his desktop materialized and, in no time at all, he was on the net, surfing from site to site, searching for who knew what, his mad scientist's brain purring like a well-oiled machine.

"You know," he said, "the song *Closing Time* by Semi-Sonic is really about being born."

"Really?" I said, still, after all these years, mildly amazed by Tom's brain switching gears in mid-thought. "Does Semi-Sonic know that?"

Tom chuckled, tapped keys. "I was merely pointing out that some things are not what they appear to be." Tap, tap. "I have access to all the equipment I should need for a complete analysis," he said returning to the topic. "And I can search the Web to find tests on how to determine if your neighbor's dog *did* in fact leave your little 'deposit'. I'll start at veterinary sites, get an idea of what to look for. First chemical analysis, find out what your 'depositor' ate; then do a bacterial analysis. Do you know anything about polymerase chain reactions?"

"Not really," I said.

"Yeah, well, neither do I. But I'm dying to try out these DNA home test kits I found on Amazon. I was going to use them on my wife; find out which species *she* belongs to, but I'm afraid the results would prove inconclusive."

"Are we fighting?" I said.

"Perpetual. She's turned it into a national pastime."

He hit a key and sat back. The screen melted away and a new web site began to unfold.

"I *will* need a sample of what's his name's shit though –"

"Rufus."

"Whatever. I'll need to make a detailed comparative analysis, and that means a trip into your neighbor's yard."

I grimaced at the thought of Tom creeping around Renko's property.

"But that can wait," he said. "First things first. I'll call you later after I do a little research. Will you be home?"

"Yes," I said nodding and getting to my feet. "Should be."

"No Summer what's-it carnival?"

"Starts tomorrow," I said. "And it's the Summer Harvest Fayre."

"Whatever," he said. "Remember, courtesy and common sense are the two things most lacking in this world. Just thought you might want to know that. I'll want a case of beer for my services. Corona Lite, please. Got to keep the ol' love machine fit, you know." He slapped his stomach and smiled.

"You'll get it," I said grinning.

"Good. Show yourself out, please. I've got work to do. And try not to irritate the Missus. She's been in a particularly nasty mood lately, and it's not even that time of the month."

* * *

I made my way to my car, supremely satisfied with my efforts. It was likely that nothing would come of the whole thing, but at least I was doing something, not taking it lying down. I really had no idea what I'd say to Renko if Tom found a match between my sample and Rufus, but at least I could prove to Joanna that I was right and being right, as a great man once said, was ninety percent of the battle.

I climbed aboard my SUV and started it up. I glanced up through the sunroof at the rising moon. It was nearly full and as big as a house. Then I remembered Fields' Bakery.

"Shit."

I checked my watch, realizing that I had only minutes before the place closed for the night. I would have a hell of a time explaining to Joanna why I hadn't made it there in time.

I backed out of the driveway and into the street. As I started to pull away, I thought I caught a fleeting glimpse of Alice watching me from one of the front windows of the house. I waved, but I don't think she saw me. When I glanced back, there was no one there.

Chapter Three

I arrived at the bakery just as they were closing and convinced a young woman with a pony tail and a Portuguese accent that I simply had to pick something up for my sick wife. Taking pity on me, she agreed.

I made my selection quickly, not wanting to press my luck, and headed home with a small Death by Chocolate Cake, brownies, and some Danish for breakfast.

I pulled into the driveway just as dusk was settling over my yard. I went inside and, from the kitchen, spied Joanna pacing in the four seasons room, the telephone pressed to her ear.

"I'm home," I said, setting my bag of sin on the island.

She looked up with a start, muttered something into the mouthpiece and ended the call.

"Death by Chocolate," I said, expecting a grin that didn't materialize. Instead, I noticed a shadow of worry clouding her face.

"Great," she said, sounding less than enthused, but managing a wan smile for my sake, "I can't wait."

***

Joanna hardly touched her cake and remained sullen for the remainder of the evening. Later, as we lay in bed with the lights out and the television on, I considered asking her what was wrong, but caught myself realizing that silence, especially in marriage, is often golden. Joanna would tell me what was bothering her when she was ready and not before; it was her way and I respected it just as she respected my numerous quirks. Perhaps the telephone call had something to do with the Fayre. Maybe one of the volunteers that she was counting on to help run the booth had backed out at the last minute. Experience reminded me

27

that this was not unusual. But if this *was* the issue, why wouldn't she confide in me?

Assuming Joanna had her reasons for not sharing the problem with me, I kept my mouth closed and reached over and touched her hand just to let her know I was there for her. She took my fingers in hers, squeezed gently and then let go. A moment later she was asleep. I soon followed.

***

I awoke to the sound of Spooky growling from the foot of the bed. Disoriented, I searched for the remote, found it and extinguished the coruscating glow of the television. Then I sat up to listen.

The window near the foot of the bed on Joanna's side was wide open and a gentle breeze was tickling the sheers. Spooky was lying at that corner of the bed with her nose aimed directly at the screen, her growling intensifying as if something outside was amiss. Concerned that she might wake Joanna, I was about to call her over to me when a bright light spilled in through the window; the sensor light mounted above the garage bay doors had been triggered.

Spooky set her paws on the windowsill as her growling deteriorated into an excited whimpering, and I realized she was shaking violently. I had never seen her behave this way. This was no skunk or alley cat that had captured her attention. Whatever was outside was scaring the hell out of her.

"Easy, girl," I whispered as I slipped out of bed and went to the window. I stroked Spooky's back and pressed my face against the screen, trying to twist my neck so as to see the front of the garage. I saw nothing unusual. There were only the two garage bay doors and the sensor light with its twin floods perched, bat-like, above them. Spooky had stopped shaking by this point and was now lying silently watching me as if I had been the cause of her concern.

I turned back to the window, craning my neck with my face pressed so close to the screen that I could smell the dusty metal mesh. The light's five-minute life span ended at that moment and darkness fell across the driveway. I felt jittery, as if a live wire had been jammed into my spine, and I decided to investigate. Spooky followed me to the kitchen door, her tiny claws clicking against the tile floor.

I gently eased the door open so as not to wake Joanna, and, once inside the service porch, I released the lock and closed the door behind me. I crossed to the screen door, pushed it open and turned to call Spooky. But instead of racing past me and bounding down the back steps as was customary, she sat quivering, pressed against the clothes dryer in the corner of the service porch.

"What's wrong, girl?"

I started to close the screen door, planning to pick the old girl up and carry her outside, figuring her hips might be bothering her as was typical with aged Lhasas, when the sensor light tripped again. Caught by surprise, I turned to the door, pushed it open and stuck my head out, hoping to catch a glimpse of whatever was triggering the beacon. I knew that flying insects and bats could activate the light, but there was nothing in sight.

Standing there, I became suddenly aware that the night was not only devoid of movement, but of sound. The night, usually alive with crickets chirping and toads croaking, was as still as a tomb. Even the moon, looking like the last ember of a dying campfire, was hiding behind a thin veil of clouds high in the southern sky.

Unnerved but curious, I pushed the screen door open and stepped out onto the porch. The wood felt cool and damp beneath my bare feet. The branches of the weeping Japanese cherry tree that guarded the gate near the base of the porch were so still they might have been etched from stone. I shifted my scrutiny to the back yard. The branches of the big red maple beside the garage were likewise motionless.

I scanned the deep shadows beneath the tree for signs of an intruder, expecting to see nothing, assuming my nocturnal visitor had fled when I opened the door as most animals would; but some fleeting movement snagged my attention. Unsure of whether I had seen anything at all, I squinted hard at a spot between the side of the garage and the trunk of the tree. Slowly, two glistening specks materialized, hovering like a pair of green fireflies deep within the shadows. A chill danced up my spine and I shivered in the sultry summer air. I blinked hard, leaned over the rail and strained to see more clearly, but the specks were gone.

Some unseen veil lifted from around me and I felt myself grinning at my own foolishness. A bat flitted by overhead. A bullfrog croaked someplace off in the distance. And, as if to mock me further, Spooky trotted past me and descended to the yard. She crossed the patio, squatted at the edge of the lawn and relieved herself, her dark eyes darting about warily. Upon finishing her business, she immediately scurried back into the house. I waited a beat, feeling uneasy about what had happened, then followed her example.

Unwilling to turn my back on the screen door and the darkness beyond, I backed across the service porch, the floorboards creaking beneath my weight. I slowly opened the kitchen door, my senses tingling, nervously awaiting the face of my green-eyed intruder to appear at the screen door, and bumped right into Joanna, who was coming back from the bathroom.

"Jesus!" I said, my heart practically bursting from my chest.

"Out for a stroll?" she said in her playful sarcastic way, sounding more like herself than she had earlier.

"Spooky had to go peeps," I said, 'peeps' being our ridiculous doggie word for urination.

"Good girl," Joanna said stooping to pat our pooch on the head and closing the kitchen door behind me, sealing out the weird night. In the darkness, I felt her eyes on me.

"My protector," she said taking me by the hand and leading me to the bedroom. The curve of her breast brushed against me as she swept past me to flick on the radio we kept on the dresser. I heard static as she scanned for her favorite Boston station, one that specialized in soft rock. Lowering the volume to a romantic, almost subliminal level, she took my hands and urged me backward until the back of my legs bumped into the edge of the mattress. Together we rolled into bed and Spooky hopped up with us.

"No, girl," Joanna said. "You stay on the floor."

I sensed Spooky giving us the canine version of a dirty look before hopping down and heading off to parts unknown. She knew as well as I that Joanna gave her the boot for only one reason.

"I'm sorry I was quiet before," my wife said, rolling over and snuggling against me. I could feel her breasts pressed against my side, her leg draped across my thighs. "I'm just a little worried about the Fayre."

"I understand," I said. "But you always make a go of it."

"I know," she said, running her fingers along my forehead, brushing a few strands of graying hair aside. "You're always wonderful when it comes to helping with the booth, the groceries and everything else."

Her lips caressed my throat and her right hand slid down across my chest, past my stomach and beneath the waistband of my shorts. Then her lips found mine and she withdrew her hand and rolled on top of me.

The night enveloped us and we became one, our bodies moving together, rhythmically, with renewed passion. We drifted lazily into that place where time ends and a soft darkness lives, a darkness where there is no danger, no unknown, only warmth.

31

Later, as Joanna slept, I lay watching the ceiling fan whirring like a phantom in the shadows above, listening to the soft tones of the radio. One song bled into another, turning time in our darkened bedroom into a slow-flowing river. The last thing I remember was Bono singing *With or Without You,* before drifting off to sleep. Spooky, having apparently forgiven us, was once again nestled at the foot of the bed.

I dozed, drifting in and out of sleep, until something awakened me from my slumber. I scanned the shadows for anything out of the ordinary, but the world appeared to be intact. I rolled onto my side and watched Joanna as she slept. I found myself counting her breaths, listening to her sighs and remembering how beautiful she looked the night we met, the night of the Fourth of July fireworks so long ago. I remembered her face, her smile, her tanned skin and her eyes alive with the fire in the sky. It occurred to me at that moment that we hadn't seen any fireworks lately. The Fayre featured fireworks; we would have our chance then.

I smiled, reached over to shut off the radio and was about to close my eyes to allow my vision to develop into a full-fledged dream, when the garage sensor light came alive again. Spooky immediately raised her head and began to growl. I sat up, my heart thudding as Spooky's growl deteriorated into an intense whimper. She made her way to my side where she rolled up in a ball, shivering, pressing against me, her dark eyes never straying from the window.

This time I didn't investigate; I just lay there waiting for the light to die. When it finally did, I waited some more. Eventually the night came alive again. Crickets began chirping and Spooky stopped shaking and fell into a deep slumber at my side. The sounds of distant cars drifted through the window, and I knew things had returned to normal. Whatever had been out there was gone; gone, at least for now. I imagined I would probably laugh at this come morning, but there is something about the night and the darkness that kills laughter, steals it away as a cat steals a baby's breath. Minutes passed. After what seemed an eternity, sleep found me and I dreamed of dark things moving unseen through dark places.

Chapter Four

The next morning I awoke to find Joanna puttering about in the kitchen. The alarm clock read eight-fifteen.

"Morning," she called, having heard me stir. Spooky, lying at the foot of the bed, raised her shaggy head and considered my wife as she peeked into the room.

"Good morning," I said.

"I figured you needed your sleep after cutting the lawn last night," she said, returning to whatever she was doing.

"Thanks," I said, not about to complain. Spooky trotted up to see me, dragged her old tongue across my face and hopped down to check on Joanna. I followed her lead, shuffling to the bathroom, wincing at the vivid bars of sunlight pouring in through the kitchen windows.

"Marge is supposed to pick up the doughnuts, but don't count on it," Joanna said.

Marge Weems was a business teacher at my school. Blessed with a genuinely kind soul, Marge's pleasant nature was often lost behind her crusty demeanor. She possessed a wry sarcastic wit fostered by years of working in the public sector and further enhanced by her truck-driver's mouth. A chain smoker since birth, Marge's voice was as craggy as her complexion. If there had ever been an actress born to play Marge in a film it would have been Thelma Ritter; though Marge was probably rougher around the edges.

"You know Marge," Joanna continued. "Something always comes up. Usually trouble with her car or her thirty-five-year-old son calling to tell her he needs something or other. She can be such an enabler."

"What time do we need to be at the Fayre?" I asked, studying my disheveled appearance in the mirror.

34

"Not until four," Joanna said. "Marge will be there and Dick Saunders will be coming over around seven."

"Dick Saunders?" I said astonished.

"He volunteered to help out this year, unfortunately. I didn't have the heart to tell him we didn't need him."

Dick Saunders was an itinerant phys-ed teacher with a bit of a drinking problem; this was no mystery. He was never drunk at school, at least not so far as anyone could determine. Dick was more of a social drinker, the sort who considered any time away from work to be social time. He was known to polish off two-thirds of the beer at a cookout, most of which he hadn't brought, and then go on a tirade about how the liberals were ruining the country. I never understood how a man working in the public sector, as a teacher no less, could possibly bad-mouth the liberals. It seemed Dick was a little confused as to which side of the bread the butter went on.

Dick's wife Janet, a quiet, unassuming woman who deserved to be canonized, would faithfully monitor Dick's degree of inebriation at any function, then, once his tank was full, she'd drive him home and probably tuck him into bed to boot. I could never understand what she saw in the man; nobody could.

"Libby Chambers will be there too," Joanna added.

This was no surprise. Like Joanna, Libby was a librarian. But rather unlike Joanna, Libby was meek and quiet. She sported a thick pair of glasses and burnt-orange hair. She was reliable, trustworthy and boring, the polar opposite of Dick Saunders. This, I suspected, should prove quite the evening.

"I'm making scrambled –" Joanna began when the telephone rang. She cursed before even picking the thing up.

I waited, the razor poised in my hand.

"All right," I heard her say before hanging up. Then she cursed again.

"Marge?" I said, knowing before she spoke.

"She can work today, but her car battery is dead. Her son is driving over from Bridgton to jump it, but she can't pick up the doughnuts."

"I'll pick them up," I said.

"Thanks," Joanna said, entering the bathroom and kissing me on the cheek, taking a face-full of shaving cream away with her. "Shamus' Doughnuts is on Grove Street and the manager's name is Kevin Olson. Just mention my name and he'll get the order."

I resumed shaving. "How many boxes?"

"Fifty dozen."

"Wow," I said, rinsing my razor. "I'm glad I have an SUV."

"I guess Macy's will just have to wait," she said, picking up the telephone and punching in some numbers. "I'd better call your sister and cancel."

Chapter Five

We finished breakfast and I took a 'Maine is Vacationland' travel mug of coffee and set out for my car.

"Remember to ask for Kevin Olson," Joanna said as we walked to the garage.

"Fifty dozen," I affirmed.

"Yes, and again, thanks, babe."

I went to the corner of the garage and unhooked a fourteen-inch wide portion of chain link fencing I kept secured by a hook so I could slip through without crossing the lawn. I clipped the fence back into place, opened the garage side door and flipped the switches that opened the bay doors. Joanna climbed into her car and started it up.

"I'll meet you at the booth," she said. "I have some things to take care of first."

I watched her back down the driveway, tooting the horn as she drove off down the street.

"And now another episode of *The Jack and Joanna Show*," I said, climbing aboard my SUV, slipping it into gear and heading out.

***

I spotted the sign for Shamus' Doughnuts, a Black Watch tartan background featuring a Scottish Terrier with a doughnut in his mouth and a tam on his head, and pulled into the lot.

Shamus' Doughnuts was by no means a juggernaut like Dunkin' Doughnuts or Krispy Kreme, but with six shops in southern New England and more on the way, its product was certainly popular with the locals and sure to be a hit at the Fayre. And the fundraiser special they featured with discounted doughnut rates perfectly suited Joanna's purpose.

The shop was packed to the rafters on this fine

morning and I began hunting for a parking space. I followed a young couple with two small children as they made their way to an over-sized SUV and slid into the space they vacated. I reluctantly buttoned up my car, realizing just how hot it would be upon my return, and set out across the broiling asphalt; it was not quite eleven o'clock, but the sun was beating down like a burning hammer.

I entered the shop and the cool breath of air conditioning washed over me, chilling the dew at the back of my neck. I wove through the throng, winding up at the pick-up counter where a young woman with a vivid smile asked me if she could be of service.

"I'm here to see Kevin Olson," I said. "It's about an order for the Summer Harvest Fayre."

"Oh, sure," she said, her smile unwavering, "I'll be right back."

She passed through some swinging doors and a moment later a middle-aged man with a freckled tan and bleached blonde hair emerged. His grin was less bright than his predecessor's and, I suspected, less genuine.

"Can I help?" he said, the grin melting into a frown.

"I'm here to pick up an order for Joanna Graves."

Olson's frown deepened as if I'd asked him who the sixtieth president of the United States would be.

"Oh," he said his nasal intonation suddenly out of sync with the world around him. "I thought Miss Graves would be picking the order up herself."

"*Mrs.* Graves couldn't," I said, unintentionally stressing the Mrs. "Is there a problem?"

"Oh, no," he said, the politician's grin returning. "It's just that, well, we've got to talking each time she's come by and, well –"

"Well, she's at the Fayre and she needs the doughnuts," I said, taken aback by Olson's overly-familiar demeanor and growing impatient. Exactly how well did this man know my wife?

"Of course, now, that was fifty dozen," he said. "Just park out back at the loading door and we'll take care of everything."

I nodded and headed for the exit.

I crossed the sweltering parking lot, passing through heat phantoms which rose like geysers from the asphalt, and climbed into my roasting car. I started it up and cranked the air conditioning all the way up, something I rarely do. Then I backed out of the space, relinquishing it to one of a line of potential customers, and drove around to the back of the shop.

I backed up to the curb and once again climbed out into the oppressive humidity, leaving the engine running this time and popping open the hatch.

I reached the loading door just as it began to rise up into its housing. Two teenage boys toting long clear plastic sleeves filled with doughnut boxes emerged.

"Where ya' want 'em, Mista?" the biggest of the boys, a sloppy looking character with greasy dark hair, asked through his braces.

I pointed.

The boy nodded and he and his partner, a thin kid with acne and an overbite, proceeded to load sleeves of doughnut boxes into my car. When they had finished I closed the hatch and slipped each of them two dollars.

"We're not supposed to take tips," the thin one said, "but what the hell."

"Yeah, thanks," the larger one said, accepting the cash, and the pair headed back inside.

I climbed aboard my car, welcoming the chilled air, and headed out of the lot. Driving west, I glanced back and spotted Olson standing just inside the open loading door. He appeared to be studying me from above the glowing tip of a cigarette. He drew in a final drag tossed the butt aside and slowly closed the big door.

Chapter Six

D riving to the Fayre with my cargo of doughnuts, The Cure's *Pictures of You* playing on the radio, I found myself wondering why 'Gospel' Tom hadn't called me with an update on his investigation. I checked my mobile for messages, found none, and clipped it to my belt.

Tom might have been a genius in the lab, but in the real world he was a bit of a scatterbrain, as evidenced by his unfinished basement and gutted lawn mower. His inability to complete tasks had become a bone of contention, adding fuel to Alice's growing disdain for the man. I wondered just how long the marriage would last. I was honestly surprised that it had lasted *this* long.

Understanding Tom's behavior better than perhaps anybody, I realized it might be days before I heard from him, and I found myself growing bored with the scheme I'd hatched. My plan required a quick response if it was to work properly. A delay would only soften the impact as well as my resolve. I decided that if Tom hadn't contacted me by that evening, I'd call him. I was, as Joanna had predicted, quickly losing interest in my little plot.

Setting aside thoughts of Tom's investigation, I found myself crossing some disused railroad tracks emerging from a stretch of densely overgrown forest where vagrants were rumored to have established a small shanty community. This was not that unusual in the summer months; our meager indigent population would migrate farther south by means of existing freight lines once winter descended. It seems that depression-era hoboes hadn't died out; they'd simply gone to ground.

I proceeded through the tree-dispersed sunlight past an endless matrix of crumbling stone walls until I spied the familiar shapes of the old state hospital's gothic-styled spires looming above the treetops. Visible amongst the greenery and brick were the metallic crests of some of the Fayre's numerous rides. I tried to remember how such sights would have affected my ten-year-old self and felt a flock of anxious butterflies traverse my stomach like ghosts on Halloween. It seemed some things never got old.

The West Wickham State Hospital consisted of several dozen buildings and houses lining a series of run-down streets and curving roads with quaint names like Juniper Grove and Maple Lane. Once the home to nearly five hundred individuals suffering from mental health issues, the sprawling array of streets and structures had served as a community unto itself.

The hospital had closed down more than a decade earlier and the residents, the hundred or so who had not already been placed in various nursing homes or in their graves, had been farmed out to private sector vendors. Government's efforts at privatization had left the facility in a state of disrepair. What had once been a thriving community with its own farm, greenhouses and hospital, was now a ghost town. A crew of groundskeepers worked to maintain the place, but they performed double duty, also servicing the grounds of a functioning mental health facility in the nearby town of Gevaudan. One glance left little doubt as to which of the two facilities took precedence.

Security had been stationed at the front entrance to keep trespassers out, but there was little for which to provide security. The busiest time of year for the lone security guard was July, when the Fayre rolled into town.

The green security trailer resembled a great dusty tortoise basking in the summer sun in a patch of sunburned grass beside the road that led onto the grounds. A heavy-set man wearing a dark blue uniform was leaning against a similarly-colored car bearing the Massachusetts State emblem on its door. He eyed me with the overactive wariness of one who takes his job too seriously, and when I waved at him, he gestured for me to pull over. I did so and

41

he sauntered over, spitting a brown wad of chewing tobacco into the dirt before knocking on my passenger side window with a clutch of thick knuckles.

I hit the remote and the window slid down, allowing dust to roll in and vital air-conditioned atmosphere to escape. The security guard leaned over and rested his thick forearms on the door.

"If you're going to the Fayre, the parking lot is down farther," he said, his words creeping past his fat tobacco-stained lips.

"I'm with the vendors," I said. "Doughnuts." I jerked my thumb in the direction of my cargo.

"Can't be too careful, ya know," he said as he studied me with droopy, blood-shot eyes, "what with the vagrants we catch sleeping in the old buildings and folks stealing copper pipe. And the ghost hunters. Most of 'em are condemned, ya know, the buildings; state just ain't got the money to tear 'em down."

A few beats passed during which his eyes drifted from my face to the back seat of my car and back to my face. Having apparently sized me up adequately, he nodded in a self-satisfied way and, with a flick of his wrist, gestured for me to proceed.

"Have a good one," he said as I rolled up the window and drove away.

Glancing in my rearview mirror, I saw the guard standing by the side of the road. Apparently satisfied with his efforts he spat at the ground and headed for his car.

I proceeded along the main entry road up a hill past some dilapidated picnic tables and benches. The road emptied into an intersection at the foot of the crumbling steps of the main administration building which stood in a perpetual state of disrepair, its gothic steeple rising proudly into the blue sky, its skeleton slowly collapsing with time. Here I turned left onto a side road that time had reduced to little more than a spider web pattern of cracks through which ambitious weeds rose in search of sunlight.

I proceeded through plumes of billowing heat phantoms until I reached an intersection where someone had painted the words 'Eat Shit' across the face of a bent and rusted stop sign. Ignoring the obscene suggestion, I turned left and drove past more rotting buildings, across more chewed-up asphalt and past a sagging array of ruined picnic tables.

An abandoned psychiatric hospital might seem an odd location for our Fayre, that is, until one got past the initial squeamishness that accompanied the idea of children enjoying themselves within a stone's throw of the desolate buildings which had once housed so many troubled souls. The remote setting of the hospital grounds, to the contrary, was in fact a logical choice. Additional security could be arranged easily, and with all the open fields, rides and trailers for carnival staff to live in would not be an issue. Electricity had long since stopped flowing to the derelict buildings, but juice was usually not a concern, as the Fayre brought with it an abundance of generators.

I turned into a cobblestone lane that meandered down a hill past more buildings, crooked curbstones, broken benches and countless weeds rising out of countless potholes until I saw the sunbaked field that served as the staff parking lot stretching out below. I turned down this new lane, passing beneath the limbs of an ancient Weeping Willow which stood like a Tolkienesque sentinel, its tendrils waving in the gentle zephyr, finally emerging into the dusty field below.

I drove through the staff parking lot past a sea of cars owned by other vendors toward two long, low gray buildings that stretched half the length of the midway. The white-washed doors at the backs of the buildings affirmed that each was portioned off into separate sections or booths. Numbering twenty-six in all, each booth was equipped with fluorescent ceiling lamps, built-in wall fans and refrigerators. The booth Joanna traditionally rented was lucky number thirteen.

Beyond the first booth, off to the right, near the visitors' entrance, the craft building, and the first aid station, stood the covered stage where bands, disc jockeys and the occasional magician and family-oriented comic would perform over the next few days. Rows of folding chairs had been positioned in front of the stage and several sections of bleachers had been erected at an angle off to one side beside the farm machinery display.

Toward the middle of the midway there stood a large tent beneath which many long tables and chairs had been set up. A few large industrial fans hummed beneath the tent in an all-but-vain attempt to chase away the oppressive summer heat. Additional picnic tables dotted the landscape for braver sun-seeking diners.

A second tent stood beyond the first, its shady innards lined with tables and cartons brimming with items to be sold or auctioned off throughout the Fayre's stay in Wickham. The western edge of the aptly-titled Anything Goes Sale tent opened onto the beginning of the midway, which was lined with an assortment of games involving oversized hydraulic hammers, air guns, darts, squirt guns, and balls of every size to be tossed or fired at targets ranging from bowling pins to goldfish bowls.

Additional vendors occupying small trailers and tents hawking everything from funnel cakes to candy apples, popcorn to cotton candy and tee shirts, littered the landscape. Beyond this, rising like the metallic bones of a mysterious race of gigantic long-dead alien creatures, were the rides, consisting first of 'kiddie' rides featuring giant caterpillars and oversized tinker toy riding cars, boats set upon submerged rails and of course a large carousel. Then came the so-called 'grown-up' rides, megaliths of steel and neon, including a one-third-sized replica of George Ferris' Great Chicago Exposition wheel, a giant slide, a roller coaster called Halley's Comet, a Round-Up, a Scrambler, a hang-gliding contraption called the Cliff Hanger, a Zipper with its swinging cages, and finally the Sea Dragon, a huge pendulous Viking Ship meant to elicit chills, screams and sometimes vomit from those who dared to embark upon it.

Beyond the rides, situated adjacent to the grove of trees that led up to the old streets and buildings, lay a seemingly endless expanse of RVs and trailers, their beige and silver hides glistening in the morning sun. It was in these portable homes that most of the carnies resided while the Fayre was in town.

I'd worked at local carnivals as a teenager, making and serving popcorn and cotton candy, so, aside from the fact that the Summer Harvest Fayre was considerably larger than those of my youth, the general atmosphere was essentially the same: rides, games, food and music. It was a tough combination to beat.

I inched my way through the field that ran directly behind the food booths, searching for Joanna's booth. It wasn't difficult to find; the numbers were printed clearly beside the back door of each, and if that weren't enough, a woman who might have been the wicked witch of the East's shorter half-sister was standing at the back door of number thirteen, chugging on a cigarette. When she saw me, she placed her pudgy knuckles on her hips and shook her head disapprovingly. I pulled up beside her, shut the engine and climbed out into the heat.

"It's about time," Marge Weems said in a voice that reminded me of rusty nails rattling around in a metal pail.

"Hi, Marge," I said. "It's good to see you, too."

Joanna emerged from the booth, a look of relief on her face.

"Thank you," she said clapping her hands together and stepping down from the back door. "Let's get these inside. Folks have been waiting for a while. I don't want to think about how much money we might have lost so far."

"Well," I said popping open the hatch to my car and offloading the first sleeve of doughnuts, "let's not keep them waiting."

Chapter Seven

Booth number thirteen measured ten feet deep by eight feet wide, with faded gray linoleum covering a plywood floor and a series of braced two-by-fours framing the roof. A half-inch thick panel of plywood hung from the ceiling at the front of the booth, such that when in the down position, it sat plumb with a counter top that ran the width of the booth. The panel, when raised, created an opening onto the midway, allowing vending to take place.

Against the wall to the left sat a long table with a small microwave oven. Six seconds was the recommended time for heating a single doughnut, but if someone wanted one unheated or in dozen or half-dozen quantities, that was fine too.

Above the long table was a framed, draped opening, perhaps two feet square, where occupants of the adjoining booth could pass or receive items. An identical opening was fitted into the opposite wall, beside which stood an old refrigerator. At the back of the booth to the left of the door were a series of wall-mounted shelves. Paper towels, folded garbage bags, boxes of vinyl gloves, and a small television set occupied these.

"For the game tonight," Marge said when she noticed me eyeing the television. "Sox and Yankees; you gotta love it."

"Now that cable's gone digital, how do you manage it?"

"There's plenty of coax running along the back of the booths for the RVs," Marge said. "The lines punch into every booth. I just bring the portable box from my kitchen TV. Basic cable, so no porn."

I nodded my approval and began sliding doughnut boxes from their sleeves and setting them on the table.

"We'll finish unloading," Joanna said, "why don't

47

you raise the flap?"

I found three folding chairs leaning against the wall beside the refrigerator and set one in the center of the room. I then unhooked two large sliding bolts situated at either end of the flap that kept the panel secured to the counter top, thus preventing anyone from breaking in when the booth was not in use, and raised the thing over my head. A wave of heat rolled in through the opening as I climbed up on the chair, securing both ends of the flap to chains dangling from the ceiling by means of two big thumb locks attached to the corners of the flap. I climbed down to inspect my handiwork and was greeted by a clutch of teenagers queuing up at the counter.

"I'd like a dozen," a lean dark-haired man with a pierced lip and a chain for a belt said. His arm was draped around a girl with multiple piercings, who was snapping a wad of bubble gum with an unrelenting fervor.

I referred to the sign tacked to the wall above the table that listed the prices. To make things easier for everyone working the booth, doughnuts had been priced in three quantities: one doughnut for seventy-five cents, a half dozen for three-fifty, and a dozen for six dollars. The increments and corresponding prices were also clearly printed on laminated signs affixed to the booth's exterior so as to avoid any confusion.

"Coming right up," I said fetching a box of doughnuts from the table and accepting the young man's money. I made change from some bills Joanna handed me and the couple thanked me and went on their way, only to be replaced by a second couple asking for a single doughnut each.

"I've got this one," Marge called and I turned to watch her scoop two doughnuts out of a box with a strip of wax paper and head for the microwave.

Joanna appeared beside me, setting the gun-metal gray money box on a shelf beneath the counter and swinging its lid open to reveal stacks of one dollar bills, a few fives and tens and a compartment full of quarters. She grinned at me and went back to the table where she continued unpacking doughnut boxes.

And so the day passed, with the three of us taking turns at the counter selling doughnuts, making change and small talk with customers, suggesting they stop in at other booths, mostly those operated by organizations with which we consorted. The day passed pleasantly, the one shortcoming being the mercury, which never dipped below ninety degrees. The vented wall fan did little to alleviate this, but things improved when a woman working in the booth adjacent to ours representing an Indian restaurant in nearby Bridgton called The Star of Delhi took pity on us and brought us a floor fan which we promptly pressed into service.

We were never bored, and, in addition to the steady flow of customers, acquaintances stopped by to chat throughout the day. Doug Redding, a retired mechanic who owned a small diner on the green and who lived in our neighborhood, enlightened me as to the latest vehicles highlighted in Motor Trend magazine and Consumers' Reports. Some teachers from my school stopped by as well to tell us how much they were enjoying their summer vacation and to take some doughnuts off our hands, at special discount prices, of course. Roy Gibson, a pharmacist who worked at the nearby Rite Aid Pharmacy, told me about the striper he caught while fishing on his brother's thirty-three foot Wellcraft in the Cape Cod Canal. And our neighbors from across the street, an elderly couple named Trimble, proceeded to tell us at great length how the grubs had consumed most of their back yard last season. Roger Trimble further elaborated on the problem by explaining how he had bought some Grubex and planned to give the grubs the same hell he'd given the North Koreans several decades earlier. I pretended to be interested, but

Sophie Trimble, the more level-headed of the two, apparently detected my boredom and dragged Roger off to parts unknown, after wishing us well in our entrepreneurial endeavors.

The vivid blue summer day eventually faded into a pink-skied evening. Around seven o'clock, the disc jockey, who had been spinning golden oldies all afternoon, packed it in right after playing Patsy Cline's *Walking after Midnight*, and a Boston-based band called Wicked Scarlett took the stage. The lead singer, an attractive waif with straight dark shoulder length hair, attired in a black cowboy hat, black tank top and matching black leather pants that laced up the sides, sauntered up to the microphone and greeted the crowd.

"Hello, all you Summer Harvesters," she said.

The crowd that had packed most of the bleachers and folding chairs surrounding the stage shouted salutations in return.

The singer picked up an acoustic guitar and set in on a better-than-decent version of Texas' *I Don't Want a Lover*, the twang of the opening guitar licks ushering in the sunset.

"I'm getting hungry," Joanna said, as she bagged a fresh load of trash and set it by the door.

"It's a little slow just now," I said, straining to be heard over the band as the lead singer passionately pleaded with an imagined lover.

"Folks are at the stage or on the rides," I said. "It's the perfect time for some Voc Tech chicken."

"Sounds good," Marge shouted from just outside the back door while smoking her latest unfiltered Camel.

"According to my husband, anytime is the perfect time for that chicken," Joanna said, rummaging through her purse for some money. "Here," she said, handing me a wad of cash. "I'd love some."

"Great," I replied, accepting the bills and heading

for the back door. "Mind the fort while I'm gone."

"Don't eat it all on the way back," Marge called after I slipped past her.

I headed for the Voc Tech booth, the last booth before the stage, picking my way across the Gordian tangle of extension cords running along the ground at the back of the booths while peeking into each booth to see what culinary delights the respective occupants were preparing. I paused to watch a heavy-set man wearing a hair-net, flipping burgers with the ease of a seasoned fry cook, before moving on to find a woman in the next booth busily lathering hot dogs with Coney Island sauce, onions, mustard and celery salt. I paused to watch a young Asian couple preparing Chinese food dishes in yet another booth. I listened to them argue in their native language about a topic that completely eluded my western ears before my attention turned to a woman in another booth slicing out portions of fudge and handing them over to voracious customers. All the while, Wicked Scarlett's singer did her best imitation of Sharleen Spiteri as other band members wailed away on harmonica and piano celebrating the woman's misery as she desperately pleaded her case, sounding every bit as forlorn as Bono had the night before on my Ipod.

I turned into the alleyway that separated booth number one, the Voc Tech booth, from the Harvest Craft building, a large shed with a picket fence where local crafts were being sold by two men sitting in beach chairs, each wearing navy blue Veterans' caps with gold-embroidered printing.

I queued up at the Voc Tech counter along with an interesting assortment of characters to sample the secret recipe (which was little more than deep-fried Tyson frozen chicken with a few spices added and fresh-cut French fries). Waiting beside me with bated appetites were a middle-aged woman talking on a mobile phone, a pair of men wearing mechanics' navy-blue jump suits, their hands rich with automotive grease, and a thin blonde woman with an extensive brood of hyper-active children. The last was wearing a grin so devoid of emotion that it could only have been induced by a considerable dose of mood stabilizers. The Fayre, it seemed, was nothing if not a slice of humanity.

The band broke into the instrumental portion of the song just then, and, as my turn to order was a ways off, I turned to watch. The lead singer stepped back from the microphone, hammering away at the acoustic guitar as the music turned darkly frenetic. It was so loud I barely felt my mobile phone vibrating against my hip. I plucked it from its case, shielded my opposing ear and, with my stomach grumbling, reluctantly stepped out of line.

"Well, well, carnival boy," 'Gospel' Tom said after I managed a 'hello.' "How's Doughnutville? Rolling in dough, are we? Get it? Dough?"

"I get it and selling doughnuts isn't so bad," I shouted into the mouthpiece to be heard above the din.

"Sounds loud there," he said. "Are the Who playing? Perhaps Rush?"

"Not exactly," I said, glancing at the stage. The lead singer had stepped back up to the microphone and was preparing to bring it home.

"I'm close to the stage," I said. "Wait a minute."

I walked past the Harvest shed into the parking lot, past a departing hay ride fully laden with Fayre-goers, until the tones of Wicked Scarlett faded to a dull roar. There I found a seat on the concrete base of a light pole situated at the edge of the staff parking lot.

"Better?"

"Much," Tom said.

"So what do you have to tell me?"

"I've made a few discoveries regarding your specimen," he said.

"I thought you'd forgotten."

"How could I forget? You happen to be my only client just now."

"So what did you find out?"

"Well," he began, "it's puzzling. I'm not sure what to make of it, so I'll need to run a few more tests. But I'll definitely call you tonight. This may turn out to be nothing, but then again, it may turn out to be quite interesting. Oh, by the by, I visited your neighbor's yard to steal a sample. It was easy picking; there was a big pile sitting right on the curb in front of that run-down rat trap he calls a house."

"Are you sure it's Rufus', uh, sample?"

"Pretty sure," he said. "Hot off the press, so to speak. So what time will you be getting home?"

"Twelve at the earliest," I said, "what with clean-up and all. And there are fireworks tonight, so we might stay to watch."

"Understood," Tom said. "You can expect to hear from me. If the results turn out to be a dud I won't call until morning so as not to disturb your romantic interlude."

I thanked him for calling, said goodbye, and started back toward the front of the booth, just as the imitation Sharleen Spiteri finished the song, waited for the applause to fade and addressed the crowd.

"How we all doin' tonight?"

A mixed sound rose up from the crowd.

"I said, how we all doin' tonight?"

The second response was more enthusiastic.

"That's what I wanna' hear," she said and the crowd howled again.

I reached the front of the booth and found myself mingling with a new batch of chicken enthusiasts, most noticeably a young couple who seemed on the verge of having sex right then and there. I thought it a miracle that they managed to keep their lips separated long enough to place an order. When my turn came I ordered three plates of chicken and fries, two diet Cokes for the women and a bottle of water for myself. The man running the booth, a local softball coach whose claim to fame was having survived Woodstock, nodded and said, "Right you are." He turned to bark out the order to the two young men at the Friolators as I stepped aside to listen to the band.

"Now, ladies," the lead singer said, "have you ever wondered if your man's been stepping out on you?"

A handful of women in the crowd broke into applause and the singer transformed before my eyes into Shania Twain and proceeded to ask that age-old question, *Whose Bed Have Your Boots Been Under?*

After a few minutes, the softball coach called my number and, after dowsing the plates with helpings of vinegar and salt and wrapping them in aluminum foil, I scooped up the dinners, carefully balancing them one on top of another and, clutching the drinks between my chest and forearm, I started back to the booth.

I was rounding the back corner of the Voc Tech booth, my mind preoccupied with the food in my arms and the band playing at my back, when abruptly a bright yellow blur loomed in front of me.

I stepped to one side, barely avoiding a collision with a man wearing a traditional yellow Summer Harvest Fayre staff tee shirt saying, "Whoops," or some equally ridiculous comment which drew what I perceived in passing to be a reprimanding glance from the tee shirt's owner. I turned in hopes of clearing the air and exchanging friendly apologies, but one look at the man told me that any chance of mutual courtesies amounted to little more than wishful thinking.

The lean grim figure I beheld possessed a harsh face seared to a dark brown color by the sun and deeply cut with crevices that only a hard life could etch. The eyes were dark and set in deep hollows beneath a sharply sloping brow that made the face and nose appear hawk-like. The

54

hair atop the head was scraggly, greasy, dark and unkempt. The arms hung like a pair of sinewy cables riddled with thick veins, the hands and fingers unusually large and knobby. Layers of grease were deeply imbedded in the creases of the knuckles and beneath the jagged fingernails.

As my initial surprise waned, I opened my mouth to apologize, still grasping at the slimmest hope that such a display might cause the stranger to reciprocate. But before I could utter a syllable, the man flashed me some oversized stained teeth, turned and vanished into the midway.

I stood, feeling foolish and oddly violated, balancing the plates of food in my arms like an apprentice juggler.

"Same to you," I mumbled in a desperate effort to maintain some degree of face before one of the plates began to slip. Catching it with my chin, I hurried back to the booth, the heat from the plates' contents searing into my flesh and making my eyes water.

Joanna and Marge met me at the back door, took the plates from me and went about setting them on the table. I crossed immediately to the counter and surveyed the midway, leaning out to the point of almost toppling forward, straining in the direction of the Voc Tech booth, anxious to catch another glimpse of the stranger with whom I'd nearly collided. But there was no sign of the man. I shifted my gaze to the midway, which was absolutely jam-packed with Fayre-goers. In all my years working the booth, I had never seen it this crowded. People were everywhere, some emerging in gluts from the chicken barbecue tent at the heart of the Fayre, others heading in, some perusing leftovers from the Anything Goes Yard Sale. Still others were streaming past on their way to the rides and games farther down the midway.

I turned my attention to the many vendor tents set up beyond the barbecue tent. A crowd had gathered beyond these to watch the pig races. Several men in farmer jeans were studying the tractors and combines squatting in the field across the street, where the equestrian event had been held that morning and the dog agility demonstration would be held tomorrow.

I turned to the audience gathered at the stage listening to the concert. The crowd occupying the bleachers to the left of the stage and the folding chairs at the front had swelled beyond capacity, reaching a point where people were sitting on the ground on blankets or standing at the back. Many were dancing to the music, but most were eating popcorn, cotton candy, and, thank goodness, Joanna's doughnuts. There was no sign of the man I had seen, but in a crowd of this size it would prove virtually impossible to pick him out, especially since all regular carnival personnel were required to wear identical bright yellow tee shirts.

I looked to the horizon where the sun was settling into a crimson pool behind the woods, its last rays passing through the spokes of the Ferris wheel like laser beams. There was a stillness in the air as if the evening was waiting with bated anticipation for the arrival of the second full moon of the month, the first having been the full Buck Moon, this one the proverbial Blue Moon or, in this particular case, the Thunder Moon.

I was suddenly aware of an oddly familiar odor, one I could only describe as mechanical in nature. Mixed in with the expected smell of food and the occasional whiff of body odor, I detected the unmistakable smell of ozone. I assumed it to be the by-product of the many generators that were needed to run the rides, but there was something strangely alien about it. The odor seemed to be coming from everywhere at once. And it was far too pungent, as if I were standing beside an immense generator.

I sensed something was going to happen. It had started Tuesday night with my discovery. Since then, the world seemed to be turning like the needle of a compass toward the strange and unfamiliar. This was the first time I consciously felt this odd sensation, the first time I sensed something moving unseen through the fabric of reality, some malevolent force hovering nearby. Like Spooky growling at the garage sensor light, I knew something was amiss. But it would not be the last time I would feel this way. Things were just beginning.

"Let's eat," Joanna said after setting out the dishes, drinks, napkins and plastic Sporks, "before the crowd picks up again."

I turned one last time to scan the crowd for my strange friend, and, though I spied several bright yellow Summer Harvest Fayre tee shirts, mostly manning gaming booths and operating rides, I failed to pick out the weathered face I'd seen.

The band had finished peeling off another song, Melissa Etheridge's *Come to my Window*, and was leading into a new tune, this one a distinctly less pop-sounding one than any of its predecessors, a song that seemed out of sync with the other numbers they had been playing. But when the lead singer set into it with her pop country twist, it all made musical sense. It was a Hal Ketchum tune, *Small Town Saturday Night*. I remember liking this song when I first heard it due to its true-to-life observations about small towns and their respective denizens.

I surveyed the midway with its crush of bodies moving past the booth as if in sync with the music. Adults, children, teenagers, carrying food, drinks and stuffed animals, wearing everything from fancy shorts and Polo shirts to grubby jeans, black leather vests, Capri pants and practically nonexistent tank tops. It was like watching a slice of humanity, the denizens of *my* small town on parade, the Ketchum song come to life before my eyes.

I felt myself grinning. Then, chuckling aloud, I joined the women at the table and we started in on supper.

Chapter Eight

Libby Chambers and Dick Saunders arrived shortly past seven. Libby was all smiles in a light summer dress that hung off her gaunt frame like a sheer tent, and Saunders his typically ruddy and gruff self but apparently sober.

"How're the Sox doing?" he asked, taking note of Marge's television.

"They're up one to nothing in the first," she said as she handed a young woman wearing a cowboy hat a warm doughnut on a napkin, "but it ain't over 'till it's over."

"Son-of-a-bitch," Dick growled and Joanna glared at him.

"Oh," he said covering his thick lips with his thicker fingers, "I forgot; customers."

Libby rolled her pale blue eyes at me and shook her head before stepping up to the counter to wait on a young couple holding what appeared to be a big stuffed wolf between them.

"Joanna, I'm going to head out," Marge said as she stepped through the back door, produced another cigarette, and set it between her lips.

"All right," Joanna said, joining her, "I'll see you tomorrow."

"Sure thing, Hon. 'Bout three, okay?"

Joanna nodded and walked the woman to her car as Libby and I set about serving a fresh batch of doughnut buyers. Dick Saunders made himself comfortable in one of the folding chairs, settling in to watch the game while munching on a doughnut.

"Don't know what all the fuss is about," he said considering the half-eaten thing as if it were a hangnail. "Doughnut's a doughnut. Nothin' special," he concluded while reaching for another.

Joanna returned and squeezed past Dick who seemed content to let her do so and she told him not to work too hard. Dick agreed and reached out with a pudgy finger to turn the ball game up while plucking a fresh doughnut from a box he had set on his lap.

***

The rest of the night passed uneventfully. The band reeled off a variety of tunes spanning decades and genres. During the band's breaks, a DJ calling himself Wild Wayne took over and spun some crowd pleasers including Elvis Presley's *Suspicious Minds*, one of my personal favorites, along with a few Beatles and Stones standards.

During all this, Dick Saunders actually managed to sell a few doughnuts. That is to say, once he got up off his ass to get a look at the band and the crowded midway. He even managed to spit out a few inappropriate comments about some of the women strolling past the booth as well as the band's female lead singer's tight leather pants. He also succeeded in using the staff bathroom, (a large shed located near the dumpster that required a key kept on a peg by the door), enough times to suggest he had a kidney disorder.

One time I stepped out back to get some fresh air and spied him returning from his pickup truck, which was parked two rows back at the opposite end of the lot. When I saw this, I got the distinct impression that Dick was secretly adding as much to his bladder as he was removing. When I returned to the counter, Libby confirmed my suspicions.

"Dick's got a cooler full of beer," she said. "He let it slip on the ride over. But he promised he wouldn't drink until he got to some late night cookout he was going to after the Fayre. For guys like Dick, life seems to be one perpetual cookout."

"I saw him sneaking one," I whispered. "And I'd bet he's been sneaking them all night long. I don't think you should ride home with him. Do you want us to give you a lift?"

"No, thanks. My sister is picking me up around nine-thirty," she said. "I would have driven myself in, but she needed my SUV to pick up a load of plants for her yard and Dick came by to help my husband move a gas stove out of the basement. When he volunteered to give me a lift, I couldn't say no, but I wasn't born last night. Dick hasn't remained sober enough to drive himself home for as long as I've known him."

"I feel better knowing you won't be riding with him," I said.

"What's the clandestine conversation about?" Joanna asked as she joined us at the counter.

"Dick is sneaking some beers out of his truck," I said.

Joanna looked to Libby who nodded in agreement.

Dick chose that moment to enter through the back door, nearly tripping as he stepped up and cursing at his own clumsiness. He plunked down in the chair in front of Marge's television and belched.

"Hey, Dick," Joanna said. "We're all set here if you have any place to be."

I turned and pretended to be inspecting the remaining stack of doughnuts on the table. We were down to six dozen and four singles, but I knew this already; I just wanted to keep an eye on Joanna in case Dick got mad that he was politely being shown the door. Rumors about Dick getting nasty after he'd had a few weren't rumors at all. Bruises don't lie; Dick's wife Janet could sadly attest to that.

"I don't mind staying," he said, his words running together like mud. "Besides, the game's not over."

"You don't have to," Joanna said. "We're almost out of doughnuts anyway and we'll be locking up soon."

"Oh," he said, glancing at the doughnut boxes on the table. "All right," he added with a shrug that sent shock waves through his entire body. But there was something in his voice, something accusatory as if he resented being asked to leave, and I found myself watching him, waiting for the other shoe to drop.

He got to his feet, roughly pushing the chair back, causing it to bang loudly against the refrigerator.

"Fuckers gave up the lead anyway," he growled. He shook his head, stroked his walrus-like moustache and waved a broad hand in our direction. Then he slurred, "Night all," and headed out the door.

"Asshole," Libby mumbled.

"How does his wife stand it?" Joanna said.

"I heard she might be leaving him," Libby volunteered.

I went to the doorway and watched Dick as he crossed to his truck.

"How bad is he?" Joanna asked, joining me in my vigil.

"He's walking straight enough," I said. "If we try to stop him, he'll make a scene. There are police around, and if he gets too loud when we confront him, he might get arrested."

"You're right," Joanna said. "I guess this isn't the best time for an intervention. Just the same, we should call Janet and let her know what's heading her way."

"I'm sure she's used to it," I said, "but that's a good idea."

"I don't think you *ever* get used to that sort of thing," Libby said. "Even if you think you have."

We all agreed that we would call Janet Saunders; Dick's apparent state warranted it. But Dick's delicate condition was hardly a secret. He'd been banned from a few local restaurants and bars, and once or twice Janet Saunders had shown up to work at the Bridgton Central Post Office with tell-tale marks on her face, marks she attributed to clumsiness. Unfortunately, as was often

61

typical in such situations, she refused to acknowledge that Dick ever hit her. I was relieved to hear Libby say she thought the woman was considering leaving for greener pastures. I silently wished her luck; we all did.

I turned back to the counter and was taken completely by surprise to see Alice Williams standing there, her stern features softening a little as she saw us, a broad grin spreading across her weathered face.

"Hi, Alice."

"Hey, Jack-o-lantern," she said, her voice friendly but typically clipped and concise.

Alice Williams was an odd duck, but I suppose I had seen odder in my day. Tonight, for instance, in spite of the heat, she was wearing a denim jacket, blue jeans and a Boston Red Sox cap pulled down over her deeply set green eyes. I found my own eyes drawn to what appeared to be bruising around her upper cheeks. She seemed to sense my scrutiny and pulled the cap down lower. I decided what I'd thought to be bruising was nothing more than the shadow caused by the cap she was wearing, coupled with my own suddenly overly-suspicious imagination. Talk of Dick Saunders' bad behavior had evidently gotten to me.

'Gospel' Tom Williams was hardly Dick Saunders. And Alice Williams was certainly *not* Janet Saunders. She might not have been a big brute of a person, but at five foot seven inches tall, she possessed a surprisingly powerful presence and would probably have killed Tom if he ever lifted a finger against her.

"Aren't you roasting in that?" I asked.

"Nah," she said. "I guess I'm just cold blooded."

"So what brings Alice to the Fayre?" Joanna asked as she joined me at the counter.

"I thought I'd find my husband here," she said surveying the bustling midway. "He went out a while ago; haven't heard from him since. No answer on his mobile, either."

"Not here," I said before catching myself. "I mean, if he *is* here, we haven't seen him." I had to be careful; for all I knew Tom was skulking around my yard at that moment searching for clues to support my argument, an argument in which I was quickly losing interest.

"Well, I'll keep looking," Alice said. "Joanna, how about a break? I want to check out the books at the Anything Goes Sale and I could use one of those fresh-squeezed lemonades the Old Dominion Road School is selling."

"Do you mind?" Joanna asked.

"Of course not," I said, realizing Joanna would never take a break under any other circumstances.

"You haven't stopped since I got here," Libby said. "Have some clam cakes while you're gone. The booth run by Chet's Garage is selling them. I hear they're great this year."

"Good idea," Joanna said and she ducked out the back door. A moment later she joined Alice at the front of the booth.

"Mind the fort," she called as they headed into the crowded midway.

"Will do," I said. "Don't stay out too late."

"Oh, I guess I should call Janet Saunders and tell her about Dick's condition," Libby said. She retrieved her purse from the top of the refrigerator and began rummaging through it. Finding her mobile phone, she stepped out back where the signal was better to make the call.

I turned back to the midway and served a pair of doughnuts to a stray middle-aged couple sharing a cotton candy, as if they were ten years old again. A lull in business set in after that and I decided to count the money in the cash box. I determined that we were considerably ahead and there were still three days remaining before the Fayre pulled up stakes. Another successful venture for Joanna Graves, I thought. I would have to start teasing her again

63

about Fortune Magazine doing a cover story about her entrepreneurial efforts.

I closed the cash box and returned to my post, but the crowd was thinning and no new customers presented themselves. Something made me think of my strange encounter earlier and I began scanning the crowded midway for signs of the carny with whom I'd nearly collided while getting supper. The bright yellow Summer Harvest Fayre tee shirts were everywhere, bobbing in and out of the crowd. But for all my effort, I could find no trace of the character I had encountered among them.

The band closed their final set with a rather dark and desperate sounding piece by Texas called *Say a Prayer*. I found myself listening to the lyrics as I watched for my 'friend' to re-appear.

In my mind's eye I relived the strange encounter, trying in vain to fathom what had evoked such a dark reaction from the strange man. I came up empty.

When the band finished, the lead vocalist bade the crowd good night and promised to return on Saturday to close the Fayre out, hoping to see familiar faces watching from the audience. She told everyone to drive safely and the crowd applauded enthusiastically, then began breaking up.

Clutches of people began spilling into the midway while others started picking their way toward the main parking lot. Many remained, some perched in their seats, others milling about, talking with friends in anticipation of the upcoming fireworks display. Some of the younger, more adventurous ones wended their way toward the other food booths, games and rides for one last dance with the Summer Harvest Fayre's pied piper.

"Janet's not home," Libby said as she joined me at the counter. "I tried her mobile, too. I didn't think it prudent to leave a message telling her that her husband is a drunken asshole."

"Not prudent at all," I said as a glut of people, fresh from the show, made a beeline for our booth.

"I'll try one more time before I go," Libby said as we set about taking fresh doughnut orders.

***

The rush ended and Joanna returned, looking drawn and pale as if she'd gotten some bad news, instead of some well-deserved relaxation.

"What's wrong?" I asked, momentarily forgetting one of the primary rules of marriage.

"Nothing," she said, distracted, forcing a grin.

I presumed that she was simply tired and decided not to press it further.

Libby's mobile phone rang and she stepped out back to talk. When she returned, she told us that her sister was on the way to pick her up.

"Thanks a bunch for your help," Joanna said, and the two women hugged.

"Call me if you need me to work again," Libby said, "but don't call Dick any more," she added with a wink. Then she picked up her purse, bade us good evening, and disappeared into the night.

***

By nine-forty we were out of doughnuts and Joanna was feeling better. She'd apparently gotten a second wind because, as fireworks time neared, she grew more enthusiastic. In spite of the speed bumps along the way, Marge not being able to pick up the doughnuts, and Dick Saunders' brush with the bottle, the night was working its way toward a perfect ending. And to top it all off, The Red Sox had come from behind and beaten the Yankees.

I packed up the last of the trash and headed for the dumpster as Joanna cleaned the table and microwave. I was tired and my body ached, but it was a good ache, a job-well-done ache.

I passed several other vendors on identical missions

and exchanged hellos with some, but most barely noticed me, clearly engrossed with their respective tasks, visions of their respective beds dancing in their respective heads.

Tossing the trash into the dumpster, I turned to gaze at the moon rising like a ball of fire from behind the stage. It was positively huge, not quite full but waxing. The jagged details of its scarred face were easy to pick out, crevices, mountains, all so close I might have reached up and touched them. It seemed the meteorologist had gotten it right this time. If only they could be as accurate about the weather.

I paused to consider the activity surrounding me, the people carrying trash to the dumpster, the Ferris wheel with its lighted spokes spinning against the black sky. Something stirred above me and I looked up to see bats flitting past the light suspended atop the bathroom shed as they gobbled up mosquitoes by the dozens. In spite of the organized chaos, the Fayre had taken on an almost serene quality and I found myself feeling oddly at peace, a welcome respite from the bustle of the day.

I listened to the sounds: popping air rifles, barkers telling people to step right up and try their luck, three balls for two dollars or six for three, the mechanical hum of rides moving through their endless paces and generators whirring with electrical life. Voices, car engines, honking horns, the snap of gravel under tires as people drove out of the parking lot, all found me in turn. Each sound was different and complete, ranging from the clang of safety bars on rides as they slammed shut to the pinging of air pellets rebounding off targets.

Thinking along these lines, I realized that, like the different sounds drifting past me, a thousand different stories had crossed the Fayre ground this night. Mine was only one. This made me feel better about the recent turn of events. Renko was Renko and the world was full of Renkos. And Rufus was just a dog, not some dime-store-novel villain up to no good, or some supernatural entity skulking through a forgotten graveyard. At that moment, my well-conceived revenge plot turned from a clever idea to a childish prank that would fade completely from my thoughts with time.

Joanna didn't know the whole story, but she had been right when she told me not to blow things out of proportion and to 'let sleeping dogs lie.' I had been a fool to involve Tom. I had inadvertently become a parishioner of my own version of the Church of I-have-way-too-much-free-time-on-my-hands. I decided that I would call Tom in the morning and tell him to forget the whole thing. I supposed I would get stuck buying him the case of beer I'd promised, but that seemed a small price to pay for the redemption of my common sense. We could drink it together, toasting to our long-lost boyhoods. Corona Light for the Love Machine, he'd said. I wondered what Alice Williams would say about that particular descriptive?

I found my gaze drawn once again to the moon. It hovered above me like a great burning stone, and I tried to imagine how early man must have felt the first time he ventured from the primeval forest and beheld such an impressive sight. It must have been terrifying. It was little wonder the lunar cycle had come to be associated with so much myth and mystery throughout history.

I was a rational human being, though, not given to flights of fancy. Superstition, according to 'Gospel' Tom, was nothing but religion without a home.

Joanna, who considered the universe to be a more mystical place than I, would respond to my pontificating by countering with the oft-told Shakespearian view of the heavens and earth holding more things than my meager philosophy could possibly conceive. Such an exchange between us, though rare, would invariably lead to an evening of friendly but opposing banter which would soon be forgotten in lieu of something more interesting on the television (or occasionally in the bedroom).

Differing views on some things can be good, even stimulating, especially in a marriage. It would make no sense to marry someone who held identical beliefs; like a civilization without objectives to overcome, boredom and decay would soon follow.

Setting my philosophical musings aside, I began to realize just how much better I was actually feeling, and I breathed in a lungful of summer night. It seems, at least sometime, that the biggest cures do indeed come in the smallest vials.

I headed back to the booth, energized and feeling better than I had all day. The moon filling the sky reminded me of the Hal Ketchum song, and I began to sing to myself as I walked.

I'd covered half the distance to the booth when a nagging sensation told me to turn around. Like Lot's wife I obeyed the urge, thinking I had perhaps dropped my wallet or car keys, and, checking my pockets, I turned to scan the shadows for any wayward belongings.

My eyes immediately fell upon a gaunt figure standing like a totem beside the bathroom, his face lost to deep shadow due to the angle of the light falling from above. Something inside me, some strange cold thing in my stomach, put a face where there was none and I knew without a doubt that my peculiar friend from behind the Voc Tech booth had found me.

He stood stock still, his arms held out from his sides as if locked in some catatonic trance, the only thing distinguishing him from a block of stone being his fists which opened and closed slowly, rhythmically, like a heart pumping blood.

"Can I help you?" I asked, my voice cracking around the words like old china and, as if in response to my question, the first round of fireworks exploded in the sky above.

68

Surprised, I turned long enough to glimpse the vivid blossom of fire eclipse the face of the moon. But my attention was torn as a new sensation, one I could only describe as sheer panic, gripped me and I spun around to confront the carny, who I felt certain was bearing down on me. But to my surprise and relief, I found him to be nowhere in sight. I was suddenly as uncomfortable with the stranger's absence as I was with his presence, remembering that it was the wolf you *don't* see that you have to worry about.

I searched the cleanly-etched darkness at the edge of the Fayre, but the only people moving through the shadows were vendors carrying garbage bags to the dumpster or pans to the sinks at the back of the bathroom for washing. The stranger was nowhere in sight; only the flitting shadows of bats circling above remained.

I found myself feeling more than a little disturbed by this new encounter. It wasn't just the man's silence that bothered me. It was the *deliberateness* of his silence. He was watching me, me *specifically*, acting as if I couldn't see him, as if he was scrutinizing me from behind a two-way fun house mirror.

I felt suddenly vulnerable. I realized that I was just a guest here; this was his Fayre, and if he wanted to elude me, he would have little difficulty doing so. I decided not to search any further and made my way back to the booth, my eyes down, the Hal Ketchum song gone from my mind, the explosions in the sky wasted on me.

There was something odd about this man, something besides his silence and his appearance, something that I could not decipher. Twice this night he had picked me out of the crowd. But why? Was he angry that we had nearly collided at the Voc Tech booth? Was he the sort who took such an accident to be a deliberate affront worthy of retaliation? Or did I simply look familiar to him?

No answers presented themselves and I kept

walking.

Joanna had finished cleaning up by the time I got back, and we switched off the overhead lights to sit there in the darkened booth watching the fireworks, me on one of the folding chairs, Joanna nestled in my lap like two high school sweethearts. It should have been relaxing, Joanna lying in my arms, her hair inches from my face and her breathing sending soft ripples through my body. But it wasn't; something was wrong. The chair I was sitting on felt like the edge of a razor. Each time the sky filled with the fire of another round of explosives, I found myself scanning the upturned faces crowding the midway for a glimpse of the carny with the dark, menacing eyes; but I didn't see him again.

There was some kissing, but no flames were rekindled; we were both tired and the feeling I'd hoped to rediscover remained elusive. When the fireworks ended, we secured the booth and drove home, exhausted.

Chapter Nine

We arrived home too tired to say much, changed out of our clothes and tumbled into bed. Spooky proceeded to barrage us with nasty looks, the sort dogs rain down upon their masters when they feel they've been slighted. But she eventually forgave us and, after taking care of her business in the yard, hopped into bed, cuddling up to Joanna and settling into a deep slumber. I turned on the news and watched in a state of semi-consciousness as a reporter standing on the edge of some woods with the big full moon hovering over his shoulder explained how coyotes were showing up everywhere and how people should be especially careful with their pets and small children.

Coyotes were not unusual in New England. I'd seen a few over the years and occasionally heard them baying at night. But I couldn't imagine one of them ever venturing onto the Fayre grounds or into someone's yard.

"Spooky, you'd better watch out for the coyotes."

Spooky snorted her disdain at my quip. I turned to Joanna, but she had dozed off. Something occurred to me then. What if my trespasser was a coyote? My yard was surrounded by a four-foot-high chain link fence and I didn't know if coyotes could jump that high, but Rufus, who was about the same size, had managed it last summer during the trash-tipping incident. Perhaps a coyote could do the same. I would have to be careful letting Spooky out at night, just in case.

A pompous-looking anchorman with perfectly coiffed hair surrendered control of the news to the meteorologist, an attractive Indian woman with jet-black hair and sharp angular features.

"The heat will be sticking around through the Thunder Moon's visit," she began. "Incidentally, for you amateur astronomers out there, in addition to the moon being a Super Moon, it is also closer to the Earth than it has been in sixty thousand years, so the tides will be abnormally high for the next few days. And along with the moon's proximity, the planet Mars is *also* closer to the Earth than it has been in about a hundred and twenty thousand years. That means the gravitational forces are at an all-time high."

"Great," I said, picking up the remote and shutting off the TV. My students were always off the wall when the moon was full, and this was not a typical full moon. Thank goodness for summer vacation. I had only the one student I tutored at the library on Saturday mornings, and he was never a problem.

I tossed the remote aside and was about to roll over and search for sleep when the phone rang.

I hopped out of bed and scooped the thing up. Covering the mouthpiece I glanced back at Joanna, who was still asleep, before heading for the four seasons' room at the front of the house.

I closed the French doors behind me and said, "Hello."

"I hope I didn't wake you," 'Gospel' Tom said.

"I wasn't asleep yet," I said, flopping down on the couch without bothering to turn on the light.

"I have interesting news about your 'night deposit,'"

"That's good, but before I forget, Alice was at the Fayre looking for you."

"Ah, there's nothing like a little mystery to keep the woman guessing."

"Whatever you say, Don Juan. So what's your news?"

"I was at your neighbor's place tonight," Tom began. "I needed a fresh sample. My research ran into a snag, and I had to confirm some things."

"Well, was it Rufus or not?" My bed was calling me. And as for my interest in revenge, it had died at the feet of the strange carny.

"It seems your depositor is quite unusual–"

"Cut to the chase Tom, I'm–"

"That sample didn't come from a dog. It came from a human being."

I sat silent, processing Tom's words.

"Are you there?"

"Yeah," I said, confused. "You're saying the sample is from–"

"–a human being," Tom finished.

"How is that possible?"

"First I ran a comparative analysis against your neighbor's dog; no match. Then I used one of the canine DNA tests, to see if I could determine *which* breed of dog left your deposit. The sample didn't come close to any dog breed. So I tried one of the human heredity kits, trying to get a baseline of some sort. And I got a match; your sample came from a human being."

"Tom–"

"Just how well do you know your neighbor?"

"You don't think–"

"I think some kid hopped your fence, found no pool to take a midnight swim in and decided to leave a calling card. That's *my* opinion."

I started to speak, but paused as a set of headlights swam across the shades at the side of the room facing Renko's house.

"Wait," I said and I went to the window.

"Something wrong?"

"Renko's home," I said prying open the blinds.

I watched the old truck pull up beside Renko's back porch. The engine coughed once and fell silent. A moment passed, but Renko failed to emerge from the darkened cab. Perhaps my neighbor had decided to spend the night passed out behind the wheel. Then the interior light came on and Robert Renko stumbled out of the driver's side, slammed the door, awkwardly mounted his back porch, and let himself into his house.

"What were we talking about?"

"I was asking, just how well do you know your neighbor?"

"I know him well enough to know he's an asshole, but not well enough to know if he's the type to crap in my yard as a joke."

"People who drink to excess tend to howl at the moon from time to time." Tom snorted as if something had struck him as funny. "Do you remember when we were undergrads and that guy, Phil something-or-other, got mad at his ex-girlfriend and took a crap in the hall of her dormitory, then wrote the word 'Bitch' across her door with his own shit?"

"How could I forget?"

"He was pretty drunk when he did that and it scared the hell out of the girl."

"He'd also taken two hits of Window Pane, if I recall."

"True," Tom said chuckling softly, clearly enjoying his little excursion down memory lane. "Perhaps your visitor has done the same. If I remember correctly, our tripping friend claimed he was *marking his territory* like an animal. Dean of students felt differently."

He paused as if collecting his thoughts and when he spoke again there was no trace of jocularity in his voice.

"But this isn't college," he said, "and Phil what's-his-name is probably not prowling around your yard leaving little 'deposits' for you to find, so be careful." I heard him sigh. "Listen, I'd like to come by tomorrow morning to take a few more samples."

"All right," I said, taking note of Tom's somber tone.

Renko's screen door creaked open, and through the blind's slats, I watched Rufus bound down the steps. The dog squatted and finished his business quickly, probably fearing retribution from his inebriated master if he moved too slowly. When finished he raised his mangy head and, after searching the night for some unknown quarry, his dark eyes locked on mine.

I let the blinds snap shut and stepped back from the window. I stood there, my heart pounding in my ears, waiting to hear Renko's voice saying, "What's the matter, boy? Someone watching us?" But the words never came.

After a few seconds I leaned forward and peered out at the pair next door. Rufus had apparently not seen me, because he darted up the stairs and vanished into the house.

I found myself suddenly filled with fresh disdain for my neighbor and I slowly allowed the blinds to close. I returned to the couch and flicked on the table light beside me, the cold sensation wriggling through my stomach. I opened my mouth to say something to Tom, but caught myself when a floorboard creaked. I sat up. I thought of Joanna waking to find me missing and got to my feet.

"So–" Tom began.

"Hang on," I whispered, reaching for the handle to the French doors that led to the living room. I caught a glimpse of movement on the other side of the lowest pane of glass and I froze, my heart hitching in my chest.

"What's wrong?" Tom asked, his voice laced with genuine concern.

I ignored him, turned the handle and opened the door. Spooky looked up at me inquisitively from the darkened living room.

"Jesus," I whispered as she trotted in and hopped up on the couch.

"What is it?" Tom asked.

"Just my dog trying to give me a heart attack," I said closing the door and joining Spooky on the sofa. She nestled in beside me and I began stroking her back.

"All right," Tom said, "that's enough excitement for tonight. We'll resume in the morning."

I said goodbye, sat back and rubbed my eyes. This day felt as if it had run into extra innings and I couldn't wait to hit the hay.

"Bed time, old girl," I said, and I made my way to the bedroom, Spooky in tow. Tonight Spooky made no move toward the back door, and I must admit I was grateful for that.

I returned the phone to its cradle, then climbed into bed, Spooky at my heels, and was asleep before my head hit the pillow. I awoke with a start to the sound of Spooky growling from the foot of the bed. I turned to the open window and realized that the garage sensor light was activated. I held my breath, listening for the sounds of the night, but they had fled for safer parts.

A feeling of Deja vu crept through me and I sat up, a big part of me dreading to look out the window, a much smaller part dying to look. Before I could muster the courage to do anything, the light went dark and, as if on the same electric timer, Spooky stopped growling and laid her shaggy head down. I had apparently awakened at the end of the light's five-minute cycle. I watched and waited, but the light remained dark. Eventually I lay back down and closed my eyes.

Sleep eventually found me and, for the third time that night, so did the carny. In my dream he was standing in the middle of the darkened, deserted midway, his face lost in deep shadow as scraps of newspaper blew across the ground like tumbleweeds in a ghost town. His fists were planted at his thighs, fingers pumping in a disturbingly mechanized manner, clenching, unclenching and clenching again as if locked in a perpetual seizure, the veins in his lean arms bulging from the effort, ready to burst. The Ferris wheel rose above the sharp slope of his right shoulder, a huge twisted tangle of steel set against the black sky, the bloated moon the only light, its scarred surface crimson as if stained with blood. And caught up on the wind like the wail of some ancient siren was the voice of the singer from Wicked Scarlett slowly cranking out the lyrics to the Hal Ketchum song, her words wavering as if she were standing at the bottom of a well.

Chapter Ten

The next day brought sun and a welcome breeze that I knew wouldn't last. Joanna left around nine, after having breakfast, to meet my sister Ellen at the Bridgton Mall. Macy's one-day sale had apparently blossomed into a two-day event and both women were anxious to get their share of bargains.

I ate breakfast, dressed in my work togs and set about servicing my yard. I began by finishing up the redressing of the peat moss, a job I had started several days earlier but failed to complete due to a surprise afternoon rain shower. As I worked, shoveling peat and leveling it with an iron rake, I found myself periodically glancing over at Renko's house. I found myself studying its badly worn roof, its rotting porch beams and sagging steps. I remembered the house being much cleaner and somehow friendlier when I was a boy. Then, with very different occupants, it had reminded me of a gingerbread house with its once-vibrant blue shingles and dark trim, though lacking a resident witch. Now, gray and somber, the place might very well have served as a hostel for witches.

Similarly, Renko's truck had fallen into such a state of disrepair that I often had to check twice to determine if the thing was in the driveway because, when present, its rusted hide blended nearly perfectly with the house's dirty facade. This morning a second glance was required for me to realize that the thing was nowhere to be seen. I found it hard to believe that Bob Renko, with his late hours and predictably typical hangover, could possibly have gotten an early start.

But with yard work pressing, I set thoughts of my neighbor aside, and in no time I was listening to the noon whistle at the silver plant across town. Pleased with my efforts, I headed for the garden hose to wash my hands.

I had barely finished cleaning up and was coiling

the hose when Tom arrived. He parked in front of my garage, climbed out of his Jeep and unloaded a small, rectangular carrying case.

"Hello," he said, proceeding to the gate, looking like some eccentric college professor in his Salvation Army clothes.

"Hello, Henry Higgins," I said, and Tom eyed me suspiciously.

It occurred to me that there were many reasons for my wife to find Tom disagreeable. He was a know-it-all, something that irked her to no end. He was often late on the rare occasions when we would meet to play cards or cook on the grill, usually because some novel notion had side-tracked him. He was a rude dinner companion interrupting as he pleased, chewing with his mouth open. And he was susceptible to fits of endless dinnertime silence which women like Joanna, who valued eating for the conversational aspects as well as the gastronomical ones, found offensive.

Each of these, I suppose, were legitimate reasons for Joanna to place Tom at the top of her 'perpetual shit list'. But I had just noticed a facet to Tom's unorthodox personality which had always escaped me and might easily surpass these other reasons in my wife's eyes and explain it all. It was clearly evident that Tom was suffering from a complete lack of fashion sense. Perhaps it was this, not his lack of promptness or dining manners that had placed him on Joanna's bad side. My musings must have brought a grin to my lips, because Tom offered me a deep frown.

"What's funny?" he asked as I opened the gate for him.

"Nothing," I said, trying to squelch my laughter. "Something I heard on the radio."

Tom nodded, cast me an impatient glance as if detecting my ridicule, and let it go.

We made our way to the patio table, where he set

79

the case down and popped it open. Contained within was a collection of equipment that would both impress and confound any Forensics expert. There were small glass test tubes resting in red felt sleeves, some nitrile gloves, a baggy containing long cotton swabs, as well as several other pieces of equipment, the precise purposes of which I couldn't begin to guess.

"You come prepared," I said sarcastically, the desire to laugh returning. I had never actually seen Tom at work, and no one who had called upon his particular talents had ever commented on his techniques.

Tom smiled and slipped one of the gloves over his right hand.

"Bend over," he said.

"Funny."

Chuckling at his brand of sick humor, he plucked a few of the big swabs and empty test tubes from the bag and headed for the big Red Maple tree that stood at the heart of my back yard.

"I've had some time to think about my conclusions regarding your prowler," he said.

"So have I, and I think you must be wrong."

"Really?" he said, pausing in mid stoop, a swab poised an inch or so from the base of the tree. "How so?"

"Well, it's ridiculous."

"Ridiculous? I checked into twenty-seven different web sites concerning fecal testing, ran several sets of DNA tests, performed a comparative chemical analysis and consulted Doctor Larson, the vet in Bridgton."

"I know Larson," I said. "He's Spooky's vet."

Spooky, who was lying at the edge of the patio, raised her head at the mention of the word 'vet'.

"It's all right, girl," I said, laughing as much at Tom as at my paranoid dog who let her head plop down with disgust.

"There is no mistake," Tom added. "Your sample

came from a human being, not a dog."

"What about a coyote?" I asked, hoping.

"Coyotes and people; two separate species," Tom said, crawling about, busily swabbing everything in sight and systematically setting the swabs in glass test tubes. "At least the last time *I* checked."

"All right, then some person paid us a visit," I said, still refusing to accept Tom's conclusions. I had been prepared for the culprit to be Rufus. I had not been prepared for this, not by a long shot.

Tom sat back on his haunches, a fresh swab in his hand. "Tell me, do either you or Joanna have any reason to suspect someone might be stalking you?"

"What?"

A shiver traversed my spine. 'Gospel' Tom, the stumbling eccentric in the blue Bermuda shorts crawling around on his hands and knees with a fistful of cotton swabs, 'Gospel' Tom, the man who I'd consulted more out of boredom than need, had struck a nerve as effectively as the best fictional detective. The truth of the matter was that there *had* been a problem, but that had been years earlier, shortly after Joanna and I had been married, and I had not thought about it since. Until now, that is.

The facts are that Joanna and I had received some strange late night calls immediately after we were married. They averaged about three to four a week and there had never been any voice, only dead silence and then a hang-up. We'd had no caller ID in those days, so the police and a trace would have been the only way to determine who was making the calls, and because there had been no threats made during the calls, it would have proved difficult to pursue such an avenue. Joanna was quick to point out that we had recently changed our telephone number and the calls might simply have been a mistake. I agreed and the police were never notified. But something was preventing me from telling Tom all this, and the cold thing in my gut wriggled to life for the first time that day.

"Well?" Tom prompted.

"No," I said, too harshly.

He paused, considering me carefully as if sensing the lie.

"I said no." My reiteration was less severe.

"All right," he said, returning to his work of collecting specimens. He might have been satisfied, and of that I was uncertain. But I was not. And the fact that I was withholding this information from him was already starting to gnaw at me. In any event I followed him, distracted, as he made his way to the Hosta bed where I'd found the first 'deposit', where I had just put down some fresh peat.

"Nice job," he said taking note of my handiwork.

I nodded, feeling creepy about his revelation regarding the nature of the droppings and the whole stalker idea. Tom had missed his true calling. He *was* a good detective, and he was making me feel damned uncomfortable.

Tom reached the back corner of the garage and I was about to fetch some beers, one for Tom as a reward for his efforts, one for me to help take the edge off, when, in true Holmesian style, he said, "Hello, what's this?"

I leaned forward, frowning. Tom was pointing at a fresh spattering of fecal matter peppering the lawn a few feet from the back corner of the garage, near the spot where I'd seen the shimmering eyes watching me from the shadows two nights earlier. I'd swear the temperature, which must have been pushing ninety, dropped several degrees at that moment. I shivered internally when I realized that what I had seen while standing on my back porch had not been my imagination at all. Someone *had* been here, hiding, watching. I couldn't begin to describe just how uncomfortable that realization made me feel, and I thought of Joanna and the strange phone calls that had come and gone in the night so long ago. The cold thing in my stomach became fully awake.

Tom studied me silently before producing a pair of small pruning shears from a case on his belt with which to snip a sample.

"It looks," he said softly, "as if your 'night depositor' has struck again."

Chapter Eleven

Tom's words were still hanging in the air when the sound of an engine drew my attention to the head of the driveway. Joanna was home. Even from this distance, I could make out the puzzled expression on her face as her eyes lit on Tom.

Joanna's dislike for Tom was never as evident as at that moment. But as I thought about it, I began to suspect that Tom's know-it-all ways and bad fashion sense might not lie at the heart of Joanna's growing disdain for the man. Perhaps it was Alice's odious feelings for her own husband which had infected Joanna like a virus.

In any case, I thought it prudent that Tom leave quickly. The last thing I wanted was for Joanna to grow suspicious. And I certainly did not want her catching wind of Tom's 'stalker' theory.

"Are you going to be long?"

Tom raised his eyes, saw Joanna's car and pursed his lips.

"No," he said. "I just want to run a quick sweep of the shrubs."

"I'd prefer Joanna not find out about your little theory."

"Agreed," he said slipping the clippings into a tube and sealing it with a plastic cap.

"Hi," Joanna said her voice chilly as she climbed from her car *sans* shopping bags.

"No luck?" I said, meeting her at the fence.

"What?"

"Macy's."

"Oh. No."

I nodded and she gestured at Tom.

"Hi," she said, the word turning to ice in the warm air.

Tom looked up, grinned then returned to what he was doing.

"Trouble?" she said.

"Oh, checking for grubs," I said amazed at the speed with which I dreamed up the lie.

"You treat the lawn for that," she said.

"You can't be too careful," Tom said. "New strain. Very stubborn."

"Sure," Joanna said and she flashed me a polite smile that possessed all the charm of a guillotine blade before heading for the house, her eyes burning into Tom as if she hoped her glare might cause him to burst into flames. She vanished into the service porch, Spooky at her heels, the screen door slamming shut behind her.

"She doesn't like me much," Tom said.

"You *are* a genius," I responded dryly.

"I don't understand," he said. "I like books; she's a librarian. We have that in common."

"You like books because you think they make you smarter than everyone else," I said, gazing at my back porch. "Joanna sees books as an escape; a way to forget yourself and see beyond the street corner. That's why she reads to kids, many who come from less than idyllic homes." I turned to watch Tom's reaction.

He nodded, looking thoughtful. "I *am* pretty smart."

I felt a grin touch my lips as I shook my head and headed for the house.

"I won't be long," Tom called after me. "But think about what I said. She'll need to know sooner or later."

I waved him off and went inside to find Joanna hanging up the phone.

"What is the mad scientist really up to?" she asked.

"Grubs," I replied.

She simply looked at me, her face revealing her true feelings, which weren't pleasant.

"Sticking to that story?"

I felt myself frowning. "What's wrong?"

"Oh, nothing," she said, throwing up her hands. "Woman issues. I need to go to the Fayre a few hours early. You don't have to come if you don't want to."

"I'd love to go," I said, speaking the truth.

Working the Summer Harvest Fayre was comfort food for me, a trip back to my youth. The only issue that had ever arisen regarding my feelings toward fairs was the strange carny I'd bumped into the night before and, having slept on it, I was beginning to realize that my concerns were absurd. It was foolish of me to spend time even thinking about him let alone obsessing over how he might, for some unknown reason, have it in for me. It was the strange events of late setting my nerves on edge and fostering my vivid imagination; nothing more.

"Well, give me time to get things straightened out there," she said. "And I've got to pick up more doughnuts. Meet me at six. That way you can fix the doorknob to the dog house like you promised."

She kissed me lightly on the forehead then went to change.

"Doorknob it is," I said. "I'll meet you at six, just in time for a supper of Voc Tech chicken and fries!"

"Oh, you and that chicken," she said, sounding happier than she had when she first saw Tom rummaging around the yard. "I swear that's the only reason you set foot in that booth!"

"I thought you knew?" I quipped, a second before my brain screeched to an abrupt halt as it was suddenly forced to consider the possibility that the mysterious carny might be a prime suspect for Tom's stalker.

The notion hung in my consciousness like a clay pigeon for less than a moment before the questions, like pellets from a shooting gallery gun, blew it to pieces. How did the man know where I lived? How had he struck the night the Fayre arrived? And, presuming he was our mysterious caller from years ago, why had he resurfaced?

The holes in the 'carny' theory were abundant and I dismissed the premise entirely. And, with that problem skewered through the heart with a stake of common sense, I set about tackling a more pressing issue: the cellar doorknob.

Chapter Twelve

In no time at all Joanna was showered, dressed and heading out the door. She kissed me in passing and I followed, Spooky watching from the shade of the maple tree.

"See you tonight," she said, before backing out of the driveway and heading down the street. Tom was long gone by this point, and, having weeks earlier gathered what I needed to replace the defective doorknob, and with no distractions looming, I set to work.

Many New England houses have bulkheads to serve as exterior access ways to the cellars; houses such as Tom's, for instance. Our house is older and my great-grandfather, who built it, chose to add what is called a 'doghouse,' a full-door access way where the bulkhead would have been.

Our doghouse provided storage space for swags and Christmas and Halloween ornaments, which hung from the walls on nails and pegs during the respective off-seasons to keep them out of the way. The doorknob to the outer door had been loose for some time and, instead of simply tightening old screws, which had probably become stripped over the years, I decided to replace the whole apparatus with a brushed nickel one to match the others. Considering Tom's suspicions, I felt better than ever about my decision to replace the old knob with a new, sturdier model.

I finished the job in no time and was in the cellar putting my tools away when I heard a voice calling from the back yard. It was a man's voice and my first thought was that Tom had forgotten something, so I went to investigate, leaving my tools lying on the table at the bottom of the doghouse steps.

"What did you—" I managed, emerging from the doghouse. But the words froze in my throat when I found

Bob Renko standing at my side gate.

"Someone broke into my garage," he grumbled.

This was the closest I'd been to my neighbor since the infamous 'trash-tipping incident,' and I was alarmed at how much he'd aged in those several months. His thinning hair had gone completely gray. A few days' worth of matching stubble clung to his jaw. His dull gray eyes were narrow and bloodshot and his teeth appeared to have had only a passing acquaintance with a toothbrush.

"Broken into?" I said, trying to focus on his words rather than the dark matter clinging to the edges of his teeth.

"Yeah. I was wonderin' if you seen anything weird lately?"

I was dying to say, 'Yeah, Bob, I've seen something weird lately: you!' But I didn't. I held my tongue, although I couldn't believe what he was asking me. In fact, I couldn't believe he was asking me anything!

Then a new angle occurred to me. What if my stalker *wasn't* my stalker? What if my stalker was actually *Renko's* stalker? One look at the man would lead anybody to conclude that Renko'd seen the inside of at least one jail cell in his day. Perhaps there was some unfinished business lurking in his past, unfinished *criminal* business.

But if that was true, why would he seek to involve me? I suppose it was possible he simply didn't realize that his past had caught up with him. Or maybe this was his effort to cover things up: by involving me, he was subtly espousing his own innocence. That made some sense.

"What happened?" I asked, figuring the only way to reach a conclusion was to hear his story.

"Come and see," he said, turning and heading toward the street.

Frowning, I considered the hammer lying on the table at the foot of the dog-house steps and wondered if I might need it.

"Come on," he insisted with an impatient gesture.

With a tremor of trepidation I followed, closing the doghouse door but, planning to return, leaving it unlocked.

We proceeded without speaking, Renko shuffling along, his worn work boots kicking up dust, me trying to ignore the invisible cloud of body odor trailing him. We rounded my fence and headed down his dirt driveway in silence. This was the second time I'd set foot on his property. The first had been to discuss Rufus' assault on our trash barrels. That visit had been enough for me to get an inkling of who Bob Renko really was, and I would always equate my experience to Scout Finch standing on Boo Radley's porch, realizing similarly that I had seen all I needed to see. This second visit was sheer overkill.

"I saw it today, but it mighta' happened a few days ago," he said with a shrug of his sloped shoulders. "I ain't sure."

I followed Renko past his decrepit back porch and around his rusted-out pick-up truck to the garage that squatted at the brink of his thickly overgrown back yard.

"Here," Renko said, gesturing lazily at the ivy choked garage with its ancient granite walls and spoiled, sagging roof. The badly-warped six-paneled wood bay door was raised, but the dense shadows within the garage's putrefying innards held most of the sunlight at bay.

A minefield of debris lay strewn at the edge of the shadows. I saw old tires, a rusted lawn mower, bits and pieces of warped lumber, and several unrecognizable odds and ends scattered about. What lay at the back of the garage remained a mystery as the darkness there proved too dense for even the bravest traces of sunlight to breach.

"That window," Renko said, pointing to the closer of two windows set into the eastern wall of the structure.

I took one hesitant step into the old garage. It was immediately evident that the glass was shattered and part of the wood frame had been torn loose. Shards of glass were winking up from a sunlit pool of dust. I squatted down to study the debris and also to search for footprints, but there was a spattering of gravel from the driveway mixed in with the debris and it was impossible to determine if there were any discernable tracks. I thought if anyone could pick tracks out of this mess, Tom could.

"I don't see where anyone might have climbed in," I said getting to my feet. "The window seems too small."

"The door was shut until a little while ago," Renko said. "I was going in to get something."

I nodded politely but could not imagine what anyone might want from inside this ramshackle building. The door looked unsafe, the guides were rusted and warped, the roof was sagging and probably leaked like a sieve and, unless there was a light somewhere, the debris-ridden floor would prove to be an obstacle course for any intruder. And to add insult to injury, there was a stench emanating from the place like nothing I had ever smelled before.

"I thought maybe you heard or seen something," he said.

"If I had, I'd have told you or called the police if you weren't home," I said. This was true. I didn't like Renko, but if a thief found one house in the neighborhood to be an easy touch, he was more likely to try another and mine was right next door. It seemed proximity made strange bedfellows.

"Have you heard or seen anything strange lately?" I asked.

Renko's eyes appeared vacant and I felt as if I was talking to a child; the pale sheen of his skin made him look like a sickly child at that. My neighborhood's Boo Radley. Or maybe Sam Berkowitz.

He shook his head. "Folks walking the graves," he said, "but I don't remember seein' anyone come *this* way."

'Walking the graves' was a local expression used to

91

explain the activity of joggers and power walkers who traversed the winding paths of St. Brigid's cemetery at the end of our street. I'd always found it ironic that the living sought to improve their health in a place that held so many of the dead.

"Rufus took to growling at night lately, like he hears somethin' out back," Renko said after a moment. "Smelled a skunk last week. Musta' sprayed my back steps, judgin' by the stink." Renko sighed and scrunched up his face as if in deep thought. "Looked out one night when Rufus woke me up, growlin' and clawin' at the back door, whining. You know what I mean, sorta' like he was mad and scared all at the same time."

I knew exactly what Renko meant; Spooky had demonstrated the same behavior.

"Did you see anything?" I asked with a sliver of apprehension.

"No. But your floodlight was on. I figured you folks had gotten in late and Rufus heard ya'." He shrugged. A fly buzzed past my face, landed on Renko's neck and inched its way toward his ear. He never noticed.

"Was anything taken?" I realized the futility of the question the second I'd uttered it. What of worth could this rotted-out garage possibly hold? And with all the clutter, would Renko be able to determine if anything *was* missing?

Renko shrugged again. "Nothin' worth takin'," he said as if it were common knowledge, which it was.

I turned to scan the shadowy contents of the garage, entertaining the slim hope that I'd missed some clue, some trace of the intruder's identity. That was when I noticed what I took to be a gutted motorcycle lying beneath a dirty ripped tarp lying between the broken window and its more fortunate mate.

I figured it to be a Harley, presuming Renko to be something other than the 'rice rocket' sort. It struck me that Renko was like the motorcycle, ruined, non-functioning.

Both he and the bike had been working models once upon a time, speeding down the highway of life until they'd hit something unexpected, like a pothole or a patch of gravel. In Renko's case it might have been a woman, one bout too many with the bottle, a death in the family. But in the end both Renko and the dismantled bike were the same: useless, beyond repair.

I felt an unexpected twinge of sadness for Bob Renko. He had no wife, no kids that I knew of and, if he had any friends, they never stopped by. Then he hawked up and spat into the dirt and my sympathy evaporated.

"Well, if you see anything let me know. I'd 'preciate it."

"Sure," I said.

Anxious to be out of there, I turned and started up Renko's driveway. I heard Rufus barking from inside the house, but I didn't glance at the window; I was in no mood to see the dog's big ugly face gaping at me. I didn't look back at Renko either, but sensed his bloodshot eyes following me. I didn't stop until I was in my house and, once there, I couldn't wait to climb into the shower.

Chapter Thirteen

When I finished showering, I phoned Tom. I couldn't wait to tell him about my visitor. He was surprised to hear about it and particularly interested in the fact that someone had apparently broken into Renko's pathetic excuse for a garage.

"You saw no sign of footprints?"

"No," I said, "but I only looked at the inside of the garage, not the outside where the prowler must have stood to break the window."

"We must assume that someone broke in for a reason. It doesn't seem likely that someone would toss a rock through the window out of malice or to get some cheap thrill. Besides, if memory serves, to throw a rock through that window would require that the perpetrator approach the structure from the back yard. And your neighbor's yard looks a little like the Amazon basin during the rainy season."

"Do ya' think?" I added sarcastically.

"I've gotten a look at your neighbor's garage, though," Tom said. "And I've gotten a look at your neighbor as well. He may be an inebriated reprobate, but I bet he can be a handful when riled."

I agreed with Tom on that point. I'd seen Renko fired up, talking on his mobile to God knew who while pacing back and forth in his driveway, swearing, threatening whoever was at the other end of the line, or at other times just yelling at Rufus when he was really drunk. And then, of course, there was Rufus. Only an idiot would seek to annoy a man who owned a dog as fearsome-looking as Rufus, not to mention be dumb enough to break into the house where such a dog lived.

"But what's interesting is that his dog is behaving the same as your dog," Tom said. "This suggests that the prowler may not be *your* prowler at all but your *neighbor's* prowler, or perhaps merely an indiscriminate prowler with no specific agenda but to prowl."

"That occurred to me."

"Then again, perhaps Renko spotted me snooping around, thinks I may be a private detective, and figures he'll hand you an alibi of sorts. If *he* has a prowler, then it follows that he can't possibly be your stalker. And judging by the condition of his place, a broken window in an unused garage hardly seems likely to be a major concern for Mr. Renko."

"So what should I do?"

"Nothing. Go about your business as usual. I'll take a look myself, maybe tonight."

"Be careful. Renko may own a gun."

"Maybe. If he has a pickup truck and a big dog, he is probably exercising his Second Amendment rights as well," Tom said laughing. "It just seems to follow."

"It's not funny," I said, genuinely concerned. "I don't need to come home from the Fayre to find you shot dead on Renko's lawn."

"Don't worry," Tom said still laughing. "It's me!"

After hanging up I made sure Spooky had food and water before heading for my car. Renko was backing his old pick-up out into the street, Rufus riding shotgun.

Standing in my yard, watching my departing neighbor, an idea lit in my brain. This was the perfect opportunity to have a closer look at the scene of the crime!

Chapter Fourteen

The best way to access Renko's place unseen was to cross behind my garage, hop the fence into his back yard and approach from the rear of the property. There was heavy foliage back there, countless overgrown shrubs, tangles of fallen branches and waist-high weeds. There were also trees abutting, and, at points, bisecting a moldy stockade fence. Even if Renko returned before I planned, he wouldn't be able to see me from the house, the driveway or the back porch. I could easily conceal myself in the heavy brush until he went inside. The one concern would be Rufus. If Rufus caught wind of me, the cat would be out of the bag.

That was a risk I was willing to take; such an opportunity might not present itself again. I would only need a quick look. I figured I might be able to spare Tom the trip, although I thought that unlikely, as Tom was the sort who trusted his own judgment above all others in matters of detective work or research. I think the real driving force for me was simply curiosity; I wanted to see what possible motive a burglar might have for breaking into Renko's garage.

I set out across my yard, moving behind my garage until I reached the chain-link fence that separated my yard from Renko's. I used an ancient moss-riddled oak tree for support and climbed over.

I landed in a thicket of branches, nearly twisting an ankle, cursing, stumbling sideways and making about as much noise as a bull in a china shop. I recovered my footing, brushed myself off, and started toward the garage, passing through clusters of unidentifiable leafy plants that had grown to thigh height. My mind was suddenly plagued by thoughts of ticks, Lyme disease and rats that might be lurking in the underbrush, waiting to pounce. I had no idea how anyone could allow his property to fall into such a state of neglect. The abandoned state hospital grounds that hosted the Fayre had nothing on my neighbor's yard.

I passed an old wood sled rotting in a heap amidst a cluster of pine trees, wondered if it had been Renko's once, decided it could not possibly have been and proceeded. I barely avoided a rusted-out lawn mower hiding in the brush like a saw-toothed predator, waiting to snag an unsuspecting ankle, and eventually emerged relatively unscathed from Renko's jungle-like back forty to find myself standing less than a dozen paces from his garage.

The east-facing side of the structure was in worse shape than the side facing the house. The sun was apparently a stranger to this part of the property, and the bulging stones that made up the lower portion of the structure were layered in a thick blanket of green moss, likening them to the trees I had left guarding the drunken stockade at the rear of the lot. The wood that comprised the upper half of the structure was in a similar state of disrepair, bare save for patches of rot and a few stubborn flakes of paint clinging barnacle-like at sparse intervals.

I searched the earth beneath the broken window and noticed several tracks. Some were boot tracks, boots that had most likely housed the big feet of Bob Renko. The huge paws of Rufus had made others. I squatted down to have a better look, but realized that only a well-trained forensic expert might decipher exactly what had transpired at the spot.

I got to my feet and peeked into the window, carefully avoiding the tracked-up area so as not to spoil potential evidence for Tom. I was also careful not to touch the remaining shards of glass that clung to the rotted frame.

The window seemed too small for a man to climb through, let alone for a man to climb through without slicing open an artery on the remaining bits of broken glass. But Renko had left the bay door open; I decided to have a look inside.

I peeked around the corner to make sure the driveway was still vacant; I hadn't heard a truck pulling in, but I was taking no chances. I quickly moved around the corner of the garage and ducked into its shadowy interior.

Renko's garage was a cave. The lower portions of the walls were hewn from stone that had turned green with age. The ceiling had partially collapsed and resembled a jagged puzzle of broken beams, complete with an array of ominous dangling wood stalactites. Thin bars of dusty light passed easily through openings and gathered in puddles on the floor, illuminating a spattering of debris consisting of bits of wood, a rusted tire iron, crinkled newspaper pages, rimmed and rimless spare tires and an assortment of unidentifiable chunks of refuse. To make matters worse, the stench I had noticed while standing in the bay doorway with Renko was severely amplified and I found myself covering my mouth and nose with my hand in a futile attempt to keep from gagging.

Determined to complete my reconnaissance, I examined my surroundings. Two filthy windows were set into the left wall of the garage, which was framed but lacked insulation or wallboard. A matching pair was set in the opposite wall, one of which was now in shambles. The rear section of the garage was another matter. Without windows, it stood behind a veil of near-impenetrable darkness, the few vaguely illuminated portions lit dimly by a dusty half-light that spilled in through the windows facing Renko's house.

Wary of the minefield of debris peppering the floor, I stood my ground as my eyes adjusted to the adverse conditions. As the shadows fled, what I took to be a large workstation running the length of the back wall swam into focus. I was able to discern cabinets and a long counter littered with what I perceived to be an assortment of unrecognizable objects, rusted, unused tools no doubt buried beneath generations of cobwebs.

I made for the workstation, crouching low to avoid cracking my head on the hanging ceiling while keeping track of the debris at my feet. It was treacherous going, and I tried to imagine how an intruder might manage it without breaking a leg.

As I neared the workstation, I became fascinated by something resembling an old coat lying across the edge of the counter. I drew closer and stretched my hand out to touch the thing. Perhaps, I assumed, it was the pelt of some animal Renko had killed while hunting. My fingers touched something cool and moist and I drew my hand back in revulsion as I realized I was staring into the dead eyes of a huge raccoon lying across the counter.

I stumbled backward, bumping into the wall, knocking a few rusted hanging tools to the floor. I waited, eyes clenched, as the cacophony of old metal striking older concrete faded into the dusty gloom. When I finally opened my eyes the first thing they fell upon was the dead raccoon with its black eyes and fly-riddled snout. I'd found the source of the terrible stench.

This was no taxidermist's effort. The animal wasn't just dead; it had been torn apart. The gut had been ripped open and the eviscerated entrails hung over the edge of the counter like spent Christmas ribbon.

My stomach rolled over like a dying animal. Renko might have been a slob, but I could not imagine him bringing a dead animal into his garage, much less leaving it to rot. I thought of Rufus and reached the same conclusion. Cats brought home gifts like birds and mice, but I'd never heard of dogs behaving in such a manner.

My mind began spinning off into uncharted territory, tracing and unraveling new threads of information. But before I allowed my imagination to get too far ahead of my common sense, I made one firm decision: I had had enough of Bob Renko's garage.

Slowly I backed away from the rotting carcass, carefully avoiding the hazards littering the floor, but never letting my eyes stray too far from the reeking corpse. I didn't know what I expected it to do; after all, it was dead. But if it was dead, then why did its glistening eyes seem to be following me? Why did its misshapen maw bristling with needle teeth seem on the verge of screeching? Something, a bird, I suspect, swept past a window and the raccoon seemed to shiver in the gloom.

I tripped over a spare tire, spun around, nearly falling over, and stepped into the doorway in time to see Renko's pickup truck pulling into the driveway!

Chapter Fifteen

Instinctively, I ducked back into the shadows beside the door, pressed my back against the wall and froze. Rusty nails bit into my shoulders, but I remained still in spite of the pain. I wasn't sure if Renko had seen me, but I was taking no chances. I listened as the truck ground to a halt, and I watched the cloud it kicked up drift past the open bay door like a Depression-era dust storm. I heard the door creak open. A jingling collar told me Rufus was out and I heard the door to the truck slam shut.

I waited, my breath catching in my chest like a fly in a spider's web, the dust biting at my throat. I felt the urge to sneeze, covered my mouth and nose and desperately tried to squelch it. I heard the welcome sound of the screen door opening and gratefully squeezed my eyes shut.

"What's the matter, boy?" Renko said and my heart stopped beating. "Get in here!"

I held my breath as a fat spider scurried across my hand and vanished into the shadows. Then I heard the screen door close and the scuffing sound of Renko's boots descending the stairs.

"What is it?" Renko said. "Somethin' there? Son-of-a-bitch come back?"

I swallowed hard and backed deeper into the shadows.

Renko's footfalls and the jingle of Rufus' collar grew louder. I squatted down and duck-walked beneath the first window. I caught my shin on a spare tire, reached out to brace myself against the rotting wood and felt something small with many legs squirm from beneath my palm. I froze, listening.

The footsteps moved slowly, stealthily. Rufus' began to growl and my insides turned sour. I began moving again, deeper into the shadows, past the second window, skipping the duck-walk entirely, assuming Renko was already too close to the bay door to glimpse me walking past the filthy glass. I reached out and touched the edge of the work station counter. It felt sticky. With a sickening sensation I realized my hand was inches from the jaws of the dead raccoon, my fingertips in a semi-dried pool of the animal's blood. I turned to find its eyes watching me, its teeth dull white in the dusty gloom of the garage. I moved my hand away, crouched down in the darkness and waited for the inevitable.

The shadows of a man and a dog fell across the dirty floor and I looked up to see Renko and Rufus silhouetted against the vivid blue sky. The dog was by his master's side, shaking, growling. Renko was shading his eyes, straining to see into the darkness that, hopefully, concealed me. I waited, inches from the dead raccoon, my breath dragging across my lungs like a heavy chain on concrete.

"What the hell is that smell?" Renko said. "Goddamn! C'mon, you full-a-shit dog, I ain't staying out here all night."

Renko turned on his worn heels and headed for the house. When Rufus remained, whining and glancing from the darkness to his master, Renko returned.

"Yeah, watch this," he said and he kicked the dog aside with his boot.

The big dog yelped and scurried away. Then Renko reached up and, grabbing the handle to the garage door, yanked it down.

The door sounded like a freight train as it fell, then a cannon as it slammed into place and the darkness covered me like the lid of a coffin. The muted sunlight pouring in through the old windows became immediately irrelevant, insignificant, as all I saw was a great block of blackness that might have been a chunk of granite resting where the

102

bay opening had been.

Claustrophobia wrapped its bony fingers around my throat and began squeezing the air out of me. I wanted to call out and run to the door and pound on it. And in that fleeting instant of panic, I didn't care that it was Renko on the other side; I just wanted to get out. But I didn't. I choked back my claustrophobic fear and waited in the suffocating heat and blackness, the stench of the dead raccoon moving around me like a putrefying phantom.

Moments passed and my heart beat began to slow. I began to breathe again. I peered through the window beside me and watched the disheveled pair mount the back porch and go inside. Then I leaned my head back against the wood-frame wall and sighed into the dismal air. I looked toward the rotting raccoon, made out its head dangling as if partially severed by some animal guillotine, its eyes little more than shiny specks in the faint light. The thing's smell had concealed my presence from Rufus. But I was hardly appreciative; just then I wanted nothing more than to be far from Bob Renko's garage.

I headed for the bay door, hugging the wall to avoid the debris field. I touched the warped wood, realizing all too well that lifting the thing would make such a racket there would be no chance Renko would not hear it. So I chose the only alternative; I would be forced to climb through the broken window.

I searched for something to use as a make-shift ladder, decided to push two of the rimmed tires across the floor, then climbed aboard. Steadying myself with my hands on either side of the shattered window, I stepped up and over the sill. But there was no such added step outside the window and the distance to the ground would be greater. I would have to negotiate the maneuver carefully.

Reaching what I felt was the best position from which to vault the rest of the way through the opening, I set one foot on the crumbling window sill and kicked off hard with the foot that remained on the tire rim. I felt at least one of the remaining glass shards protruding from the sill snap off against the weight of my inner thigh and I flopped down like a rag doll in the dirt beneath the window. I realized as I got to my feet that I had probably contaminated the site of the break-in, but I was so relieved to be out of the God-forsaken place that I could not bring myself to care. I had started brushing myself off and inspecting myself for damage when Rufus began barking from inside the house.

I started for the back fence but stopped to check my left hand, which felt sticky, and spied blood smeared across my fingers; I had cut myself on the broken glass. Renko yelled something from inside the house; he was probably getting pretty fed up with Rufus' behavior. I thought about going back to inspect the broken window for evidence of my intrusion, but Rufus' barking drove that thought from my mind and I ran toward the back fence. Rufus let out a single yelp as I reached the tall weeds, then fell silent; I guess Renko had decided that enough was enough.

I pushed my way through the thickets, pausing to catch my breath, crouching down beside the rusted-out lawn mower to look back at the house to be certain Renko wasn't standing in his driveway watching me. But there was no sign of man or beast, and I went to the fence and climbed back into my yard.

I crossed behind my garage, my lungs aching, my body drenched in sweat, my clothes covered in dust, and my injured hand throbbing. It was nearing six o'clock, but I couldn't go to the Fayre in this condition, so I went inside, took another shower and tended to my injured hand.

The cut turned out to be less than I feared and, after wrapping it, I checked on Spooky and found her resting in her bed in the four seasons room, clearly the one member of this family with an ounce of sense.

I set out for the Fayre with two new disturbing bits of information tucked away in my head, the first being that a man *could* climb through Renko's garage window. The second being that whoever *had* climbed through my neighbor's window had brought with him a new type of 'deposit', one that was sicker and more frightening than either of the ones I had stumbled upon.

Neither one of these facts was liable to help me sleep nights. I was beginning to doubt whether or not I would ever sleep soundly again. And I was beginning to wonder if it was safe to try.

Chapter Sixteen

I drove with the windows and sunroof open, hoping the flowing air would wash the remnants of Renko's garage from my senses. In my mind, I could still see the dead raccoon's lifeless eyes, like two black marbles watching me from the shadows. I could still hear Rufus' pathetic yelp as Renko kicked him to shut him up. Too much was happening. This was summer; I should be relaxing.

I needed a distraction to drown out the grumbling of facts and ideas in my head, so I flipped on the radio. An old favorite by a Boston-based band called Face to Face was playing. The tune was a fiddler's dream called *The Grass Grows Greener after the Fire*. I listened as Laurie Sargent, the lead singer, wove her tale of the trials a relationship must too often endure if it is to survive. I found myself analyzing the lyrics as if they held clues to life's ordeals and discovered myself wondering why the grass couldn't grow greener *without* the fire?

It all seemed so ridiculous, but inescapably logical. Why was it always darkest before the dawn? I sensed my marriage heading for a blaze of its own, the kind of conflagration that reduces feelings to cinders, though I had never smelled the smoke and could not yet see the flames. I sensed them there in the darkness around the next bend, though, smoldering, waiting to engulf us just as surely as the coming moon.

I drove on toward the Fayre, the sad prophetic lyrics drifting around the cabin of my car, working their way into my being.

By the time the song reached the fiddle solo, my thoughts had turned so dark I shut off the radio. I had no idea what I should or shouldn't tell Joanna. My little discovery had certainly opened a can of worms. I wished I could let the goddamned issue sink to the bottom of the ocean so I could forget all about it, but the 'deposits' weren't the problem; the problem was the *depositor*. My hope that Tom's imagination was simply running away with him was fading with each passing second. There was something happening on our little dead-end street, something I wasn't prepared to deal with, something involving someone who was more than a little twisted and very determined.

"Is there anyone from your past who might want something from you?" Tom said from someplace inside my head. I remembered the phone calls, my picking up the receiver and listening to nothing, but knowing there was someone there, someone who was listening to *me*. And then there would be a click, followed by the inevitable dial tone.

Joanna had refused to call the police then, but now someone was setting foot on our property. Perhaps it was time to involve the police.

I thought about the evidence I'd collected: funny feelings, droppings, and a broken window on a garage that should be condemned. Oh yes, and my mysterious carny, the one who had no idea where I lived, but just enjoyed staring at me and visiting my dreams. There wasn't much. There was, in fact, nothing.

I decided it was best to let Tom handle things, for the time being, at least. I imagined him sneaking into Renko's garage, but with the dead raccoon, I figured Rufus would never smell him. Still, it didn't make me very comfortable knowing that Tom was going to try to repeat my stupid stunt.

I turned west into the sunset. As I neared the Fayre, I could hear a band playing Grace Potter and the Nocturnals' *Stars*. I could see the Ferris wheel turning slowly against the sun-streaked sky.

Enough, I said to myself. I called Tom from my mobile phone and left a message on his voicemail telling him to call me about something I'd discovered. Now he was on his own.

I reached the entrance to the state hospital, waved to the security guard as I drove past, watched him wave back, and continued on past the old buildings to the Fayre grounds. The in-dash clock read six-forty. Joanna had expected me at six. I was pondering what excuse I would hand her for being late as I rounded the old willow tree and started down into the staff lot when I saw something that drove any thoughts of excuses from my mind.

An ambulance was parked at the back of the booths with its lights flashing and its bay doors wide open. I could see a clutch of onlookers gathered there and from this distance I'd swear I could see Marge Weems standing among them!

Horrible thoughts lit in my brain and I stomped on the accelerator, my heart filling my throat like a fist.

Chapter Seventeen

I drew to an abrupt halt behind our booth and was momentarily and perhaps selfishly relieved to see that the ambulance was sitting behind a different booth. A clutch of thirty or forty onlookers had gathered around the vehicle and, though I'd swear I'd seen Marge among them, there was no sign of her now.

I climbed out of my car and started toward our booth as Joanna emerged, her face ashen and her eyes wide with fright.

"What's wrong?"

"A little girl wandered off into the woods and a coyote attacked her," Joanna said.

"Jesus, is she all right?"

Marge appeared fresh from the scene with the scoop.

"She's okay, just frightened," she said in her sandpaper voice. "The damned thing never got hold of her. A couple of cops are looking for it now. At least a dozen people saw it chase the girl out of the woods. When it realized where it was, it turned and ran. The girl fell, skinned her knees." Marge let out a breath and shook her head. "Christ, I need a cigarette."

She entered the booth, presumably to get one, and Joanna put her arm around my waist. I could feel her trembling.

"I knew there were coyotes around, but I've never heard of one coming so close to so many people in broad daylight," she said, her voice catching in her throat.

"Oh, they get brazen sometime," Marge said stepping down from the booth, a fresh glowing Camel clenched between her teeth. "One of the bastards attacked a little kid on Cosgrove Street the other day. Kid was just playing in a sandbox in the back yard. It's the heat," she

109

said, pointing up at the sun. "Makes 'em crazy. And the full moon isn't helping."

I watched a female EMT with close-cropped blonde hair hop out of the back of the ambulance and begin speaking with a second EMT, a young man with a shaved head. He said something to her, then turned and spoke with someone else inside the ambulance's cargo bay, someone I couldn't see but presumed to be the little girl's parent. Then the female EMT closed the ambulance bay doors, went around to the front of the vehicle, pushing her way through the rubberneckers, nearly bumping into a heavyset man with slicked back, thinning gray hair who was hovering at the driver's door, before hopping aboard. The man exchanged words with the woman, then turned toward us.

I could see him clearly now; he wore an ill-fitting bowling shirt that had seen one season too many and was holding a stubby cigar in one hand. His face was a mixed palate of emotions, worry, anger, confusion and something else, something dark that was hiding behind his small dark eyes.

The man turned back to the driver's side door and began speaking with the female EMT again. He nodded several times and stepped away from the vehicle, presumably satisfied with the outcome of the conversation.

"That's Vern Cross," Joanna said, "the carnival owner."

"What a specimen of manhood," Marge said sarcastically before taking a long drag on the half-spent Camel. "Johnny Depp better watch out."

The ambulance siren squawked briefly and the vehicle slowly pulled away, picking its way through pockets of concerned bystanders as it made its way toward the main entrance. Once the vehicle had gone from view, the crowd began to disperse. Cross remained. He took the cigar from his mouth, spat into the dirt and looked my way. Our eyes met for a moment and it was like staring at the dark lifeless eyes of the dead raccoon in Renko's garage. Then he walked away, toward the RVs.

"The Fayre is supposed to be *fun*," Marge said, stomping out the Camel and stepping up into the booth.

I shared a worried glance with Joanna and, as she followed Marge into the booth, we heard a loud report. Joanna turned toward the sound, which had emanated from the woods beyond the RVs.

Marge poked her head out of the doorway. "Was that-?"

"I guess they found the coyote," I said. I looked up and caught a glimpse of Joanna glaring down at me from the doorway. She turned suddenly and went inside.

Curious, I moved toward the bathrooms to get a better look. I watched as a pair of police officers emerged from the woods; one was holstering his weapon. A truck pulled up beside the officers and two men wearing beige coveralls climbed out and spoke briefly with the police. Then, after retrieving a large brown duffel bag from the bed of the truck, they followed the officers into the woods.

Several minutes passed before the four men emerged from the tree-line carrying the bag, which was fully laden, reminding me of Rufus yelping as Renko's boot found his flank. I waited until they had loaded their cargo into the truck-bed then watched them pull away. The officers headed off toward two cruisers parked farther up the dirt road.

"Something's got to 'em," someone growled and I looked over to find a heavily tattooed man standing beside me. He was wearing jeans and black motorcycle boots. I could see a leather knife pouch dangling from his belt and a chain that secured his wallet to his belt loop gleaming in the late day sun. He was shielding his eyes from the sun's rays and smiling around teeth that looked like a broken picket fence.

"What?" I said absently.

"Coyotes," he said pointing a thick forearm at the scene unfolding at the edge of the woods. "Something's getting' under their skin. Even here. The dogs wouldn't run over the obstacles in the dog show, the horses wouldn't jump their jumps. Hell, even the pigs at the pig races were acting spooked. Maybe it's the moon." He pursed his leathery lips. "Chased a coyote outta' my yard the other night. Damned near attacked my chained-up Pit."

"Yeah," I said, unsure of what else to say. "Coyotes."

He looked my way long enough to flash a gap-toothed smile and then turned away, his long gray ponytail flipping across the back of his neck as he headed for the midway.

I turned back to the action. I felt strange, detached, overtired. It was as if I'd been staring at a map of some alien landscape for the longest time and only now realized that I was on the verge of falling *into* that strange new land.

The officers reached their respective cruisers, climbed aboard and turned the engines over. I waited until the cruisers had driven off then headed back to the booth. It was hot. Too hot. Too much had happened. I tried Tom on my mobile, but there was no answer. I gave up and went inside the booth to sell doughnuts.

I found Joanna standing at the counter with her back to me. She was leaning forward, apparently talking to somebody.

"I'm heading to the bathroom," Marge said waving the bathroom key in my face. "Be back."

I nodded and walked up to the counter. My heart skipped a beat when I saw Kevin Olson, the doughnut shop manager, standing on the other side of the counter.

"You know my husband, Jack," Joanna said.

"Yes," the man said, the broad smile on his lips faltering. He hesitated for a moment then offered me his hand. I considered it, took it. His flesh was soft, hot and

112

sweaty and I felt a sudden urge to wash my hands.

"Well," he began in that squeaky voice of his, "I just thought I'd, uh, stop by to see how things were going. Good, I'd say, judgin' by the crowd." He laughed a nervous laugh. "Terrible business about the coyote and the little girl."

"Yes," Joanna said. "At least no one was seriously hurt."

"Yes," he said, his eyes shifting nervously. "Well," he said lowering his gaze and shuffling from one foot to another, "I'll be off, then. Good luck."

Joanna said goodbye and I waved a chilly hand in Olson's direction. The funny little man shoved his hands into his pockets and walked away, turning back only once to cast us a sheepish grin before the bustling midway consumed him.

Chapter Eighteen

Joanna was quiet for some time after the coyote incident, but she eventually snapped out of it. I never really understood what had been bothering her. She was simply not herself, hadn't been for days. I decided to give her some time to sort it out, as per rule number one of being a good spouse. If she didn't come around, I'd be forced to pursue the issue, but at that moment we were too busy to talk about much of anything, and perhaps that was for the best.

The booth, however, was a success. Doughnuts were flying out of the boxes faster than we could keep up. The coyote incident had done little to decrease people's appetites. Word that the little girl had not been seriously hurt further eased any apprehension that might have been growing, and soon people passing by were heard to be once again talking about the summer and the heat and the Red Sox's chances at a World Series appearance.

Speculation among doughnut buyers and other booth staffers who stopped by to visit suggested that the coyote might simply have been protecting some nearby young. But no hard conclusions were reached. I did notice a police presence on the perimeter of the Fayre that had not been there earlier. Something was happening, something strange. I could sense the world turning, the wind changing, and the moon watching.

***

We ran out of doughnuts around nine forty-five and once again Marge bid us good night. Joanna and I cleaned up and I took the trash to the dumpster, uneventfully this time. When we had finished with the clean-up, we killed the overhead lights and sat back to relax and listen to the band, a Boston-based rock-and-blues group called Genuine Risk whose original songs informed the crowd that women, like black widows, could bite, and that fear was a rumor, like a gun in the hand of a desperate man.

Joanna and I dined on clam cakes from the booth run by Chet's Garage and chicken and fries from the Voc Tech booth, after which we called it a night. We locked the booth, tucked the cash box into the trunk of Joanna's car and set off separately for home, beating most of the soon-to-be departing multitude. I was exhausted and looking forward to an ice-cold beer and a little television before bed. I didn't know it then, but I was on the verge of being terribly disappointed.

Joanna was driving ahead of me and I'd lost track of her at some point, but as I neared our neighborhood, it became evident that something was happening. I could see the coruscating flash of multi-colored LED's rebounding off the tombstones at the edge of the cemetery and the alleyways between houses. I felt the color drain from my face and the cold thing that had been living in my stomach these past few days squirmed to life.

With a feeling of dread cinched tightly around me, I turned into our street and was confronted by the ghostly outlines of our neighbors milling about on their front lawns, their faces zombie-like before the flashing lights of a police cruiser perched across the street from my house.

My heart sped up when I spied Joanna's Honda parked at the head of our driveway, the driver's side door open, the cabin light aglow. As I drew closer I noticed a second cruiser parked in the Trimbles' driveway, its lights casting an icy pall over the neighborhood.

I felt suddenly woozy, exhausted, as if trapped in a dream I couldn't escape. And I thought of Tom. What if Tom had come snooping and run into Renko?

There was no time to speculate; I had to find out what had happened. And I had to find Joanna!

Chapter Nineteen

I pulled up behind Joanna's Honda, killed the engine, and climbed out. I scanned the scene quickly, concerned not only for Tom but also for Joanna, who was nowhere in sight. A sliver of panic embedded itself in my heart and I nearly screamed out her name, but before I could form the words, I spied her waving to me from the Trimbles' driveway. Relieved, I jogged over as Joanna began explaining my presence to a lanky young police officer standing on the bottom step of the Trimbles' deck.

"Mr. Graves," the officer said as I approached.

Winded, I nodded and said, "Yes." I noticed he was writing things down in a small note pad.

"We had a prowler," Sophie Trimble said appearing at the base of the steps and taking my wrist with her bony fingers.

"I was washing the dishes and someone ran right under the window," Roger Trimble said as he emerged from his back door, nodding his narrow, weathered head. "Dropped one of the Waterfords. Smash! All over the goddamned kitchen floor."

"Don't swear, dear," Sophie prompted.

"If a prowler don't warrant a cuss, I don't know what does," Roger shot back before turning and heading back into his house. "My mother gave us those damned dishes —" His voice trailed off as the screen door slammed shut behind him.

"But you didn't see his face, ma'am?" the officer prompted.

"No," Sophie said, shaking her head and clutching at the collar of her bathrobe. "Just Roger hollering to call the police."

A second officer, a short stocky woman with a knot

of blonde hair fastened above the nape of her neck, appeared from around the corner of the Trimbles' garage with a flashlight in her hand. She swung the light our way, inspecting each of us in turn.

"Nothing out there," she said, having apparently ascertained that we were no threat.

"Oh, dear," Sophie said, gripping Joanna's hand.

Roger reappeared, carrying a cinched plastic bag.

"Waterford, no less," he mumbled as the remains of the broken dish clinked around in the bag. He went to the barrels at the side of his garage, pried open the lid to the nearest one and deposited the bag. Then he turned, mumbled some displeasure, and, mounting the steps, went back inside.

"Well, ma'am," the male officer began, "there's no sign of anyone. Our shift is over, but I'll leave word for the next shift to cruise by, just in case. But I think whoever it was is long gone."

"Oh, I hope so," Sophie said, her lean fingers laced through Joanna's. "I'd hate to run out of dishes." Sophie managed a smile and everyone laughed.

"Probably a kid taking a short cut," the female officer said. "Your husband probably scared the bejesus out of him."

"Thank you," Sophie said, "but I don't think Roger could scare the bejesus out of a squirrel."

The officers bid us good night and went to their respective cruisers. A second later the flashing LED's went dark. Then the first cruiser backed out of the Trimbles' driveway and drove off followed a moment later by the second. I watched them move slowly down the street, our curious neighbors turning and going into their houses as they passed.

"C'mon, Mrs. T.," Joanna said – she always called Sophie Mrs. T. "Let's go inside and I'll make some tea."

"Oh, that would be lovely," Sophie said and Joanna

led the woman toward the door.

"I'll put the cars away," I said.

Joanna nodded. "Come over when you're finished, if you like, but this won't take long."

"I'll let Spooky out," I said.

Joanna nodded as she led Mrs. Trimble into the house.

I ran my fingers through my hair in a vain attempt to wipe away the worry and headed toward the street. I still had no idea what had become of Tom. I needed to call him before Joanna returned from the Trimbles'.

Joanna's car was in front of mine; she had started to pull into the driveway but must have given up on it when she saw Sophie and Roger talking with the police. I hopped into her car, started it up, and slipped it into gear. I hit the remote and waited for the garage door to open, but nothing happened. In addition to this, the sensor light failed to brighten.

"What the hell?" I growled. It had been a long day and an even longer night and the last thing I needed was to have to deal with a malfunctioning garage door opener.

I parked Joanna's car in front of the left bay door, killed the engine and pocketed the keys. I was walking back up my driveway when I heard somebody cough. My head flicked to the right and my eyes picked out a shape near the base of my neighbor's porch. It was Renko sitting in what appeared to be a kitchen chair, the porch light above him dark. I saw the glowing tip of a cigarette in his hand and heard the tinkle of Rufus' collar as he emerged from the shadows to pace back and forth in front of his master. I thought about waving but decided against it. The last thing I needed just then was a diatribe from my drunken neighbor.

I reached my car and climbed aboard. I turned into my driveway and pulled up in front of my bay. I tried my remote, but, as with Joanna's, nothing happened.

"Goddamn it," I hissed climbing out and tramping off toward the door at the side of the garage, imagining Renko laughing quietly at my dilemma from the shadows.

I reached the corner of the garage where the fence bent at a ninety-degree angle. I did my best to ignore Renko, keeping my back to him as I unhooked the section of chain link fence and peeled it back. Stepping through the gap, I reattached it. I couldn't risk Spooky getting out; things were getting too weird around here to have her wandering off anytime soon, and my old dog had the street sense of a newborn. I remembered the coyote incident at the Fayre and realized that we were less than two miles from the state hospital grounds. A coyote would make short work of our old Lhasa.

I turned the doorknob to the garage door and pushed it open. I reached for the light switch, which was just inside. From my position I could see Renko's porch and I watched as he tossed his spent cigarette aside, lifted his kitchen chair and carried it into the house, Rufus at his heels.

"Asshole," I muttered and flicked the switch. Nothing happened. Everything was dead, which was odd. There were two circuits in my garage; one circuit for the doors and the sensor light and a second for the internal lights. I could not imagine how both circuits could have tripped.

"Strange," I muttered.

I was reaching up to the place above the switch where I knew the circuit breakers to be when I sensed movement in front of me. Before I could call out a set of fingers reached out of nowhere, gripped my wrist and yanked. Then I was falling forward into the darkened garage!

119

Chapter Twenty

The fingers gripping my wrist released me and I fought to maintain my balance. I caught the doorframe to avoid falling and was just regaining my footing when a flashlight beam stabbed at my eyes. I raised my hand to fend off the glare, tossing out threats and obscenities and the beam, as if offended by my tirade, swung up into the face of its operator.

"Close the door," Tom prompted, and, confused but relieved, I obeyed.

"What are you doing here?" I hissed. "What the hell happened? Where's your car?"

"One question at a time," he said. "I don't want anyone to know I'm here. I parked at the other side of the block and cut across the field. I hopped your neighbor's fence, but his garage door was shut. I figured it would make a racket if I tried to open it, so I managed to shinny through that broken window. See?"

Tom aimed the light at a blood-smeared hand.

"Jesus, Tom!"

"Oh, it's not as bad as it looks; just a nick."

"Did you see the raccoon?"

"Yes," he said. "Do you have a rag for this?"

"Sure," I said. "But I'll need the flashlight. Let's keep the circuits off until you leave."

Tom handed me the light and I crossed the garage to the workstation at the back. I opened a cabinet door and took down my car cleaning supplies; I always kept fresh rags there.

"Here," I said, handing a clean white rag to Tom. "So what happened?"

"Hold the light steady, will you?"

I held the light above Tom's injured hand as he wrapped the rag around it. I could see the cut was no worse than mine; it appeared to have already stopped bleeding.

"Between the crap on the floor and that low-hanging ceiling, Renko should be thrown in jail for maintaining a hazardous building," Tom growled.

"But you *did see* the thing."

"Yes. Something tore that raccoon apart and with no intention of eating it, not that I know what might eat a raccoon. Dogs wouldn't do that, and dogs wouldn't bring something like that home and set it on a worktable to boot. No, that carcass was put there for a specific reason."

"Maybe as a warning," I volunteered.

Tom finished wrapping his hand and shrugged off my suggestion.

"If it *was* a warning, why put it in the garage where Mr. Clean over there was hardly likely to see it?" Tom said. "Why not on the front or back porch?"

"Maybe someone did as you suggested and Renko tossed it in the garage."

"Why not toss it in the back of his pick-up truck to dispose of later on or even in his own backyard? You could hide the Chrysler building in the brush he's got back there."

"All right, so it's not meant as a warning," I said. "What then?"

"You said the dog didn't detect you due to the smell."

"Sure," I said. "It seems logical. Why else couldn't Rufus find me hiding there? I mean, dogs have good noses, don't they?"

"Dogs have excellent olfactory senses. And I believe you're right about the raccoon's purpose being to conceal the smell of someone hiding in the garage. You benefited from someone else's idea."

"So someone put that thing in there so they could do what? Hide and watch Renko?"

"Did you look around while you were in there?"

"A little, but I was too busy trying not to get

caught."

"If you stand at the front window on the side facing your neighbor's house, you'd find it provides a commanding view of the north side of your house and patio."

"Oh, cut the shit, Tom. Why the hell would someone want to watch Joanna and me?"

"I think you know who's watching your house, Jack," Tom said.

I stiffened. "What the hell does that mean?"

"It means that somewhere in your past there's a clue as to who this is and why he or she is doing this. You've got to unlock your memory and figure this out, because someone is going through an awful lot of trouble to keep an eye on you and your wife."

Tom's words washed over me like icy water.

"You should tell Joanna," he said. "She may know who it is."

I remained silent. I had no intention of telling Joanna. The last thing she needed was to hear that someone was stalking us, someone who thought nothing of bringing a dead animal along for the ride or, worse, maybe killing it just to hide their scent from Rufus.

I breathed a heavy sigh. I wanted to go back in time to the simpler life I'd known before I found the first 'deposit,' to a time before Tom's crazy notions.

"So how did old man Trimble see you?"

"What?" Tom said, adjusting his make-shift bandage.

"The police were here. Someone ran past the kitchen window of the Trimble's house. It was you, wasn't it?"

Tom shook his head slowly.

"But the cops *were* here. There were two police cruisers sitting out front."

"I saw them coming; that's why I hid in here," he

said. "But I had no idea why they were here. I figured maybe there was an ambulance coming, too. I thought one of the old farts had had a heart attack. And I never crossed the street," Tom added softly. "I had only been in Renko's garage for a few minutes when I heard something. I figured Renko had come back out to poke around or have a butt, though I never heard that damned squeaky screen door of his." Tom paused. I could sense him frowning there in the dark. "The Trimbles saw someone else."

My stomach felt cold and queasy.

"I think your stalker was here tonight," he said, his voice suddenly low, "though I can't imagine why."

"What do you mean?"

"If your stalker is worth his weight in salt, he would have known you two were at the Fayre tonight."

"Maybe he didn't know."

"Maybe." I could sense Tom's frown growing darker. "Maybe he was here for another reason. Maybe he wanted to take a tour of your garage, or your house, take home a few tokens, souvenirs. Joanna's underwear."

"Tom!"

"*Your* underwear." Tom shrugged.

"And you wonder why I don't want to tell Joanna any of this!"

"Or maybe," he continued, as if I had said nothing, "he was here to see someone else."

"Jack!"

I froze. It was Joanna calling from the yard. Tom extinguished the light.

"Jack!"

She was close, moving toward us. I turned on a dime and threw open the door, stepped out into the yard and caught Joanna before she reached the garage.

"Mrs. T's doing okay," she said looking past me to the open door. "Why are the cars still in the driveway? And what's wrong with the sensor light?"

"Circuit for the doors must have tripped," I said, trying to sound convincing.

She nodded slowly while considering the darkened doorway behind me.

"Use a flashlight so you don't kill yourself," she said.

"Yeah," I said. "Flashlight."

"I'm done in," she said. "I'm going to hit the hay. Has Spooky been out?"

"No, I'll let her out when I'm done."

"The cars are fine in the driveway." She turned and waved to me. "Fix the circuit tomorrow."

"I'll be right in," I said.

"All right, Mr. Obsessive-compulsive," she said, walking away. "Have it your way."

I waited until Joanna had crossed the yard and gone inside, then I went back into the garage and closed the door behind me.

"Tom," I called.

"Over here," he said, his voice coming from the other side of the garage. I strained to see in the dark and detected his silhouette against the window closest to the bay door on Renko's side. He was gazing out at something.

"You do know how to re-set the circuits, don't you?" he said.

"Of course."

"I haven't had to touch one in years," he added. "Alice always beats me to it. My wife is a regular Norm Abrams."

"Good skills to have," I said, a little annoyed at his joking. "So what the hell's so interesting?"

"I'm just watching your neighbor's garage," he said. "The house is dark; looks like he's gone to bed."

"I'm going in," I said. "Let yourself out later."

"Will do," Tom said, his eyes never straying.

"How's the paw?" I thought to ask.

"Stopped bleeding; still attached."

"Will Alice say anything?"

"Nah. She hardly notices me these days. Besides, if she does notice, she'll figure I did it working on some project."

I nodded, more to myself than to Tom, as his eyes were still glued to Renko's place.

"Turn my circuit breakers back on before you go, would you?"

"You really don't know how to re-set them, do you?" he said with a snort.

"Funny."

"I'll call you tomorrow. Are you working the Fayre?"

"Tomorrow night definitely and probably the afternoon, too," I said after opening the door.

"Sleep tight," he said. "Don't let the prowlers bite."

I ignored this last bit of advice, closed the door behind me and left Tom to my darkened garage.

Chapter Twenty-One

I found Joanna in bed asleep when I got in, Spooky lying at her side. My dog raised her head to consider me with disdain for having left her cooped up for so long without a bathroom break.

"C'mon, girl," I said apologetically and led her to the service porch, where I clipped her leash to her collar. I couldn't afford to have her catching a whiff of Tom and barking. This night had already seen enough activity.

We descended the steps, crossed the patio and headed for the side gate, a favorite spot for Spooky. She took care of her business quickly as I watched the side door of my garage for movement, wondering if Tom was still inside or if he'd already crept off into the night. I wondered just how far he would go to satisfy his insatiable curiosity. He was like a man with an addiction, once he got going.

I leaned over the top of the fence, waved my hand, and watched as the sensor light slowly grew brighter, signaling that the circuits had been reset and Tom had gone.

Movement near the head of my driveway drew my attention and I noticed a police cruiser slowly rolling into view. It paused in front of the Trimbles' house, and I watched as a spotlight crept across my elderly neighbors' front yard. Spooky began to growl and I picked her up. The light swept my way and when it found me I waved. It went out and the cruiser slowly backed away.

"Are you trying to get me in trouble, girl?" Spooky dragged her tongue across my chin. "Let's turn in," I said, and I carried her inside.

I changed and brushed my teeth, considered a few cans of Corona Light staring at me from the top shelf of the refrigerator, decided against them and closed the door. I went to the four seasons room and was about to flip on the television to see what was left of the late night lineup when the telephone rang. I scooped it up before the second ring was done and said "Hello," clearly expecting to hear Tom's voice telling me he was home, safe and sound. But I was oddly surprised when no familiar voice responded to my greeting. In fact no voice responded at all. "Hello," I said again and the dial tone resumed.

I eyed the receiver suspiciously for a long time before hanging up. I sat down and watched the telephone as if it might start crawling toward me. It didn't. It didn't ring again, either. I picked it up and searched through caller ID. The LCD screen listed the number as private.

I hung up and sat back on the couch. I had a sick feeling in my stomach; the cold thing had returned. I went to the window and cracked the blinds open with my fingers. Renko's house was shrouded in darkness. I slowly let the slats close, sat back down and recalled Tom's words. It was in my memory, he'd said. The stalker was there, hiding, waiting for me to reveal his identity. But I saw no one. There was only the new phone call, just like the others years ago. It was starting again.

At some point, I dozed off and dreamed of the Fayre. I found myself standing in the midway; it was dark and the rides were silent, the crowd gone. The boarded-up food booths were situated to my left, and the tents, where jewelry and tee shirts and novelties were sold, to my right, their flaps tightly drawn and laced shut. Looming before me was the Ferris wheel, silhouetted against the bloated orange face of the full moon. I became gradually aware of music like the distant wail of a train whistle. It was the Hal Ketchum song being sung by the lead singer from Wicked Scarlett. But there was something haunting and ethereal about the voice, as if the woman was standing in a cave and singing the song at half-speed. The words drifted past me as if caught up on ribbons of mist, undulating, moving in and out of the shadows like ghosts, the pitch wavering.

My eyes were drawn to the base of the Ferris wheel to a lone motionless figure. It was the carny; he had found me again, and a cold feeling of dread settled over me. I called out to him, asking who he was and what he wanted. He didn't answer. He only stood there, his face buried in shadow, his arms at his sides.

I opened my eyes and found Spooky staring up at me with a curious expression on her face, as if questioning her master's sanity. I must confess that at that moment, she was not alone in her concerns. I remembered my dream and I felt compelled to put a name to the carny's face. Perhaps *this* was the memory Tom was talking about. Perhaps I *did* know who our stalker was after all.

I considered my dog gazing up at me, telling me in her way that it was time to go to bed, that no good could come from me waiting up all night for something to happen. I took her advice, scooped her up, and joined Joanna.

Spooky never growled that night. And, so far as I know, the sensor light on the garage never brightened. And, for the rest of that night at least, the mysterious carny left me in peace.

Chapter Twenty-Two

Morning was slow to arrive, and when it finally did, it proved to be a gray, drab one, moving sluggishly across the horizon like an old man with a hangover. Joanna had apparently gone out for a walk by the time I rolled out of bed; she did this occasionally, especially during the summer months. She claimed it gave her a chance to collect her thoughts and get some exercise at the same time. She was always trying to find new ways to multi-task. Spooky was nowhere to be found and I assumed Joanna had taken her along. This, too, was not uncommon.

'Walking the graves' at St. Brigid's cemetery at the head of our street provided Joanna with a way to release her pent-up stress. My own stress level was usually lower, and a brisk bike ride or workout on the Bowflex in my basement usually suited my needs. This morning I decided a cup of coffee would do the trick, and I poured myself one from the pot Joanna had made, silently wishing my wife luck in her efforts to exorcize whatever demons were plaguing her as of late.

Java in hand, I stepped outside to consider the slate-gray sky and was immediately overcome by the oppressive humidity that was a trade mark of July in New England. I remembered the meteorologist talking about the moon and Mars being closer to the Earth than they had been in centuries and wondered if those facts had any bearing on the lingering heat wave. I knew the occurrences were probably unrelated, but I found it interesting to wonder about the mysteries of the universe and how they might interlock like cosmic puzzle pieces.

The truth behind my musings was simple: I was trying to keep my mind off the bizarre incidents plaguing my neighborhood. The routine of life on my street had been broken and, as my wife can surely attest, I do cherish my routines.

I took up a position at the patio table and sipped my coffee, letting my mind turn back to the events of the previous night. In my head, I saw the police cruisers parked in front of the Trimbles' house with their flashing lights. I saw Joanna's car sitting at the head of our driveway, the driver's seat disturbingly vacant. And I sensed the cold, sick feeling that had been creeping through my insides since discovering the first 'deposit' coming alive, and I shivered in the heat.

I sat back, closed my eyes and sighed. My efforts to cast the recent events aside were failing. Then, as if adding insult to injury, I remembered my dream of the mysterious carny standing in the shadow of the Ferris wheel. And I remembered staring into the darkness beneath the maple tree in my yard, searching for two glistening specks that might have been eyes, and I shivered again.

I was suddenly overcome by the sensation that something was happening, something big, looming just beyond my range of vision like a shark swimming beneath the smooth surface of the sea, and I realized that part of me was truly frightened. I had imagined the whole thing to be a joke, a sick gag and nothing more. I hoped I would look back at it all someday with laughter. Now, though, I was beginning to realize that I'd been wrong. Whatever was happening was no joke, and I suddenly felt like a man trapped in what he thought to be a dark comedy, only to discover that there was no comedy, only deepening layers of darkness and dread.

Tom hadn't helped matters. He had planted seeds of paranoia in my brain, and I found myself suddenly worried for Joanna.

I consulted the slate-colored tile clock hanging above the party cart in the corner of the patio. It read nearly nine o'clock, but I had no idea what time Joanna had left the house. There had been no note, no indication of when she might return. Her walks seldom exceeded thirty minutes.

I remembered news of a woman being assaulted in the cemetery last fall. The culprits had been two homeless men who lived in the woods that abutted the back portion of the cemetery. They had attacked her looking for money. I remember seeing the woman on television when the local cable news network interviewed her. Her face was bruised, some of her hair had been torn out and her lip was bleeding. When she spoke, she sounded shaken and she kept telling the interviewer how lucky she was to have gotten away with only some bumps and bruises.

I got to my feet, my chair banging against the outer wall of the doghouse, and I went to the driveway. I threw open the gate and uncharacteristically left it ajar, something I am normally meticulously cautious about due to Spooky's lack of street sense, and jogged to the head of the driveway.

I reached the street, spied Mrs. Trimble standing beside her garage watering her tomato plants and watched her wave at me as if in a dream. Distracted, I managed to wave back, but my fevered brain never thought to ask her if she'd seen Joanna. But then again, Sophie Trimble held my wife in high regard, almost considering her to be a substitute for the daughter she had lost years earlier to a car crash, and if I'd asked her then about Joanna's whereabouts, the woman would surely have seen the concern in my eyes and started in on her own batch of worry.

Panicky, the thick air enveloping me, I headed down the street, the asphalt hot against my bare feet, the occasional pebble biting into my flesh. I found myself in front of Renko's house. Breathless, I considered its sick drooping facade before realizing that there was a figure moving toward me from the head of the street. It was Joanna with Spooky, tethered to her leash, tooling along by her side.

"Thinking of joining me?" she called as we met in the middle of the street. There was a sliver of disgust in her voice.

"Well–" I fumbled, still short of breath but immensely relieved.

"I just needed some time alone," she said curtly.

Then, without further explanation, she moved around me and headed back toward our house, Spooky in tow.

I stood in the middle of the street, drawing in desperate chunks of humid air, confused, my mind racing. I couldn't decide whether I should be angry with Joanna for not caring about my concerns for her safety or merely relieved. For the moment, I chose the latter.

I turned to consider the cemetery as if hoping for some sign that I had simply overreacted. Perched on the grassy shoulder that abutted the chain link fence surrounding the cemetery was a big, black, early seventies muscle car, a Chevelle, I thought, its engine purring like a jungle cat, deep and powerful. I was certain the car hadn't been there a moment earlier.

I strained to see the driver, but the tinted windows were fully raised and I could make out little more than a vague shape behind the wheel.

The engine revved and the car pulled slowly off the shoulder, moved off down the street and in a moment was gone. I watched, mesmerized, as it left my field of vision. Then I turned to see Joanna heading down our driveway. A beat passed and I followed.

Chapter Twenty-Three

Joanna remained quiet and distant for the rest of the morning. I considered Spooky, who was nestled in her bed, her big dark eyes studying me, hoping silently that she could tell me what was bothering my wife. I figured the incident with the Trimbles' prowler had further set Joanna's nerves on edge. She didn't know about Tom hiding in the garage, or at least I didn't *think* she knew, though that revelation would certainly have sent her over the edge entirely and might easily explain her abruptness.

I considered my cold coffee, poured it out and started making some eggs. I tossed a couple of slices of raisin bread into the toaster oven and poured myself some orange juice.

"That will make the house hot," Joanna said, emerging from the bathroom after showering and heading for the bedroom.

"Yes, it will," I said then caught myself. Whatever was bothering Joanna, it would not be chased away by my childish sarcasm. "I'll be quick," I said.

She said nothing.

"What time are you due at the Fayre?"

"Not until one," she said and I detected a softening in her voice. "But I have a few things to take care of first."

"Need help?"

"No," she said with a tone of friendly finality, and I decided it best not to push the issue.

I finished cooking and turned to the breakfast island, my plate in hand, to find Joanna standing in the bedroom doorway, fully dressed, her hair hanging in dark wet strands at her shoulders. I nearly dropped my plate. In all our years of marriage I had never known Joanna to leave the house without at least attempting to style her hair. I was about to ask her if she was all right, but decided it best to give her space. There would be time later for disclosures.

"Should I meet you?"

"Huh?" she said, distracted, rifling through her purse as if searching for something. "Oh, yeah," she said, producing her mobile phone and tucking it into her pocket. Then she went to the door, paused, glanced down at Spooky who was considering her with big eyes, and turned to me.

"I'm all right," she said in a refreshingly lucid tone. "I just have a lot on my mind. I'll see you at the Fayre. We'll eat Voc Tech Chicken and listen to rock and roll."

I nodded. "Sounds good."

Joanna actually grinned, blew me a kiss and headed out.

I glanced down at Spooky, who'd set about napping again as if nothing could possibly be wrong. Then I sat at the breakfast island and, Spooky, who had not missed a meal in her entire life, shuffled over to mooch. As I listened to Joanna's car backing out of the driveway, I was overcome with the distinct feeling that it was going to be another long day.

Chapter Twenty-Four

I finished eating, tucked the dishes into the dishwasher, got dressed and started in on the yard work. I had just finished watering the shrubs at the front of the house, paying special attention to the Hydrangeas, which were fairly new and always thirsty, and was moving on to the Hostas by the garage when Tom pulled into the driveway. He parked beside my car, which I hadn't bothered putting in the garage the night before, and met me at the gate.

"What a night," he said, grinning.

"I prefer a more serene environment," I said, pushing the gate open and leading the way to the patio chairs. "Police, prowlers, and spies hiding in my garage set my nerves on edge."

Tom's grin broadened as if it was all great fun for him, and I found myself resenting his light-hearted mood.

"Moon's getting big," he said, his eyes finding the horizon.

"Blue moon," I said.

"Looked pink to me," he said, "like that song by the English guy."

"Nick Drake."

"Yeah," Tom said, sounding distant and thoughtful, "Nick Drake."

"Pink moon is in autumn, I think," I added matter-of-factly, plucking that particular nugget of astronomical information from some forgotten corner of my brain.

"I heard about a poet who tried to kiss the moon's reflection in a pond," Tom added.

"I heard he drowned," I added flatly, unimpressed with Tom's musings.

"I guess," Tom said nodding thoughtfully, "that poet was after something that could never really be his,

135

even if he thought it was."

"I should tell you that things haven't changed," I said, feeling inclined to remind him of the recent events. "I still have a stalker, at least according to the cheap detective I've hired." My tone was more than a little sarcastic, but I didn't care. Things were going from bad to worse.

"True," he said, his gaze finding me. "But something occurred to me last night after I got home."

"And what was that?" I was growing impatient with Tom's beating around the bush for dramatic effect, not to mention Joanna's mood swings and, most of all, the mysterious person who was creeping around my neighborhood after hours.

"How about a beer?" Tom said. "You look strung out."

"It's not even noon."

"No time like the present," he said, his eyes straying to the field behind my house.

"Tom, I'm sorry, but I'm not in the mood for–"

"Millard Fillmore once said that it is not strange to mistake change for progress."

"What does that mean?"

"Simply," Tom replied, "that change is inevitable, but not all change qualifies as progress. Good change is desirable." Tom sighed. "Tell me, what has *changed* in your life lately?"

"Just the stalker," I said with a shrug.

"That's all?"

Again I shrugged. "Yes, unless I'm missing something."

Tom grinned. "There's the rub."

"Wha–?"

"Tell me, when did your stalker first appear?"

"When did he first ...? Haven't we covered this?"

"Not really," he said pursing his lips. "When did you find the first 'deposit'? You brought me the sample on

Blue Moon

Tuesday night, but you never really mentioned if you had found it that day. And I was so taken aback that I never thought to ask."

"Well, I found the first 'deposit' that same evening."

Tom grinned. His right leg was bouncing around as if he was bursting with news or in desperate need of a trip to the bathroom. I found myself not caring which. I wanted him to leave and let me sort this out in my head.

"You keep a well-maintained yard," he said, his brain skipping across topics like a needle across an old phonograph record.

"My yard?"

"I mean to say you keep a tidy yard, and you would have noticed if the 'deposit' had been left earlier than Tuesday, perhaps on Monday or Sunday. The air had been humid and the specimen might have kept, not that I'm an expert on such things, but I suspect you would have known."

I frowned around Tom's words. The only reason I had noticed the specimen was because I had been cutting the grass. I suppose it could have been left there a day earlier. Then I remembered having gone out back on Monday to pick up branches that had fallen Sunday morning during a bout of wind gusts. Some had landed in the Hosta bed, and there had been no sign of any 'deposit' at the time, so I concluded the specimen must have been left at some point between Monday morning and Tuesday afternoon. That left Monday night as the most likely time.

"And you saw no sign of the deposit on Monday morning?"

"No," I said, picturing it all in my mind.

"Are you sure?"

I explained about my 'stick-picking' and how it worked into the time frame I'd established.

Tom turned back to the field and nodded slowly, his

137

jaw moving back and forth as if he was literally chewing on some new notion.

"What else made its first appearance Monday night?"

I shrugged, raising my hands and letting them flop down into my lap. "I don't know," I said, feeling abandoned as if I had been on the verge of some important revelation which turned to smoke before my eyes. "The Yankees came to Fenway. The full moon arrived."

Tom's leg stopped moving and he turned to me, his eyes intense and somehow darker than usual. "I'll tell you what else happened Monday night," he said softly, a sliver of a grin touching his lips. "The Fayre came to town."

I paused in the middle of a smart-ass remark, my mouth half-open.

Tom leaned back in his chair, his gaze returning to the field.

"Close your mouth before a fly goes in," he said. "Now, how about that beer?"

Slowly, lost in deep thought, I got to my feet, went inside and got Tom his beer, letting Spooky out in the process. She greeted my guest, then took up position beneath the table as Tom pried open his beer.

"What, no lime?" he said before taking a long sip.

"What are we talking about here?"

He set the bottle down, pausing for dramatic effect, his eyes fixed on the field.

"Do you know anyone at the Fayre, that is, anyone beside teachers and librarians?"

"Uh, no."

"Does Joanna know anyone that you might *not* know?"

"I don't think so," I said shaking my head, "at least not in a social sense."

"Think carefully," he said.

I leaned closer, a trickle of sweat inching its way

down my spine.

"Is there anyone at the Fayre that seems out of place, someone who might be paying an unusual bit of attention to either you or Joanna? Perhaps a repeat customer, a real doughnut lover."

I wanted to grin at Tom's sick attempt at humor in the midst of all this, but I couldn't manage it. The fact was he had hit the nail on the head.

"Yes," I said the moisture in my mouth evaporating. "There is."

Tom pursed his lips and nodded slowly. "When exactly did the Fayre arrive?"

"Sometime Monday night; set up all day Tuesday. They were up and running by Wednesday."

Tom sat back, drew in a deep breath and blew it out. His face was clouded over, his brow deeply furrowed.

"Yes, it's their business to be quick," he said. "Time is money. That would give someone time to find out exactly where Joanna lived, or where *you* lived. It all fits."

"But why?" I asked, that cold slithery sensation in my stomach returning.

"As I said, that answer is probably buried someplace in either your memory or Joanna's." Tom finished his beer. "This person you've noticed, what can you tell me about him or her?"

"He's a carny," I said, trying to picture the man's face in my brain. "Skinny, quiet, weird. Rough around the edges. He hasn't bought any doughnuts, but I keep bumping into him."

"And how does he behave?"

"He doesn't talk, he just stares at me. Strange. Suspicious character. Loner."

"Has he spoken to Joanna?"

I shook my head. "No. I don't think so."

Tom let his gaze stray back to the field.

"If he *is* a carny, he's probably staying in a motel or

139

a trailer."

"There are a slew of mobile homes behind the midway," I said.

Tom nodded thoughtfully. "Then that's a good place to start," he said turning to me. "It looks as if I'll be going to the Fayre tonight after all." He handed me the empty beer bottle and got to his feet. "You should redeem that."

I studied the bottle. "Thanks for the advice."

"Ray Bradbury wrote a story about a very strange Fayre that came to a small town. As a teacher of English Language Arts, I'm sure you're well acquainted with it."

"*Something Wicked This Way Comes*," I said.

"The title was borrowed from *Macbeth*," Tom said nodding. "The Scottish play." His grin had gone and a solemn expression had replaced it. He looked suddenly older to me, as if he'd aged several years in the past few moments. It was as if some strange, youth-draining radioactivity existed in my yard, doubtless the lingering effects of my mysterious stalker. Maybe for the first time Tom was taking this seriously. That was exactly what I'd wanted. But somehow, now that I'd gotten my wish, now that the situation had moved from the theoretical to the real, I'd have done anything to wish it away. Maybe I *should* have let sleeping dogs lie.

"Something wicked came to town with the Fayre, I'd say," Tom added before nodding slowly and walking toward his car. "Yes, sir."

I sat in silence, watching him back out of my driveway. The trickle of sweat running down my back had swelled to a river. Could the carny be my stalker? That idea had occurred to me, but I had dismissed it with little effort; there just seemed to be no connection, no thread linking the man to Joanna or me. There was nothing but my gut instincts.

But some things are like that. Intuition is often the

deciding factor that prevents someone from climbing aboard a doomed plane or leaving an appliance plugged in when going on a trip. And if the carny *was* our stalker, what possible motive could he have? Had he picked us at random? Or had he worked the Fayre last year and taken a shine to Joanna – or *me*, for that matter? If that was the case, why had he waited an entire year to put his twisted scheme into action? I couldn't begin to guess, but I had to assume that Tom might be right this time. Perhaps something wicked *had* come to town with the Summer Harvest Fayre.

I felt panicky, as if something was happening that I should be a part of, and I suddenly wanted to be with Joanna. I looked at my watch. It was barely noon, but I had a nagging feeling, like a premonition, my own brand of intuition, if you will, that something was wrong. Unimaginably wrong.

Chapter Twenty-Five

I stood at the gate, my mind racing around Tom's suspicions like one of the Indy slot cars at the Fayre. I could sense something on the horizon, something ominous, and I wanted to join Joanna as quickly as possible. But first, I would need to retrieve my dog.

I called for Spooky, but she was nowhere to be found. Annoyed, I checked the driveway just in case the old girl had taken advantage of my momentary lapse of reason and followed Tom through the gate, but there was no sign of her. I called her again and, much to my relief, she poked her head out from behind the garage. Before I could entice her with promises of a biscuit, though, she glanced back at something behind the garage that had apparently piqued her interest and then vanished around the corner.

Spooky had grown stubborn with age and I usually didn't mind her infrequent bouts of disobedience, but I was in a rush now and in no mood for games. I decided to give her a last chance, called her one more time and, when she didn't appear, I set off after her.

I found her behind the garage scratching at a branch that had apparently fallen from the huge moss-covered oak that stood in the corner of Renko's yard. I had been meaning to ask him to trim the upper portion back because it hung directly over my garage, but simply hadn't gotten around to it.

I lifted the branch, which measured more than six feet in length and at least two inches thick at its widest point. Angrily I pitched it over the fence into my unruly neighbor's yard. I was about to chastise Spooky for disobeying me when I realized that it wasn't the branch that had fascinated her but rather something lying *beneath* the branch.

I looked closer and saw that she was clawing and

sniffing at a few sheets of roofing shingles lying by the fence. I stooped down beside my dog, stroking her back, realizing then that she was whimpering and shaking.

"It's all right, girl," I said, trying to soothe her but realizing that I was not only failing to alleviate her fears but stoking my own as well. There had been no excessive wind since Sunday, at least not enough to tear a large branch or some shingles free, and as Tom had pointed out I was nothing if not fastidious about my yard. I certainly would have noticed a branch the size of the one I had just tossed into Renko's yard. I also would have checked on the condition of the garage roof if I'd seen the shingles.

Concerned, I picked up one of the shingles and examined it. The edges were torn and there were several deep gouges in the top portion, as if Spooky had been digging at it with her claws. But Spooky was not a big dog, and the gouges were large and deep. Something else had been worrying these shingles, something considerably larger than my fourteen-pound Lhasa.

I glanced up at the garage roof, then went to fetch my ladder. I wrestled the thing out from where it hung on the garage wall and, under the watchful eyes of my dog, set it against the back of the garage. With no one to foot the thing for me, I hopped on the lowest rung a few times, hoping to embed it in the earth and prevent it from slipping out from beneath me. Reasonably satisfied that I was not going to kill myself, I started to climb.

Heights have never been my friend and I moved gingerly, one rung at a time, making certain my footing was solid before moving upward, until I found myself at eye level with the slightly pitched roof. It didn't take long to find the site of the missing shingles. Several others were lying there as well, having been torn loose by something that simply could not have been a gust of wind. The corners were raised up as if someone had pried them loose deliberately. And an entire four-foot-square section was marred with scratches similar to those gouged into the ones I'd left on the ground. If I didn't know better, I'd say Rufus had been up here digging at my roof.

I reached out to touch the damage, slid my fingers in and out of the deep gouges, and felt something tucked beneath one of the shingles. I slipped my fingers beneath the upturned portion, tightened my grip around something pliable and plucked it free. I found myself staring at a large, mangled oak leaf. Perplexed, I raised my eyes to the leafy canopy above and saw where a good-sized branch hung by splintery threads.

The cold thing in my stomach moved and I looked back at the damaged shingles. Someone had been in the tree. The branch had broken under the climber's weight, and he had landed on my garage roof and caused the damage.

I decided to take advantage of my lofty position and scanned the neighborhood for anything suspicious, anything out of the ordinary. I could see past Renko's hovel to St. Brigid's with its joggers, the Trimbles' house across the street, other houses on adjacent streets, well-maintained yards, driveways, chimneys. There was nothing unusual about any of it. Then my eyes settled on the large field behind my house with its small trees and tall grasses and weeds. There I sensed the memory of something ominous, something dark and frightening, moving beneath the surface of James Joyce's proverbial 'summer afternoon.' My once-peaceful neighborhood had been corrupted and tainted by this mysterious presence which left traces everywhere. Everything had changed, subtly, imperceptibly to most, but definitely nonetheless.

I climbed back down and began scanning the area by the fence for tracks. If someone *had* jumped down from the garage roof, they might have left a footprint in the soft earth. But after several minutes of searching, I found nothing. I realized that whoever had fallen onto the roof had probably climbed down at the northeast corner of the garage, where the tree was closest and their movements would be hidden. They could have used the chain link fence as a ladder, because it was at that corner that a small portion jutted in from the main run and met with the garage.

I inspected the section of fence for signs that someone had used it for support and found some of the spines to be bent. I turned my attention to the back length of fence and the field beyond. The waist-high weeds that thrived there would thwart any detective's efforts at finding tracks, presuming this was in fact the escape-route the tree-climber had taken. And despite the gouges that looked canine in nature, Rufus was off the hook; dogs don't climb trees. Neither do coyotes.

I looked up into Renko's oak at the dangling branch; it had to be a good thirty feet above the ground and at least ten feet above the roof of the garage. Whoever had been up there was an astute climber. Perhaps my stalker was a rock climber or an acrobat. My brain began sorting through this new information. Where would one find an acrobat? The answer was almost rhetorical. Acrobats would most likely be found at circuses, carnivals and, of course, at the Fayre.

The chill in my stomach intensified as I carried the ladder back to the garage. Then I picked up Spooky and headed for the house. I would need to tell Tom about this.

***

There was no answer when I tried Tom's mobile phone, so I hopped into the shower. Tom planned to be at the Fayre that night; I could talk to him then.

As I stood beneath the hot water, I tried to imagine the state of mind required for someone to climb a tree and risk breaking his neck just to watch someone putter around their yard. I stopped scrubbing my hair when I realized that climbing the tree might have been an act of desperation.

The stalker had been seen by Roger Trimble and needed to escape. There are houses behind the Trimble place, so he couldn't go that way, especially if he suspected the police were on their way. The neighborhood is old and zoning has become stricter over the years, so several houses are built so close they're practically on top of one another, but the field behind my house with its tall grass could easily conceal a man lying on his stomach.

I ducked my head under the stream of water. I was thinking like Tom, and that bothered me. I tried to imagine how the scenario might have played out. I envisioned the stalker taking a shortcut through the Trimbles' yard. Then he's spotted by Roger Trimble as he passes beneath the man's kitchen window and he scrambles for cover. He bolts across the street, runs through Renko's yard, but not by the driveway; Renko might emerge at any moment and find him making his escape. He would use the section of yard to the north, which is almost as overgrown as the back portion. But maybe Rufus starts barking at him as he passes. He knows his way around Renko's yard because he's visited Renko's garage. He can't risk going to ground, not there; Renko might let Rufus out and there would be no dead raccoon to conceal his scent.

In an act of desperation, he climbs the tree in the back corner of Renko's yard, skillfully, quietly. He has every intention of waiting up there until things quiet down, and, when they do, when the police have gone, he starts to climb down, but the branch breaks and he falls. He has to wonder if someone heard him fall. He has no choice now but to climb down from the roof, hop the fence and run for it, into the field where he can lay low until he's sure it's safe to leave.

But what about Tom? Tom had taken cover in my garage as soon as the Trimbles started the commotion. That meant that the prowler could not have escaped *before* Tom hid in my garage. There simply hadn't been time. And Tom

146

would certainly have heard someone crashing down on the garage roof above him.

The stalker must have escaped *after* Tom left my garage. That meant that our stalker was in the tree above us all the while. He must have watched as Joanna came to get me. He must have seen me go into the house. And he must have waited until Tom sneaked away through the back field before making his escape. If that was the case, and no other scenario seemed plausible, the stalker had gotten a good look at all of us, Tom included. He might even have followed Tom to his car!

I climbed out of the shower, dried off and dressed, my mind racing. I made sure Spooky had fresh food and water, then went outside.

Renko was walking toward his garage, Rufus at his heels. He was carrying a hammer in one hand and his old kitchen chair in the other. His pick-up truck was parked in his driveway; I could see several sheets of plywood stacked in the truck's bed.

Ordinarily I would have been happy to see that the man was planning to do some work on his rat-trap house, but my mind was preoccupied and I didn't think any more of it as I went to my car, started it up and backed out of my driveway. My thoughts were consumed with my need to get to the Fayre. If Tom was going to do some snooping, I wanted to be in on it. I had to tell him about my mysterious tree-climber, too. But most of all, I figured it was time to have a little talk with my anonymous carny to hopefully determine once and for all if he and my stalker were one in the same. All in all, it was shaping up to be very a busy night.

Chapter Twenty-Six

I drove beneath the slate-gray sky, which acted like an immense shroud, trapping in the heat, bringing the world around me to a near-boil. The dead air only served to amplify the jumble of thoughts in my fevered brain. Images flashed through my mind as if on a thread of film, images of the carny standing by the Ferris wheel, images of Tom asking me when my stalker first appeared and grinning when I told him. In my mind, I saw Renko walking toward his garage with a hammer in one hand and an old kitchen chair in the other. I saw cold black eyes gazing at me from the shadowy innards of Renko's garage and I saw the tattered shingles on the roof of my own. In the middle of it all was Joanna, her green eyes glinting in the moonlight. Things were spinning all around me as if trapped in the vortex of a tornado. But try as I might, I simply couldn't put order to them.

I passed a police cruiser that had pulled up beside an accident and caught a glimpse of two young women arguing with one another as the officer, a young woman who reminded me of the one who had investigated the Trimbles' prowler, tried to calm them down. It was hot. People got crazy when it got hot. Tempers flared, fights broke out. It would be crowded and hot at the Fayre. And the moon would be closer than ever, a burning stone in the sky, disturbing the human internal gyroscope, tipping its needle askew.

The clock in the dash read one forty-five. A pickup pulled out of a side street and slowed me down.

"Relax," I told myself as I dug a shred of logic from a forgotten crevice of my brain. Worrying was a useless distraction, one destined to defeat our best efforts. I couldn't remember where I'd heard that, but it rang true.

The pickup finally veered into a side street and

vanished into a seedy-looking neighborhood. I hit the gas. Not far now, I told myself. Not far.

***

I reached the edge of the state hospital grounds and felt my eyes drawn to the woods where the little girl had been chased by the coyote. I turned into the main drive and waved to the security guard sitting in his car before proceeding toward the administration building atop the hill. I drove past the boarded-up buildings, past several teenagers skateboarding beneath the big weeping willow tree and on to the lot below.

The dust billowed around me as I drew to a halt at the back of the concession booths. I watched Marge Weems emerge from the back door, an unlit Camel clenched between her teeth, frowning.

"Bored?" she asked as I climbed out of my car into the residual cloud of dust.

"Yeah," I answered, not sure what reason for my presence I could possibly offer.

"Joanna's checking out the Anything Goes Sale," she said, her gravelly voice sounding worse than usual. "Slow day. Too hot."

"Hot. Yes. I'm going to have a look around."

Marge shrugged her sloping shoulders. "Suit yourself."

I moved off toward the midway, and when I reached the last booth in our row, I turned back to locate Marge. She was at the back door talking with the woman from the Star of Delhi booth. She wasn't watching me so, instead of turning into the alleyway that separated the rows of booths and moving into the midway, I headed for the RVs.

"Hot one, isn't it?" a woman said, surprising me as she stepped out from the iced tea and coffee booth, wiping her forehead with a towel.

"Yes," I agreed, trying not to be rude, before proceeding.

149

I reached the end of the second set of booths. I stepped over some hoses and power cords, but paused at the edge of the trailer park when I sensed some urgent activity on the midway. Throngs of people were slowly moving toward the rides and I wondered if another coyote had been spotted. Curious, I moved through the alleyway into the midway.

I emerged perhaps ten yards from the Ferris wheel beside the water-balloon game, which was devoid of contestants as were all the gaming booths. All eyes were on the Ferris wheel. Its seats were near-full to capacity, but the ride stood motionless and it became immediately evident that something was wrong.

A curious crowd was gathering at the boarding ramp. The man I had seen talking with the EMT the previous day, the man Joanna identified as Vern Cross, the owner of the Fayre, was standing on the big wheel's passenger loading platform talking into a handheld radio. Everyone was staring up at the motionless wheel. It was clear that the ride had malfunctioned and people were trapped in the gondolas, unable to debark. With everyone's attention on the wheel, this would prove a perfect opportunity to search the trailer park for my carny.

I turned with renewed purpose and managed to squeeze off two steps when the mysterious carny emerged from the growing crowd of onlookers, brushed past me, ignoring me completely, and made straight for the failed ride. Momentarily taken aback but gathering my wits, I turned to follow.

I trailed along behind him, pushing through the rubberneckers so as not to lose my quarry. He was easy to track, clearly becoming the focal point of everybody's attention as he approached the ride. He was wearing a tool belt and a grease-stained version of the yellow tee shirt worn by the other Fayre employees. He climbed up onto the Ferris wheel's loading platform and paused to speak

150

with Cross.

The carnival boss nodded and turned to address the other workers. Within seconds, they began ushering people away from the ride. A short, stocky police officer with a mustache that made him look like a walrus emerged from the crowd, tramped up the loading platform and began bending Cross' ear.

I moved closer, keeping an eye on the carny as he inspected his tool belt. Then, ignoring Cross and the officer, he climbed up into the only empty gondola on the ride, the one in the loading position. A man I presumed to be the ride's operator approached, and he and the carny exchanged words. The man nodded, stepped back and, with the agility of a seasoned rock climber, the carny climbed up into the superstructure of the Ferris wheel.

I watched as he wound his way deftly through the steel frame-work, higher and higher, moving to the outside and finally reaching an outcropping of metal just below the hub of the big wheel. At this point he went to work, picking tools from his work belt, fiddling with the mechanism and replacing each piece of equipment in its proper sleeve on his belt.

After a few minutes he began his descent. Even from this distance, I could make out the veins in his forearms bulging and the cords in his neck standing out like steel cables as he worked his way down through the wheel's superstructure. He stepped down onto the loading platform like a returning astronaut to a meager spattering of cheers from the crowd, then spoke to the ride operator who immediately went to the control panel and started the thing up.

The Ferris wheel lurched to life and the crowd on the ground broke into a full-blown round of applause. The first occupied gondola reached the loading platform and the operator helped the couple out of their seats. The carny walked down the ramp and talked to Cross, who clapped a big hand on his lean shoulder. Then the carny turned and vanished into the crowd.

Remembering my mission, I forced my way through the glut of people but quickly realized I would never catch up with the carny. I decided I would wait for him at the edge of the RV lot.

I turned to head back that way and literally bumped into 'Gospel' Tom.

"Follow me," I said before he could speak, and together we rounded the corner of the water-balloon game. But when we reached the field behind the booths, the carny was nowhere in sight.

"What's going on?" Tom asked.

"Our man just fixed that Ferris wheel; climbed it like a flight of stairs. Now I can't find him."

"So he's a good climber," Tom said. "What has–"

I rattled off what I had found in my back yard that afternoon. Tom's frown grew deeper as I explained about the broken branch and the shingles and my theory about the stalker having some acrobatic skills. When I finished, I waited for his comment.

"You could be right," he said after some consideration. I didn't understand his hesitation; it seemed so obvious.

"Did he see you just now?"

"Yes, I think so. But he didn't react at all."

"Maybe–"

"Hi," Joanna said as she emerged from the crowd with a paper bag tucked under her arm. "What's going on?"

"I thought I'd join you a little early," I said.

She nodded. "All right." She looked to Tom and, for a change her gaze didn't turn to ice.

"Is Alice with you?"

"No," Tom said. "Her asthma's been bad lately; must be the humidity." Tom cleared his throat. "Well, I'd better be going."

152

"Say hi to Alice," Joanna said and she turned toward the booth. "Coming?"

"In a minute," I said. "I want to get some lunch."

"Ah," she said grinning. "It wasn't me that drew you here, it was that damned Voc Tech chicken."

I shrugged playfully and she shook her head. Then she cast Tom a tepid glance, told me she'd meet me at the booth, and disappeared into the crowd.

Tom immediately led me to the side of the water-balloon booth, now surrounded by kids waiting to play, where we could talk undisturbed.

"You said he fixed the Ferris wheel?"

"Yes," I said. "I *know* it's him. Who the hell else could climb like that?"

"There's not much we can do in broad daylight," he said. "I'm going to have a look around your yard. You go sell doughnuts. But if you get a chance, try to find out which trailer belongs to your friend. Are you packing?"

I tapped the phone clipped to my belt.

"I'll call you later," he said. "Oh, this latest batch of tests might be ready tonight; bacterial cultures. Should shed some light on our little mystery."

"Why bother?" I said. "I'm sure we've got our man."

"I just think it's prudent to research every avenue that presents itself," Tom said. "But based on what you just told me, you're probably right. In any event, I'll talk to you later. Good luck with your little piece of detective work."

"You, too," I added.

With that Tom turned and entered the crowded midway while I was left standing there alone amidst the chaos. A voice on a loudspeaker announced that the Ferris wheel would be closed until further notice but was expected to be up and running by nightfall. A small cheer rose up from the crowd closest to the towering ride.

Nightfall, I thought. I looked up at the slate-colored

153

sky. The sun was a silver coin hiding behind the thick blanket of clouds, working its way down to the western horizon, but I could still feel its relentless heat and had to shield my eyes from its diffused glare.

I headed back to the booth to sell doughnuts and wait for Tom's call. I kept an eye out for my mysterious carny as I walked, but I saw no sign of him. I considered the RVs in passing, but there was little movement there. A couple of women were hanging clothes on cords strung between some of the smaller, less fully-equipped units. One man was working on his car, a beat-up Chrysler, parked beside his trailer, but most of the residents were occupied with the task of running the Fayre. This would be a perfect time to do some snooping of my own, but I would never know which RV belonged to the mystery man. For all I knew, he might be staying at a nearby motel. I would have to wait until I saw him again. Besides, I'd made a commitment to Joanna and she needed me.

I returned to the booth where I found Marge and Joanna knee-deep in doughnut orders. It seemed potential Ferris wheel riders needed something with which to bide their time while waiting for the ride to start up again and our doughnuts apparently fit the need.

I jumped right in and, before long, night was falling all around us like a veil. The neon came alive, the Ferris wheel was back up and running and a country and western band took to the stage, telling all concerned that Lucinda Williams felt that she loved her man righteously. The sky started to clear and the big glowing molten face of the Thunder moon made its first appearance of the evening, peeking out from behind some wispy clouds, reminding me of the Angel of Death scene from The Ten Commandments movie. Hanging below the moon like a curious child was a bright red speck. Mars, the god of war, inching closer to Earth than it had in centuries. I could feel the pull of those heavenly bodies tugging at the baser instincts of the crowd, seeking to drag their primordial urges out into the moonlight for all to see.

A strange energy was building around me; I could almost see its luminosity drifting about, phantom-like. People were excited about nothing in particular. It was as if the ground and air were suddenly functioning as batteries, absorbing the power of the moon and Mars and feeding it to the Fayre goers. It was the same feeling I'd had the other night when I smelled ozone, only stronger. I was filled with an irrepressible feeling that something was going to happen, that we were standing on the edge of a precipice waiting to step off, needing only a slight nudge to send us all pin-wheeling down into who knows what.

I didn't realize it then, but across town, my premonition was unfolding. My unruly neighbor, Bob Renko, was about to have a most unwelcome visitor; a visitor like no other.

Chapter Twenty-Seven

We ran out of doughnuts shortly past nine. Marge said her goodbyes and set out into the parking lot, a wisp of cigarette smoke in her wake. I bagged the last of the trash as Joanna counted up the day's profits.

"Be back," I said and I set out into the night, making my way through a multitude of staffers off-loading supplies from the backs of SUVs and cars for the next day's business and joining the ranks of others dutifully carrying their own bags of refuse to the dumpster. The sinks at the back of the bathrooms were fully engaged and prospective dishwashers were forming a queue. Bats were circling beneath the street lamp by the dumpster, greedily gobbling up mosquitoes, as I heaved the bag into the big blue receptacle. I turned to head back and nearly collided with a man I recognized as the Ferris wheel operator.

"Sorry," he mumbled, his breath as rancid as spoiled meat.

"Excuse me," I said too harshly, the mysterious lunar energy apparently having affected me as well. I thought of apologizing when an idea lit in my brain.

"I watched the mechanic fix the Ferris wheel," I said.

The man turned to consider me, frowning.

"That weren't my fault," he said. "That wheel's as old as dirt. And the bearings in that hub assembly–"

"Oh no," I said shaking my head. "I wasn't–"

"Well, what then?" he said crossing his heavily tattooed arms and setting his unshaven jaw defensively.

"I have a friend," I began, stumbling, trudging deeper into unfamiliar territory, "who has a show, a small one, nothing like this, in Rhode Island, and he's looking for a mechanic."

The operator shook his head slowly. "Cross ain't

gonna' like you tryn' to steal Judd."

Judd, I thought excitedly; the face had a name.

"Well, it would be more as a consultant," I said. I couldn't believe how well I was slinging it. My heart was thudding. "My friend knows good ride mechanics are tough to find."

The operator snorted his agreement, glanced around as if checking to see if anyone was listening, then looked down at my hand. It took me a second to understand the cue to grease his palm and I reached into my pocket and produced the first bill I found, a twenty as it turned out, handed it over, and watched the man stuff it into his pocket.

"Big ol' silver Airstream with the classic sittin' behind it," he said, looking around as if the cigar-chomping carnival boss might leap out of the dark at any moment and throttle him. "Judd's so good Cross hauls his rig with one of the carnival trucks. Only don't tell 'em I sent you," the operator added and, with those final words, the man headed toward the midway.

I turned my attention to the sea of RVs. Judd was in one of them. Perhaps I would manage to accomplish my goal for this evening after all. I only hoped Tom was having as much luck.

Chapter Twenty-Eight

I wound my way through the swarm of people heading to the dumpster, never losing sight of the first batch of RVs squatting at the edge of the trailer park like prehistoric tortoises. I was, on some level, aware of the conversations going on among the people I passed, but, as before, their words amounted to little more than white noise to my preoccupied brain. I was on a mission; I was focused. But it was more than that, much more than simply a matter of tuning it all out. Everyday conversations had ceased to interest me. It was as if I were no longer part of the everyday world. I had been teetering on the edge of the 'everyday world' for days and more than ever, felt on the verge of slipping off. I was becoming a phantom, able to limit my contact with those still clinging to their routines, those still functioning in the 'everyday world.'

My parents had left enough inheritance to keep Joanna and me comfortable, so I had no summer job to keep me grounded, no day-to-day grind to consume my thoughts. I was, instead, alone with my notions about the strange events transpiring on my street. This ability to disassociate myself from reality was nothing less than a skill I was honing, a skill practiced by the obsessed, by the fearful and, perhaps, the insane. I felt alienated, my mind obsessed with the abnormal, the strange, my world comprised of suspicions and fears. I had grown paranoid, and Tom's ideas had fed my psychosis. Everyone was a suspect. Then there was this new premonition nagging at me like a dog worrying a bone, an inexplicable sensation that something was going to happen, something incomprehensible.

I moved through the bleached grass, my imagination taking hold. Scenarios began unfolding in my brain, most ending with Judd producing a shotgun and blowing my head off as I stood at the door to his trailer. Grisly scenarios involving Tom's fate emerged as well. And at the heart of all my dark meditations, there lurked a faceless figure climbing through the window of my mind, carrying with it terrible plans for Joanna.

I struggled to shake off the feelings of despair, but with the possibility of meeting Judd finally at hand, my efforts proved futile. I was filling up with dread and my efforts to stem the rising tide were failing dismally.

A thud shook my concentration and I spun toward the sound, nearly toppling over as if lightning had struck nearby. The sound proved to be nothing more than a man loading gear into the back of a Volvo wagon parked behind one of the booths. His wife emerged from the booth's back door, a slight, brunette woman with a jovial face. She said something inaudible, the two of them laughed and she went back inside, wiping her hands on her apron. Life went on, it seemed, in spite of my troubles.

Floodlights perched atop light poles high above the midway came alive, signaling closing time, forcing a vivid white light into each nook and cranny of the Fayre. The only portions spared the antiseptic brilliance were those specifically reserved for carnies and staffers, like the patch of field behind the booths and the trailer park. These places, by contrast, seemed to grow darker, as if some entity within them was deliberately resisting the light, and the glare created by the contrast served only to bite at my eyes, making it twice as difficult to find my way.

Lost in that glare, I was too late to avoid bumping into someone. Before I could mutter an apology a deep gravelly voice said, "Watch it." I managed an apology nonetheless, nearly tripping over some power cords in the process.

I reached the edge of the trailer park without further incident and stood studying the seemingly endless jumble of vehicles, all connected by a complex array of clotheslines and extension cords, much like arteries in some massive metal beast. I wondered which of the makeshift lanes running between the vehicles would lead me to Judd.

Determined, I forged ahead, knowingly crossing the barrier at the edge of the 'everyday world' I had so cautiously clung to for so long and began picking my way through the first gathering of RVs.

This initial batch was spotless, layered in fresh paint, rich with every imaginable option. Judd's old Airstream, though perhaps pristine, was not among them.

I moved deeper into the park, scanning the rows and narrow alleyways, the quality of the motor homes deteriorating as I progressed. It seemed there was a hierarchy among trailers and Judd's silver-skinned Airstream was apparently situated near the lowest rung of the ladder.

I reached the back portion of the lot where the trailers were likened to houses in a slum. Tattered and rusted, patched with everything from chicken wire to duct tape, these trailers were carefully situated so as to remain hidden from the prying eyes of the public. This was the Whitechapel of the trailer park and these RVs the ramshackle tenements of the Summer Harvest Fayre. I felt certain that I would find Judd's trailer here; it suited him.

I rounded the end of the lane and saw in the distance, sitting just beyond the rides, the largest and most luxurious of the RVs. Obviously a converted Greyhound bus, this mansion on wheels was doubtless the traveling homestead of Vern Cross, the Fayre's owner. Beyond this there were only trees.

I turned away, discouraged, certain that the Ferris wheel operator had sent me on a wild goose chase for his own amusement. I was about to call it quits when I saw it.

At first I thought it to be a trick of moonlight, a sliver of foil from a candy apple wrapper lying on the ground. But as I strained to see deeper into the shadows, I realized that a muted strip of moonlight had found the silver skin of the trailer for which I searched.

My feet ground to a halt. I had found Judd's lair. Hidden beneath the arms of a huge twisted oak tree, it was sheer luck I'd spotted it at all. If not for the moon's intervention, I would have missed it entirely.

I approached the RV, suddenly conscious of carnies gathering in the makeshift yard of a large Bayliner at the end of the nearest row. They seemed preoccupied with a small television's flickering image. I presumed that most of the trailer park residents were still busily preparing to close down the midway and its rides, seeking to milk the last bit of money from those who simply could not get enough of the fun and games.

Grim but determined, I crept forward, passing through alternating stretches of deep shadow and soft moonlight, the former leaving me temporarily blind, the later leaving me vulnerable to detection. The trailers were off limits to Fayre-goers and the last thing I needed was for Cross' security people to find me and escort me from the premises.

I paused less than twenty feet from the Airstream to evaluate the situation. The trailer was bigger than I'd presumed, reaching a length of perhaps thirty feet or more, resembling, if nothing else, a spaceship from some nineteen-fifties sci-fi movie. A single step led up to a hatch-like door in the thing's side. There were no lights visible through the windows, and there seemed to be no porch light. There was no way of knowing if Judd was inside, and I didn't have all night to stand around waiting for him to come home; Joanna would worry.

I was suddenly unsure how to proceed, doubting my weakening conviction. One nagging possibility remained: the person who had despoiled my yard and broken into my neighbor's garage with the gutted carcass of a raccoon simply to distract Rufus so he could watch

Joanna and me might be just beyond that door. If I was wrong, there was no harm done. But if I was right...

I tried to think of what I should say to Judd if he was home. And I tried to imagine what to do if he produced a weapon. The truth was I had no idea *what* I would do if Judd became violent. But I knew that in the end, there was only one way to find out.

Propelled by an invisible hand, I started for the trailer. But something lurking behind the Airstream caught my eye, and the Ferris wheel operator's words came back to me like ghosts crossing my path.

'The one with the classic parked behind it,' he'd said.

The man had been right and I stood transfixed, unable to move.

There it was, the same jet-black Chevelle I had seen at the cemetery. The rims were the same, the racing stripe identical. There was no mistake. Judd had been watching Joanna as she returned from her walk and had, in all likelihood, been watching us since the Fayre arrived in town.

A cold sensation gripped me like a vise; without question I had found our stalker.

Chapter Twenty-Nine

Gazing at Judd's Chevelle, the cold thing in my stomach slithered to life. I understood that a stalker worth his weight would know the behavior of those he was stalking. Judd had probably been watching our house all morning long, perhaps since the Fayre closed the night before. Perhaps he had parked in some dark section of the cemetery and waited for the sun to creep over the tops of the tombstones. Maybe he felt comfortable among the dead, resting among the graves. Maybe he dreamed of the dead lying in the ground all around him as he slept; maybe he dreamed of things he would like to do with the bodies. Maybe he even despoiled the stones as he had my yard. Perhaps he had spoken to Joanna as she walked the cemetery paths that morning. He might have asked directions or worse, asked if she still cared for him. That might explain her sullen mood upon returning from her walk.

The cold thing in my gut wriggled as I thought about Joanna exchanging words with Judd. He might even have tried to touch her. Perhaps he *had* touched her, dragged his callused filthy hand across her flesh. Perhaps he imagined wrapping his long bony fingers around her throat and squeezing until she fell silent. And then a new thought caught like a jagged thorn in my brain: was Joanna protecting Judd? Had she been protecting him all along?

I had interrupted more than one suspicious phone call over the past few days. And then there had been the hang-up call I'd answered like the ones years ago.

The thought sickened me. Pieces of a wretched puzzle began falling into place. I'd been a fool. Joanna's strange behavior coincided with the arrival of the Fayre. Our stalker had arrived at the same time, and Judd had come to town with the Fayre. He had climbed the Ferris wheel with ease. A tree would prove a small obstacle for Judd.

I considered the door to the Airstream and what might be lurking behind it. I had to do this. I needed to know; I needed to finish what I'd started. Time was wasting. Joanna would be looking for me and I would be looking for her armed with questions and, depending upon what happened in the next few moments, perhaps accusations.

I crossed to the step, drew in a deep breath, blew it out and climbed. Reaching the door, I raised my fist. It felt like a block of lead in my hand. I brought my fist down and knocked on Judd's door.

Chapter Thirty

I stood with my heart pounding as the sound of my fist thudding against the old metal faded. Nothing happened. I knocked again, secretly wishing I'd brought a weapon. I thought of the baseball bat in my SUV and wondered how it would feel in my hand. I couldn't believe the thoughts running through my brain. I raised my fist to knock a third time, but the door swung outward before my knuckles could strike and I stumbled backward, nearly losing my balance.

Judd considered me carefully from the darkness, his deep-set eyes caged by crow's feet etched by a long, hard life. His hands, too big and sinewy for a man his weight, hung by his side, one wrapped around a bottle of beer. His eyes moved across my face, my shoulders, as if sizing me up, determining whether or not I might pose a threat. Then, apparently satisfied with his evaluation of me, he spoke.

"Help you?" he said in a voice that was too deep for his lean frame, the cords in his neck straining.

"I was looking for the bathroom," I said, nearly kicking myself for choosing such a lame excuse.

A sliver of a grin split Judd's razor-thin lips and he cocked his narrow head to one side.

"No, you ain't," he hissed.

I could smell the liquor on his breath. It was not the smell of a few beers but the rancid odor of a lifetime of inebriation. He wiped his big hand on the stained and torn tank top he was wearing and, for a fleeting moment, I thought he might take a swipe at me. But the vein-riddled hand slid quietly down against his thigh where it hung like a slab of meat. I felt like a child swimming in dark water who looks back at the beach, only to realize he's out too far. I began searching for a defense for my pathetic excuse, for a better lie, when I detected a glint of realization in

Judd's dark eyes.

"I know who you are," he said and my blood ran cold. The grin on the cut in his face that served as a mouth widened and he said, "you're the *husband*."

I felt something inside of me tear open and the cold thing in my gut slithered serpent-like into this new space. My fears were coming true.

Cold revulsion filled my being, revulsion over the realization that Joanna might actually have *been with* this man. I felt anger growing. But most of all, I felt fear, the sort that comes when things turn suddenly bad. *I* was the boy swimming out too far, suddenly feeling something cold slip past his leg.

"How do you know–" I began.

"Be careful," he said, and the grin melted away as his eyes narrowed to slits.

I started to speak, but he cut me off.

"Be careful, is all."

Judd stepped back into the darkened Airstream, closing the door. I heard a dead-bolt click into place; the meeting had come to an end.

I stood for a moment, stunned, my hands shaking, my heart pounding. What the hell had just happened?

Confused, I climbed down from the step, dazed, my mouth as dry as the Sahara, and looked up to find myself gazing at two of the dirtiest people I'd ever seen. The woman, who must have been pushing sixty, was wearing a pair of worn black leather chaps and a black skin-tight tank top. The man was short and stocky with a pockmarked face and heavily tattooed arms.

"You don't belong here," the woman growled.

I looked to the man who was considering me with tiny eyes surrounded on three sides by a sea of yellowish-white. The alcohol-induced grin that exposed his badly-stained teeth was so broad and filled with such ecstasy that he might as well have been accepting a check for ten

166

million dollars rather than looking at me standing in front of Judd's old Airstream.

"You hear?" the woman prompted. "You don't belong here."

"No, I don't," I said with more force than I thought possible and I walked past them, granting them a wide berth, passing through a cloud of booze and body odor. I glanced back when I heard them laughing and saw them stumbling away, deeper into the shadows of the big oak tree.

Still stunned, my ears ringing as if I'd heard a shotgun blast, I made my way back to the booth where Joanna asked where I'd been.

"Oh, talking with an admirer of your doughnuts."

She nodded, apparently either accepting my explanation or not caring.

"I'm ready," she said after giving the place a final once-over. "Let's get the hell out of Dodge."

I secured the panel over the counter, killed the light and fans, and locked the door. I walked Joanna to her car and waited as she climbed in.

"Money box?" I said, my tone unintentionally chilly.

"I already put it in the back," she said, starting the engine. "See you at home."

I stepped away to allow her to back out, but she reached for my hand instead. I took it and she squeezed my fingers between hers.

"Thanks for doing this," she said.

I smiled, trying desperately to force the image of Judd's face from my mind. There had to be a mistake. And what about Judd's cryptic warning?

"Something wrong?"

"No," I said. "Tired, I guess. It's been a long day."

She smiled a wan smile and waved to me, then backed out into the staff parking lot, which was emptying quickly. I watched her drive off toward the exit road, then went to my car and climbed aboard. I couldn't help but take one last look at the RVs sitting in the dusty distance. Then I headed home.

***

The drive home was a quiet one. I didn't turn on any music; my senses had had enough input for one night. I just let the warm summer air wash over me through the open windows and sunroof. I was more confused than ever. I'd thought a trip to Judd's RV would have laid everything to rest, one way or another. But it hadn't. Things had grown more complex than ever. The light, as Macbeth observed, had thickened. I kept seeing Judd's face in my brain, kept hearing him telling me to be careful. Be careful of what?

There was, however, one element to the mystery I was more than willing to put to bed. I didn't believe Joanna had had an affair with Judd; I couldn't imagine when she might have had the opportunity. And in spite of the fevered visions I had experienced while standing on Judd's step, I couldn't bring myself to believe that they'd ever made love. I considered the doughnut shop manager and wished *he'd* been the one. I would have known how to deal with him. But this was different, *completely* different.

The Joanna I knew would never have gone near a man like Judd. I suppose it was possible that Judd had fallen on hard times, but that didn't seem likely; Judd had been Judd since the day he was born. Perhaps he'd met Joanna at some point in the distant past and had been carrying a torch for her ever since. That made some sense to my tired brain.

Stalkers are usually people who have dreamt up a different reality, one where they are romantically or personally involved with the object of their stalking. If this were true, and there was a thickening ribbon of logic suggesting that it was, then Judd could conceivably have been the mysterious caller who plagued us years ago. And perhaps Joanna's mood upon returning from the cemetery was due to the fact that Judd had spoken to her and she'd told him to leave her alone.

I was beginning to like this new theory very much. Joanna probably wouldn't have told me about Judd's previous advances, hoping that he'd gone from her life forever. But these new advances might force her to confide in me, perhaps not immediately, but eventually. Yes, I liked this new scenario more with each passing second.

I felt at least a portion of the load I had been carrying for days being lifted from my shoulders, and I breathed a sigh of relief. Joanna and I could deal with the likes of Judd together. After all, we were husband and wife.

The streets were quiet at this hour. I felt alone. Most people were already in bed; it was, after all, Friday night and Wickham was not exactly the glowing hot center of New England.

I glanced up at the bloated face of the moon through the open sunroof. The clouds had gone and it was alone in the sky, save for Mars, its distant red companion hovering beside it.

"Thunder moon," I mused aloud.

I glimpsed the flashing blue and red lights before I ever turned into my street. The air fled my lungs and my sleepy heart came suddenly alive, thudding against my ribs. It was like Deja vu, a replay of the previous night's events. Only tonight, what awaited me was a thousand times worse.

Chapter Thirty-One

My once-peaceful dead-end street had been turned upside down. Three police cruisers with their LED lights flashing sat at the end of the street, one parked directly in front of my house, another at the end of the Trimbles' driveway and the third in front of Renko's house. The lawns to the first few houses were rich with onlookers busily cinching robes and talking anxiously about the newest event to plague their once-sedate neighborhood.

The red glare of a fourth emergency vehicle was evident and, as I drew near, I spied the nose of an ambulance poking out from Renko's driveway. My heart became an ice chip. Renko had found Tom!

A figure stepped out of the shadow and signaled for me to stop.

"Do you live here, sir?" the police officer asked.

"Yes," I said. "That's my house at the end. What happened?"

"Move along," he said, ignoring my question and waving me on.

I slowly pulled into my driveway. The bay door to Joanna's side of the garage was open and her car was parked inside. I didn't bother opening the bay door to my side; instead I anxiously shut the engine and hopped out. I felt suddenly dizzy, as if I had stood up too quickly. It was like a terrible dream. Everything looked alarmingly like the previous night, only amplified.

It was immediately apparent that the crux of the activity was centered at Renko's back door. I could see that the screen door had been chucked open as well as the inner wood paneled door and two police officers were standing on the top step, talking softly. A third officer was standing at the base of the stairs, leaning on the black wrought-iron rail, listening to the other two. The ambulance was parked a few yards from the back porch, its bay doors open, the bay vacant.

A sudden flash from Renko's doorway caught my eye; then another. Someone inside was taking pictures.

"Hello," the police officer at the bottom of the stairs said as he took a step toward me.

"I live here," I volunteered defensively, "there, I mean," I added jerking a thumb over my shoulder.

The officer nodded and said, "Have you been out all night?"

"My wife runs a concession booth at the Fayre," I blurted, moving toward the fence to meet him. It was then that I noticed two more officers moving through the deep shadows at the side of Renko's garage, near the now boarded up broken window. They were aiming their flashlights at the ground and moving slowly as if looking for something; tracks, I surmised.

The beam of one light fell across something near the corner of the garage, some three-dimensional collection of angles that seemed out of place. At first I couldn't determine what I was looking at, but after a moment it became clear and I realized the police had stumbled upon a kitchen chair. It was the same chair Renko had been sitting in the night before while the Trimbles' prowler incident was winding down. It was the chair I'd seen Renko carrying from his house earlier that evening. I figured he'd used the thing as a makeshift stepladder while raising the sheet of plywood into place to block off the broken window and thought no more about it.

"Well, sir, why don't you go in your house," the officer said, apparently unhappy with my streak of curiosity. "Someone will be along to talk to you soon."

"Yes," I said. "I have to get my wife. She's at our neighbors' house across the street."

He glanced in the direction of the Trimbles' house, nodded, and returned to his station at the bottom of the porch.

I headed for the street just as a fourth officer, this one carrying a large clear plastic bag in one hand, appeared in Renko's doorway. He paused to remove a pair of plastic sleeves from his shoes, tucked them into his pocket and began talking with the two officers on the top step. He showed them the thing he was holding, this drawing some head-shaking from one and an astonished whistle from the other, before descending to the dirt driveway and heading for the street. I paced him slowly, hoping to catch a better glimpse of whatever was in the bag.

The man reached the street and walked to the cruiser sitting in front of Renko's place. He set the bag on the cruiser's roof and began fishing through a jangle of keys he drew from his pocket. In that instant I came to the head of my driveway and got a pretty good look at the thing in the baggy.

At first I wasn't sure what I was looking at. Logic told me that what I was seeing was impossible. But the longer I stared at the thing, the more clearly it came into focus and I found myself being forced to accept what I was seeing as fact.

The baggy the officer had placed on the cruiser's roof contained a rifle, or, more precisely, it contained what *remained* of a rifle. The first thought that popped into my brain was that Tom had been right; Renko *did* own a gun. The second thought was less reassuring and infinitely darker. This gun looked as if it had been fed through a wood chipper. The once lethal weapon had been reduced to a useless mass of metal and wood, its barrel twisted into a shape no gun manufacturer ever intended, its stock reduced to splinters.

"Help you?" said the officer, who, having opened the trunk, had come around from the back of the car to pluck the ruined gun from the roof of the vehicle.

"No," I said, taken aback, and I started toward the

172

Trimbles'.

The officer watched me intently until I was halfway across the street, then tucked the gun away in the trunk and slammed it shut.

I reached the Trimbles' front yard with the image of the shattered gun burning in my brain when the lights of an approaching car fell across my face. I looked up to see a big SUV draw to a halt in the middle of the street. The officer who had stopped me stepped out of the shadows to greet the driver. After speaking quietly to whoever was behind the wheel, he stepped back and ushered the vehicle through.

The SUV inched its way down the street, pulling up beside some hedges that ran along the northern portion of the Trimbles' yard, perpendicular to the street. Without delay, the driver's side door opened and a tall, efficient-looking woman with straight, shoulder length brown hair, attired in a light-colored blouse and dark slacks emerged. She closed the car door and turned toward Renko's house, her gaze rising to the peak and falling to the foundation as if taking it all in. Then she turned to me and our eyes locked.

I felt suddenly like a deer caught in a pair of headlights, unable to move. The flashing light from the cruisers caught in her cold, steel-blue eyes. I opened my mouth to speak, but, apparently satisfied with what she saw, the woman turned and strode deliberately across the street to head down Renko's driveway.

She showed the police officers at the back porch what I presumed to be some form of official identification and their relaxed demeanor changed drastically. Then she climbed the steps and disappeared into Renko's house.

Wickham was too small a town to have any detectives on its police force, but when one was needed the nearby towns of Bridgton or perhaps Gevaudan, each considerably larger than Wickham, usually supplied one. I figured I had just seen a detective from one of those towns enter my neighbor's house.

"Jack."

It was Joanna calling to me from the end of the Trimbles' driveway, near the base of their deck. She was standing alongside the same female police officer who had investigated the prowler incident the previous night.

"This is my husband," Joanna said, introducing me to the officer.

"I remember," the officer said, taking a brief break from jotting down some information in a note pad.

I noticed a second officer standing near the corner of the Trimbles' garage, talking to Roger Trimble. My neighbor was going on about something, his words running together like mud. All the while the officer was dutifully jotting everything down, nodding.

"Joanna, what happened? Where's Mrs. Trimble?" But before my wife could respond, Sophie Trimble emerged from her kitchen, her face grim, her cheeks stained with dried tears.

"He's dead," she said flatly.

"What?" I said. "Who's dead?"

"Mr. Renko," she said, her words as cold as stones brought up from the bottom of a deep mountain lake. "Somebody killed him!"

Chapter Thirty-Two

I couldn't believe the words Sophie Trimble had spoken. Bob Renko was dead. I looked around at the excessive police presence. Renko *was* dead; that was the only possible explanation for what was happening. The air had suddenly grown impossibly thick and people seemed to be moving in slow motion. I hadn't liked Renko, but I had never wished him dead.

"How?" I asked, hoping the police officer would supply some information.

"We can't elaborate at this time," the officer said finishing her last notation and flipping her notebook shut. "Please stay clear of Mr. Renko's house," she added before heading for the street. "Behind the tape."

"There was a noise," Mrs. Trimble said. "Like a fight, and that dog of his–"

"Rufus," I said.

"Rufus," she continued, "was barking and howling. Oh," she said, ringing her hands, "it was terrible."

"Why don't we go inside," Joanna said, taking Sophie Trimble by the arm and leading her toward the door.

"I'm going to check on Spooky," I said.

"Be careful," Joanna said as they reached the door. Then, in a whisper designed to elude the old ears of Mrs. Trimble, she added, "Whoever did this might still be around."

I nodded and it was at that moment that I fully appreciated what had happened. My neighbor, a formidable sort to be sure, armed, no less, with what appeared to be a rifle, was dead and it was just possible that my stalker was responsible.

The cold thing that had started moving through my stomach spread to my entire body and I shivered in the summer heat. I thought of Tom. I had to reach him.

The officer who had been interviewing Roger Trimble nodded, turned, and walked past me, heading toward the nearest of the cruisers. Roger Trimble moved up beside me and together we watched the officer climb aboard the cruiser. I turned to Roger to offer solace but was struck by the fear and confusion in his eyes. He reached out with his lean fingers and gripped my forearm.

"I was taking out the trash," he said, his old face grim and ashen. "I was walking back in when I heard it, the ruckus over there." He gestured with his chin in the direction of Renko's house. "I walked to the edge of the driveway. I actually thought about going over there to see what the hell was going on, but I didn't. I didn't. I just stood there, not knowing what to do. I heard the sound of things breaking and I heard the dog barking and howling, making noises like the animal was…" He paused, his eyes wavering, his head shaking as if uncertain as to how to continue.

"Roger–" I said, but his fingers tightened another notch and he moved his face in close to mine. I smelled bath powder and a trace of what might have been brandy on his breath.

"And I heard something else," he hissed.

"What?" I asked, frowning.

He opened his mouth as if hoping the word he sought was waiting there and shook his head when it didn't appear.

"I don't know," he said, and his eyes, like two ancient crystals, found mine, "but it weren't no dog. And it sure as hell weren't no man."

Something cold danced across my spine and I glanced back at the activity encompassing Renko's house.

"Did you tell the police?"

Trimble nodded. "They said when a person is being killed, he makes all sorts of noises." Slowly, as if realizing what he was doing and perhaps regretting it, Roger Trimble released his grip. He studied his spider-like hand for a moment as if seeing the crags and wrinkles that had once been his skin for the first time. Then he hitched his 'old man' legs into gear and started for his deck. He looked drained, defeated, his old shoulders hunched more than usual. I watched him climb the stairs and shuffle in his house slippers toward the screen door. When he reached it, he turned slowly.

"I'm old," he said, his voice jagged like broken china, "and I ain't as sharp as what I used to be. But I know what I heard. It weren't no dog. It weren't no man, neither. But," he added with a shrug of resignation, "I suppose in all the confusion, it might have been a little of both."

His old eyes remained fixed on mine for a moment and the despair I saw there was insurmountable. Whatever had happened had happened on Roger Trimble's watch, and the retired Navy man was having a hard time dealing with that. Then he lowered his gaze and disappeared inside.

I stood, watching, long after the screen door banged shut, Roger Trimble's words sitting in my brain like stones in a road. Then some new activity across the street snapped me out of my spell and I watched the cruiser with the mangled rifle in the trunk swing slowly out into the street, perform a classic three-point turn, and drive away.

Dazed, much as Roger Trimble must have been while listening to Bob Renko being murdered, I walked across the street into the flashing glare of the assorted lights. Ignoring the growing number of onlookers now spilling off the lawns into the street, I headed down my driveway. I passed through my gate ghost-like, drifted across my patio and ascended my porch, letting myself into my house. I found Spooky huddled in her bed growling, no doubt nervous due to the commotion outside. I scooped her up; she was shaking with excitement and fear.

"It's all right, girl," I soothed her, gathered her leash

and we went outside.

Skittishly she considered the activity next door, but went about her business, casting worried glances my way as if seeking reassurance that the world was not ending. As I stood waiting for her to finish, two EMTs appeared at Renko's back door. They considered the stairs and studied the width of the doorway as if planning some repairs, then went back inside. They emerged a moment later and I watched them wrestle a gurney through the door and down the steps to the open bay doors of the waiting ambulance. Strapped to the gurney, wrapped in gray plastic, was what I presumed to be the last of Bob Renko.

Watching them set the gurney down in the driveway and listening to them complain about the heat and what a 'bitch' it had been getting the 'Goddamned thing' through the 'fucking doorway,' I found myself feeling remorse for my neighbor. I had seen him that afternoon unloading plywood from the bed of his truck. Now he was gone. I wondered if Renko had any family left to notify or whether they'd care.

My legs felt suddenly weak and I remembered how drained and exhausted I'd felt before turning into my street and being confronted with all the adrenaline-pumping confusion. It was nothing a good night's sleep wouldn't cure. The same could not be said for Bob Renko. His hard times were over.

The taller of the EMTs, a lean man with short blonde hair, climbed into the back of the ambulance and guided the second EMT's efforts in sliding the collapsible gurney into the bay. The two men exchanged words, then the shorter of the two, a stocky man with slicked-back dark hair, closed the bay doors, went around to the driver's door and climbed aboard. A moment passed, the siren let out a whoop and the ambulance with its grim cargo moved to the head of Renko's driveway. Another whoop and the ambulance turned onto the street and drove slowly away.

The flashing red light seemed to linger, caressing the houses like a bloody phantom lover before following its master and fading from view. Then, just like Bob Renko, it was gone.

I considered Spooky, who was studying me the way a child might study an adult, with a mixture of awe and inquisitiveness.

"Let's go inside, girl," I said.

I looked to Renko's place one last time, only to find myself staring at the female detective who had arrived in the big SUV. She was standing on the top step of Renko's porch, her eyes once again searing into mine. A uniformed police officer was saying something to her, but her attention was on me.

I lowered my gaze, gave Spooky's leash a tug, and started for the house, sensing the woman's eyes at the back of my head.

Once inside I set Spooky free, hung her leash and thought again of Tom. I went to the answering machine in the four seasons' room to see if he had called. Sure enough, it was blinking. I hit the recall switch and a mechanical voice told me I had one new message. A second later Tom's breathless voice filled the room with instructions for me to call him as soon as possible.

I felt a weight lift from my shoulders, realizing that Tom hadn't been caught in the cross-fire of whatever had happened next door. I would never forgive myself if something had happened to him.

I took the telephone receiver to the window abutting my driveway, pried open the blinds and punched in Tom's number. The world outside hadn't changed. Police were milling about, poking into shrubs, talking to the people who had come to investigate the chaos. The detective was nowhere to be seen, but her SUV was still at the curb, its silver skin glistening in the moonlight much like that of Judd the carny's Airstream trailer.

"Hello," Tom said.

"Tom, what the hell happened?"

"The shit hit the fan tonight," he said, sounding tired and a little hoarse. "I had to get out of there when the old man across the street came out. I thought sure he'd seen me, but he only stood in his driveway and listened to that ruckus, then went inside, presumably to call the police. I didn't need to stick around to see how *that* turned out. People creeping through bushes after dark tend to bring suspicion upon themselves, even if their motives are completely innocent."

"Did you see anything?" I asked, my eye pressed to the window.

"No. I'd just gotten there. Then your neighbor's dog started barking loud enough to wake the dead over in St. Brigid's. I heard Renko yelling at the mutt, telling him to shut up. Then all hell broke loose. The barking turned to some kind of shrieking and I heard Renko yelling and then the smashing started and that's when the old man across the street got into it."

"Jesus Tom," I said leaving the window and sitting on the sofa. "I thought you had gotten arrested or killed when I saw the commotion."

"Still ticking," he said. "Any luck with your man?"

"Yes, I talked to him and he said something strange."

"You actually *spoke* with him?"

There was a knock at the door.

"Hang on," I said before covering the mouthpiece and yelling, "Who is it?"

"Police," a woman's voice said.

"Uh, coming." I uncovered the phone. "Tom, the police are here."

"At your door?"

"Yes. Tom, Renko's dead."

"What?"

180

The knocking came again, more deliberate this time.

"I'll call you later," I said and I hung up and went to the door, Spooky bounding along at my side. I was reaching for the knob when the door swung open and Joanna appeared, her face as grim as Roger Trimble's had been. For a second I saw only Joanna, then I noticed the female detective standing behind her.

"The police need to talk to us," Joanna said, entering the kitchen.

"I'm Detective Teschal," the woman said offering me a glimpse of her badge, number 1767, as she too entered the kitchen. "I'm from the Gevaudan Police Department. I need to talk to you about your neighbor, Robert W. Renko."

Chapter Thirty-Three

Detective Teschal was not an unattractive woman. Tall and lean with fairly wide shoulders, a slim athletic waist and steel-blue eyes, she might have been an Olympic swimmer if not for the badge hanging on a thin chain about her neck. Her hair was a deep shade of brown, shoulder length, blunt cut. An air of practicality hung about her like perfume. There was a stern quality to her face that only added to her professional, efficient demeanor.

"I need to ask you a few questions," she said, her voice curt but polite.

Spooky shuffled across the floor and sniffed Teschal's leg, an act that drew a quick glance from the detective and little more. Feeling jilted, Spooky waddled back to her bed, where she flopped down for a nap.

"Would you care to sit?" Joanna offered, gesturing toward the high-backed bar stools at the breakfast island. Teschal declined.

Joanna looked to me, then sat down. I remained standing, moving to the opposite side of the island and leaning on it.

"To begin with," Teschal said, "I suppose you are well aware that Robert Renko is dead."

Joanna nodded. Her skin was ashen.

"How did it happen?" I asked.

Teschal raised her eyes and I realized then just how flinty and cold they were.

"As this is an ongoing investigation, Mr. Graves, I'm not at liberty to discuss the specifics."

Joanna lowered her gaze.

"Just how well did you know Mr. Renko?" Teschal proceeded.

"Not well," Joanna said staring at the floor.

"Fences make good neighbors," I added.

Teschal studied me and cocked her head. "That's an interesting observation, Mr. Graves. Did you get along with Mr. Renko?"

"I guess so," I said shrugging, sensing a grain of suspicion in Teschal's voice. Perhaps I'd been too honest with the detective and immediately realized I'd have to tread carefully through the rest of the interview. "I mean, we weren't fighting, if that's what you're suggesting."

"I'm not suggesting anything, Mr. Graves, just asking," she said coolly, and I felt like a fly considering the glistening strands of a spider web.

Joanna lifted her gaze and looked my way, clearly remembering my general attitude toward Renko, but hopefully not showing too much to our guest. I was feeling suddenly guilty, but of what I couldn't say.

Teschal glanced sideways at my wife, pursed her thin lips then grinned ever-so-slightly as if mere observation had answered some un-stated question.

"He wasn't exactly the sort of person we'd associate with," Joanna said, feeling compelled to add something to our statement.

"How so?" Teschal asked, her eyes locking on Joanna.

"Well–" Joanna began, but I cut in.

"He was a little rough around the edges. You know the sort who drinks too much, might blow his nose with his thumb and spit on the floor. I'm a teacher, my wife's a librarian. We didn't have a lot in common with Mr. Renko."

Teschal shifted her gaze to me and nodded slowly. "Do you know if he had any enemies?"

Joanna looked to me and we said 'no' nearly in unison.

"Did he gamble, so far as you knew?"

Once again Joanna and I exchanged glances and

shrugs.

"Detective," Joanna said, "we hardly knew the man. I don't think anyone in the neighborhood really knew Bob Renko." Joanna glanced my way and I nodded in agreement.

"Well, then," Teschal said, "has anything strange happened lately?"

"Strange?" Joanna said, frowning.

"Oh, unfamiliar cars parked on the street, people walking around, maybe looking at Mr. Renko's house. Has he had any parties lately, guests coming and going, perhaps at odd hours? Has his general behavior changed in any way you might have noticed?"

I looked to Joanna, who did not return my glance this time. My wife was unaware of the changes in Renko's behavior that I had witnessed. He had asked me about the broken garage window. And I had seen nothing but that and the dead raccoon to suggest that he was experiencing any trouble. If there *had* been anything else, he had not confided in me.

"Not that I've noticed," I said keeping my eyes on my wife.

"Mrs. Graves?" Teschal prompted.

"Oh, no," Joanna said as if returning from some far off place. "No."

"Are you sure?"

I waited for Joanna to answer. I thought of telling Teschal at least a little about our stalker, but caught myself. I wasn't sure how much was *too* much and didn't want to drag Tom into something in which he was only peripherally involved. I thought of mentioning Renko's broken window, figuring that it wouldn't incriminate Joanna or me, but caught myself again before saying anything. The whole thing was too dicey. Once something like that was started, the questions would begin to pile up. Besides, I would have to reach Tom to get him to corroborate the story, and I was convinced that the break-in next door was part of my stalker's efforts to get a better view of our activities. I decided it best to remain silent, for the time being, at least.

"No," Joanna said with more intensity than I think she'd intended.

If Teschal noticed, she did not respond, but I found my mind swimming. The whole situation was taking a turn that I had never foreseen.

"This is early in our investigation and I understand that these are difficult questions under the circumstances, but I need to ask them so please don't be offended," Teschal said, sounding suddenly human.

Joanna studied her hands.

"You do know about our neighbors' report of a prowler the other night?" I interjected.

"We're aware of that," she said. "Probably kids taking a short cut." She looked my way and let a small grin touch her lips.

I nodded in feigned agreement.

"I think that's all for now," Teschal said. "Oh, by the way, there will be a police cruiser stationed outside Mr. Renko's house for the remainder of the night and for the next day or so while our forensics team goes through the place." Teschal pursed her lips as if in deep thought. "Well, thank you for your help—"

"What about the dog?" I asked.

"Yes," Joanna said, coming back to life, her eyes looking hurt.

"The dog is missing," Teschal said coolly. "The food and water dish is pretty full and we found evidence that the animal might have been locked in the basement, but there's no sign of it. One of the basement windows was broken. It may have served as a means of entry for our assailant. But based upon the condition of the property, it may have been broken for some time. The dog most likely got out that way. If it should turn up, please call us."

185

Teschal reached into an inner jacket pocket, produced a card and handed it over to me. My paranoia could see the wheels turning behind her eyes and when her fingers brushed against mine I felt a deep cold. She'd been trying to lull us into a false sense of security while carefully studying our reactions. I often used the same technique with my students when trying to determine who was responsible for some misdeed committed at school. It was a deceitful tactic to be used on a child and I found myself resenting Teschal for having utilized such a crude trick. I suspect Joanna did as well. But I suppose under the circumstances it was to be expected; police procedure.

Each and every move on Teschal's part, each glance, each statement since the moment she'd walked through the door, had been the work of a seasoned detective searching the nooks and crannies for the truth. And, unlike the uniformed officers combing the neighborhood, Teschal had taken no notes during the interview.

In spite of my bruised ego, I found myself admiring the woman for her thoroughness, and because I knew that there was more here than met the eye, I found myself fearing her as well.

"Gevaudan," I said, studying the card, affirming my earlier suspicion.

"Yes, if you call the local police they'll have to connect you, which may take time. That's my mobile number."

Nodding, I set the card on the island.

"Sorry to disturb," Teschal said. "Good night."

Chapter Thirty-Four

Detective Teschal let herself out and I closed the door behind her. I watched Joanna as she absentmindedly secured Teschal's card to the refrigerator beside the magnets she kept there, the ones she'd collected from our various trips. She paused a moment as if considering this new souvenir, then went into the bedroom. I heard her rummaging through drawers, probably changing for bed.

I went to the refrigerator where I studied Teschal's card which was held in place by a shell-basket magnet Joanna had gotten in Rockport. I couldn't help but notice the other magnets, the Brachiosaur skeleton from the airport in Chicago, the Nubble lighthouse from southern Maine, a small placard featuring the Zen expression stating that if you leap the net will appear. There were many more, each acquired with the intention of adding it to a sort of scrapbook comprised of experiences Joanna and I shared. I imagined how lonely the refrigerator would look if our ridiculous little magnets weren't there and how out of place, how obscene, Detective Teschal's card looked among them. This collection was meant to be a testament to our happier times, not our sadder ones.

I left the card where it was, hoping that one day very soon I could toss it in the trash and be done with everything it represented. Spooky must have sensed my discomfort, as she made her way to my feet and nuzzled my ankle, momentarily rescuing me from the somber mood that was trying to steal me away. I vowed right then and there that no matter what happened, no matter how bad things got, I wouldn't let this be the end of Joanna and me. We would add many more ridiculous little magnets to our refrigerator, many more memorable experiences to our lives together.

I looked down at Spooky's big black upturned eyes,

thanking her silently for intervening. I bent down and picked her up. She kissed my nose gently. Dogs, with their unconditional love, have a funny way of rescuing you when you needed it most.

I set the old girl down in her bed and she considered me for a moment before laying her shaggy head down and closing her eyes.

I shook off the cobwebs as best I could and went out front to the four seasons room, where I peeked through the blinds at the scene outside. Teschal was standing at the head of Renko's driveway, talking with the female police officer who had responded to the Trimbles' prowler call the night before. Another officer was busy stretching bright yellow crime scene tape across Renko's driveway, closing the remaining gap in the perimeter now that the ambulance had departed. He was dutifully pushing his way through the cluster of ivy and shrubs that had grown unbidden against the front of the house, effectively cordoning off Renko's all-but-forgotten front porch. I shook my head despairingly. What the hell was happening?

"I'm going to bed," Joanna said from behind me, startling me, and I turned to see that she was dressed in an old pair of lightweight sweats, her favorites, the ones she'd worn the night we brought Spooky home from the animal shelter four years earlier.

"Are you all right?" I asked, understanding that the outfit she was wearing served two purposes, only one being that of clothing. The question was all but rhetorical. She shook her head and I noticed her lower lip quivering. I stepped forward and she fell into my arms, sobbing.

"What's happening?" she sighed.

"I don't know," I said, and that was the truth. "But we'll be all right." I added, this bit of reassurance for Joanna's sake. But it was a lie. In spite of the vow I had taken, I realized that some things were out of our control, and I wasn't sure of the ultimate outcome at all. There was more transpiring than Joanna knew. There was more transpiring than *I* knew and I really had no idea what was going to happen next. Despite all the vows and best intentions, there was no telling if we would ever be all right again.

Chapter Thirty-Five

J oanna was asleep in no time, but I lay awake long after midnight, watching the blades of the ceiling fan revolve in the shadows above the bed. What *was* happening? I had reluctantly accepted the idea that someone might be stalking us, but Renko winding up dead was never part of any scenario I'd imagined. I'd had no use for the man, but I could not imagine who might hate him enough to kill him. Tom had suggested that the answer to the mystery might lie in either my past or Joanna's. I had to suppose that the answer might actually lie somewhere in *Renko's* past. That was a place that was, in all likelihood, out of reach, at least for anyone but professionals like Teschal.

I suspected Judd of being the stalker. But what could Judd possibly have against Renko? Then again, Judd had been at the Fayre tonight while Renko was being killed. Or had he been?

I tried to recall the timeframe of this evening's events. I set out for the Fayre at just past one-thirty. I arrived to find the Ferris wheel out of commission and had watched Judd complete his repairs on the ride well before three. I lost sight of him immediately after and didn't see him again until I spoke with him at his trailer. We had run out of doughnuts shortly past nine-thirty. I had found Judd's trailer at around ten o'clock. He'd been unaccounted for between three and ten PM, and I had deliberately kept an eye out for him.

I supposed it was possible for Judd to have committed the murder and still made it back to his trailer in time for me to speak with him around ten, but that brought me back to the elusive motive.

Renko may very well have been Judd's target all along. Perhaps Teschal was right about Renko having enemies. Judd might have risen up from Renko's past to kill him as retaliation for some unresolved issue. But then what was behind Judd's cryptic warning?

I gritted my teeth and rolled onto my side where I could see through the open window to the driveway. From this angle I could see the front third of Renko's house, but not the police cruiser I knew to be sitting at the curb.

Spooky raised her head for a moment to consider me thoughtfully, then lay back down. The sensor light above the garage was dark. The only movement outside was the occasional moth flitting against the screen; the only sounds the chirping of crickets, the infrequent noise of distant cars and the thrumming of the gas station generator around the corner.

I rolled onto my back and let my gaze return to the blades of the ceiling fan. I began searching their sweeping motion for answers. They reminded me of the Ferris wheel turning in the waning sunset, its neon strips blinking in time with the music playing on the loudspeakers, Echo and the Bunnymen performing *Killing Moon*, of all things, the last song I'd heard as I'd made my way to the dumpster. The details were there in my mind, but I was missing something, some unknown piece to the puzzle that was eluding me. Judd, Joanna, Renko and me; there had to be a thread connecting us.

I climbed out of bed. The box spring creaked and I paused to check on Joanna before proceeding. Spooky raised her head.

"Stay," I whispered, realizing the futility of my words. Spooky had taken after the people she lived with; if she wanted to tag along, she was damned well going to do it.

I went to the back door and let myself into the service porch. I slipped on the flip flops I kept by the washer and turned to close the door but found Spooky pushing at it with her paw, her dark eyes considering me as if to say, 'You're not going without me.' The sight of my dog trotting to the screen door ahead of me, acting as if everything had returned to normal, made me feel better than I had in some time.

I pushed open the screen door and Spooky bounded down the steps and crossed the patio. She made a beeline for the deep shadows beneath the maple tree, a favorite spot of hers, and I followed.

A sound drifted down the driveway and Spooky stopped in her tracks, raised her head and began to growl. I turned to see the police cruiser perched curbside in front of my late neighbor's house. The windows were lowered and I detected movement inside. I waved but no one waved back, and Spooky, apparently satisfied that there was nothing overtly interesting to see, set her nose in gear once again and made tracks for the maple tree.

I followed her and, as she took care of her business, it slowly dawned on me that I was close to the spot where I'd found the first 'deposit'. I also realized that I was near the spot where I'd seen the glistening specks, specks my brain had insisted were fireflies in spite of my imagination's efforts to convince me otherwise. Then there had been the second 'deposit' and, most recently, the tree limb and shingles. This portion of my yard had certainly seen a lot of activity lately.

Curious, I turned to consider my back porch and immediately understood why my stalker had chosen this spot; it was the perfect vantage point for someone wishing to see but remain unseen.

Something bumped into my ankle and my heart skipped a beat. I looked down to see a pair of iridescent eyes at my feet and realized Spooky was staring up at me. I listened to the gentle jingling of the tiny bell on her collar as she turned and made tracks for the gate.

I set my sights once again on the darkness behind the garage, darkness so thick it might be possible to cut it with a knife. And I waited for something to happen, waited for some bony shape to lunge at me from the shadows, for a voice with the slightest twinge of a southern drawl to tell me once again to 'be careful.'

But nothing happened. The crickets chirped. A car horn blared somewhere and I found myself feeling a little like Scout Finch after she'd gotten too close to the Radley house. Suspecting I'd overstayed my welcome, I headed for my house.

I had traveled less than a yard when I heard what might have been a twig snapping someplace behind me. Chilled, I spun around, expecting an apparition to leap at me, better late than never. But again, there was nothing. I strained to see through the black folds and for a fleeting second imagined that I saw something dart across my field of vision, something man-sized, draped in shadows, and I almost cried out in surprise. Spooky saved me the trouble by letting out a brief, crisp rattle of barks.

"Relax, there." It was a man's voice coming from my driveway and I twisted around so hard and fast I nearly toppled over.

Spooky was at the gate sitting up on her haunches as the police officer from the stakeout at the front of Renko's house reached over the fence and patted her on the head.

"Hello," the officer said.

"Hey," I managed, finding some bit of my own voice.

"It's okay," the officer said, his eyes on Spooky as she begged for attention. "I was just wondering if everything was all right."

"Yeah," I said, my voice becoming clearer and stronger. "I couldn't sleep."

The man nodded. "I understand," he said. "It's a nice night; too bad about the business next door."

I trudged toward the fence, glancing warily over my

shoulder, searching for the shadowy figure I thought I'd seen, but the darkness was impenetrable. I waved my hand over the fence as I approached the officer and the sensor light above my garage came alive, flooding the driveway with vivid white light, illuminating the officer's surprisingly young face.

"Nasty business," he said. "Did you know him well?"

I shook my head, suddenly uncertain as to whether this was idle conversation resulting from a chance meeting or some new, carefully-planned form of interrogation. Teschal might just have set this up deliberately. Young officer, opportune late night conversation; I wouldn't put it past her. But at that moment I wouldn't put it past my own paranoia, either.

"Just small talk," I said shrugging.

He nodded.

"How'd you draw the duty?" I asked. "I mean, overnight details can't be high on the popularity list."

He smiled, reached over the fence again to pet Spooky. "I've only been on the force one year," he said. "Still a rookie, I guess. Rookies all start on third shift. I'm getting married in the spring and I need the cash. Tonight's supposed to be my night off; guess I'm lucky to draw the extra detail."

"What if he comes back?"

The man stopped petting Spooky. "Who?"

"Whoever did this," I said, gesturing toward Renko's darkened house. "I mean, Detective Teschal was pretty tight-lipped with the details, but it seems to me that whoever killed Bob Renko might come back."

The man glanced at Renko's house then shook his head.

"That's very unlikely," he said, stiffening noticeably as if offended by the notion that he had not considered that possibility. "Most crimes of this sort resolve themselves quickly. And perps, for better or worse, are a lot like lightning; they rarely strike twice in the same place. I'm just here to keep the nosy kids and reporters away. Whatever motive was behind this," he said gesturing over his shoulder with a thumb, "won't stay hidden for long. You can count on that."

I wasn't sure if he was simply handing me the company line or if he really believed what he was saying. But then again, there was always the possibility that Teschal was on to someone. I just hoped she wasn't aiming her suspicions in my direction.

"Well, good night, sir," the officer said as if suddenly sensing he'd said too much. The man headed up my driveway, his heels thudding against the asphalt.

The exhaustion I had experienced earlier came crashing down on me; it seemed the adrenaline rush I'd succumbed to when I first saw the police cruisers was finally wearing off.

"C'mon girl," I called. "I think we've had enough of the great outdoors for tonight."

Spooky followed me up the stairs, through the service porch and into the house.

I found my way back to bed and lay there waiting for the sensor light I had activated to die. After a few moments it did, and at some point my own internal light went out and I fell asleep.

Chapter Thirty-Six

That night I dreamed of Renko. In my dream, I was working in my yard beside my garage, trimming back the long purple flower-tipped stalks that grow from the Hostas during dry spells, when I noticed my dead neighbor standing at his fence, staring at me. I set my shears down and got to my feet.

"Can I help you?" I asked, my voice sounding clipped as if I were being suffocated by the stagnant air that filled my dream. I was angry with Renko for intruding on my peace, not acknowledging or caring that I knew he was dead.

He didn't respond; he just stood there, looking lost. His dull eyes seemed to be looking past me, and I glanced over my shoulder to see what was drawing his gaze. Storm clouds were gathering on a blood-red horizon. I turned back to find him walking away.

I called after him; he turned back for a moment. I moved to my fence where I could see his face more clearly. He looked haggard, his temples thick with gray, his skin worn, cracked by the sun and time. Ignoring me, he turned and shuffled toward his back porch.

Again I called after him, but when he failed to respond, I opened my gate and walked quickly up my driveway.

Renko had reached the base of his back porch by the time I got to the street and, as I proceeded down his driveway, he began climbing the steps. I watched him open the screen door. It creaked loudly.

I reached the porch just as he vanished inside. I watched the screen door slam shut. I was lost in indecision, uncertain as to why I had followed him in the first place, a feeling of dread growing within me. That's when I noticed the vegetation in Renko's back yard, vegetation that had grown completely out of control, engulfing the old garage and thickening into an impenetrable rain forest that might have been a garden in hell.

The kitchen chair I'd seen Renko carrying to his garage the previous night sat by the boarded-up window. Vines were wrapped tightly around its worn finish. The entire house looked as if it had risen from the ground like a tombstone and might at any moment be swallowed up by the strange earth that inhabited my dream.

I considered the screen door with its flaking paint and rusted hinges. It looked ancient, as if it were a relic from some lost temple in an Indiana Jones story.

Finally, propelled by unknown forces, I climbed the steps and took hold of the screen door handle. As my fingers wrapped around the old metal, the sky above me changed from vivid blue to pitch black and a ripple of thunder stirred in the distance. I hauled the screen door open, winced at the deafening creak of its hinges, and stepped inside.

The door slammed shut behind me and I found myself standing in a closet-sized mud room. The warped and scarred floor was littered with old sneakers and worn work boots. Oddly, the walls in this room were lined with smooth beige cinder blocks that would have seemed completely out of place in reality but fit in perfectly with my dreamscape. They were the sort of cinder blocks one might find lining the walls of an institution like the state hospital at the Fayre grounds. The room was a mixture of themes, as if many elements had infiltrated my dream and had blended together in some twisted fashion, making even mundane things feel uncomfortable. It was like being trapped in a Salvadore Dali painting and watching the world blur around me.

Dangling from an array of hooks set in one wall were several well-worn jackets and what I took to be faded blue scrubs, the sort one might also find in a hospital.

Above me hung a tattered drop ceiling; I noticed some of the tiles were missing while others were badly water-stained, the metal framework being slowly consumed by rust.

A sound like shuffling feet drew my attention and I crossed through a curtained archway and found myself in what appeared to be a living room. I sensed the air evaporate around me, as if I had stepped into a vacuum chamber. I looked for Renko, but he was nowhere to be found. The room itself was similar to its owner in that it was crudely furnished and unkempt, its walls composed of old pine tongue and groove paneling, a style that had been ripe fifty years earlier, but was now long out of date. To the left were three large windows in an alcove where a moth-eaten sofa sagged. Drawn dingy shades filled the windows, successfully keeping light from the outside world at bay.

Most of the floor was covered by a large faded oval shaped rug with torn, tattered edges. Newspapers, magazines and pieces of well-worn furniture were crammed into every nook and cranny of the room, each layered in dust. Jumbles of plugs and extension cords that would frighten any fire inspector hung from each outlet, winding off into shadowy corners and disappearing beneath tattered pieces of furniture. Dusty prints of western scenes, cowboys huddled around campfires drinking coffee and trains cruising depression-era landscapes, hung at odd angles on the shabby walls. And an old wagon-wheel chandelier, its frontier-scene shades askew and thick with dust, hung glowing, sentinel-like, above it all.

Perched atop a scarred pressboard entertainment center situated between two darkened doorways at the far end of the room was a television. The screen was alive with the chaotic jumble of a channel that had gone dead, a thick wash of white noise drifting aimlessly from its speaker. In front of this reliquary, like the captain's chair on the bridge of a weather-beaten fishing boat, sat a bedraggled green vinyl recliner patched with silver duct tape.

This, then, was Renko's world, the television, the source of the glow that brightened the perpetually-drawn shades at night, the chair, the place where Renko rested his weary bones, nursing the various alcoholic concoctions that got him through the days and nights. Immediately to the left of the chair, in a state of perpetual readiness to receive beverages, stood a metal TV tray, its edges bent, rings of rust peppering the covered bridge print that adorned it.

I moved closer, the floor creaking beneath my weight like the noisy screen door, too loud for any world other than this imaginary one, serving only to betray my position until I concluded that the recliner was empty. The shuffling feet I had heard had not belonged to Renko; they had apparently belonged to no one.

A sensation of cold dread broke over me and I knew in my gut that it was time to leave. I did my best to obey this urge, but my movements slowed to a crawl as if time within my dream had ground nearly to a halt. I struggled, my feet dragging, my muscles aching from the effort. I bumped into a table and watched a stack of magazines that had been resting there topple over in slow motion, spilling, domino-like, across the floor. The top-most came to rest in the far corner of the room. A chill broke across my spine as I saw the image of the jet-black Chevelle that graced its cover. I took a step toward the magazine, but my attention was suddenly drawn to something new, something that I would have sworn had not been there a moment earlier.

Inches from the magazine, tucked away beneath a jutting angle of wood I took to be the bottom of a flight of stairs, stood a half-sized door with a tongue-in-groove face. Perhaps this was the door to the cellar.

I crossed the room, my feet moving normally again, as if some force functioning within my dream wanted me to investigate. Perhaps I had been brought here for the express purpose of looking behind that door and putting an end to the mystery once and for all.

I felt certain this was the case, but as I drew near the thing the feeling of dread returned, as palpable as a pulse, and the last thing in the world I wanted was to see what lay behind that door; so far as I was concerned, the tiny door could remain shut forever.

Nevertheless, I found myself in front of the thing, my eyes drawn to a large padlock dangling unlocked from a rusted clasp just above the tiny crystal doorknob. A frantic voice in my head told me to secure the lock, and I was reaching out to do just that when something collided with the other side of the door with such force that the entire room shook violently. Instinctively I backed away, but I slipped on the spilled magazines and joined them in a heap on the floor as my horrified eyes watched the padlock fall from the clasp and land inches from my feet. Thunder rattled the old house. Movement above me drew my gaze and I looked up to see the wagon wheel chandelier swaying, its lights flickering. Again something collided with the door, this time with such force that a huge crack split the old wood from top to bottom. That was when I noticed the blood.

The walls, floor and ceiling had, moments earlier, been drab, boring, old, but devoid of blood. Now streaks of red were everywhere, splattered across the walls, the ceiling, the floor, the window shades, and the door in the corner, which was disintegrating before my disbelieving eyes. More pounding rattled the old wood. The room quivered and I struggled to get to my feet. A terrible shrieking filled my dream, a sound like nothing I'd heard before and I briefly wondered if a rabid Rufus was locked in the cellar before realizing that no dog on Earth had ever made a sound like this.

"It weren't no dog," Roger Trimble said from someplace in my head. "And it weren't no man, neither. But maybe it was a little bit of both."

The other voice in my head, a voice that sounded suddenly like Joanna's, told me the time had come to run.

Determined to obey this time, I turned, but felt a cold shock pass through my body, pinning me to the spot. Someone was sitting in the recliner. I could see a hand draped across the arm of the chair and reflected in the heart of the television screen's bug fights, there was a dark shape that had not been there earlier. The feeling of dread exploded inside me. In my dream I broke out in a sick cold sweat.

A deafening shriek, like a jagged shard of glass, lacerated the air and I turned to see the small door explode in a shower of splinters. The wagon wheel chandelier above me went dark and I covered my face to fend off the flying debris. In that fleeting instant, I glimpsed a dark, unrecognizable shape looming in the doorway.

Then my eyes snapped open and I raised my hands in a desperate attempt to fight off an attacker, an attacker who, in a blur of shadows, faded into the spinning blades of the ceiling fan far above my bed. I stopped struggling and lay panting, my heart a jackhammer in my chest. I turned to check on Joanna, who was sleeping soundly. I was thankful for not having disturbed her. Spooky had raised her head and was watching me from the foot of the bed the way a psychiatrist might study a new patient. After a moment she laid her head down, sighing, probably wondering what my next trick might be.

I turned to the clock. It read three-thirty-seven. Bathed in sweat, I went to the window. The fresh air was still warm but a slight breeze proved rewarding. I drew in several deep breaths as the sweat dried into chilly droplets on my skin. The generator at the gas station around the corner thrummed like a mechanical heartbeat. The echo of a police siren someplace far away found me and I considered Bob Renko's empty house. I had never been inside, yet my dream had seemed so real, so detailed. I spied the police cruiser parked at the curb, but its presence did little to assuage my feelings of uneasiness.

I went to the bathroom where I splashed water on my face and dabbed it dry with a towel I got from the linen closet. Then I climbed back into bed and set about trying to decipher my dream. Renko had been dead in the dream, that much was certain. I had watched the EMTs carry his body out to the ambulance before going to sleep, so there was little wonder I dreamed of death. But then what about the blood? Teschal had said nothing regarding the condition of the body or the grisly details of the crime. Perhaps this lovely little embellishment was nothing more than the product of my overworked imagination.

I grimaced at this avenue of detection and decided it best left for daylight; I hoped for more sleep and, thinking along these lines, I was not likely to find any.

I rolled onto my side, my thoughts growing fuzzy around the edges, the adrenaline injection my nightmare had effused me with fading. I watched the clock until, sometime past four, I lapsed into sleep. The last thing I remember was hearing the sound of a train in the distance; a freight heading to parts unknown. Just like me.

Chapter Thirty-Seven

The next day found the sun sitting high and bright in the sky, making everything seem as if the horror of the previous night had been a figment of my imagination. I found Joanna making breakfast, so I went to the bathroom to shave. I finished around the same time she did and we sat in near silence, picking at the food on our plates and watching the little television on the counter.

When we finished eating, Joanna set the dishes in the dishwasher and headed for the bathroom to brush her teeth. The morning news was on and I stayed to watch, certain there would be a piece about Renko. My morbid curiosity was not disappointed.

A cartoon sketch of the chalk outline of a dead body and a ribbon of police tape bearing the words *Police Line, Do Not Cross*, appeared in the upper left-hand corner of the screen and the anchorman, a middle-aged man wearing an appropriately grim countenance, delivered the unsettling news. He explained that there had been two murders in Wickham, both having occurred in the last twenty-four hours, both apparently similar in nature.

My ears perked up and Joanna appeared in the bathroom doorway, the toothbrush poised in her hand.

"Last night Robert W. Renko was killed in his home at Six Cranberry Road," the man said. "Sources also confirm that a *second* body was found early this morning in the woods adjacent to the grounds of the state hospital where the Summer Harvest Fayre is set up. The man found in the woods, an elderly man who has not yet been identified is presumed to be a vagrant who lived in a shanty off the Number Four Fire road at the west end of the state hospital campus. Police are not commenting on the details of *either* murder, but a jogger who found the body of the man in the woods is talking exclusively to Live on Five.

Here's more from Shelby Sanders."

The face of a young woman with long blonde hair and an over-abundance of makeup filled the screen. Behind her, appearing every bit as grim as the anchorman's face was the faded facade of Bob Renko's house.

"That's right, John, the police have cordoned off the site of the latest murder, that of Robert W. Renko, who was killed in his home last night. Neighbors heard a scuffle and called police."

Roger Trimble's disgruntled face filled the screen, a microphone thrust in it.

"I heard a ruckus and called the cops," was all he said before the camera cut back to Shelby.

"Early this morning, another body was found adjacent to the grounds of the now-defunct West Wickham State Hospital by Andy Westcott, a jogger who claims to have seen the murdered man before."

The face of a middle-aged man standing on what appeared to be a wooded trail replaced Shelby's.

"I was jogging down this way," he said pointing off to the left, to a spot where the trees met some heavy brush, "when I noticed what looked like a pile of clothes by the side of the trail. I knew this homeless guy lived in a shack up a ways, because I seen him from time to time when I was out running. So I figured maybe the clothes was his. I went over to investigate and realized it was more than just clothes. There was blood everywhere. Most of the body was by the edge of the trail, but the head was over there."

There was a click as Joanna's toothbrush hit the floor.

"Do you want me to turn it off?" I asked, turning to face her.

She shook her head. Her face was the color of bone.

The old man's face had been replaced by an exterior shot of Renko's house. The camera backed off to find Shelby Sanders standing at the edge of Renko's front lawn.

Behind her the yellow tape cordoning off Renko's front porch flapped in the breeze. The nose of the police cruiser was also visible.

"It was right here," she said, "in this unassuming house on Cranberry Road, where Robert Renko met his end. Police are not speculating as to whether or not these two murders are related or whether or not the killings were indeed similar in nature as rumors suggest, but they *are* asking for help. They are looking for anyone who might have seen or heard anything strange in the vicinity of Cranberry Road and St. Brigid's Cemetery yesterday afternoon or evening. And they are also looking for a German shepherd that answers to the name Rufus. The dog belonged to Mr. Renko and, though police are not suggesting it at this time, it is barely possible that the dog may have turned on its master. That's all for now, John. Shelby Sanders reporting live from Cranberry Road."

The image of the anchorman returned.

"Well, how about those Red Sox," he said, his expression changing like the tide, "winning their sixth–"

I went to the four seasons room, Joanna at my heels. Prying open the blinds, I spied a van with the Channel Five logo painted on its side parked adjacent to the Trimbles' driveway. I could see Shelby Sanders talking to the cameraman.

I let the blinds snap shut and turned to find Joanna standing in the doorway, her retrieved toothbrush in her hand, her mouth hanging open in shock. She considered the toothbrush as if it were an ancient relic she had just dug up in the back yard and headed back to the bathroom to finish what she'd started.

I sat down on the couch and switched on the television, hoping for more details on another station, but came up empty. The situation had changed dramatically. There had been *two* murders. But what could a homeless man possibly have in common with Joanna or Renko?

205

Perhaps there was no relationship. News people were always looking for stories, a conspiracy here, hidden meaning there; it didn't necessarily follow that they were right. The media had a job to do and that was to make people watch, read, listen, and stay tuned for more details, and to do that they had to make it spectacular. Murder was spectacular. *Two* murders were gold.

I thought of the coyote that had chased the little girl at the Fayre. I supposed that it was possible that a coyote *could* have killed the homeless man. The witness said that the body had been mangled. In fact he'd spoken of decapitation. That might explain the official concern over finding Rufus. The elements of my dream became more disturbing than ever. But two canine-related deaths happening days apart with less than two miles distance between them committed by two different animals? What were the odds?

I remembered the biker at the Fayre telling me that something was making the coyotes act weird. He'd also said he had chased one out of his yard. Marge had talked about a coyote attacking a boy in his sand box.

I supposed that it was remotely possible that a coyote had gotten into Renko's house, most likely through the broken basement window Teschal had mentioned, probably rummaging for scraps, which I'm sure Renko, being the slob I knew him to have been, had left lying around. Then, when an inebriated Renko had confronted the animal, possibly even cornering it, the thing had killed him.

This notion seemed implausible but Renko was lying dead at the morgue and other explanations were not exactly forthcoming. Rufus might have started barking when he smelled the thing but had been unable to protect his master. That would certainly explain the ruckus Roger Trimble had heard. Perhaps Rufus, driven to a fit of rage by the coyote's attack, escaped from wherever Renko had put him and pursued the fleeing animal. Or animals. I suppose there could have been a pack of coyotes.

This explanation was thin enough to be transparent. A coyote might wander too close to the Fayre or a neighborhood, but the idea that one might break into a house was ridiculous. And a pack of coyotes? It also didn't explain what had happened to Rufus. If Renko had been killed by coyotes, why hadn't Rufus returned once they'd been driven off?

I thought for a moment and decided that Rufus might have been killed or injured by one or more coyotes while chasing the one that had killed Renko. This actually made some sense. But would a coyote kill a raccoon and drag it into Renko's garage?

It seemed very unlikely. Coyotes might be daring, especially when their territory was infringed upon or when food was scarce, but to take up residence in a yard where a big German shepherd lived seemed ludicrous. But what if the coyote was rabid? And what about Renko's rifle?

A door slammed and I went to the kitchen. I found Spooky standing at the back door, her big eyes brimming with dejection.

I ran through the service porch, down the stairs and across the yard. I caught a glimpse of Joanna heading up the driveway.

"Joanna, wait!" I called. "Where are you going?"

"Walking," she called back without offering me so much as a glance.

Something was terribly wrong. The Renko situation was bad enough, but there was something else, something I was missing.

I watched her turn right at the head of the driveway, walking briskly past the police cruiser and the news van.

I waited until she was out of sight, then went back inside, a confused Spooky at my heels. I went to the four seasons room, angrily picked up the remote and shut off the television. The last thing I heard was the female meteorologist talking about the Thunder moon as if that had anything whatsoever to do with what was happening.

Chapter Thirty-Eight

No sooner had I switched off the television than the telephone rang. Annoyed at how the day was going and dreading what could possibly happen next, I scooped up the thing and growled, "Hello."

"I understand your attitude, but please don't shoot the messenger," Tom said.

I sighed, flopping down on the sofa. Spooky saw her chance and jumped up with me, nestling in beside my leg.

"I'm sorry, but this Renko thing has hit Joanna pretty hard. And if that isn't enough, the police are trying to tie this murder in with another."

"Yes, the tramp in the woods," Tom said flatly.

"The police are suggesting that Renko may have been killed by his dog."

"Yes, I see that. But why would anyone try to tie–" His voice trailed off into nothingness.

"Tom?"

"Sorry, I just thought of something."

"Coyotes?"

"Yes," he said, "now that you mention it. A coyote might have killed the vagrant. Didn't I hear that one of the critters chased a little girl at the Fayre?"

"Yes," I said, "but she's all right. I suppose that a coyote might be rabid–"

"Maybe," Tom said. "But I'm having trouble thinking that a coyote has been prowling about your neighborhood."

"Don't forget about the dead raccoon. Could a coyote be responsible for that?"

"I suppose so, but then how and why did it end up in Renko's garage? And don't forget your tree-climbing acrobat. Coyotes don't climb trees."

"The whole thing is getting sickening," I said, sighing. "And Renko's rifle was destroyed."

"Rifle?"

"I didn't get a chance to tell you last night. I saw it being loaded into a squad car; you should have seen it. It was mangled almost beyond recognition."

"That's interesting," he said, sounding thoughtful. "Very interesting."

I opened my mouth to tell Tom about my encounter with Judd at his trailer and about his cryptic warning regarding Joanna, but for reasons I didn't understand, I remained silent.

"Anything else regarding your Ferris wheel climber?"

"No," I said, confused as to why I was not being more forthcoming with the very person I had entrusted with the job of solving the mystery. I was not only withholding information from Joanna and the police but from Tom as well. For the first time since this whole thing started, I was feeling completely alone.

"If I could only get inside your neighbor's house," Tom mused. "Visit the crime scene, so to speak."

"Forget it," I said. "There's a police cruiser parked out front until further notice."

"Hmm," he said and I could almost hear the wheels turning. "Maybe there's another way."

I had no idea what he meant and was not in the mood to play guessing games. I needed concrete answers. I needed to figure out why I was unwilling to tell him about Judd's comment, too.

"What about those tests?" I said, forging off in a different direction.

"Nothing yet," he said. "Our lab should have the bacterial results by tonight."

"You're not going to get in trouble at work, are you?"

"Nah." Tom chuckled. "I'll call you after the Fayre or if I get the results sooner. Can I reach you on your mobile?"

"Sure."

"Good. I suppose it's just possible that Renko was the real target of the stalker after all."

"I've considered that," I said, wanting very much to believe it, but somehow not being able to fully grasp the idea. Joanna's moodiness was preventing me; that, coupled with Judd's words. I had seen Judd's Chevelle near the cemetery, too. That last tidbit *couldn't* be coincidental. The car was one tangible element that had made its way into my dream. Even my subconscious was trying to unravel the mystery.

"Keep looking at the bright side," Tom said, but I didn't appreciate his optimism; things were looking pretty dreary from where I was sitting.

"Keep an eye on your carny if you can, but I wouldn't put too much faith in his involvement. There's no link that I can detect."

"You're probably right," I said, biting my tongue. The last thing I said was, "I'll wait to hear from you."

I was heading for the bathroom to shower when Spooky let out a quick bark. A knock at the door followed. My first thought was that Joanna had forgotten her key, but then I noticed the door wasn't locked.

"Mr. Graves?" It was a familiar, chilly voice.

I felt the cold presence in my stomach rear its head. I opened the door to find Detective Teschal standing in my service porch.

"Mr. Graves, how lucky to find you at home," she said, trying to appear friendly and casual but sounding as businesslike as ever. "May I have a word? It won't take long."

Chapter Thirty-Nine

I gestured for Teschal to enter, but she declined my hospitality by ignoring the offer entirely and remained in the service porch. Spooky, who had followed me into the kitchen, glanced at Teschal but, apparently remembering the cold shoulder the detective had offered her the night before, simply took to her bed.

"Is your wife at home?" The detective glanced over my shoulder.

"No," I said. "She's pretty upset. She's out walking."

"Yes," Teschal said. "We're all upset."

Her words were clearly meant to be empathetic, but I couldn't imagine anything that might rattle the good detective, even murder. Teschal seemed completely unshaken. I considered the cream-colored suit she was wearing; though attractive and flattering to her athletic figure, it did little to soften the stern demeanor to which I was growing accustomed. I imagined Teschal spending evenings at home alone or perhaps with an independent-thinking feline companion, watching CSI reruns, scoffing at Hollywood's flashy interpretation of crime detection while nursing containers of bottled water or perhaps, on weekend nights, the occasional glass of wine. At the same time, she would be perusing with unending admiration the framed photographs of police officer relatives, deeply satisfied with her position in life as the whip hand of justice, thoughts of marriage and children never troubling her precise brain.

"To the point, then," she said curtly, clasping her hands at her waist. "I suppose you've heard about the other victim."

"Yes," I said, "the homeless man by the state hospital."

I suspected that the only reason Teschal was broaching the subject was due to the story having been splashed all over the news. If the local reporters hadn't run with the piece, suggesting that the two murders were somehow connected, my guest would probably not have mentioned it.

"We don't think the deaths are related," she said, reading my mind with ease.

"But you're not sure."

She paused, her eyes locked on mine as if waiting for me to flinch. It was as if she was unwilling to accept the slightest hint of insubordination from a civilian.

"The reason I stopped by," she said, dodging my query, "was to see if you remembered anything else that might help the investigation and to remind you that this *is* a police matter."

"I don't follow?"

"The incident occurred next door to your home. Some people might be tempted to take matters into their own hands."

I felt a deep frown settle into my face and the cold sensation in my stomach grew colder. Was Teschal aware of Tom's investigation?

"This is an ongoing murder investigation, and we wouldn't appreciate you or anyone else getting into the middle of it," she said firmly.

I remembered the conversation I'd had with the officer in my driveway the previous night and tried to recall if I'd said anything leading, anything that might have reached the ears of Teschal. I must admit I hadn't cared for the good detective's not-so-subtle accusatory tone from the start, and I was learning to like it less with each passing second.

"Sure," I said. "I understand."

"By the way, Mr. Graves, it might interest you to know that approximately two hours prior to the call that resulted in the discovery of Mr. Renko's body, a police dispatcher received several complaints from this area concerning what sounded like a car backfiring or fireworks."

She paused as if waiting for me to respond. When I didn't she continued.

"We believe the sound was a gun shot. Did you know your neighbor owned a .22 caliber rifle?"

"I didn't know he owned one, not until I saw one of your men carrying it out in a baggie last night," I said.

Teschal's eyebrows arched up slightly and a hint of a smile touched her lips. She hadn't known I'd noticed the rifle being carried out of Renko's place. I suspected I'd risen up a notch in her estimation.

"We found the weapon in the house," she said, "as well as an open box of cartridges on the kitchen table. We have reason to believe that the weapon was loaded and fired recently, probably last night." She paused, pursing her lips as if waiting for me to add something. When I remained silent she proceeded.

"Mr. Graves, do you have any idea why Mr. Renko might have fired that weapon?"

I was taken completely aback by this question. Why was Teschal offering this information? "I have no idea," I said with a shrug. "But as I said, I didn't even know he owned a gun until I saw it being carried out of the house. Maybe he saw a coyote."

"Yes, they are on the prowl these days."

She paused again as if waiting for me to offer more, but once again I remained silent. Her thin lips formed a chilly smile and Teschal turned to leave.

"Thank you, Mr. Graves," she said.

I waited without closing the door, suspecting that Teschal had a final question to pose, much as she had the night before. I was not disappointed.

"Mr. Graves," she added as she reached the screen

214

door, "have you seen Mr. Renko's dog?"

"Rufus? No sign of him."

"No tracks, no tipped-over trash barrels? No unsightly deposits in your yard? Dogs do that sort of thing."

The cold thing in my gut reached up into my throat. Was she guessing, poking around in the dark like a detective, or did she know more than she was saying?

"No," I said, forcing a grin in hopes of taking the edge off my surprise. I sensed I was too late. Like a fortune-teller, I suspected that Teschal had seen the shadow of surprise in my face and was prepared to run with it.

She nodded, forced a grin of her own, although with greater ease I suspected, and bid me goodbye.

I closed the door, pressing my forehead to the wood and cursing silently, angry with myself for being unprepared for the shrewd detective. I was sinking deeper into a quicksand of defensiveness and, guilty or not, the signals I was sending were bad for my cause.

I went to the four seasons room and watched Teschal through the blinds as she made her way toward her SUV, which was parked across from the cruiser. The news van had departed. Teschal stopped to exchange a few words with the officer in the cruiser, then got into her vehicle and headed up the street just as Joanna came walking the other way. My wife considered Teschal as she drove past before continuing in my direction. I could see from where I stood that my wife's face was streaked with tears.

Chapter Forty

I greeted Joanna as she entered the kitchen, and she studied me for a long moment as if on the verge of saying something important. But then she only nodded, as if reassuring herself of something she'd already decided upon.

"I have to ask," I said.

"I'll be all right," she said softly, using her fingers to wipe away what remained of the tears on her cheeks. "It's just that, well, a lot is happening ... *has* happened."

"I'm here," I said, trying to sound reassuring.

Spooky had left her bed and was whimpering at my wife's feet.

"Spooky's here too," I said. "We're your family. Things haven't fallen entirely off the edge."

I had never seen Joanna this distraught. There had been arguments over the years, mostly over things long forgotten that must have seemed important at the time. But whatever had been plaguing my wife for the past few days was different. Whatever this was, it was not leaving any time soon. To the contrary, it seemed to be taking up residence in her soul; I could see it in her tired eyes, lurking there like a parasite sapping her strength, her joy, and, perhaps, her love for me as well. And once again, I sensed that there was so much more here than either of us understood. It was as if something was moving beneath it all, like rushing water beneath a deceptively thin layer of ice. One false step and we would plunge through.

"Do you want to stay home tonight?" I suggested, certain of the answer before the words passed my lips. "Marge could cover–"

"No," Joanna said, shaking her head and wiping more moisture from her face. "Busy is good," she said. "Busy is what I need."

I nodded in agreement. Busy had always worked for Joanna.

"Then I'll be busy with you, if that's okay."

She smiled and Spooky reached up with a fuzzy paw and touched her leg.

"I didn't forget you," Joanna said and she reached down and patted Spooky. "But would you mind picking up the doughnuts for me today?" She looked my way, providing me with a clear view of just how reddened her eyes were. "I don't need the drive and it's getting late."

"Sure," I said nodding and mustering a grin.

"Thanks," she said putting her arms around my neck. "What would I do without my rock?" She kissed me and I tasted tears. Then she hugged me tight. "Don't ever leave me," she whispered in my ear. "And don't let me go, no matter what happens."

She turned and went into the bathroom. I was still pondering her words when I heard the shower starting up.

Chapter Forty-One

J oanna was first to leave, saying something about getting things in order. She was distracted and barely noticed the fact that I kissed her goodbye in the driveway. She thanked me for agreeing to get the doughnuts and I watched her back out into the street. Once she'd driven away, I hopped into my car and set out in the other direction, toward the town library, Joanna's usual stomping ground. I had to meet a student I'd been tutoring before picking up the doughnuts.

***

I parked in the Wickham Town Library back lot and made my way toward the main entrance, across the smoldering asphalt, then beneath the shade of the big oaks that guarded the granite steps. I proceeded past the main desk with its dark Victorian-age wood, ornate Gilded Age globe-topped columns of brass, and Mrs. Crandall, its silver-haired guardian, who cast a cautious, though familiar, eye in my direction, before arriving in the cool recesses of the main reading room where my student awaited me.

"So," Angus Duncan began, after we settled in for our session, "we were talking about Andrew Jackson."

Angus was fifteen and as precocious as Tom Sawyer, but with the street sense of a nun.

"Yes, the man on the twenty-dollar bill," I said as I flipped open my favorite worn text, certain that anyone whose face graced currency would impress my young companion.

"Mr. G., why do you use that old book? They have new shiny ones with bigger pictures."

"I like these old books," I said, studying the worn text on the table before me. "These old books are solid; classics." I patted the faded tan cover. "You know where you stand with them. No surprises."

"Whatever," Angus said with a shrug of his sloped shoulders.

"Back to Jackson," I said. "A bit of a contradiction."

"Sure, you mean the way he fought alongside freed blacks and Indians and even pirates at the Battle of New Orleans, then totally ignored the Supreme Court's ruling which would've let Indians set up their own constitutions and then screwed them over?"

"Um, yeah," I said, mildly taken aback by Angus' teenage interpretation of the historical facts. "Tell me again, why am I tutoring you?"

"Because my mom acquaints school attendance with retained knowledge," Angus said, before snapping his bubble gum.

"That's right."

"And Jackson completely opposed the Supreme Court and moved the Indians out to reservations in Oklahoma, along the Trail of Tears, where they were exposed to blankets contaminated with smallpox and other gross diseases that make your skin erupt in pustules and ooze all over the place."

"That's actually not correct; there was no smallpox at that point," I said, grimacing. "That had been the idea of the British. But the forced relocation is accurate. So what does that tell us about Jackson?"

"It tells us he was a prick," Angus said. "Oh, sorry Mr. Graves, about the 'P' word."

"That's okay," I said clearing my throat and glancing around the big room for potential eavesdroppers. I spied only one other person in the chamber, an elderly man sitting in the far corner pretending to read a newspaper but really napping.

"That's why the Indians today hate his guts," Angus added. "I think you said that it might have been his mother's influence that made him hate the Indians."

I nodded. "And?"

"And it just goes to show that no matter how well you think you know a person, you might not know them at all."

I opened my mouth to speak but found the round-faced Angus Duncan's words to be oddly impactful. How well did anyone know the people in their lives? I began to wonder, not for the first time, about Joanna.

"Mr. Graves."

I turned to Angus, a little dubious about hearing his next offering of wisdom.

"I need to go take a leak," he said, grinning.

"Sure," I said, mildly relieved.

Angus got to his feet and trotted off toward the bathroom, his sneakered footfalls fading into the distance, leaving me alone with my thoughts. My eyes strayed to the big windows in the far wall and the dusty mote-riddled bars of sunlight cascading through them. "Christ," I thought, "out of the mouths of babes."

***

One hour later, with Angus Duncan set free to loot and pillage, I made my way to the doughnut shop, the heat building around me like a tsunami. It was Saturday and weekend traffic was heavier than usual, with people jockeying for position to get on Route 495 for a Cape Cod excursion. I wasn't headed that way but inevitably got caught up in the rush nonetheless. I didn't mind all that much, because it gave me time to think.

I had decided at some point between my shower and the sight of Angus Duncan jogging down the library steps that Teschal was simply acting like a cop. It was her job to turn over every stone in search of Renko's killer, and she struck me as the type who would do just that. Besides, the fact that there had been two homicides in the past week in a relatively sleepy New England town like Wickham was enough to send anyone into a tailspin. I felt certain that political pressures would be brought to bear if they hadn't been already. Teschal was on the hot seat.

My primary concern was how to avoid dragging Tom into it. It wouldn't surprise me a bit to find that someone in the neighborhood had seen him skulking about, or spied his Jeep parked around the corner and wondered to whom it belonged. Everyone's senses became heightened under such circumstances, and license plates could be traced. Tom was in the mix because I had invited him, so I was feeling responsible for his involvement and his safety. Proving once again that he was a good clairvoyant, Tom chose that instant to call me on my mobile.

"Good day, friend," he said. "Quite the business in your neck of the woods, eh?"

"Yeah, I'm rolling with laughter."

"Relax, I have a plan."

"What sort of plan?" I didn't like the sound of Tom's voice. "You're not going to try to sneak into Renko's place, are you? I told you there's a cop–"

"Time out," he said. "I know I'm crazy, but who ever said I was stupid?"

"I did."

"Well, there you have it. The truth of the matter is I may not need to sneak in, not that I find that possibility very likely what with Barney Fife on guard."

"Then what are you talking about?"

"I spoke with a polka buddy this morning," he said. "He works at Mercy General. Well, as you know bodies are stored at the morgue there before they are shipped off to Boston for autopsy. My friend hopes to get me details about the condition of your corpse, I mean *the* corpse. He works the graveyard shift, so I won't hear from him until late, or early as it were, but, if this checks out, I can forego a trip into the deceased's abode."

"Good," I said definitively. I didn't know how to

221

break it to Tom, but, for his own good, and my peace of mind, I wanted him off the case. This had become a matter for the police, but I knew that if I asked him to step aside, he would plow ahead, more determined than ever. It was his way. His sitting around waiting for phone calls wouldn't hurt anyone, and Teschal would have no reason to suspect anyone else was nosing around in her professional backyard. I hoped.

"So keep your phone on and I'll call you. Or maybe I'll get a hankering for some doughnuts and pay you another visit."

"What about Judd?" I asked tempted more than ever to tell him about Judd's warning.

"Let's see what my friend turns up before we go roasting carnies at the spit, shall we?"

"All right," I said, relieved that Tom had provided me with a way to avoid having to tell him about Judd's warning. "Then I'll wait for your call."

"Good enough," he said.

He hung up and I tossed the phone aside. I was feeling better but not healthy yet, not by a long shot. At least Tom was temporarily off my 'things to worry about' list.

The traffic started breaking up and I veered off the main drag, determined to take the less-traversed back roads to the doughnut shop. I'd had enough time to think, too much, to tell the truth. I had a troubling feeling that tonight, my stalker would reveal himself to me, and I wanted to be ready.

Chapter Forty-Two

The doughnut shop was overflowing with the Saturday morning crowd, and I had to wait for a parking space. I finally found one close to the loading door and climbed out into the oppressive heat. I crossed the steaming asphalt and entered the shop.

The air conditioning felt like heaven and, for the first time in days, my thoughts began to lose their edge. I waited in line and asked a chipper young man if I could see Olson.

"He doesn't work here anymore," the young man said flatly. "Quit."

"Oh," I said, genuinely surprised. "Well, I'm here to pick up an order of doughnuts for Joanna Graves."

"Let me check with the new manager," he said, and he disappeared into the back room emerging a moment later with a short, heavy-set woman whose face was as pale as the white linoleum beneath my feet.

"Hello, sir," she said, grinning. "I'll have your order ready at the loading door."

I thanked her and headed back out into the heat.

I reached the loading door and huddled in the archway that housed the big metal door, seeking even the slightest relief from the merciless sun. After a moment, I heard a mechanical grinding sound and the big door began to inch its way up into its housing.

I stepped aside as three young men wearing the traditional navy-blue uniforms emerged, carrying the familiar plastic sleeves full of doughnut boxes. I popped the hatch on my SUV and returned to the shade of the door just as the manager appeared.

"Fifty dozen," she said. "You can count them if you like." Her pale skin made her look vampire-like in daylight.

"That won't be necessary," I said. The young men

returned for a second load of doughnuts and I took this opportunity to pry.

"Say, whatever happened to Kevin Olson?"

"Oh, you hadn't heard?" she said, her eyes brightening.

"Heard what?" I asked, trying to sound coy and hoping she was as much of a gossip as I was starting to suspect.

She led me away, to a small section of lawn surrounding a tiny cluster of trees.

"Well," she began, "I guess Kevin was caught stalking a woman over in Bridgton." She nodded with the dutiful affirmation of someone who had just related a grim fact that she had long suspected.

"You don't say?" I couldn't believe my luck, or surprise.

"She caught him one night peeking in her bedroom window," she said with what was becoming a perpetual nod.

"The woman recognized him?"

"He lived up the street!" she said with a gleeful grin. "I bet he's been doing this for years. He just never got caught. He was probably sneaking peeks at me and the other girls. Sick," she added, shaking her head slowly with conviction.

"So is he in jail?" Was it possible, I wondered? Had Olson been the one all along? If so, then Renko's murder was unrelated.

"It's good to see someone like that behind bars," I added.

"It will be, if they ever catch him."

"But you said–"

"I said she recognized him, but he took off and hasn't been seen since. He lived with his parents, and if they know where he is, they're not talking. I never liked him, anyway. I always knew the company had passed me

224

over for the manager's position because he could kiss ass. I guess they finally saw the error of their ways," she said with a definitive nod.

"All set, sir," one of the kids loading doughnuts said, eyeing the manager as if hoping for a tip, but realizing that, with the woman present, the odds of that happening had just dropped to nothing.

In spite of the manager's presence, I dug into my pocket for cash, withdrew some singles and forced the money into the kid's hand. He glanced at the manager warily before heading back into the loading bay with his partners. I turned toward my car and had made it halfway there when the manager's voice broke into the din of traffic.

"Sir, we don't accept tips!"

I waved her off and climbed aboard my SUV, still reeling from the news about Olson. This information put a new spin on everything.

I twisted the key in the ignition and drove out of the parking lot in such a distracted state that I inadvertently cut off at least one other car along the way. Horns blared in protest, but my brain was buzzing so loudly I barely noticed.

Chapter Forty-Three

I could see that the midway was overflowing with people as I approached the state hospital grounds. Rows of cars were filing into the already-jammed visitors' parking lot, and I was glad I would be using the staff entrance. But as I veered into the entranceway, I noticed a state police cruiser parked beside the security trailer. A burly state police officer wearing the typical broad-brimmed hat climbed out of the cruiser as I slowed to a stop.

"Is there a problem?" I said.

The security guard emerged from the trailer, shrugging.

"Identification, please," the officer said in a deep, gravelly, voice, sounding like a male version of Marge Weems.

I dug into my back pocket for my wallet, flipped it open and handed the man my ID. He studied it as if doubting its authenticity, comparing my face to the picture several times until he was satisfied. Then, stone-faced, he handed the license back to me.

"He's with the food vendors–" the security guard offered, but the cop cut him off.

"We have to check everyone, sir," the officer said. "Routine. Sorry for the inconvenience. May I check your cargo?"

"Sure," I said realizing the futility of the situation and I killed the engine and climbed out into the heat. I met the trooper at the back of the car and popped open the hatch.

Keeping his hands on his gun belt the officer leaned in and looked around. Reaching into one of the plastic sleeves he drew out a box of Shamus' finest. He looked at me, then at the box before popping it open. He nodded when he saw the contents.

"So you're the one selling these," he said.

"My wife, actually," I said. "She raises money for the library."

The officer's demeanor softened as he stood there looking suddenly like an incredibly huge kid studying a bike he wanted for Christmas in a store window.

"Keep those, if you like," I said.

The man looked at me and, for a second, I wondered if he might bust me for trying to bribe him. But after a moment he grinned, nodded, thanked me, and then sent me on my way. As I drove off, I checked my rear-view mirror and saw the pair picking doughnuts from the box.

I made my way to the staff parking lot, realizing that there would be an extra police presence on the Fayre grounds tonight due to the recent turn of events. Such precautions were to be expected under the circumstances, and I wondered how the additional security might affect Judd's behavior. But then again, I still wasn't sure about Judd or how he fit into what was happening. I didn't even know the man's last name.

I slowed before the turn to the staff lot when I spied a local police cruiser parked beside the big willow tree. My initial assumption was that I had run into more security and I resigned myself to being questioned again. But when I saw the officer from the cruiser standing amidst a group of teenagers armed with skateboards, I decided he had probably busted them for skateboarding on state property.

I drove slowly past and the officer turned to consider me with mild interest. One of the kids, a tall thin boy with bleached blonde hair and a particularly extensive collection of piercings, chose that moment to flash the man a middle finger. Satisfied that I was not a potential danger, the officer turned back to the crew of kids and continued with what I took to be a lecture, one they had probably heard many times before regarding society's norms and how they should get jobs. I had to confess I had actually heard just such a speech once or twice when I was their age. At that moment I couldn't decide whether such lectures had eventually taken root in my brain or if I'd simply grown bored with bucking the system and chosen to hop aboard the conformity train. In any event, I suspected I had, somehow, over time, become a conductor on that train and I felt a minor pang of loss for the long-forgotten joys of my rebellious boyhood.

Leaving the officer and the kids behind, I followed the road to the lot and crossed it, kicking up a cloud of dust that followed me like a persistent phantom, until I pulled into my usual space at the back of the booth. The familiar image of Marge sitting on the back step smoking one of her Camels greeted me. I killed the engine and climbed out into the settling dust shroud.

"Hot enough to boil eggs," she said, extinguishing the butt beneath the heel of her sandal and coming over to help me unload. "We've been waiting for you. Folks are lined up three deep."

"Sorry," I said. "Traffic."

Marge's nod was laced with empathy as she followed me around to the hatch where we began offloading the doughnuts.

"What's eating Joanna?" Marge whispered doughnut sleeves in hand. "She's not herself. Hasn't been for days, so I know it's not just that horrible business with your neighbor that's bothering her."

Surprised at the question, I glanced around the side of the car to be sure Joanna was not approaching. I could see her inside the booth at the counter, apparently talking to someone in the queue.

"I don't know," I said, not wanting to go into details.

Marge simply shook her head. "Well," she said, "it's too hot for pissing and moaning and I'm not getting paid for this shit."

She raised an eyebrow in my direction as if daring me to disagree with her, then turned and headed toward the booth when I didn't. I watched her go, then grabbed sleeves of doughnuts and followed.

Joanna had finished her conversation by the time I stepped into the booth and I set the sleeves of doughnuts on the big table.

"I'll do that," Joanna said curtly. "People are waiting."

I glanced toward the counter; there were several faces there, but none looked remotely familiar. I turned back to Marge, who raised a second eyebrow to emphasize her point, before we headed back out for another haul of doughnuts.

I waited until Marge and I were out of earshot before asking, "Has she been talking to anyone strange?"

Marge paused, leaned against the rear bumper and frowned, an act that caused the deep creases in her face to become bottomless.

"Not that I've seen, unless you consider talking to Libby Chambers or our alcoholic gym teacher strange, which, let's face it, you very well might."

"No, I mean one of the carnies, the people who run the rides, the ones who live in those," I said, pointing to the RV park.

Marge squinted against the sun, then looked at me, her expression one of utter puzzlement.

"She might talk to one every now and then, I suppose. They work here. But if you're asking if she's friendly with any of them, the answer's no. At least not so far as I can tell. But you should know better than I."

I sighed and picked up a load of doughnuts. She was right; I should know better.

"Hey," Marge said, wrapping her thick fingers around my wrist. "I just thought she was being a little quick is all, a little crabby. Women are crazy. I'm one, so I should know."

"I don't know what's bothering her," I said. "Maybe the stress, the Fayre, you know."

Marge grinned, slapped me on the arm and picked up a few sleeves of doughnut boxes.

"Hey Marge," I said as she headed back toward the booth.

She paused, peering at me around the corner of the car.

"I'd appreciate it if you'd keep our conversation to yourself."

She nodded, winked and started back toward the door.

"And Marge."

She leaned back again, a look of impatience lighting on her craggy face.

"Let me know if you see her talking with any carnies, or anyone unusual, for that matter."

Marge stood running her tongue around the inside of her lower lip as if chewing on my words.

"Someday," she said, "you're going to tell me what's going on here."

She set one sleeve of doughnuts down on the ground long enough to point a pudgy arthritic finger in my direction to emphasize her point, then picked it up and went into the booth.

I sighed and scooped up my load. I will Marge, I thought. Someday I'll tell you everything. That is, if I ever figure it out myself.

Chapter Forty-Four

The afternoon crawled by like a snail on a garden walkway, and the unrelenting heat didn't fade one bit as night settled over the Fayre. The doughnuts moved quickly at first, but just when I thought we'd sell out by nine o'clock, the demand dropped off to nothing.

"Eight dozen left," Marge said as she stood outside the back door, smoking. "And I forgot my television and the Sox are playing the Evil Empire again."

Joanna, who had been wiping down the counter, tossed her rag in a bucket of soapy water we kept beside the refrigerator and sighed.

"It's hot," she said, her eyes low, her face pale. "I'm going for a walk."

I stopped cleaning the microwave and asked her if she was all right.

"Sure," she said, flipping the lid of the money box closed. "Swell."

She cast me a stony glance then headed out the back door.

"I won't be long," she called back.

Marge stamped out her latest butt and climbed up into the booth.

"That's what I mean," she said. "Just not right, you know?"

"Well, maybe the walk will relax her," I said, starting back in on the microwave.

"They usually do," Marge said, and she went to the counter where a young girl with ponytails was smiling in anticipation of one of Shamus' finest.

I picked up the spray bottle of cleaner and gave the microwave's guts a good blast before Marge's words hit home.

"Walk?" I whispered. Joanna took walks while I

wasn't here? "Marge?"

"How many would you like?" Marge asked the little girl who held up two fingers in response.

"Marge?"

"What, Jack?" she asked as she retrieved some wax paper and scooped two doughnuts out of an open box.

"This may sound stupid but–" I stopped myself before telling Marge more than I'd planned. Yet I had to follow Joanna.

"Marge, do you mind if I take a walk to the bathroom? I mean, can you handle this for a few minutes?"

"Here you go, honey," she said, handing the girl the two doughnuts and accepting the money. "Enjoy the Fayre."

"Marge," I prompted, impatiently. She turned to me, smirking.

"I get it," she said. "A little moonlight stroll at the Fayre; a brief encounter under the bug lights." She nodded approvingly. "Just the thing to get a woman out of the doldrums, you romantic devil!" She winked at me. "Go get her, tiger."

I forced a sheepish smile, thanked her and set off into the night. This would not be a guessing game; I knew exactly where to look.

I crossed behind the booths, winding through batches of people carrying dirty dishes to the sinks or clean ones back to the booths. I stepped over the lengths of hoses and power cords, walked around the milk crates, cardboard boxes and trash barrels, ignoring the talk, the laughter of people enjoying themselves, living their lives as if nothing mattered. I could hear the band Wicked Scarlett, reeling out a decent version of Creedence Clearwater Revivals' *Bad Moon Rising*, doubtless in honor of the full Thunder moon.

But all of this amounted to little more than background noise. My mind had once again switched over to automatic pilot. I was on course and there was no stopping me, though I possessed not the slightest inkling of what I would do if my suspicions proved correct. I didn't care about that. All I could see was my destination and the visions flashing in my head of what I might find there.

I reached the last booth in our row and nearly stumbled over some debris I neither recognized nor stopped to move. I ignored the strange glance a bearded man carrying a load of dirty dishes cast me and veered left toward the trailers and Judd.

Chapter Forty-Five

I found the edge of the trailer park where I'd left it, but a new element presented itself: two police officers had positioned themselves along the perimeter. I had been right about the increased police presence. They hadn't yet taken special notice of me, though one was scanning the area as the other busily bent his ear. They had clearly been posted to cordon off the trailer park from the general public. But this meant that Joanna would have been turned away as well.

"Hello," one of the officers, a tall thin man with close-cropped hair and a dusty mustache, said.

"Can we help you, sir?" added his partner, a short, stocky man with little hair remaining and the general demeanor of a Marine drill instructor.

I considered concocting a story, perhaps about visiting a friend who traveled with the carnival. But not knowing Judd's last name, I quickly decided it would only steer suspicion in my direction.

I scanned the area, searching for another way into the trailer park, but a rope boundary had been slung on waist-high stakes around the perimeter. I decided to stick to my lame story about searching for the bathroom.

"You need a pass to get in here," the shorter of the officers said, firming up my belief that Joanna had not made it through, either.

"I was looking for the bathroom," I said.

The two men glanced at each other as if not buying my excuse and the taller of the two leveled a lanky arm in the direction from which I'd come.

"If you're working one of the booths," he said, "you can use the one at the sinks. If not, you need to use the Porta-johns. They're set up behind the stage."

"If you're going to use the staff bathrooms, you'll

234

need the key from your booth," his partner added.

"Key, right," I said backing away. "I'll get that. I'm just working here tonight; they didn't tell me about the key."

The tall officer nodded and his friend resumed talking.

I retraced my steps, sensing eyes at my back. I glanced back once and, sure enough, the shorter of the two was watching me. I greeted a woman who was returning from the sinks with a basin full of freshly washed dishes. She smiled in return. My hope was to alleviate any suspicion my own stupidity may have brought upon me. I dared to glance back one more time and, to my relief, found the pair considering the buildings on the hill instead of me.

Feeling ridiculous, I returned to the booth where I found Marge selling the last of the doughnuts. Joanna was nowhere in sight.

"Have a great night," she said, as the couple who'd purchased the last dozen faded into the crowd. Marge turned to me, rolled her eyes and said, "I think I'll have a butt. I hope you two had a nice chat."

She walked past me and barely made it to the back door before sparking up a Camel. I watched her sit down on the step and blow smoke into the night. Then I went to the counter and studied the thrumming midway. Tonight was the last night of the Fayre. I wondered what that meant for me. Would Joanna disappear during the night like some phantom I had only imagined? Was I trying to kiss the moon's reflection? Or was Judd's plan stranger and more frightening than I could possibly have foreseen? This was his last opportunity to do whatever he was planning. I thought of my mobile phone, checked to make sure it was active. Where the hell was Tom? I was feeling suddenly desperate and helpless.

I surveyed the seemingly endless sea of people. They were everywhere, on the rides, playing the games, sitting and eating on picnic tables or in the barbecue chicken tent. They were gathered in clots at the stage, on the bleachers, at the booths, the tents, looking at exhibits, tractors, harvest crafts, buying souvenirs, tee shirts, jewelry, old books left over from the Anything Goes Sale. Yet there was no trace of Joanna or Judd.

The band was finishing up with *Bad Moon Rising.* I looked up at the bloated orange face of the Thunder moon and found myself wondering if it knew where Joanna was, if it knew what was going to happen. If the moon held any secrets, it remained as tight-lipped as ever and I was left pondering my fate, the electric strumming from the stage washing over me like cold rain.

Chapter Forty-Six

Joanna showed up at the booth soon after, clearly agitated as if something had not gone her way but unwilling to talk beyond monosyllabic responses, which drew puzzled glances from Marge. I decided to wait it out, at least until Marge had gone. I walked toward the counter where, to my surprise, I found Marge talking with Dick Saunders. It took only seconds to determine that the man was thoroughly inebriated.

"Great fucking doughnuts," Dick growled as I approached. Behind him I saw several wide-eyed young girls backing away.

"Hi, Dick," I said, and he glared at me. Marge shot me a troubled glance. I heard something behind me and turned to see Joanna talking quietly on her mobile at the back door.

"What brings you back?" I said, and Dick's face flushed red.

"She left," he said, slurring. "The fucking bitch left!"

A group of middle-aged couples walking past the booth paused, shaking their heads disapprovingly.

"What–?" Marge began, but Dick pounded a fist into the countertop, cutting her off.

"If I find her–?" he hissed.

The two police officers I had encountered at the trailer park's entrance appeared suddenly and Dick glared at them. But in his condition, it was clear he could do little but bark, and he looked back at me, his eyes swollen with tears and booze, his face no longer filled with anger but with a bottomless sadness. He sighed as the officers moved up beside him.

"Now, sir, we hope you're not going to give us a hard time," the taller officer said and he wrapped a sinewy hand around Dick's wrist. The second officer took hold of the beefy gym teacher's other forearm. I realized that a crowd was forming, rubberneckers watching a tragedy, waiting for blood.

Dick looked up at me and any trace of fight his hefty frame may have housed faded.

"They all leave," he said sadly, his words running together like rain water, "in the end."

"All right, we're going to move along now," the tall officer said and together he and his partner led Dick Saunders to the last booth in our row, then spirited him around the corner toward the staff parking lot.

I looked to Joanna whose face was the color of bone. She punched some fresh numbers into her mobile and settled into one of the chairs by the table.

"Jesus," Marge said. "I need a butt."

She walked to the back door and lit up a Camel.

"There he goes," she said between drags.

I joined her and together Marge and I watched as a police cruiser moved silently toward the main exit.

"Poor Janet," Marge said.

"She's all right," Joanna said, joining us at the door. "I just spoke to Libby Chambers. Janet is staying with her for a bit."

I watched the cruiser vanish into the distance, the cloud of dust following like a pesky bystander.

"What a fucking night," Marge said, plopping down on the back step to finish her smoke. "What the hell else can happen?"

Chapter Forty-Seven

Things settled down after the 'Dick Saunders incident'. Marge bid us good night and I walked her to her car as Joanna cleaned.

"I gather you two didn't 'hook up' 'neath the Thunder moon," Marge said as she climbed into her old Chevy.

I shook my head and studied the vacant building near the edge of the staff parking lot. It was dark and lonely, like a huge tombstone.

"It's not my business, but I like your wife," she said. "She doesn't judge folks based on their bad habits or less-than-charming personalities. But something's not right with that woman, and it's not her period or a mid-life crisis. And for some Godforsaken reason, I like you, too. So keep me posted, will you?"

I nodded and tried to grin, for Marge's sake if not my own. Maybe if she thought it was just a fight Joanna and I were wrapped up in, she wouldn't lose sleep over it.

She sparked up a Camel, waved to me then drove off, kicking up a trail of dust in her wake.

I stood for a moment, studying the dust cloud, watching how it rose up into the air and passed specter-like before the moon. Then I headed back to the booth.

By the time I got there, Joanna had finished with the cleanup and she asked me to take out the last of the trash. She was putting the broom away as I scooped up the final two bags.

"You know," I said, unable to hold it in any longer, "I wish you'd tell me what's going on."

She turned to me, or rather *on* me, her eyes narrow, lips quivering.

"I'm just being quiet," she hissed. "Can't you leave me alone?"

She grabbed up her car keys and pushed past me.

"I have the cash box in my car," she called back. "Would you please finish locking up?"

I stood alone with the trash bags in my hands, watching my wife walk into the shadows.

"Mister," someone called.

I turned to the counter where a teenage couple was standing. They shared matching dog collars, their hair spiky strands of black, blonde, and green.

"You got any doughnuts left?" the boy asked.

"No," I said, shell-shocked. "We ran out."

He nodded and his waif-like date rolled her heavily rouged eyes.

"C'mon," he said. "Let's get some candy apples. I'm jonesin' for sugar."

I watched them fade into the throng. Remembering the bags of trash in my hands, I headed for the dumpster.

I spied two new police officers standing at the trailer park perimeter as I disposed of the trash. The trailer park was alive with activity. I saw the flicker of television sets. I smelled wood stoves and barbecues. I envisioned Judd sitting in his trailer nursing a beer and watching television, much as my recently deceased neighbor had done.

I headed back to the booth, dragging my soul behind me. There were supposed to be fireworks later on, but clouds were moving in across the moon and I wondered if they'd get them off before the rain arrived. I realized I could not have cared less.

I reached the booth, pausing a few feet from the doorway. The light was off and for the life of me I could not recall having shut it. Frowning, I stepped inside, tripped the switch by the door and nearly dropped dead of shock.

"Hi, Jackie boy," Alice Williams said from a chair by the counter. "Where's our girl?"

Chapter Forty-Eight

"Jesus, Alice, you scared the hell out of me!"

"Sorry, fluorescent's not my best color." Grinning, she adjusted her Red Sox cap. As she did this, I couldn't help but notice what appeared to be bruising on her wrist.

This sort of bruising was not uncommon with Alice, at least not as of late. She claimed it was all part of her condition, which she attributed to asthma, severe allergies and a plethora of mysterious ailments. I was no physician, but I had an aunt who suffered from diabetes and I recalled that the slightest bump left bruising on her skin. This led me to suspect that Alice's condition was more serious than she chose to disclose.

"Joanna's gone," I said. "She's tired."

"You let our girl work too hard, Jackie boy," she said shaking a long lean finger at me. "I'll be having a word with you about that someday."

"Alice knows best," I said grinning through my dejection and exhaustion.

"That's right," she said. "You don't want to get on my bad side."

She pushed herself to her feet with a grunt. I offered to help, but, as usual, she refused.

"I can do it," she said, waving me off. "This is just one of my bad days. You should see Alice when she's ten feet tall."

I nodded, remembering Alice as she'd been when I first met her, athletic, spry. But lately her mysterious ailments seemed to be sapping her strength, draining her very being. I was starting to suspect that arthritis might be the culprit, based upon the way she moved, the way she needed time to get out of the car or a chair. I remember my mother struggling with it in her knees toward the end. It had not been pleasant.

She crossed the booth, wrapped her long fingers around my upper arm, gave it a solid squeeze and said, "Goodnight, Jackie boy. I've got to be finding that no-good husband of mine. I'll be having a word with *him* one of these days, too."

"Likewise," I said, hoping it would be tonight as I ran my fingers across the silent mobile clipped to my belt. "Then you haven't seen him?"

Alice climbed down from the booth, shaking her head.

"No," she said. "He's waist deep in one of his little projects. Top secret, you know," she said placing a bone pretending to be a finger to her lips and then cackling at her own strange brand of humor. "You don't know what the hell he's been up to, do you, Jack-o-lantern?"

I didn't want to lie to Alice about Tom's activities, but found myself backed into a corner of my own making and shrugged, feigning ignorance.

"No idea. With Tom, it could be anything."

She nodded, saluted me and set off into the night. "Ain't that the truth," she called from the darkness.

I breathed a heavy sigh and plopped down into the chair she had vacated. It was still warm.

"Ladies and Gentlemen," the lead singer from Wicked Scarlett said over the sound system, "folks at the Summer Harvest Fayre and Vern Cross Entertainment hope you've enjoyed tonight's festivities but, due to impending bad weather, they regretfully have to postpone tonight's fireworks display."

A collective moan of disappointment rose up from the crowd.

"But don't fret," she added. "Though the carnival will be packing up and moving on, the fireworks will happen tomorrow night, weather permitting."

A subdued cheer followed and, as if on cue, the

242

entire mob shifted like a school of fish avoiding a predator, and began their exodus.

"But here's one for the road," the singer added, "in honor of this fine Saturday night," and the band broke into the Hal Ketchum tune, the one about the small town and a man who wanted to howl at the moon and shoot out a light. I took this as my cue to leave and dropped the counter board into place, shut the fans, killed the light and locked the booth. At some point next week, Joanna and I would give the booth a final sprucing up. All around me vendors were doing the same, making last-minute trips to the sinks to wash utensils, loading supplies into cars, making final visits to the bathroom, inviting each other out for drinks or late-night snacks. But there were no late-night festivities on my agenda. I no longer fit into the world I'd once occupied. I was heading home, alone. To what, I didn't know.

I searched for the all-too-familiar face of the moon, my silent, brooding companion throughout this seemingly endless week, but its face was lost behind thickening clouds; all that was evident of its presence was a ruddy glow in the sky.

I made my way to my car and drove out the back, avoiding the exiting multitude, which resembled a huge dust-choked snake with a thousand glowing eyes, coiling slowly toward the front gate. As I veered away from fatigued Fayre-goers in their equally fatigued vehicles, I caught a glimpse of a familiar face behind the wheel of a small SUV. It took a second before I put a name to the pudgy face, but when I did, the cold thing in my stomach wriggled to life. It was Kevin Olson, the doughnut shop manager, the one the police were searching for, the one who enjoyed peeking through windows after dark.

I strained to see through the rising dust cloud, but was unable to find him again. The glimpse I had gotten had been a brief one and I began doubting what I'd seen. I couldn't imagine that the man would be stupid enough to show up here. But then again, if Olson *was* our stalker, where else would he be?

I tried to convince myself that I had imagined him, and, while driving across the staff lot, had nearly succeeded, when I noticed something strange beneath the big willow tree at the head of the cobblestone road that was *definitely* not the product of my imagination.

I took the corner at a crawl so as to get a better look at the commotion. Several people were gathered near the base of the big willow tree, teenagers in baggy clothes. I thought of Tom, who'd once commented that teenage girls of today looked as if they were searching for a street lamp to stand under while the boys might very well be trying to locate the Bozo the Clown auditions. The observation sounded funnier coming from Tom; at that moment, with all that was running through my head, it just sounded sad.

The police officer I'd noticed earlier talking to the skateboarders was at the heart of the disturbance. The number of teenagers had doubled. The officer was aiming a flashlight beam at a dark mass lying at the base of the tree.

I squinted to see what it was and, as I did, the light seemed to glint off slivers of white. Teeth, I realized; lots of them. I was looking at the carcass of a coyote. It was lying on its side at the edge of the road, broad smears of blood like brush strokes across its flank.

Noticing my car, the officer swung the light my way and I raised my hand to shield my eyes. He signaled for me to stop and approached.

"Excuse me, sir," he said reaching the passenger door as I lowered the window. "Do you work at the Fayre?"

"Yes," I said, in no mood for an interrogation.

"I'm sorry, sir, but could I trouble you for your ID?"

"Sure," I nodded, slipped the car into park and reached for my wallet, wondering if I should tell him about my Kevin Olson sighting. I decided against it for more reasons than I could count, the most prevalent being that I wasn't even sure I'd seen the man.

I succeeded in wrestling my wallet out of my pocket and set about rummaging through the thing with sleepy fingers, awkwardly plucking my license from its sleeve.

"Is that a dead coyote over there or have I been working too long?"

"I don't know if you've been working too long, but that is a dead coyote," the officer said, accepting my license and studying it. "I thought maybe a car hit it, but no car does that to an animal." He raised the light, aimed it at me and studied my face. I squinted and he lowered the light, glanced back at my license then handed it back to me. "Sorry for the inconvenience, it's just that most folks use the other exit."

I nodded my understanding.

"Something's bothering them," he said as I replaced my license and wallet. "The coyotes."

"How so?" I asked remembering the biker's similar observation.

"We're getting reports from all over town about small animals being mauled. Even a few deer have been found torn up."

"But what would attack a coyote?" I asked, feeling suddenly queasy.

"Another coyote, maybe," he said. "Or a wolf. I'd say there's something big and mean out there. Be careful if you have a dog, especially at night." He glanced back at the scene unfolding by the big tree. "The kids found the thing over behind that building. The idiots dragged the carcass over here! God knows why. Looks as if it's been dead a while; blood's all dried up." The man shrugged, adjusted his cap. "Long, hot night; I'll be glad when it's over."

I nodded, the cold thing that had been living in my stomach rearing its head.

"Well, sorry to bother you, sir," he said. "Have a good night."

He turned and walked back to the group of kids while I closed the passenger window.

I drove on, feeling more uneasy than ever, remembering the coyote that had chased the little girl through the woods. The cold thing in my stomach was wide awake and I concluded that I'd had more than enough of the Summer Harvest Fayre, at least for this lifetime.

I made my way past the lonely buildings with their boarded-up windows to the main gate, where the security guard and the state police officer were standing. The officer frowned as I approached, but then waved me past. The security guard raised the spent doughnut box from where it sat on the hood of his car and gave me a thumbs-up. I lowered the driver's side window to wave back. In the distance I heard the band winding down, the music hanging in the air like summer smoke.

The music stopped and the last thing I heard before I raised the window, sealing the world out, was Wicked Scarlett's lead singer saying, "Goodnight, everybody. Drive safe and come back next year." Then I flipped on the AC and headed for home.

Chapter Forty-Nine

The ride home was a somber one. Fear of what I might find as I turned into my street had almost become a tangible thing, and I half-expected it to materialize on the seat beside me in the form of a dark, cancerous mass. Finding Joanna heading to her car with a suitcase in her hand was just one of the scenarios at which my mind was wincing. Finding her heading to her car with a suitcase in her hand and Judd by her side was another, darker one.

I considered the sky through the open sunroof. The moon had been reduced to a radiant glow seeping through a thickening veil of clouds. A distant flash drew my attention, and I watched the western horizon explode with a vibrant sliver of lightning that split the darkness open like a wound. It was like seeing the edge of the world, beyond which loomed a black hole waiting to devour everything in its path.

Shutting the sunroof, I flicked on the radio, switched to AM and scanned around until I found a clear station and waited for a weather report. I wasn't too concerned about the impending storm; the yard was pretty self-sufficient. *Our* yard was self-sufficient. I grimly wondered how long it would continue to be *our* yard.

Something made me think of the day we brought Spooky home from the animal shelter. Joanna had seen her photograph on the bulletin board of the local Stop & Shop and had fallen in love with the dark-eyed Lhasa. Joanna talked me into going down to the shelter to have a look. She had been relentless as if sensing she was predestined to adopt the orphaned dog.

One look and we were both sold. We brought Spooky home two days later, never knowing the name her former owner had given her. It didn't matter; the old girl took to her new name like a duck to water.

It had been fall and leaves had covered the back yard. Spooky was nearly ten years old at the time, an apparent stranger to the outside world and she didn't care for the way the dead leaves sounded as they crackled beneath her feet. She would chase Joanna to the edge of the leaves, stopping short as if an invisible force field had suddenly been raised, tipping her head to one side and whining. Joanna laughed each time; it was the most wonderful sound I'd ever heard.

We had been married three years by then. Now, after seven, I wondered if it was all coming to an end. And if our days as husband and wife were numbered, what was the reason? Because some mistake from her past had returned to claim her? Perhaps Judd had something over her, some shred of dirty laundry that he was not willing to forget. Perhaps *that* was what lay at the core of the whole thing. Maybe Judd was capable of unspeakable things and Joanna knew it. Perhaps Joanna was protecting me from Judd, at least in her mind.

I didn't know. The only thing I could attest to was that I was sick and tired, the sort of tired one must experience after crawling through a desert, reaching the edge and seeing a vast mountain range with snow-capped peaks waiting to chew you up next. My strength had fled; happiness had become a distant memory. I tried to imagine life after Joanna and couldn't; I didn't *want* to imagine it.

I grew suddenly angry. Not angry with Judd, or even with Joanna, but with myself. I'd dug a hole in the middle of my life and was about to toss my marriage into it. And for what? Suspicions? Inconclusive evidence?

I slammed my palm into the steering wheel. I was not about to give up so easily.

"And now for the weather," a female voice on the radio said, interrupting my chain of thought, and, welcoming the emotional respite, I turned up the volume.

"Good evening, New England, this is Glynnis Jensen at the weather center here on WBZ. Well, batten down the hatches, because we're in for a soaker tonight. Heavy rains at times, possibly two inches in isolated spots, are on the meteorological menu for this evening. The winds could get a little gusty as well, perhaps exceeding thirty knots."

"Lovely," I said. I didn't really mind the rain; my lawn needed it. It was just that the rain always brought a gloomy feeling with it, one that I knew affected Joanna. Things had been gloomy enough already without it.

The meteorologist started in again, but I'd heard all I needed to hear and shut off the radio. I was practically home, anyway.

I turned into my street and was relieved not to see a chaotic crunch of police units gathered. But grim reminders of what had transpired remained in the guise of a single, silent police cruiser parked in front of Renko's house and the yellow Police Line tape secured to his porch.

I drove past the cruiser; the officer was sitting behind the wheel, his face bathed in the glow of a laptop. He raised his eyes as I passed and I nodded at him. He nodded in response.

I turned into my driveway, hit the trigger for the garage door and drove into the open bay. I killed the engine and sat for a moment absorbing the summer night. Crickets were chirping. A dog was yapping somewhere off in the distance. I paused to consider whether it could be Rufus, but the barking was too shrill, shriller even than Spooky's. The noisy animal was *not* Rufus.

Joanna's car was sitting in the opposite bay. I could still hear the sound of the engine clicking as it cooled. I didn't think she'd have parked in the garage if packing a bag and leaving was her plan. I felt a trickle of relief.

I climbed out, closed the garage door, continued to the back porch and let myself in.

249

Spooky greeted me at the door, her tail wagging. I reached down and patted her, then went to the bedroom to look in on Joanna.

The television was off and the room was in darkness. I heard the gentle whoosh of the ceiling fan spinning in the shadows above me and sensed Joanna lying on the bed, probably asleep. I was tired but realized that sleep would prove to be elusive. I hoped that some television in the four seasons' room might relax me.

"Hi."

I paused. The mattress creaked as Joanna turned toward me. I could barely make out her shadowy shape.

"I thought you were asleep."

"No," she said softly. The edge that had filled her voice earlier had faded.

"I don't–" I began, but she told me not to bother.

"Just come and sit with me for a minute."

I sat on the edge of the bed. Her hand crept out of the darkness, found mine, and she drew my hand to her lips, kissed it and held it to her face. Her skin was warm and moist with tears.

"Jack, I need you to remember something."

"What?" I said, confused but relieved that some semblance of the Joanna I knew had found her way home.

"Do you remember the time your sister, Ellen's ex showed up at her door, drunk, looking for trouble?"

"Sure," I said. "I told her she should never have gotten mixed up with that idiot."

It would have been difficult to forget that situation. Ellen had been dating a smooth character named Dave something-or-other about six years earlier, just after Joanna and I married. He showed his stripes after a few months by turning up in his Corvette with another woman outside a local club. My sister, hardly the type to take such nonsense, promptly handed him his walking papers. Dave seemed content to move on, until one night, when he showed up at her door, demanding explanations. She called me, scared, the sounds of Dave's fists striking the front door providing background noise for her frightened sobs. I told her to call the police and that I would be right over.

She did as I instructed and the situation ended peacefully. The police arrived before I did and Dave cooled his heels in a Bridgton jail cell before vanishing into the sunset, thanks in no small part to a restraining order.

"How could I forget?" I said.

"I begged you not to go because I was scared, but you went anyway. You had to go," she said. "I know. I knew it then. It was just something you had to do, something you couldn't explain fully to me at the time because I didn't completely understand that your parents wanted you to take care of your little sister."

I shifted on the bed. I had no idea where Joanna was going with this.

"You explained the whole thing to me later," she said, "and over time, I came to understand."

"Yes," I said, waiting for her to reach a point. "I–"

She raised her finger to my lips and made a soft shushing sound. Then she squeezed my hand. Her hand was impossibly warm, feverish.

"Remember," she said, her voice quivering with fresh tears. "I love you more than anything."

I shook my head, my relief eroding like sand on a stormy beach. I started to speak, to ask for clarification, but at that moment, the telephone rang.

"You'd better get that," she said. Releasing my hand, I felt her turn away and roll onto her side to face the window.

I reached out to touch her shoulder, but the ringing of the phone dragged me away. It's amazing how the smallest things can interfere with the most important ones, and we rarely recognize it until it's too late.

I suspected the caller to be Tom, his timing as

horrendous as ever, and scooped up the cordless wall phone in the kitchen.

"What?" I said, my voice edgier than I'd intended.

"Can you talk?" Tom asked, his voice anxious.

I turned back to the bedroom, but Joanna had fallen silent and still. I decided to go out to the four seasons room to get rid of Tom. Whatever had been bothering Joanna as of late was showing itself, and I was not about to allow the tip of that iceberg to submerge again.

"Tom" I said, closing the French doors behind me, "your timing is terrible. I–"

"Just listen," he said, and I sensed something in his voice, an urgency I didn't recognize. "There's something wrong. The tests," he said, "the bacterial analysis; the results came back."

"Slow down," I said going to the window to check on the local constable. To my surprise, the police car was nowhere to be found and for reasons I couldn't explain, I felt a splinter of panic slip into my heart. Perhaps, I thought, searching my bag of rationalizations for a good one, the man had gone for a coffee or maybe Teschal, realizing the need had passed, had simply called off the detail.

"I got the results from the lab," Tom said. "The results on the 'deposits'–"

"Yeah, yeah, go on," I prodded, still scanning the street for signs of a police presence, hoping the officer might simply have moved to a less conspicuous spot.

"The first results, the DNA kits, the comparative chemical analysis, all indicated that the specimen *had* to belong to a human being and that there was *no way* it came from your neighbor's dog. That much is certain."

"So?"

"Well this second series of tests, the ones that came through tonight, they ran them three times because they thought there was a mistake in the findings."

"Tom, spit it out!" I was losing my patience. I was actually thinking about calling the police to ask about the cruiser's whereabouts.

"The 'deposits' contained unusual types of bacteria, bacteria *never* found in humans. Aside from e-coli, there were other forms of fecal coliform bacteria and traces of salmonella and giardia–"

"Well, maybe the samples were cross-contaminated like you said. I mean I keep a clean yard but–"

"The conclusions were that it had been there long before leaving the intestinal tract of the animal that produced the samples."

"Animal?" I said, confused. "You mean the *person*? You said–"

"The samples *did* come from a person, a person whose excrement contains bacteria only found in certain animals, dogs, coyotes and wolves, to be precise."

"What?" I wasn't sure what to say. "Tom, this has to be some form of cross-contamination. No one is part human and part dog."

"Listen, Jack, I'm really worried. There's something wrong here. Is Joanna home? Is she all right?"

"She's sleeping. What–"

"Stay there," he said. "Is that cop still outside?"

"Not right now," I said, pulling open the blinds to check again. There was still no sign of the cruiser. "But he was there when I pulled up. He's probably on a coffee break."

"Well, I think we need to let the police in on this."

"Let them in on *what*?" I was scared, though I wasn't sure why. First there was Renko's murder, then my dream and now Tom going off full tilt. This was completely out of character for the usually calm, cool and collected 'Gospel' Tom Williams. And the idea of filling Detective Teschal in on things at this late date was not sitting well with me at all.

"Just stay there," Tom said firmly, almost desperately, his voice cracking over what I presumed to be the edge of panic, "I'll be–"

But before he could finish, there was an abrupt click and the line went completely dead.

Chapter Fifty

I stood in the darkness of my four seasons room, holding the receiver to my ear, calling Tom's name. But it was no use; the line was completely dead.

I turned the thing off, then on again, but still there was nothing. I cursed cordless phones and their temperamental batteries.

Panicky and unsure, Tom's worried tone still ringing in my head, my instinct was to check on the status of the missing police cruiser, which I found to be still missing. My next instinct was to check the cordless phone's cradle in the kitchen, just in case. If that failed, I could always try the land line in the cellar.

I opened the French doors, nearly tripping over Spooky, who was cringing and whimpering on the other side, and stepped over her as she scrambled into the four seasons' room while I headed for the kitchen.

I reached the wall cradle and, in the darkness, felt for the flash button, flicked it and put the receiver to my ear. There was no sound; the line was dead. I turned to try one last time, but something reached out of the shadows and took the receiver from my hand.

Leathery skin wrapped in coarse hairs brushed against my fingers and I released the handset and backed away, toward the bedroom where Joanna slept. I heard the dull click as the intruder set the handset down on the island and I realized my visitor was standing directly in front of the refrigerator.

"Who are you?" I hissed, trying to sound threatening but realizing with dread that there was more fear in my voice than anger.

The intruder uttered a low sobbing sound that sent my flesh crawling, and I took another step back toward the bedroom, stopping only after the doorframe bit into the back of my skull. The pain brightened my mind and sparked my courage and I asked my question again with a sharper edge of anger this time.

"Who are you?" I was confused as to why Joanna had not awakened and joined me in my confrontation. Then, through the deafening pounding of my heart, it occurred to me that Joanna was no longer in the bedroom.

"Don't you know?" A raspy voice laced with terrible familiarity drifted through the darkened kitchen. The cold thing in my stomach came wide-awake. Joanna was not in the bedroom; she was standing in front of me.

"What–?" I managed, tears stinging my eyes, my voice catching as if on a hook buried in my throat.

"Goodbye," she said, side-stepping my question, her voice growing raspier with each syllable, quickly losing any human quality.

She moved away and I watched a crooked shape with terribly long, bony limbs lope through the bars of diffused moonlight seeping in through the kitchen windows. I glimpsed its hide, dark and matted, its body all angles and knobby protrusions where joints should have been, moving with the awkward gait of a man walking on legs for the first time. There came a sound like twigs clicking against the tiles in the vicinity of the door. Then there was a skittering sound that reminded me of rats scurrying across concrete and the door to the service porch creaked open.

The cold sensation in my stomach turned sickly sour and I fought to keep the food I had eaten throughout the day down. The dark shape passed through the doorway to the service porch, a shadowy phantom of monstrous proportion. I heard the screen door open and shut and I stood frozen, my feet desperately clinging to the tiles like the roots of a dying tree clutching the earth as a hurricane tore mercilessly at its limbs. A terrible moment passed before the sound of breaking glass shattered my spell and, like a ghost, barely aware I was even moving, I passed through the kitchen door and crossed the service porch.

I gingerly pushed open the screen door, oblivious as to what I would do when I confronted Joanna, but realizing that I had to do something. In a cold sweat I stepped out onto the porch.

Shards of glass crackled beneath my sneakers, remnants of the porch light that had been shattered by Joanna, probably in an effort to conceal what was happening, to hide what she had become from prying eyes. I was about to call out to her, but the words died in my throat as my eyes lit on a second twisted shape lurking at the edge of the patio.

Chapter Fifty-One

The light of the Thunder moon, like molten metal, spilled into my yard, casting a blood-red pallor across everything it touched. The maple tree alone resisted the moon's power, casting instead a deep shadowy darkness of its own that reached like bony talons to the edge of the patio. There a hideous gargoyle crouched, strategically wrapping its twisted shape in the dense shadows, a terrible predator breaching the surface of a dark sea.

The breath fled my lungs and my heart hitched in my chest. My knees buckled and I leaned back against the screen door for support. I felt dizzy, sick, as if I had stepped off a cliff and was hovering above some dark abyss waiting for the inevitable plunge. But I was not dreaming. The vision was as real as the edge of a razor, and as deadly.

I had been teetering at the edge of my map of reason for days, daring myself to step off, flirting with the darkness. Now I had fallen off the map entirely, landing in some shadow-world, and my stalker had been revealed.

Part of me wanted to retreat, but I didn't. To the contrary, I found myself oddly astonished by what I saw and what I saw was the barest glimpse of a thing that must have spent its entire existence in darkness, a secretive creature that had somehow stolen across the fields of time and lore to make its way to the edge of my patio on this moon-drenched night.

I chided myself for having suspected Renko and his mangy dog of defiling my patch of land. I had been as wrong as it was possible to be, due to my inability to think beyond my chain link fence, beyond my own little world.

The eyes of the intruder impressed me the most, the mere sight of them driving a jagged shiver into my spine like a steel railroad spike, and I knew with cold certainty that I had seen them before. These had been the eyes watching me from the darkness beneath the maple tree as I stood on the steps trying to coax Spooky out of the service porch. They were unmistakable. Emeralds set against a palate of night, rat-like, intense, crystalline and alive with hellish green fire as if the thing were burning from within.

The face surrounding the eyes was lost to the shadows, and for that, I was grateful. But my own eyes refused to look away and continued to probe the darkness for details in spite of my mind's efforts to send me cringing into the house. My eyes traced the shadowy outline of the forelimbs, followed the sinewy lines down from the hunched shoulders to what might have been the knotty stumps of two small trees poking out of the lawn, lit only by a shaft of moonlight. But these were not the stumps of trees but hands, horrible, twisted, impossibly powerful hands with huge knobby knuckles bulging with fat worm-like veins.

Tom's scientific findings suddenly made perfect sense. The thing in my yard was part human *and* part animal, part dog or coyote or wolf, though it bore similarities to other creatures as well. Its limbs were thick and powerful like those of an ape, yet disproportionately long, like those of a monstrous spider. Tom had deduced the nature of my stalker all too well, though he could make no sense of his own conclusions. 'Gospel' Tom could not possibly have imagined the other half of the puzzle; whatever my visitor was, Joanna was one too.

I watched, transfixed, as my wife moved through the molten moonlight, becoming more comfortable with her newly acquired form with each step, until she reached the *other*. Then the pair coiled around each other like cats, their bodies intertwining, each emitting a deep, guttural purring that reminded me of big jungle cats: powerful, deadly.

I watched as the pair moved off into the yard. The smaller of the two, Joanna, looked back one last time, her eyes not as vivid as the other's, but evident nonetheless, flickering ever so briefly before the deep shadows beneath the maple tree claimed them entirely.

I waited, breathless, lost in the suddenly alien landscape of my own mind. What I was seeing was impossible. But the broken glass beneath my feet was real, as was the leathery skin that had caressed my hand in the kitchen. I was being forced to accept that what I was seeing *was* real.

There came a sound at the back of the yard, a faint chink of metal against metal. It was the sound of them vaulting the fence. A moment later I spied them crossing the field I had played baseball in as a boy, moving gracefully, like two wild things returning to a primeval forest, shadows, not human but not quite animal. Then they were gone, swallowed up by the night, and I found myself alone save for the silent, cloud-shrouded Thunder moon.

Blood Moon: **A moon with a distinct red hue often associated with blood.**

Chapter Fifty-Two

Stumbling, glass crunching beneath my feet, I struggled to brace myself against the screen door. My legs failed and I slid down until I found myself sitting on the top step with the cool metal surface of the screen door pressed against my back, the dewy dampness of the wood steps seeping into my clothes. The cloudy sky had turned to a burnt orange as the moon spread its bloody pallor across the heavens, and I became gradually aware of a sound, a distant yet intensifying sound mingling with the mechanical heart-beat thrumming of the gas station generator a block away. It was Spooky. I had failed to secure the French doors to the four seasons room, and she had made her way into the service porch and was whining and whimpering on the other side of the screen door.

Twisting my body, I reached up with trembling fingers and opened the door. Spooky squeezed through and wound her way across the top step, climbing into my lap and rising up on her haunches until she was pressed against my chest. She dug her claws into my shoulder, pressed her face into my throat, hugging me like a terrified child.

My senses kept telling me that the laws of nature had ceased to function on Cranberry Road. But rational thought, like a long-awaited sunrise, was creeping over the horizon of my mind, telling me that what I had seen was simply the imaginings of an overwrought, exhausted brain. Debates would have to wait; my first priority was Joanna.

Joanna had gone with our stalker, with Judd, or rather with the thing Judd had become. Whether she had gone willingly or unwillingly was irrelevant. I had to believe that the thing I had seen might harm her. It could have harmed me if it wanted; I suspected that Joanna had prevented that by simply accompanying it. But the most sobering piece of all was accepting the fact that I had just encountered Renko's killer, though what purpose lay hidden behind the murder of my neighbor was well beyond my grasp at that frantic moment. Then I remembered Teschal's words concerning a reported gunshot and everything fell into place.

Renko was unloading plywood from his truck when I saw him last, plywood he'd used to board up his broken garage window. This attempt by Renko to reclaim his property may have angered the intruder, who had already marked my property with excrement and urine. But to make matters worse, Renko had taken his rifle and, using one of his kitchen chairs to sit on, took up a vigil beside his garage, waiting with the gun in his lap for the intruder to return. And though I don't believe he'd gotten a good look at the thing, (he would surely have called the police if he had), I believe my neighbor heard it moving through the brush in his back yard and fired a warning shot that sealed his fate. Satisfied that he had frightened off the intruder, Renko had gone inside to celebrate with a few beers and some television.

This explained the two police officers poking around Renko's backyard the night of the murder. I mistakenly assumed they had been looking for footprints. What they had been searching for was the spent cartridge case. Then, furious over Renko's transgressions, Judd had returned and, under the cloak of darkness, killed my neighbor.

My mind began turning like a wheel, each spoke offering up a new angle to the mystery, a gruesome new possibility to be fathomed. The Fayre had visited many places this summer and summers past. I tried to imagine the bloody trail Judd might have left in his wake. How many unexplained disappearances? How many mangled bodies left in lonely out-of-the-way places? The vagrant in the woods near the Fayre grounds had surely been a victim as well.

Tom had unknowingly stated the facts when he said that something wicked had come to town with the Fayre. I had taken his overly-dramatic musings to be typically those of 'Gospel' Tom Williams, the result of an over-stimulated imagination with too much time on its hands, much as my own. But I had been wrong, *dead* wrong, and my mistake had finally revealed itself.

I looked to the moon as though I expected an answer to be written across its shrouded orange face and was reminded of an old saying that compared holding onto someone to holding onto moonlight. The words played over in my mind, forcing me to think about the wisdom contained in them, about the impossible nature of either task, and I thought how oddly appropriate they were suited to my present situation. I realized, too, how the slightest things can change the world irreparably. Then I heard thunder in the distance, and the rumblings in the sky freed me from my dark dream.

The world swam suddenly into focus and one fact crystallized in my mind: my wife was in terrible danger. Anyone who encountered Judd this night would be in grave danger. They were out there, crossing town, skulking through back alleys, through fields, moving like phantoms through the shadows. I had to do something.

I would need a weapon. I got to my feet and carried Spooky inside to search for one. I knew where I would find Judd if I hurried, and I was starting to realize what I would have to do when I did.

Chapter Fifty-Three

I put Spooky in the bedroom and began frantically ransacking the kitchen for a suitable knife. I didn't own a gun, never believed in them, but in my feverish state, I figured that a decent knife might at least serve as a deterrent once I met up with Judd. I found a good one in the drawer beside the stove, a sturdy one with an eight-inch blade made for slicing through roasts and vegetables. It struck me that it had, in fact, been the knife Joanna had been using to slice vegetables the night I found the first 'deposit'.

I slipped it from its plastic sheath, studied its broad blade and slid it back into its protective covering. I went to the door and stopped to consider Spooky, who was sitting in the bedroom doorway whimpering and shaking. I felt a terrible pang of remorse for her and tried to imagine what this situation would have been like if Joanna and I had children.

Another idea slipped into my brain as if it were an open mailbox, and I wondered if this condition my wife was suffering from was the reason she could not have children. I also had to consider the possibility that if Joanna *had* given birth, she might have passed along her horrible affliction and that she had simply made up the lie to forestall any potential discussion regarding the subject.

I squinted against the barrage of ideas assaulting my brain and tore open the door. There would be time to speculate later, if there was a later.

I closed and locked the door and headed for the back porch. I remembered the baseball bat I kept in the hatch of my car, the baseball bat I jokingly told Joanna I kept in case of 'close encounters,' a situation which had never materialized until tonight. I felt the knife in my hand and hoped that it, too, would remain unused.

I crossed the yard, carefully avoiding the patch of ground where Judd had stood, pushed open the door to the garage and flipped the switch for the bay door. I shook off a cobweb of fear that something might be lurking in the darkened garage and was less than completely relieved to find nothing waiting for me but my car. I wondered if I would ever feel comfortable in the dark again or whether I would always imagine that something was waiting just beyond the next shadow.

I opened the hatch to my car and made a hasty search for the baseball bat, which I found under an old New England Patriots sweatshirt Johanna kept there, and held the bat up to the light. The lettering on its shaft had faded with time, but the age-darkened wood still felt solid in my hand.

I closed the hatch, let myself in the driver's side and set the bat on the floor of the passenger side. I backed out hurriedly, nearly clipping the side of the bay. I reached the street, keeping an eye out for the police cruiser, which was still missing; it was clear I could expect no help from the authorities.

I hit the remote, closing the bay door, and sped off around the corner, past the cemetery with its leaning tombstones. Paying little heed to speed limits or stop signs, I soon found myself nearing the Fayre grounds. I repeatedly glanced at the knife on the seat beside me as if it might prove a mirage, silently hoping it would vanish and I would wake up. But there it remained, a grim reminder of what had happened thus far. And what still lay ahead.

My mobile phone beeped. I awkwardly plucked the thing from my belt, hoping against hopes that it was Joanna, who, having escaped from Judd, was calling to tell me where I could find her. My heart sank when I heard Tom's voice at the other end.

"Tom–" I began, but words failed me. In addition to my state of mind, the signal was bad; perhaps because I was jostling the receiver as I drove or due to the approaching storm.

"Something's wrong with your phone," he said through a layer of static. "I've been trying to reach you. Now listen, this is important. My friend from the morgue called me. He said your neighbor's body was torn to pieces. One of the responding EMTs told him it looked like a cyclone had gone through that place. It took time for the cops to find the head, which had been stuffed in a trash barrel in the kitchen. My friend also said that the vagrant found in the woods by the Fayre was in a similar state. Jack, we need to talk to the police right away–"

"Joanna's gone," I said, spitting the words out.

"Gone?"

"Something took her."

"What do you mean, *something took her?*"

"I don't have time to explain," I said, swerving to compensate for my reckless driving.

"Jack, whoever is doing this means business!" Tom said. "We absolutely need to let the police in on this. Now, I want you to stay put. I'll be right–"

I hit a pothole and the phone slipped from my hands and bounced across the seat. I reached down and grabbed it before it could travel further. Swerving, cursing, I put the phone to my ear, but found the signal to be broken and the line dead. I cursed again and tossed it into the back seat. This time Tom would have to fend for himself.

Chapter Fifty-Four

The Fayre grounds were drowning in darkness by the time I arrived. The rides had long since fallen silent, their neon lights extinguished, and the dust that had been kicked up in the wake of the crowd's exodus had settled back into the parched earth.

I drove past the main entrance, my headlights panning across the darkened security trailer. There was no sign of the security guard or his state trooper companion. It had never entered my mind to ask either of them for help and I had no idea what I could have said to secure their assistance, but their absence further reminded me of my solitude. Resigned to that fact, I left the empty trailer behind and made my way up the hill toward the cluster of derelict buildings.

I reached the main thoroughfare and drove past the central administration and hospital buildings, the cobblestones thudding beneath my tires. The darkness seemed sentient. The old buildings were brooding brick giants, the ruined benches and signposts the skeletal remains of long-dead animals. Night, somber and complete, had darkened the character of all that surrounded me, and the thickening cloud cover had all but eradicated any trace of light the huge pink moon might have provided.

I reached the big willow tree where I had seen the dead coyote, the police officer, and the teenagers. But there was nothing there now, only weeds, cracked curbstones and a litter of spent cigarettes.

I turned and drove through the night following the road as it sloped down to the staff parking lot as raindrops began to pelt my windshield. I killed the headlights, so as not to announce my arrival, and cautiously I picked my way through the murk. I pulled up behind the booth closest to the stage, the Voc Tech booth, now silent, and shut off the engine. Through the drizzle on my window, I could see that several of the trailers were missing, most likely on their way to the Fayre's next destination. Those that remained were steeped in darkness, their occupants either asleep or in town for one last hurrah before pulling up stakes.

I leaned back and closed my eyes, dreading what lay ahead. I listened to the drizzle striking the roof and my pulse pounding in my temples. Part of me wanted to lose myself in those sounds, to drown in them, to lay back in the darkness and sleep as I have never slept before. The child in me wanted to forget all that had happened, to retreat into a warm madness where evil things could not exist.

One more moment might have found me settling into that soft haze where reality and madness meet. But a clap of thunder shattered the mood and I opened my eyes with a start. My mind turned to Joanna. I saw her standing at the sink cutting vegetables, her back to me, her hair the color of night, and I knew I could never forget her, no matter how hard I tried. I reached over and picked up the knife. Then I opened the door and climbed out.

I stood for a moment with the rain falling around me. The night had settled into some dreamlike state, some surreal place where reality ceased to exist. The world around me seemed to stretch out into impossible distances, twisting into unimaginable angles where light bent as if trapped in a black hole. A fresh flurry of doubt lit in my brain and I wondered if I had in fact seen what I believed I had seen. Or had my mind slipped its gears? Was I really standing on the old state hospital grounds? Or was I at that moment strapped to a gurney in a psychiatric ward, Joanna at my side, holding my hand and begging me to return from the dark precipice to which my mind had dragged me?

I squeezed the handle of the knife. It was real. I struggled to convince myself that the rest *had* to be real. I had watched my wife change into some unimaginable

268

horror, and I had seen Judd crouching like a feral demon waiting to carry her away.

I raised my face to the rain. It felt real. I fought to shake off the confusion that was trying to steal away my will and started out across the lot, the raindrops tiny needles against my face. Time would answer all my questions, and time was wasting.

I passed our booth, empty and dark, and imagined Joanna appearing at the back door, smiling. I would love to have seen that. But that was an image left over from last summer, a ghost from a time when there were no worries, no fears, only Joanna and I and the warm days stretching out before us. This summer had turned out to be quite different.

I found myself close to the trailers and I could see the rain glistening on their smooth metallic skins. Something fluttered beside the dumpster, and for a fleeting second I imagined it was Judd lying in wait for me and I fumbled with the knife. A heavy sigh rattled my windpipe as I realized that what I had seen had been nothing more than the edge of a discarded cardboard box, flapping in the breeze.

Dowsed with a fresh dose of adrenaline, I pressed on, finally reaching the edge of the trailer park as the drizzle turned to rain. The police I had encountered earlier had gone, and I climbed over the rope barricade, unimpeded, and wound my way deeper into the rows of RVs. It occurred to me that I had not stopped to consider what I would do if Judd had packed up and gone.

My worries proved pointless because, after winding my way through the makeshift avenues, I found Judd's trailer right where I'd left it. I checked to see if the Chevelle was still behind the trailer, and found its black grill poking out like the snub nose of an old police revolver. Judd had not gone anywhere.

From the base of the step I could detect no sign of

life; there were no lights in any of the windows. It was then that I sensed something was wrong. Either Judd had misjudged me and simply assumed I'd stay away, or I'd caught him before he could escape with Joanna. But I also had to suspect a trap; perhaps Joanna had cooperated with Judd at the house, going with him willingly to buy my safety. But now that she was his, maybe he wanted me dead like Renko.

I climbed the step and reached for the door handle, the sheathed knife at my side. A sound crept from the trailer, the muffled sound of a woman crying out. Anger and fear forced my hand and I took hold of the handle and slowly pulled open the door.

The sounds of sex filled the trailer; moans and grunts emanating from some unknown source. I stepped into the darkened trailer, gingerly closing the door behind me. I remembered clearly the vicious-looking claws of the thing I had seen in my yard, the thing Judd had become, and I realized that surprise might prove my only ally, surprise and the sheathed blade in my trembling hand.

I scanned the deep shadows for movement, but all was still. My eyes swept to the right, past what appeared to be a kitchenette until they fell upon a darkened doorway. I took a tentative step forward, but something snagged my attention and I swung my gaze to the left, past a built in bench-seat with an oval-shaped table to a doorway which was emitting a coruscating light. Slowly I moved toward the door realizing that the flickering glow was coming from a television set, the sounds I'd heard that of a porn movie. I reached the doorway and peered inside.

The room smelled of grease and I suspected that it had once been a storage compartment now converted into a crude living room. At the far end of the room were several curved windows, each crudely draped with roughly cut fabric probably designed to serve as curtains which explained why I had not seen the glow from outside.

Secured to the outer wall and partly covering the innermost windows was a large flat screen television. And between me and the television was a beaten recliner.

I took another step forward, but my foot snagged on the edge of the rug, which appeared to have been hastily laid out during the room's conversion from storage bay to living room. I raised my eyes and my heart turned to ice. There was a hand draped over the arm of the recliner. Someone was sitting there.

I remained frozen to the spot, the rain dripping from my hair and face, watching, waiting for Judd to spin around in the recliner and confront me. My dream was coming true, but it wasn't Renko in the recliner, it was *Judd*.

A dozen heartbeats passed by and still nothing happened. Perhaps he was asleep or simply hadn't heard me, what with the racket from the television.

Stealthily, my heart thudding like a locomotive, I inched forward. I had covered half the distance between the door and the recliner when a squeaky floor betrayed my presence.

I froze. Again my dream was becoming reality. More heartbeats passed; still no movement, no response from the chair's occupant. Judd was toying with me, waiting for me to draw near so he could spring at me. I imagined him changing into the horrific thing I had seen in my yard and wondered how those claws would feel as they tore through my throat. The element of surprise was gone and I swallowed hard and squeezed the handle of the knife.

"Get up!" I said, my voice cracking around the edges. I waited a beat, wincing once when I mistook a change of scene on the television to be movement on Judd's part. But Judd was not moving. He remained seated, his back to me.

I moved closer, my palm sweating against the knife's handle. I slipped the plastic sheath from the blade and let it fall to the floor.

"Judd!" I called, my voice surprisingly firm, and I raised my foot and kicked the back of the recliner. Something unseen fell from the chair and landed with a thud. But the hand draped across the armrest remained motionless.

Judd was passed out, unconscious. Anger flared in my brain. I felt the knife in my hand and moved up beside the chair, where the glare of the television screen provided me with an irrevocable explanation as to why Judd had not reacted to my intrusion.

He was sitting upright in the recliner, his chest and stomach soaked in blood, his hands draped casually over the arms of the chair. The reason for all the blood was immediately evident as my eyes fell upon a knob of bone poking up from a bloody gash where Judd's throat should have been.

Repulsed and shocked, I fell backward, landing hard on the old rug. The knife fell from my hand and the back of my head collided with a series of shelves secured to the wall. Knick-knacks toppled and rained down on me. I turned to the blood-streaked television screen in time to watch a die-cast race car flop down on the rug beside Judd's lifeless face. I had dislodged the thing from its resting-place in Judd's lap when I kicked the recliner and now it lay on the floor, its dead eyes locked on mine.

I clapped my hand across my mouth to muffle my scream, pushed myself to my feet and stumbled for the door. I burst out into the night and slid down the step, landing hard on the wet ground. Rain assaulted my eyes and the thudding of thunder devoured the sound of my dry heaves. Judd was dead. But where was Joanna?

Possibilities like writhing snakes filled my brain and two facts rose to the top of the nest: there was a killer on the loose and Joanna was still missing. I needed to call the police and, more importantly, I needed to find Joanna.

I searched my belt loop with fumbling fingers for

my mobile phone, remembered tossing it into the back seat of my car, and laced my fingers across my face as I screamed in complete disgust at my ineptitude. A thought pierced my consciousness like a splinter piercing the skin. Judd might have a phone!

I turned to the Airstream's door, which had closed of its own accord, and realized that my time with Judd's mangled corpse was not over; I needed to go back inside to search for Joanna and to call the police.

Chapter Fifty-Five

I climbed the step to Judd's trailer on the weakest knees imaginable and pulled open the door. Dripping wet, I moved reluctantly into the room toward the recliner with its terrible cargo, in hopes that a phone might be somewhere in the vicinity. I discovered my knife lying on the floor beside the recliner and hesitantly picked it up. I searched the immediate area, but found no phone.

I moved back toward the doorway, running my fingers along the wall until they fell upon a switch. A dingy overhead light came alive granting me an unabated view of Judd's lifeless face staring up at me from its place by the television. The skin had been bled white and the face looked as if it had been fashioned from wax. The eyes were shriveled and sunken and the mouth hung open in a silent scream. The expression was more one of puzzlement than horror, as if whatever Judd had seen in the last moment of his life had amazed him. Remembering what I had seen in my back yard, I completely understood.

I turned away from the horrible exhibit and went to the kitchenette. Running my hands along the back-splash and counter top, searching for a light switch, I stumbled upon a mobile phone. I picked it up and punched in 911. I waited through one ring and listened as a woman told me I had reached the Gevaudan Police Department and that my call was being recorded.

"I need to speak with Detective Teschal," I said with as much authority as my breathless voice could muster.

"Detective Teschal is off duty," the woman said. "If this is an emergency–"

"It is," I said, interrupting her. "Someone's been murdered."

"I need your name and location, sir," the woman said, her voice becoming icily efficient.

"My name is Jack Graves," I said, immediately regretting having provided the dispatcher with my name. "Someone at the Summer Harvest Fayre has been killed."

"Are you on the scene, sir?"

"Yes," I said, growing impatient, realizing that each second I spent talking on the telephone was one second I could have spent searching for Joanna.

"He's in the silver Airstream trailer in the northwest corner of the trailer park," I said. "Hurry." I hung up. It was perhaps not the brightest thing I could have done, realizing immediately that my actions would seem suspicious, but I didn't care. Judd was dead; finding Joanna was the priority.

I headed toward the door at the far end, the only room I hadn't explored, suddenly unconcerned for my own safety, not caring if Judd's killer was lurking in the shadows.

The phone rang, doubtless the police calling back because the 911 call had ended abruptly.

I ignored the ringing and entered this new room, running my fingers along the wall in search of a light switch; finding one, I flicked it. The light revealed a cramped little chamber with a built-in bed. There were several curved windows encircling the bed that would not prove a sufficiently large enough escape route even for a child. But remembering my experience with Renko's garage window, I checked them anyway and found them to be locked.

I turned my attention to the bed which was strewn with clothes and disheveled blankets. Several pairs of work boots, rich with grime, lined the floor in the alleyway between bed and wall.

I turned suddenly when a flicker of movement startled me and found myself gazing into a wall-mounted wood-framed mirror. Tucked into the space between the

275

glass and the wood around the edge of the mirror were ticket stubs from tractor pulls, monster-truck shows and stock car races.

Relieved, I stepped outside the cluttered bedroom. Immediately to the right was a small bathroom plastered in a thick layer of grime and black mold. The medicine cabinet mirror was afflicted with a large crack that ran the height of the glass. I found myself staring into it, momentarily entranced by the way my face seemed to be split in two with the right side appearing to fall away into some unknown dimension. Something about the image made my stomach complain.

I withdrew from the bathroom and went back to the make-shift living room where Judd was reeking in his own gore. Through the bloody drippings on the television screen, I could make out the image of a woman, tied to a bed, being whipped by a heavy-set man in a black mask. The woman would let out a shrill, all-too-realistic shriek with each slash of the whip.

The flickering image was eating its way into my brain like a parasite, the woman's voice becoming that of Joanna. All the while, the phone kept on ringing. The oppressive heat of the trailer was making me sick, and I became conscious of an odor like rotting meat hanging in the air. I had to get out, get into the fresh air, and once again I broke for the door.

The rain had become steady and the air outside was nearly as warm and stifling as that in the trailer and did little to refresh me. I looked up into the torrent, my brain brimming with images of Joanna. I saw her lying at the bottom of a dark pit, her body broken and blood gushing from a wound in her throat.

I squeezed my eyes shut, desperately hoping to kill the vision. But it persisted, and I sat down on the steps, dropped the knife into the mud, and screamed into my palms. I felt helpless, lost. I had no idea if Joanna was still alive or if Judd's murderer had killed her. Then the final wound opened in my side as the worst scenario of all presented itself to me: what if Joanna had gone willingly? Had she been plotting all along to leave with this unknown lover from her past? Was Joanna's own plotting at the heart of the moodiness and the mysterious telephone calls? Her last words, telling me she would always love me, sounded in my brain like thunder. There had been remorse in those words, in her affect. I'd swear to it.

No. She had gone reluctantly, to save me, and I would find her.

I thought of the teenagers and the dead coyote, and I remembered something the security guard told me about homeless people using the old buildings as refuge. It was a logical place to start, if logic could be applied to this situation.

I looked toward the old buildings which rose, crag-like, on the hill above the Fayre grounds. Nearly three dozen of these structures dotted the tired landscape, if memory served, most of them boarded-up and dangerously in need of repair. Some few were still accessible, mostly those closest to the Fayre grounds; those that had been the last to shut down.

Judd's phone was ringing again and there was a sound rising in the distance: a siren. The police were coming. If I were to find Joanna alive, I would need to move quickly before the police arrived with their questions.

I found the knife, plucked it from the mud and got to my feet, the rain falling in my eyes. Something occurred to me then and I went back into Judd's trailer.

I went to the kitchenette where I ransacked some drawers, pushing aside eating utensils, stray tools, and old photographs, until I found what I needed. I shoved the small flashlight into my back pocket and headed back outside.

I trudged off through the descending curtain of

water, up the muddying slope toward the grove of trees and the buildings beyond. In the distance, the police siren grew louder. A fearsome dagger of lightning split the sky. I was halfway to the trees by the time the thunder arrived.

Chapter Fifty-Six

The branches of the trees caught most of the deluge before it reached me as I made my way up the hill toward the old willow. Breathless, I reached my destination and panned the light around. There was no trace of the coyote carcass; the animal control officers must have hauled it away as they had the previous one.

The screech of an approaching siren drew my attention and I killed the light and hugged the base of the old tree for cover, suddenly remembering too vividly the hazards of standing beneath trees during electrical storms. The smell of wet wood and earth enveloped me as I watched the flashing lights appear in the distance and move along the main service road far below. As if in response to the siren, a spattering of lights appeared in the trailer park. It was time to move.

Crouching low, I crossed the cobblestone street, my feet splashing through the deepening puddles. I passed beneath a cage-like archway that was slowly being consumed by rust and arrived at a formidable metal door in a similar state, set into the building's facade. I tried the handle, found the door to be unlocked and wrestled it open. Grimacing at the sound of the creaking hinges, I slipped into a small foyer.

The light revealed smooth, beige cinder block walls set off by strips of faded grout that had begun falling away long ago. The light also revealed a bank of dead fluorescent lights, dangling above me like rusted stalactites. A large bulletin board hung on one wall, its black-tracked face dotted with stray shreds of paper, reminding me of the decorative magnets adorning our refrigerator back home.

The light glinted off a wall switch beside the board and I flicked it. Nothing happened. The power was out, had been for years.

I made my way to the inner door, stepping over trash and beer cans. It seemed the security guard's stories of homeless people using the old buildings for shelter were true.

The inner door was as large and imposing as the outer one, with a square of reinforced glass set into the upper portion. I reached for the handle, but a strange grinding sound drifted down from above and I paused, instinctively casting the beam up into the blackness. It revealed nothing but the dead bank of lights and a prickly forest of peeling paint flakes sprouting from the water-stained ceiling. A fresh wave of thunder crashed around me and in its rippling aftermath, I managed to half-convince myself that the roiling atmosphere accounted for the mysterious sound as well.

Turning back to the inner door, I gripped its handle, but having learned my lesson twice this night, first with the creaking floor in Judd's trailer, and then with the outside door to this building, I gingerly pried open the door, just enough to squeeze through. Managing to contain most of the old hinges' complaints, I closed the thing behind me.

I found myself in a corridor that ran off in both directions. The glow of the light suggested that the building had been constructed in the shape of a cross, or cruciform as often described, a popular post-World War II design for institutions. I knew from my point of entry that the main junction would be situated farther to the right, and, using the light as my guide, I struck off toward the heart of the building.

Large wooden doors lined the darkened corridor, each featuring a placard in the upper portion stating what might be found within. Assistant Unit Director, Utility Closet, Director of Nurses. I lost track after the first few, but tried each knob in turn, finding each to be locked.

I reached the central junction, where I found an office to the right sealed off by a half-wall topped with a large pane of safety glass. I pressed my face against the glass and angled the beam so as not to cause its reflection to blind me, and peered into the room.

The space beyond the glass partition was crammed with desks and chairs stacked precariously from floor to ceiling. A placard on the wall at the back of the room told me I had found the Pelham West Central Nursing Office. A door set in the glass led into the office and I tried it. Like its predecessors, it proved to be locked.

I turned to consider the corridor that branched off to the left, away from the one I currently occupied, and stabbed the light at its shadowy depths. This corridor was wider and the doors lining it were larger.

I wiped rain and sweat from my face with my soaking sleeve and struggled with my options, realizing that time was ticking. I decided to try this main corridor and was about to proceed when something stirred back by the main entrance. I swung the light that way; it revealed nothing. I did, however, notice a large door leading into what looked to be a stairwell beyond the door that had granted me access to the building.

I listened for any indication of movement. Hearing only the distant rumble of thunder and the steady patter of rain, I decided against this new corridor and headed back toward the stairwell.

Retracing my steps, I moved beyond the main entrance past more doors, each locked, until I reached the door at the end of the corridor. As I'd guessed, the light revealed the word Stairwell.

Awkwardly holding the flashlight and the knife in one hand, I fumbled with the knob and pushed the door open. It moved easily at first, its hinges barely squealing, and through the opening I glimpsed a pitch-black void. Then abruptly the door refused to move any further.

I halted my efforts, cursing silently, waiting for the sound of something toppling over to break the stillness, or worse, a voice of complaint from some sleeping vagrant I had awakened. Neither materialized and I tried again. Still the door stuck, but I felt certain that a faulty mechanical device such as a damaged piston was not the cause of the problem. I was sure the obstacle was an object, some piece of furniture set in the stairwell for storage or to discourage visitors.

Determined, I put my shoulder to the door and pushed. Whatever was impeding my effort gave way. I tried again, and after some effort, I'd produced enough space for me to fit through. I shinnied into the stairwell.

Curious as to what had stalled my progress, I aimed the light at a dark mass lying behind the door.

At first I thought I was looking at a pile of clothes someone had used as a bed. But then I saw the blood, fresh blood, spattered across the floor and the wall.

I recoiled as if struck, backing away until the stair rail ground painfully into the small of my back. I managed to catch myself before tumbling down the stairs, but the flashlight was less fortunate. It slipped from my fingers and tumbled down into the gloom. It came to rest on the lower landing, its beam thankfully still alive, revealing the same beige cinder blocks I had seen in the foyer and the corridor. Cursing aloud, fighting back a need to vomit, and struggling to catch a lungful of stale hot air, I cautiously started down the stairs.

Arriving at the lower landing, I stooped down to retrieve the light. But while lifting it, the beam fell across the blanched, blood-streaked face of a young woman.

Shock and surprise drove themselves into my stomach like fists, and I stumbled backward, colliding with the cinder block wall. There I remained, trembling, the light illuminating my feet and the dusty floor. The image had left its imprint in my mind like a branding iron, an image that would haunt my dreams until my dying day. I envisioned the dead eyes staring at me, the mouth hanging open and the swollen tongue lolling to one side. Then it struck me: the face in the corner might be that of Joanna.

With trembling fingers I lifted the light until the beam lit upon the grisly thing, and a misplaced wave of relief washed over me; the face in the corner was *not* that of my missing wife. It was in fact that of a young girl, more precisely one of the teenagers I'd seen earlier that terrible evening, studying the dead coyote beneath the willow tree.

I crouched there in the dark, relief and remorse twisting through my heart like snakes. I studied the young face as if in a trance and felt the sting of tears.

Anger replaced my feelings of remorse and I steadied the light. The face was still horrific to behold, but it was no longer something to be feared; it was something to be pitied, and I inched forward, past the dead eyes and matted black hair and ashen skin, and climbed back up to the first floor landing. Outside, thunder boomed as if announcing my ascent.

Chapter Fifty-Seven

The air in the stairwell grew hotter and more oppressive with each step. More thunder bellowed overhead, causing the railing to rattle beneath my fingers. I moved past the dark shape lying behind the door to the first floor corridor and pressed on to the second floor landing, where I tried the big metal door. It was locked. There was no chance of breaking through, so I aimed the light upward and resumed my climb.

The heat had risen to the third floor stairwell and had gathered there in a suffocating knot; sweat dribbled down my face and along my back as I was borne into it. A wedge of thunder split the air above the building, closer than ever, sounding like a bomb being detonated on the roof, and the stairwell shook. I waited for the rumbling to subside, then made my way up the final steps to the topmost landing and tried the big metal door. The latch clicked and I hauled the thing open.

A strong breeze riffled past me; somehow, the outside world had gained access to this floor. There was a sound like running water in the distance.

The flashlight beam traced its way down a long corridor, illuminating what appeared to be a large rotunda at the intersection of the arms of the crucifix. I stepped into the corridor and tried to close the door behind me, but found it wouldn't close all the way; it was as if the metal frame had shifted over the years and would no longer accommodate the door. I left it as it was and proceeded.

There were more doors lining this corridor, and, as before, I tried each in turn, finding each locked, until I reached the last door before the rotunda, which I found to be ajar. What appeared to be the flickering glow of a candle was visible within. My mouth was suddenly as dry as Death Valley. I inched closer, knife at the ready, the flashlight beam pooling on the floor at my feet so as not to startle anyone lurking inside. I gently nudged the door open. The candlelight played across the placard in the upper portion of the door as it receded into the coruscating gloom, allowing me to decipher the words: Aversive Therapy.

The door ground to a halt and I stood transfixed, my eyes adjusting to the flickering light within the office. Furniture was piled everywhere. The rain was falling torrentially beyond the barred and partially boarded-up window, filling the room with a terrible drumming sound. In the center of the room sat a large wooden spool; the sort telephone lines are coiled around. Squatting in its center was the melted remnant of a smoldering black candle, the dying flame the source of the glow. Shelves lined the walls, each layered with hospital supplies, unidentifiable pieces of small equipment wrapped in old plastic, stacks of hospital scrubs, small cardboard boxes.

I moved deeper into the room and the flesh on the back of my neck began to crawl. Instinctively I turned and aimed the light into the darkness behind the door and the air fled my lungs.

A second body, this one that of a teenage boy, sat propped in the corner of the room. Its legs were akimbo and its lifeless hands were lying in its lap, framing its severed head.

A wave of dizziness washed over me, and I stumbled into the corridor. I pressed my back against the cool cinder block wall and fought to squelch my roiling stomach. I had barely stopped gagging when a deep thud jolted my frayed nerves. I swung the light toward the stairwell, anticipating the worse. But instead of the beam revealing some horrible apparition bearing down on me, it glinted harmlessly off the stairwell door, which had apparently settled properly into its disused frame. I would have felt foolish, but I was too terrified to feel much of anything.

Another sound found me, a thudding that seemed to emanate from the rotunda. I swung the light that way and watched for signs of movement. Lightning must have flashed at that instant because the rotunda and the portion of corridor that intersected it were suddenly bathed in a vivid white light. A deafening report of thunder followed.

Grimly determined, I started forward, but paused when I realized that the floor was wet and getting wetter. I proceeded, conscious of my footing, the water deepening with each step. I reached the end of the corridor and, lowering the beam so as not to draw unwanted attention, peered around the corner into the rotunda.

The space was rectangular in shape, some forty feet wide and at least as deep, its walls comprised of the same shiny beige cinder blocks that lined the rest of the building. Perhaps a dozen doors lined the perimeter, each large and imposing, each closed. I swung the light upward until it revealed four huge pyramid-shaped skylights arching up into the night sky, each lined with panes of reinforced glass crudely patched with black caulking to keep out the rain. Years of neglect had taken their toll, however, and water was liberally pouring in through cracked panes, turning the whole of the rotunda into a giant waterfall and the floor below into a roiling sea, complete with an archipelago of ruined furniture.

Thunder and lightning split the night, tossing shadowy shapes in each direction, freezing the water as if in a strobe light and making the whole scene appear surreal. The flash also revealed that I was alone.

I moved forward, hugging the nearest wall, my feet sloshing through the water. I reached the first door, marked Janitorial Supplies, and routinely reached for the knob to determine if it was locked. My fingers brushed against a jumble of keys dangling from the lock and, as if bitten by a snake, I pulled my hand away. I sensed movement within the closet, a stirring, as if the jangling of the keys had awakened something. I thought of Joanna. Could she be locked inside?

Cautiously I pressed my ear to the metal and was about to call her name when something inside the closet collided with the door with such force that the doorframe shuddered and I fell to the floor. The knife skidded from my hand and I scrambled for it. I felt the handle slide further away into the turbid water. The door shuddered again, more forcefully this time, and I aimed the light into the heart of the commotion.

Whatever was locked inside crashed into the door a third time and the metal frame shifted in its housing. The keys shook in the lock, working their way out of the knob. The flashlight beam found its way to a slatted metal grating in the lower portion of the door. Whoever was in the closet must have seen the beam of light pass through the slats and, before I could switch the thing off or even turn it aside, the grating exploded in a shower of twisted metal.

I covered my face as ruined slats bounced off my arms, then looked up to see what remained of the venting break away from the door as a terrible, twisted hand clawed at the grate's remaining edging. Long, lean fingers held together by huge knobby joints layered in dark wet coarse hair tore gouges into the metal and clamored across the soaking floor. All the while, a terrible sound, a mixture of wailing and unearthly growling, rose up from within the closet. This was the sound Roger Trimble had heard, the sound that had driven him to call the police, a sound he had described as being neither man nor dog but something in between.

The hand withdrew and another great thud rattled the doorframe. The door inched further away from the masonry and the keys shook again, sliding farther out of the lock. Another jolt shook the door and a large crease appeared in the upper portion of the metal. *Could* it be

287

Joanna locked inside, trapped in the form of the thing I had seen in the kitchen? Had she, in fact, been the one who killed Judd? Could she have locked herself in the closet somehow to protect me from the thing she had become?

But Joanna wouldn't hurt me. She couldn't!

Another jolt rocked the door. The keys slipped from the lock and plunked down into the water, near the base of the door. And, as if sensing the keys were no longer in the lock, the thing in the closet fell silent.

"Joanna!" I shouted.

The hand broke from the spent grill again, clamoring around on the floor, searching for the keys. The thing's claws brushed against them and they skittered away. The hand paused, sensing its objective was near. If I could get the keys, I could free Joanna. She wouldn't harm me. I was sure of it and I was willing to bet my life on it.

I lunged forward to grab for the keys, but the hand cut me off, bumping the keys again and pushing them farther aside.

"Joanna, wait!" I cried.

The hand froze as if its owner recognized my voice and slowly pulled back into the vent. Tenuously, my heart thudding wildly, I leaned forward and extended my hand. My fingers were inches from the keys; I could see them glistening beneath the water before the beam of the flashlight.

"I've almost got them," I said.

Suddenly something was in front of me, some dark shape that seemed to appear as if out of nowhere, and I drew back with a start, dropping the flashlight into the water and watching its beam wink out. I barely made out the shape before me kicking the keys aside and I heard the metallic jingle as they flew off into the darkness. Then someone was leaning over me and I heard a familiar voice pierce the din of the rushing water.

"Take my hand!" Joanna shouted. "Now!"

288

Chapter Fifty-Eight

Turning aside my shock, I reached out and took my wife's hand. I struggled to my feet and together we ran toward the corridor, thunder and lightning exploding all around us. Behind us, the rotunda echoed with the unearthly wail of the thing in the closet as it bellowed and howled in inhuman rage. The sound of the closet door disintegrating joined with the echoing thunderclaps and falling water as we made for the stairwell. We had barely pushed the stairwell door open when the deafening sound of metal crashing to the ground filled the corridor and I knew the thing was free.

Joanna and I tumbled into darkness, she leading me down the stairs, me following blindly, trusting her instincts. We reached the first floor and Joanna tightened her grip on my hand, signaling me to slow my pace while she led me past the corpse behind the door. Then we exploded into the first floor corridor, running at full tilt to the front door and out into the night.

The rain was torrential and lightning erupted around us. By the time the thunderclaps caught up with the vivid streaks of electricity, we had passed beyond the sweeping arms of the willow tree and were running down the hill toward the staff parking lot.

We crossed the muddy lot, water sloshing around us, rain and wind tearing at our faces. My clothes were soaked through and the blue hospital scrubs Joanna was wearing were equally drenched. I glanced down at her feet, realized she was barefoot.

"Don't stop!" she yelled.

I didn't.

We reached my car and I fumbled for my keys. I, dropped them, bent to retrieve them, cursing, found them, and slipped them awkwardly into the lock. I climbed in the driver's side and Joanna tumbled into the back seat. I struggled with the keys again, slid them into the ignition on the third try and turned the engine over. I dropped the car into reverse, peeled backward through the mud and slammed it into drive. The car lurched forward, thick rivulets of mud splattering against the windshield and side windows.

"Hang on!" I yelled as I pushed the accelerator to the floor.

I veered toward the exit road, the car fishtailing through the mud. Reaching it, I spun the wheel to the left, nearly flipping us over, and swerved onto the road. I had traveled less than sixty feet when two sets of headlights appeared, the second topped off by flashing blue LEDs.

I pounded the brakes, slammed the car into park and climbed out into the storm. Both cars came to screeching halts in front of me and I watched three dark shapes emerge from the gloom. I could tell from their posture that weapons were trained on me. I threw my hands up and began spouting what must have sounded like pure gibberish.

"Just freeze!" Detective Teschal shouted. In a second, both she and another officer were standing before me, their weapons drawn but lowered; their dark-colored raincoats flapping in the gale. Another officer was running around to the far side of my car.

"My wife is hurt," I said, managing to sound intelligible.

Teschal gestured for the officer at her side to investigate. He ran around me and tore open the back door to my car.

"She's unconscious," the officer yelled above the din.

"Call an ambulance," Teschal said, and the officer closed the door and ran back to the cruiser. At the same instant the second officer appeared from the far side of my car and shook his head, apparently satisfied that there was no one else in the car.

Teschal holstered her gun.

"What the hell are you doing here, Mr. Graves?" she growled. "And what happened to your wife?'

Chapter Fifty-Nine

S tanding in the rain, I realized that time was crucial, but if I told Teschal all I knew, all I'd seen, she was likely to put the cuffs on me and pack me off to the nearest psychiatric hospital, or at the very least, the nearest police station. So I quickly conjured a tale that would, hopefully, explain the scene she had stumbled upon, carefully choosing the most necessary, more believable points.

"My wife had forgotten to check the inventory in the booth," I said. "She insisted on coming back out here. So I dropped her off and was heading to Dunkin' Doughnuts to get some coffees when she called me on her mobile phone and told me she'd been attacked."

"Attacked? How?" Teschal's voice was harsh, angry.

"She said someone was hiding in the booth. She got away, ran to one of the buildings and called me on her mobile."

"Did you call the police?"

"I dropped my mobile phone somewhere and thought that if I stopped to look for it, I might be too late."

She paused, soaking my words in with the rain. "I understand you reported a dead body in one of these trailers."

"Yes," I said, growing impatient. "Detective, I'll tell you everything, but the man responsible is in *that* building up there."

Teschal's gaze shifted from me to the dark outline of the Pelham West building, then back to me. I wasn't sure whether I saw doubt or amazement in those steel-blue eyes. Perhaps both.

"Joanna locked him in a closet, but he was practically free by the time I found her."

"Let's get your wife's side of the story," Teschal said and she led me to the back of my vehicle, where the third police officer was leaning into the back seat taking Joanna's pulse and trying to rouse her.

"Well?" Teschal said.

"Still unconscious," the man said, shaking his head and wiping rain from his face. "Her pulse is strong, but she's unresponsive."

"All right, Abrams," she said, "Malick is calling for an ambulance. Stay with her until it arrives. Make sure she gets off okay and then get your ass up to that building." She pointed at the grim structure atop the hill and the officer nodded.

Teschal turned to me. "Where's the dead body you reported?"

"There are three," I said, wincing, and I watched her face turn to stone. "There's a man named Judd; he's in a silver Airstream in the trailer park. I made the call from there. Then there are two dead teenagers in the building up there."

Teschal looked to Abrams, whose face betrayed his confusion, then both turned to study me.

"I'm not crazy," I said.

"No offense, Mr. Graves, but the jury is still out."

She turned and waved to Officer Malick, who emerged from the police cruiser and joined us at the side of my car.

"Ambulance is on its way," he said.

"Good," Teschal said. "Do you know what an Airstream trailer looks like?"

"I think so–"

"It's rounded and silver-skinned, aluminum," I said. "It's the only one like that and there's a black muscle car, a Chevelle, parked behind it."

Malick nodded. "Okay."

"You'll find it in the back corner of the trailer park,

293

under a big oak tree."

"Go check it out," Teschal said, her voice riddled with impatience. "Mr. Graves says there's a dead body inside. Call me as soon as you check."

Malick nodded, looked at me as if I was something the cat had dragged in, and jogged off into the rain toward the trailers.

Teschal turned to me. "Let's go, Mr. Graves."

I started to protest but she cut me off.

"Your wife is in good hands," she said, "and I need you to show me the way. Something weird is going on and you seem to be at the center of it all."

I glanced at Joanna's motionless form, then into Officer Abrams' face.

"I'll take good care of her, sir," he said and I believed him.

"We need to go now, Mr. Graves," Teschal prompted and I reluctantly followed her to her car.

Chapter Sixty

Teschal ushered me into her SUV and we drove through the back of the staff lot. The smell of the well-appointed leather was a sharp contrast to my 'wet dog' odor. I was out of my element in every possible way.

She killed the lights and we parked beside the building, a dozen yards or so from the big willow. We proceeded on foot, taking up position beside a rotting picnic table beneath a tattered canvas awning that was attached to the building some yards from the main entrance.

"Your story about coming out here with your wife is a little thin, Mr. Graves," she said.

"Thin?" I echoed, an ice chip rubbing against my heart.

She studied the metal cage archway above the entrance to the Pelham building.

"Enough, Mr. Graves," she said, turning on me, her voice edged with broken glass. "Why *did* you come out here tonight?"

I felt trapped. I had to tell her something, but how could I tell her what I had really seen, about the thing that had taken Joanna, about the terrible transformation my wife had undergone? The answer was simple: I couldn't. If Teschal hauled me in for questioning, I wouldn't be able to protect Joanna, and I knew that with the thing I'd seen on the loose, Joanna was not safe. It had come for her after all these years. It would surely return, perhaps not tonight or the next, but some night soon.

At the same time, Teschal was no fool; I knew I had to tell her something, *anything* to keep her guessing at just what the truth might be.

I opened my mouth to speak, but the radio clipped to Teschal's belt came alive at that moment, sparing me.

"What have you got?" she said, scooping the thing up.

"Malick here," a voice said through a thin wall of static. "The story checks out."

"Roger that," she said, her face as grim as death, her eyes locked on mine. "Call Abrams; have him call for another ambulance and lots of backup. State police too; this is their turf. And find the carnival owner or manager or whoever the hell is in charge down there and wake him up."

"Roger that. Out," Malick said.

Teschal switched the thing off and clipped it to her belt, her steel-blue eyes never leaving mine.

"Well, Mr. Graves, it seems this situation is getting darker every minute. I think you and I will be having a very serious talk later. Just now I have to see what's in that building," she said, producing a small flashlight from her jacket pocket. "You don't need to come, but I don't like leaving you here and you know the way."

"I'll come with you," I said.

She nodded slowly.

Shivering, my clothes soaked, I watched Teschal draw her weapon and start for the entrance. I hesitated, my heart suddenly thudding like a sledgehammer over the thought of paying another visit to the Pelham West building. I looked back at the Fayre grounds below. The rides looked like broken tombstones silhouetted against the cloudy sky, the Ferris wheel a huge spider's web. The storm had ebbed and the sky was beginning to clear. I could make out the moon's orange shape muted behind the clouds and the image made me shiver.

Reluctantly I moved out from beneath the shelter of the awning and followed Teschal toward the entrance to the Pelham West building.

Chapter Sixty-One

We reached the entrance to the building and Teschal led me through the caged archway to the big metal door. She pulled it open, ignoring its complaining hinges, and stepped inside. I watched the glow of her light sweep around the small foyer, then her hand appeared, ghost-like, beckoning for me to follow.

"Which way?" she whispered, shrugging off her raincoat and tossing it in the corner of the foyer.

"That way," I said, pointing.

She nodded and we set off, Teschal in the lead, me a few paces behind. We had gone less than ten feet when something shifted somewhere above us. Teschal stabbed the light at the water-stained ceiling. A distant clap of thunder broke the silence and she cast me a worried look.

"It's not too late for you to turn back," she said.

"I'm all right," I said, lying.

She looked me over, pausing long enough to consider my trembling hands, which I conspicuously shoved into my pockets.

"Cold," I said, shivering almost intentionally.

The glint of worry I'd seen faded and a slight grin touched Teschal's lips. She made for the stairwell, the beam of the flashlight skimming along the smooth cinder block walls.

"Which floor?"

"Third," I said. "The second is locked."

Teschal seemed to chew on this fact for a moment before pushing the door open.

"The first body is wedged behind the door," I said, lending my shoulder to the effort.

The door opened enough for her to squeeze through and she turned and told me to wait. Then she closed the door and I was left alone in the dark. I heard her moving in the stairwell. More thunder boomed; the storm was moving away from us. Then I heard something else, something that might have been footsteps. I looked warily back at the entrance, but the darkness had closed in behind me. If something was lurking back there, I would never see it until it was too late. The footsteps, or whatever they'd been, faded and then there was only the rain.

The door opened suddenly, much wider than before and I realized that Teschal had moved the body farther into the stairwell.

"It's clear," she said, and I felt like a child following the lead of an overly-cautious parent.

"The rest is down there," I said stepping through the doorway.

"I saw," she replied flatly.

"Shouldn't we do something?" My stomach was complaining again. It was the heat and the darkness wrapping around me.

Teschal detected my suffering and she cast the light at me.

"Mr. Graves, you need to calm down or this won't work."

I nodded and struggled to gather my wits. I closed my eyes and concentrated, telling myself to relax. A moment passed and I sensed my heart slowing, my breathing returning to some semblance of normalcy.

"What about the body?"

"This is like finding an unconscious person," Teschal said, lowering the light. "First you make sure the area is safe. Then you intervene. In this case, intervention is useless. My job now is to make sure no one else ends up dead."

Realizing the cold logic of her words, I nodded briskly.

"Do you think you can continue?"

"Yes." My legs felt weak and thoughts of the

impending climb proved daunting.

"Good," she said, before leading the way up the stairs.

I found myself staring down into the darkness. I was unable to see the woman's remains, but I could still sense her dead eyes watching me.

We climbed through the shadows, pausing at the second floor landing to try the door, which was still locked, and waited a moment when we heard a sound like metal scraping against metal drift down from above. We exchanged glances, hers born from curiosity, mine almost certainly laced with fear, before continuing upward.

We reached the third floor landing and Teschal paused at the door where, for a fleeting second, I thought I saw doubt in her posture. But when I realized she was checking to make sure her radio had been switched off, I knew I'd been wrong. She tried the door knob. It turned freely.

"The door sticks," I said. "It doesn't close too well and falls back into place after a few minutes."

She nodded and whispered that I should stand back. I obeyed.

The door opened with a dull scraping sound and I realized that at least one of the sounds we'd heard on our way up the stairs was the sound of this door opening or closing. A deep chill passed through my spine and Teschal cast me a look of genuine concern, realizing herself that someone was fully aware that we were here.

She nodded and stepped into the corridor, the gun drawn. I followed. She was moving quickly, the element of surprise no longer ours. She tried each doorknob as she progressed until she reached the door marked Aversive Therapy. I had left the door nearly wide open; now it was barely ajar. I started to warn her, but she seemed already aware. Slowly, she pushed the door open, then vanished inside. I moved forward, taking up a flanking position

299

beside the door, feeling useless. She emerged suddenly and the expression on her face was deadly serious.

"Where's the closet?"

I pointed to the rotunda. She raised the gun and started off, moving quickly through the inch-deep water. She reached the rotunda seconds before I did, raised her weapon and moved briskly around the corner. I waited a beat, then moved closer, peering after her.

The torrential waterfall had slowed to a trickle and pale bars of diffused moonlight were cascading through the ruined skylights. Teschal was standing in front of the closet bathed in one of those bars of moonlight. I moved up beside her.

The closet door was lying in a shattered heap. Some of the metal doorframe hung twisted from its mounting. Teschal aimed the light into the closet. It revealed bent and twisted metal shelving.

She panned the light across the door, which was now resting a few feet from the doorway with the inner side facing up. Deep gouges were visible in the metal. I was reminded of the dream about Renko and the gouges in my garage shingles. I also remembered the claws of the thing I had seen at the edge of my lawn and then again as it broke through the grating in the closet door. I closed my eyes, trying desperately not to imagine what those hands could do to Joanna now that she had angered it. Or what they could do to me.

"Mr. Graves," Teschal said softly as she slowly turned in a circle, the beam of the flashlight piercing each shadow, "I have no idea what's going on here, but one thing is clear: this is no place for you." Her eyes found mine. "We will *definitely* be talking later, but just now I want you out of here."

I started to speak but she raised a finger to silence me as she drew the radio from her belt and switched it on.

"Malick, Abrams," she said. "What's your

location?"

"On the first floor," a voice said.

"Stairwell is to the left at the end of the corridor. I'm on the third floor. I'm sending Mr. Graves down. Is the unit outside?"

"Affirmative," the voice said.

"One of you is to escort Mr. Graves to the unit and see him safely inside. He's not under arrest, but I am very concerned about his safety and about our suspect's whereabouts."

"Roger that," the voice said. "State police are on their way and local units are securing the trailer. Mrs. Graves is away to Mercy General."

"Good," Teschal said. "I need one of you up here. I'm sending Graves down."

"Roger that."

"Get out of here, Mr. Graves," she said.

I didn't wait for her to tell me twice.

Chapter Sixty-Two

I reached the stairwell just as the door burst open and Officer Malick emerged. He looked startled, his eyes opening wide, his hand dropping to his holstered pistol.

"Mr. Graves," he said, quickly assessing things, "my partner is waiting for you downstairs."

I walked past Malick into the stairwell. I heard him talking into his radio, telling Abrams I was heading down. Then the door behind me closed and I was alone in the darkened stairwell. A beam of light appeared, beacon-like, rising out of the gloom. It was Abrams aiming a light up from the first floor landing.

I started down and found him squatting beside the body, which Teschal had moved into the far corner near the base of the stairs.

"Sir," Abrams said, rising to his feet as I arrived, "I'm to accompany you to the cruiser."

I nodded, breathing heavily, not about to argue. The heat was bearing down on me again. I followed Abrams down the corridor to the front door.

The rain had stopped by the time we reached the road, and Abrams led me to a black-and-white unit parked beneath the big willow tree across the street, precisely where I'd seen the teenagers studying the dead coyote. He opened the back door and ushered me inside.

"Now, Mr. Graves," he said, flipping the child-proof catch in the door's leading edge, "we can't leave you locked in, so this will allow the door release to function. But I'd advise you to remain here." He started to close the door. "As a matter of fact, sir," he said, holding the door open and leaning close enough that I smelled coffee on his breath, "I insist." He paused, letting his words sink in, then stepped back, shut the door, and disappeared into the building.

I sat back, breathing deeply, closing my eyes. Exhaustion was waiting to claim me, but I knew that no sedative could make me sleep; sleep would have to wait until this was over. I thought of Joanna; I could see her standing at the kitchen sink cutting vegetables, the sunlight on her tanned shoulders.

The radio in the dashboard crackled and the whoop of an approaching siren rose up in the distance. Abrams said Joanna was being taken to Mercy General. I thought of using my mobile phone to check on her but remembered I'd left it in my car. I listened to the last few raindrops as they struck the roof of the cruiser. The world was spinning out of control. Five people were dead and my wife was at the heart of it all. I still had no idea why. I had suspected Judd, with good reason. But that theory was as dead as he was.

The radio crackled again. The siren was closer, but I didn't think it had made it onto the grounds yet. I looked to the old building with its few non-boarded up windows like dark eyes, watching me. A man's voice broke through the static.

"Anything?" The voice was ragged as if out of breath or scared.

I leaned sideways, my ear pressed against the metal grill partition that separated the back seat from the front, straining to hear through the crackle.

"Down to the left," another man said, "back door."

Then the static consumed everything and I turned to the window. The building known as Pelham West was shrouded in a grim silence, an impossible contradiction to what was happening within its rotted walls. Then something, some stone or bit of wood, fell from the roof and bounced off the metal archway. My eyes were immediately drawn upward to the perceived source and, through the rivulets of water tracing their way down the window glass I glimpsed a crooked figure crouching at the

303

roof's edge.

I strained to see better, pressing my forehead firmly against the cool glass, but the figure was gone.

I pushed at the door, but it refused to budge. I remembered Abrams releasing the child-proof lock in the leading edge of the door. Or at least I remember him *saying* he released it. Perhaps he hadn't completed the motion? Perhaps the thing was faulty? Or maybe he wanted to make sure I stayed put and had only *pretended* to release it. And with the door closed it was impossible for me to reach the switch.

I was growing frantic. I tried the door again with no luck. I had to warn Teschal before the thing got away. I felt my breathing growing heavy. I glanced hurriedly around the darkened back seat then up at the side window.

"Jesus," I heard myself saying as I realized what I had to do.

I flopped down onto my back and, using my outstretched arms and hands to brace myself against the opposite door, I kicked at the glass with all the force I could muster. The glass splintered but remained intact. I braced myself, kicked again, harder, shouting some primordial rage and the glass fell to pieces.

I clamored up onto my knees and, using my sleeve, brushed as much residual glass away from the frame as I could. Then I shinnied through the ruined window. I stumbled out onto the cobbled road and leaned back against the car, craning my neck to see the roof of the building. But the figure was nowhere in sight.

"Where are you?" The muffled voice from the radio was drowned out by a screeching wail of static.

"Heading down," someone said, "north stairwell." Then the static devoured everything again.

I struggled to get a grip on my bearings. I was standing outside the main entrance, at the southernmost part of the building. The voices' owners were heading north, heading down. They were going the wrong way!

I had to warn Teschal. I tried the driver's side door but found it to be locked. I could climb back into the rear seat but the metal grill would prevent me from accessing the radio.

My head was spinning. If the killer escaped, he would find Joanna. I began searching for a stone with which to break the window, but there was nothing.

I heard the radio through the glass, a series of frantic garbled sounds. Sirens in the distance were growing louder. There was no time to wait.

I headed for the building entrance, determined to beat every existing record for climbing three flights of stairs, but as I reached the door I glimpsed something I had missed. The nose of a car was poking out from behind the adjacent building.

Relieved, I ran toward the car. I reached the vehicle; it was the security guard's from the front gate.

It was impossible to tell if anyone was inside because the windows were thick with rainy rivulets and fog. I imagined the guard, sneaking a nap or eating his supper, the ear buds to an MP3 player securely tucked into place, completely unaware of what was transpiring a hundred feet from his location.

Desperately I pounded my fists on the hood.

"Hey," I said. "It's me, the doughnut guy."

Perhaps he had been recruited by Teschal and was at that moment guiding Malick and Abrams through the guts of the Pelham West building. But the car should have a radio!

The vehicle was parked too close to the building for me to access the driver's side door, so I ran around to the passenger side. I tore open the door and, spouting what must have amounted to panicky babble, stuck my head into the car's broiling innards.

My ranting abruptly ended when I saw the mangled

body of the security guard slumped over the wheel. In a split second, my senses registered the entire grisly scene, the streaks of blood, the head drooping forward, suspended by bloody cords, the eyes half-closed, the swollen tongue poking from between the ruined teeth.

Caught up in an uncontrollable knee-jerk response, I drove myself backward with explosive force, cracking my head on the door jamb and spilling out onto the wet asphalt.

In a single powerful motion I raised my foot and kicked the door shut. I pushed myself to my feet, my palms stinging from where they'd scraped the asphalt, my fingers finding the spattering of blood at the back of my skull, barely conscious of the fact that I was muttering something incoherent. And in the middle of all the horror, one thought kept pounding at my brain: I had to warn Teschal! The thing had to be stopped before it could escape, before it could find Joanna.

Still probing the jagged tear in my scalp, I sensed myself running toward the building as if on borrowed legs, then around to the front and through the main entrance. By the time I fully regained my senses, I was in the darkened corridor, running toward the stairs.

Chapter Sixty-Three

I burst through the door to the stairwell and started up through the oppressive heat, taking the steps two at a time. I reached the second floor stairway, picking my way through the darkness, using the rail as a guide, and continued my ascent. I stopped just before the third floor landing to catch my breath and, amidst the rumbling thunder and impenetrable darkness, sensed someone move past me.

I froze, my heart pounding, sweat washing liberally down my spine, listening intently for audible evidence of an unseen trespasser, but the only sounds I could detect were those of my labored breathing and the distant grumbling of thunder. The rational part of my brain told me I had imagined it. Perhaps the logical portion of my brain was right. Perhaps the only other thing in the stairwell was my imagination. Perhaps.

Shaking off the eerie sensation, I found the door to the third floor and hauled it open. I started down the empty corridor, past the office where I'd found the corpse and continued on to the rotunda. The waterfall had ceased; all that remained were a few thin trickles at the corners of the skylights. My eyes were immediately drawn to the far corner of the rotunda where I spied an open door nestled in a small alcove. I was certain no doors had been open earlier.

I crossed the rotunda, sidestepping the wrecked furniture keeping distance between me and the ruined closet. Still my eyes were drawn to the darkened space and, for a fleeting second, I imagined the glint of eyes returning my gaze from the shadows. Chilled, I bolted for the door in the corner but as I was about to breach the doorway two figures suddenly appeared.

"Jesus!" Abrams growled, raising his gun and

pointing it heavenward. "I almost–" His words trailed off and I realized that the man had come very close to shooting me.

"You were supposed to stay in the car, Mr. Graves!" Malick barked as he moved past me into the rotunda.

"Malick," Teschal called over his radio and, scowling at me, the man hit the talk button.

"Graves is here," he said.

"Tell him–" Teschal said, sounding as angry as a wasp. "Never mind," she said. "I think we missed our man."

"Roger that," Malick said.

Abrams cursed and tucked his weapon into its holster.

"Wait," I breathed. "You can't give up."

I must have struck a nerve because Malick's eyes turned red as flame and he grabbed me by the upper arm and pulled me close.

"Listen, Mr. Graves," he began his tone acidic. Abrams put a hand on the man's shoulder and Malick released me.

"Sir," Abrams said as Malick stalked away from me, toward the corridor, his shoulders shaking as if he was ranting silently, "we understand your concern, but the perpetrator is gone."

I sighed and shook my head. "You don't under–"

"Yes sir, I think I *do* understand," he said. He leaned in close; he smelled like a wet dog, as did I. "We'll find him. Now I think you should come with me. Detective Teschal is downstairs and she wants to have a word with you."

I nodded. "You checked the roof–"

"Thoroughly," Abrams broke in. "There's nothing up there."

I nodded and when the man headed for the stairs, I

followed. I glanced back at the door that led to the roof, then up at the skylight. I half-expected to see the *thing* glaring down at me from behind the broken glass, grinning. But all I saw was my old friend, the Thunder Moon, peeking out from behind the clouds.

Chapter Sixty-Four

The lobby of the building was bustling with police activity by the time I reached it. Large battery-operated work lights were being erected everywhere. Some local officers from Wickham, Bridgton, and Gevaudan had arrived as well as some state police, looking somehow taller and more official in their black slickers and broad-brimmed plastic-wrapped hats. They all eyed me with a degree of curiosity and suspicion as Abrams led me past. I was not one of them and therefore automatically suspect.

What I presumed to be the remains of the young woman from the stairwell was now lying on a sheet-draped gurney pushed against one wall, where a young blonde woman wearing the familiar navy-blue attire of an EMT was making notes on some clipboard-mounted forms. Two more EMTs emerged from the clutch of police officers and rushed past me carrying their kits, presumably heading to the third floor to claim the other body.

Abrams gestured with his jaw that I proceed to the glassed-in office at the heart of the building. I passed Malick, who was still scowling; he turned away as I walked past.

I entered the office and found Teschal leaning against one of the old metal desks, her arms crossed, a badge hanging around her neck. She was wearing a navy blue track suit with a light jacket. Her hair was plastered to her head and face. Her boots and legs were coated with mud. A set of portable lights stood off to one side casting heavy shadows against the wall. I could only imagine how bad I looked just then. She reached back, plucked a towel from the desk top and tossed it to me. I began toweling my hair.

"Close the door," she said and I obeyed.

The place was full of stacked furniture, some of which had been hastily shoved aside to create a makeshift office space.

"Mr. Graves, we have six bodies on our hands," Teschal said, her steel blue eyes unwavering.

"You found the security guard," I said, draping the towel around my neck.

She cocked her head.

"That's what I was coming to tell you," I said.

"I see."

"And I think I saw the thing on the roof–"

"Thing?" she said.

"I mean the person who killed those people and attacked my wife."

She nodded slowly, her eyes focusing on mine. I wanted to look away but didn't dare. Teschal might perceive such an action as a sign of guilt or perhaps weakness.

"The perp got away," she said. "We never got a look at him and we don't know how he escaped. Any ideas?"

"There are trees at the back and north side of the building," I offered.

"A leap from the roof?" Teschal said. "Risky. Even under the best conditions."

"Desperation makes us do strange things."

"Indeed?"

I tossed the towel aside.

"Description?"

"I didn't get a look at him."

"Mr. Graves, did your wife know her attacker?"

Some aspect of my demeanor must have shifted, because Teschal nodded as if some elusive piece of information had just fallen within her grasp.

"So that's it," she said.

I felt suddenly exhausted beyond imagining and I

slumped down into a tattered vinyl chair by the door.

"Why don't you tell me everything, Mr. Graves? While there's still time."

I leaned forward, running my fingers through my damp hair, then wiping my palms on the towel. She had known from the start I'd been hiding something, as I suspected she had. I had to tell her at least part of what had happened. The situation had gotten quite beyond anything Tom and I could handle. Six people were dead. Joanna was in danger as well as anyone who got in the thing's way.

"Mr. Graves?"

"Several years ago," I began, starting at the beginning, "shortly after we were married, my wife and I began receiving strange phone calls."

Teschal frowned. "Go on."

"The calls were always at night. The line would stay open for a few seconds, just long enough for me to realize that there was someone listening on the other end. And then that someone would hang up. The caller ID listed the call as private, so there was no way to trace it. Anyway, they eventually stopped."

"How many calls, would you say?"

I shrugged, not remembering clearly. "I must have answered at least a dozen. I couldn't speak for my wife; she told me about a few."

"Did you believe her?"

My head snapped up.

"Perhaps the caller spoke with her and she kept it from you."

I shook my head after hearing Teschal suggest something I had suspected. "I don't know if the caller spoke with her."

Teschal nodded.

"Anyway, they stopped after a while. Then, a few days ago, I started to suspect that someone was watching my house, mostly from the back yard and maybe up in the trees. And Renko, the man who was murdered next door, told me that someone had broken a window in his garage. When he showed me, I realized you could see my house perfectly, see *us*, Joanna and me, through one of the windows from inside his garage."

"What did your wife think of all this?"

I shook my head. "I didn't tell Joanna about any of this. I suppose I didn't want to worry her. You see, I have a friend, 'Gospel'–" I cleared my throat. "Tom Williams–"

"I'll need an address," she said cutting me off.

"Yes," I said, resignedly. "He was helping me look into it."

"Look into it? Is he a licensed private investigator?"

"No," I said, stumbling around in my own head over how to explain the part about the 'deposits.' Teschal saved me the trouble.

"What indications did you find to suggest that someone was stalking you?"

I laughed unintentionally.

"Something funny here I've missed?"

I looked her square in the eye. "No," I said flatly, "nothing funny at all. The intruder had … defecated and urinated in my yard. I thought it was Renko's dog, and I brought Tom in to analyze it."

"Is he a forensic specialist?" Teschal's frown deepened.

"He's a chemical engineer. He's good at this sort of thing, analyzing pools and lawns."

"Pools and lawns. And his findings were …?"

There was a trace of contempt in Teschal's voice, as if she considered Tom's efforts to be far less than adequate. I suppose they were, in her eyes.

"He said that based on the chemical analysis and DNA test kits, it had been a human being that had left the specimen," I said. "And then it happened again, also human." I sat back, drained, feeling like a fool, but not fool

313

enough to tell Teschal about the canine bacteria Tom's tests had uncovered. Or what I'd seen.

"Why didn't you contact the police?"

I shrugged hopelessly. "I thought it was Renko's dog at first. Then I figured some kids were playing a sick joke. Then when Renko turned up dead..."

There was a knock at the door and Abrams appeared.

"Excuse me, Detective," he said, glancing from Teschal to me and then back again as if wondering how much he should divulge.

"Thrill me," Teschal said, sounding agitated.

"We found it," Abrams said.

"Good," Teschal said. "I've got something to show you, Mr. Graves."

Chapter Sixty-Five

Abrams led Teschal and me down the main corridor toward the back of the building, past several doors that opened into shadowy rooms crammed with stacks of furniture illuminated sporadically by the shafts of numerous flashlight beams as officers searched. Someone found the circuit breakers at that moment because several banks of fluorescent lights flickered to life.

"I see someone got the power turned back on," Teschal noted.

"Down here," Abrams said, leading us past a heavy-set police officer guarding a large metal door. The man eyed me with the routine suspicion I had come to expect before stepping aside to let us pass.

Abrams pushed open the big door, which complained loudly, and we entered a dimly lit stairwell. The air inside was dead and hot. We proceeded down past two landings, each lacking a door, until the stairs petered out and we found ourselves in a plain concrete chamber replete with a yellow and black fallout shelter emblem on the wall. A tall, lanky police officer with a hard face emerged from the shadows and led us to a large metal door that might have been borrowed from a World War II battleship.

"Where does this lead?" Teschal asked.

"State put a call into the Department of Mental Health," Abrams said, panning his light across the big door, "see if they still have blueprints." The beam revealed a series of deep gouges in the metal surface not unlike those I'd seen on the closet door in the rotunda. Then he focused the light on a large badly bent hasp hanging from the doorframe.

"There's a whole system of tunnels down here under the buildings," Abrams continued. "They were used to transport pay to the workers. It was also a way to move residents and staff around from building to building when the weather was bad. Or at least that's how the stories go."

"Are these tunnels safe?" Teschal asked, pushing past Abrams and running her fingers along the door's scarred metal.

"Don't know," the other officer said. His voice was deeper than his lean form suggested. "Nobody comes down here anymore, except maybe transients. But it's a sure bet our guy knows his way around." He pointed to the ruined hasp. "Transients didn't do that."

"Are the other entrances locked?" Abrams said.

"Sure," the officer said. "Just like this one."

The officer took hold of the door and hauled it open. It made a deafening grinding sound that echoed through the chamber.

"He might be hiding in one of the tunnels or in another building," Abrams said, as the officer pushed the door back until it clanged against the concrete wall.

"Or he might be miles away by now," Teschal said, stepping into the entranceway and aiming her light into the shadows.

From where I stood, at the base of the stairs, I could see smooth concrete walls, rich with green scum, and a dark muddied floor. A few stubborn roots, having punched their way through the concrete ceiling, hung down like skeletal fingers grasping at the shadows. Beyond the beam of light was only thick and impenetrable darkness.

"Dogs?" Teschal said.

"They're on the way," Abrams said before sighing. "But the smells down here..." He let his words trail off and sniffed the air. "Does anyone smell smoke?"

Teschal sniffed at the air. "All I smell is sewer," she said, before turning to look at me.

"Mr. Graves, we have a lot of work to do here and I don't need you in the way. I know how to find you if I need you. Don't leave town, but I suppose with your wife in the hospital, that wouldn't be likely."

I felt like a child who was being scolded for something I hadn't done, and my thoughts turned to Joanna.

"Abrams," Teschal said, "escort Mr. Graves to his vehicle and see him safely away."

Abrams nodded.

Teschal turned back to me. "This isn't over, Mr. Graves." Her words were firm, grim. "I'll be in touch."

Abrams followed me up the stairs, and I glanced back once to find Teschal glaring at me from beside the open door. Then I was out of her reach, and I found myself back in the main corridor following Abrams toward the intersecting point of the cruciform.

We reached the junction, where a stocky gruff-looking man wearing a dark-colored jogging suit was having words with an African-American police officer. I recognized the man immediately, though this was the closest to him I had ever been.

"This is bullshit!" Vern Cross growled as I approached. "We got a show to set up in two days at the other end of the state."

Cross turned my way, and I saw his face clearly for the first time. He was nearly bald; all that remained of his hair was a laurel wreath of gray strands that hung nearly to his sloping shoulders. His stomach hung down generously over his worn belt and the fleshy folds beneath his chin seemed endless. He shoved a chewed-down cigar between his stained teeth and considered me with cold, deep-set eyes that were practically devoid of color. A feeling of dread washed over me and I turned away, following Abrams toward the door. I felt those icy chips on my back, glaring at me each step of the way. The sensation lingered until I'd left the building.

The sky was clearing by the time Abrams and I

317

reached the cobblestone lane and the bloated moon was becoming visible, emerging from the wispy remnants of the storm. I noticed the flickering red lights of an ambulance behind the next building, near the spot where I'd seen the security guard's car. There were also several police vehicles, both state and local, parked at the side of the building, near Teschal's SUV. The air smelled of dampness, and I thought I smelled a wood stove in the distance, an odor I usually associated with Christmas. But tonight it made me think of darker things.

"Something you want to tell me Mr. Graves?" Abrams said as he considered the police cruiser's ruined window.

"The door wouldn't open," I said sheepishly. "I had to get out."

Just then a large blue van with the words Bridgton Police K-9 Patrol stenciled in gold lettering on the door pulled in and parked behind the cruiser. Several uniformed officers debarked and began offloading some large, fearsome-looking German shepherds from the bay doors. One of the dogs paused to consider me, the red light from the ambulance playing across its dark eyes, and I thought of Rufus.

The handler gave the dog's leash a tug and led it toward the building's main entrance. All the dogs were suddenly whining and shifting nervously as their handlers tried to lead them across the road; it was as if something was frightening them. It's said that dogs are more sensitive to strange occurrences, impending natural disasters and such, than are humans. I couldn't help but wonder what those dogs were experiencing. And I wondered if, like me, they were afraid.

Chapter Sixty-Six

Abrams and I walked in silence past the big willow with its swaying tendrils, through the grove of trees, down the hill and across the muddy flats past the trailer park, where several of the occupants were milling around in their respective front yards. I felt many eyes studying me as I passed.

"Hang that dirty fuck!" someone growled from the nearest clutch of people.

"Shut up!" a woman with a gravelly voice hissed, making me think of Marge Weems. "Mind your goddamned business."

I glanced at Abrams, who was behaving as if he hadn't heard a thing.

We passed the staff bathrooms and moved along behind the darkened booths through the slop that had once been solid earth to where my car was parked. Several police cruisers were parked along the edge of the dirt road that led into the Fayre, some state, some local, LEDs flashing. Flashlight beams were slicing through the murky underbrush at the edge of the woods across the street. The search, it appeared, was on in full force.

Another cruiser moved slowly along the road heading west, its lights joining with the others, turning the dark trees into malevolent phantoms with jagged talons. Somewhere in the distance, I heard the sound of a helicopter moving through the murky sky. As I suspected from the first, Teschal was leaving no stone un-turned.

Standing numb beside my car, I searched my pockets for my keys, fought off a twinge of panic when I failed to find them before remembering I'd left them in the ignition.

Devoid of even an ounce of energy, I climbed into my car on legs that might have belonged to another man for all the sensation left in them. My wet clothes clung to my body like a second skin, one that was two sizes too big. My shoes were filled with mud and my body ached. But I had accomplished my goal; Joanna was safe, at least for the time being. The problem was keeping her that way, and myself as well.

Starting my car, my eyes scanned the endless stretch of woods sprawling beyond the Fayre grounds along the opposite side of the access road, sensing that my feelings of relief might be short lived. The killer was out there somewhere. Several steps ahead of me from the beginning, he was now eluding the police as well. And Joanna had worked her way to the top of his list because of what she had done, because she had betrayed him by locking him in that closet, because she had chosen *me*.

I thought about calling Tom and decided to wait until I got home, or maybe until morning. The clock in my car read eleven thirty-seven. It felt like four AM.

I glanced over my shoulder at the back seat where, earlier, Joanna had collapsed. There was nothing there but shadow, and the cold empty darkness drove a thorn of apprehension deep into my soul.

I lowered my window and started to say something to Abrams, but the words never quite took shape. Abrams evidently detected my disorientation and approached the driver's side window. He set his thick forearms on the top of the door and leaned close.

"Your wife was doing better when the ambulance took her," he said. "She asked for you. She's at Mercy General; that was the closest. You know how to get there?"

I nodded but never managed to bring myself to meet the man's gaze. I suspected he blamed me for everything that had happened; they all did. Especially Teschal. Perhaps if she had met up with the thing I'd seen, she might feel differently.

I finally opened my mouth to speak, but a scream

rose up from the direction of the trailer park.

Abrams spun around. The reason for the scream was immediately evident.

Our position at the edge of the staff parking lot granted us an excellent view of the first few buildings squatting atop the hill, their gothic steeple-like edifices rising above the trees. I knew the main administration building was situated to the right of the Pelham building and recognized its tall church-like spire silhouetted perfectly against the once darkened night sky, a sky that was now alive with the undulating glow of a huge fire.

"Jesus!" Abrams hissed as he fished for his radio, found it and flicked the talk button. "This is Abrams, we've got a fire, Goddamn it!"

His words had barely passed his lips when a dull whooshing sound filled the night and the dry old structure of whatever was burning behind the administration building seemed to collapse in upon itself, throwing sparks, tongues of flame and thick black smoke billowing high into the sky. Abrams' radio crackled and a screech of static-rich voices responded.

Abrams, now fully engrossed with the fire that had, in all likelihood, been the result of either the newly activated power surging through a damaged power line or the thing I had seen covering its escape, stepped back and frantically waved me on as he barked into his radio. I slipped the car into gear and drove off, the stench of what I'd thought to be a wood stove now pungent and overwhelming.

I raised my window, sealing out the burnt offerings, and wound my way out of the staff parking lot onto the main access road, moving past the police cruisers lining the lane, flashlight beams stabbing at me from the brush by the side of the road as their shadowy owners considered me with well-warranted suspicion, flashing lights acting like multiple strobes adding layers of chaos to insanity. The last thing I noticed in my rearview mirror was the Ferris wheel looking like a huge spider web silhouetted against both the angry burning sky and the glowing face of the Thunder moon. In the distance I heard the wail of approaching sirens.

Chapter Sixty-Seven

I drove through the night wrapped in a blanket of sheer exhaustion, my eyes powered by nervous energy, darting from shadow to shadow, sensing fleeting movement where there was none, in search of a monster. It was possible that the thing was hiding somewhere on the state hospital grounds, holed up in a forgotten stretch of tunnel or in some dingy corner of one of the abandoned buildings, watching the police activity through the slats of a boarded-up window, waiting for the growing conflagration to draw them away, providing it with an avenue of escape. That seemed possible, even likely. I just couldn't help but study the shadows as I drove, just in case. I wondered if Teschal had arranged for police protection for Joanna and realized that amidst the confusion, I had neglected to ask.

I stopped at a red light and gazed dazedly into the empty intersection. The hospital was another two miles away. I grew impatient and decided to run the light. I had barely started forward when a small black sports coupe sped through the intersection and I slammed on the brake.

One of the occupants yelled an obscenity, pegging a finger and a burning cigarette in my direction. I sat there, my heart pounding, watching taillights fade into the distance. I thought that if I could have gotten my hands on that kid right then, I might have killed him. I felt my eyes well up with tears and I was very grateful that the car hadn't stopped. I was not myself; my rational brain had gone to sleep. The bare nerve that remained was running on a steady diet of pure adrenaline.

The light turned green, and I proceeded through the empty intersection as the tears began.

After a few blocks, the tears dried up. I dragged my sleeve across my swollen eyes and choked back what remained of my boiling emotions. The night was not over; Joanna needed me to keep control. And for her sake as well as my own, I would do just that.

The houses I passed were mostly dark, but a few windows glowed with the flickering life of television sets. It was Saturday night. People were nestled on couches, eating popcorn, drinking beer, perhaps making love or wrapping up dinner parties that had run late. But I was doing none of these things; I was going to visit my wife in the hospital, hoping desperately that her kidnapper was not waiting somewhere along the way.

Mercy General became visible in the distance, rising above the trees like a prosaic ancient citadel. The Thunder moon was hovering above it, apparently unwilling to leave before the grisly show was over.

I veered into a curving drive with a lighted sign that read Visitors and Emergency Walk In. I followed the road, which wound up the hill toward the hospital. The sign for Visitor Parking sent me to the left, down to a vacant lot nearly surrounded by trees. I pulled in beneath a street lamp and warily considered the dark enveloping woods.

I climbed out of the car and proceeded up the hill toward the main entrance. The night seemed impossibly still; it was as if everything that called the night its home was waiting for something to happen. The pungent aroma of smoke was everywhere reminding me of October, of Halloween, but this was July and not a trick or treat in sight.

The sound of a twig snapping shattered the eerie silence and I spun around, but there was nothing there. At least nothing I could see. I continued on, my pace quickening with each step, my pulse racing. By the time I reached the ambulance debarking zone, I was jogging.

I crossed beneath the overhang that covered the main entrance to the hospital and paused long enough to consider the woods below. The sky beyond was aglow.

Leaving the eerie scene behind, I passed through the automatic doors.

The vivid antiseptic light of the lobby stung my eyes as I crossed the empty waiting room. At the far end was an information desk behind which sat an elderly man. He looked up from his crossword puzzle, lowered his reading glasses. A small television set occupied a shelf behind him, its tiny screen flickering with the images of a sports wrap-up program.

"Yes, sir?" he said as I approached.

"I'm here to see my wife, Joanna Graves," I said, my voice faltering.

"Graves," the man said and, after chewing on nothing in particular for a moment, he turned to a computer terminal and began pecking away at the keyboard. A moment passed. "Is she a new admittance?"

"Yes, tonight," I said. "She was brought in by ambulance."

"Here we are," he said. "She's in the ICU. Bit late but, under the circumstances, it shouldn't be an issue. Now, you go down this corridor and you'll see two elevators on the left and two on the right. The ones on the left go to the fourth floor, that's the ICU. The other two are closed for repairs."

I thanked him and headed into the corridor.

"Remember, fourth floor," he called after me.

I found the elevators with no trouble, hit the button and waited. I was amazed at how quiet the place was; I guessed business was slow. The corridor ahead of me was lighted for another thirty feet or so. Beyond that point there was only darkness. Doubtless an energy-saving move, but it reminded me of the tunnel beneath the Pelham building and I began to wonder if someone might be watching me from the gloom. I gazed into the darkened corridor, picking out stray bits of medical equipment lining the walls, Gurneys, IV poles and other items; I was searching for the specks of

325

light I'd seen beneath my maple tree that dark night, so long ago. All the while, my mind was calculating how long it should take for an elevator to descend a few floors.

I was studying the numbers above the elevator doors, willing the number one to brighten, when some pin-drop of a sound drew my attention and I peered hard into the blackness, my heart thudding against my ribs.

The light above the elevator door pinged, startling me, and when the doors finally opened, I anxiously stepped inside. I hit the key marked 4 several times until the doors slid into place, sealing out the eerie feeling that lurked in the corridor beyond. The elevator lurched to life, then began to rise and I breathed a sigh of relief.

I listened to the sound of the mechanical winch lifting me through the elevator shaft, trying not to think of what I would find on the fourth floor. Would Joanna be conscious? Would she be able or willing to explain?

The elevator came to a halt, the doors parted and I found myself in a short, stark corridor. At the end hung a pair of swinging doors with stainless steel handles and matching kick plates. The place reminded me of a morgue I'd seen on television. I walked the length of the corridor, dreading each echoing footstep, touched the automatic pad with the wheelchair insignia and stood back as the doors swung slowly open.

The ICU was dimly lit and comprised of glass enclosed cubicles that served as patients' rooms, its hub a nursing station where a few women in scrubs were gathered. A middle-aged woman with a ruddy complexion and dark hair pulled back into a short ponytail considered me from above her bifocals as she typed at a portable computer terminal.

"Can I help you?"

Before I could speak, a short, stocky police officer appeared from around a corner and studied me with stern gray eyes.

"Joanna Graves is my wife," I said.

The nurse moved from behind the desk studying me dubiously, glancing at the officer as if waiting for his approval. Then she stepped aside as a younger nurse with shoulder-length blonde hair took her place. The officer took a step closer as the blonde nurse approached.

"We need to see some identification," she said, and in less than a heartbeat the officer was at her side.

I fumbled for my wallet and managed to produce my driver's license with less effort than I'd anticipated. I handed it to the nurse who offered it to the officer. He studied it before nodding his head. He handed it back to me and I slipped it back into my wallet.

"This way," the nurse said, leading me past the nursing station and halfway around the ICU, the officer hovering a few feet behind us. We reached a room marked Number Twelve. The chamber was sparsely lit and a faded white curtain had been drawn nearly all the way across the reinforced glass wall preventing me from seeing inside.

"She's here," the nurse said, leading me into the dimly-lit space.

The chamber was perhaps eight feet by twelve. A large window filled the wall directly across from the door. The curtains were drawn back and I could see part of the roof below where large air conditioning units hummed, filling the room with a dull thrumming sound like the gas station generator near my house. Beyond this there was only the parking lot and the distant trees silhouetted by the glow of the state hospital fire. Above it all was the luminous red face of the Thunder Moon.

"The radio says it's one of the buildings at the state hospital that's on fire," the nurse said, pointing to the orange-streaked horizon. "They won't say how it started, though."

I grunted a response as I turned to consider the rest of the room. To the left was an elaborate bed with raised

327

safety rails. Joanna lay sleeping, a sprig of tubes running from her left wrist to a bottle hanging from an IV rack attached to the wall above the head of the bed.

"Dextrose and fluids," the nurse affirmed. "She was dehydrated. SOP. Not to worry."

I moved around to the far side of the bed where I practically collapsed into an orange metal chair that sat beside the night stand.

"Dr. Chalmers is the physician," the nurse said, her voice sounding empathetic. "She'll be along in a minute."

I leaned closer, my chin resting against the cool metal safety railing. "Joanna," I whispered.

"She's been sedated," the nurse said.

The officer must have figured he'd seen enough and left the doorway, where he'd been leaning against the jamb. I watched him take up position in a chair in the hall by the nursing station, where he retrieved a newspaper from the floor and resumed reading.

I turned back to Joanna, reaching out to touch her hand below the place where the IV's protruded from her flesh. Her skin was cool. I remembered how feverish she'd felt in our bedroom earlier, before the *change*. I whispered, "I love you." That was when I noticed the bruising on her forearm.

I leaned closer to get a better look. The room's dim lighting had concealed it initially, but now that my eyes were adjusting I could plainly see deep purple bruises running along Joanna's forearm. The damage didn't stop there.

Attached to the wall above the bed was a gooseneck lamp. I reached up and flicked the switch and swung it over so that its beam spread across Joanna's upper body. Bruises were visible everywhere, running along her forearms, across her face, especially around her eyes and jaw line and down along her throat. She looked as if she'd been in a car wreck. The cold thing that had plagued my stomach since

328

the discovery of the first 'deposit' awoke.

"Please, Mr. Graves!" the nurse, who had been watching from the doorway, protested.

"What happened to her?" I asked, my voice sounding like breaking china.

"Sir," the nurse complained, moving around to the far side of the bed and swinging the light away.

"What happened to my wife?" I said, anger sprouting in my voice.

"Sir, if you'll wait–"

"No," I said my fingers tightening on the bed rail. "Tell me what happened to my wife?"

"Sir–"

The officer looked up from his newspaper.

"Mr. Graves."

I turned to the doorway where a thin, raven-haired Indian woman stood with her hands buried in the pockets of a white lab coat.

"Mr. Graves, I'm Dr. Chalmers," the woman said. "Your wife is resting comfortably, I assure you. But there are things you need to know. And I would be glad to speak with you in my office."

Chapter Sixty-Eight

I followed Dr. Chalmers down a corridor that ran between the nursing station and more glass-enclosed rooms. The other chambers were empty.

"Quiet night," she said. "Two patients were downgraded earlier; moved down to the second floor. Your wife is our only guest."

Chalmers turned into an abrupt little corridor with a window that looked out over a parking lot. Adjacent to the window at a right angle to the outer wall was a door with the words Stairwell and Emergency Exit stenciled across its upper third. Opposite the stairwell was a cramped little office.

"Please come in, Mr. Graves."

Chalmers made me feel surprisingly at ease by sitting in a vinyl and metal chair set in front of a utilitarian desk. Relieved to get off my feet, I took up a seat opposite her. My legs were wobbly and the hard plastic chair felt wonderful.

Chalmers reached behind her and took a chart from the top of her desk, which, like the office itself, was practically devoid of any personal touches. She took a pair of glasses draped about her neck on a beaded string, set them on the bridge of her nose and proceeded to read from the chart.

"Your wife has undergone a trauma of unknown origin," she said, and my heart skipped a beat.

"Unknown? But–"

Chalmers raised her slender fingers to calm me.

"Just wait," she said her voice low and soothing, in sharp contrast to mine, which was riddled with panic and fear.

"She was semi-conscious when she arrived, but responsive. She asked for you several times."

"Why is she sedated?"

"A precaution; she was quite agitated. The bruising is what concerned us. We ran some x-rays, but they were negative." She scanned the chart with her finger. "The x-rays did reveal what appears to be extensive effusion, swelling, but we'll need an MRI to confirm that. All her vital signs are good, but she is suffering from exhaustion and dehydration and that was part of the reason why we sedated her."

"So what caused the bruising and swelling?" A dark, unwelcome idea had crept into my head.

"Who is your wife's primary care physician?"

"Um, Dr. Ackers at West Grove Clinic," I said. "Why?"

"We will need to see her records, find out about any medical history."

I nodded realizing I should have known this.

"Do you know of anything that we might need to address at this time? Allergies? Asthma? Special conditions such as diabetes? The clinic is closed for the night, but we may be able to reach a physician on call."

"No." I shrugged. "Joanna's always been healthy. She sprained her ankle a few years ago and complained of back pain last year, but other than colds and bouts of flu, she's been fine."

Chalmers nodded slowly and let her eyes scan the chart.

"Where was your wife born?"

"She's from a town in Oregon called Claudoch, though I've never been there. I didn't know her before eight years ago."

"Does she have any children either by you or anyone else?"

"No," I said, snapping unintentionally, then immediately regretting it and apologizing. I wasn't angry with Chalmers; it was simply that her questions had begun to open doors, doors that had always been there, doors that I had deliberately kept closed.

Joanna rarely talked about her past, only to say that her parents were dead and her relatives were scattered to the four points of the compass. It had never struck me as particularly odd that Joanna maintained no contact with them. But, sitting in Dr. Chalmers' cramped little office, trying to answer her questions, I was beginning to realize just how little I really knew about my wife and that fact was beginning to gnaw at me.

Chalmers sighed. "Mr. Graves, I need you to sign some forms so that I can perform further tests. The bruising may be nothing but blunt trauma or mildly inflamed muscles, but, due to its extensive nature… Well, I need to rule certain things out."

"Things like what?"

Chalmers pursed her lips. "Auto-immune diseases and skin cancer for starters, not that the bruising resembles any I've ever seen, but we need to be sure. A woman your wife's age should have regular exams."

I nodded in full agreement. Chalmers considered me for a long moment, then got to her feet.

"I will have the nurse bring you the forms to sign in your wife's room and we can get started in the morning." She placed a lithe hand on my shoulder and squeezed gently. "We will do everything possible for your wife, I assure you, Mr. Graves. Would you like to spend the night here?"

I looked into Chalmers' dark eyes and nodded.

"Good. I'll arrange for you to sleep in here. We can bring in a cot, but unfortunately it won't fit in your wife's room."

I rose, dazed, barely aware I was moving and followed Chalmers to the door. I paused when I noticed something resting atop a bookcase beside the door, something I hadn't noticed earlier.

"Ah, you've found my Buddha," Chalmers said, gesturing to the tiny statue of the ancient wise man. "I've only just moved into this office and that's the first item I thought to bring."

"I didn't know India was Buddhist," I said. "I mean other than the Himalayas and Nepal."

"Once wealthy families in India embraced Buddhism," Chalmers said. "But the Turks destroyed many of the temples and artifacts when they invaded. Today only a few sections of the country follow the old ways. My family is from Sri Lanka, which is predominantly Buddhist. My mother gave that to me when I came to America to study medicine. She told me it would ward off evil. I don't believe in such things, but I suppose every bit helps."

I had never held stock in such things either, but my vision of a once-ordered universe had fallen to pieces revealing something darker beneath, something where legends and superstitions were more than mere tales. And at that moment something made me reach out and touch the tiny figure.

"I wonder, Doctor," I said, stumbling over the words.

Chalmers moved up beside me and gently scooped up the carving.

"Why don't we put it in your wife's room, for tonight at least," she said studying the figure's round, serene face.

I nodded, found her dark eyes and managed a half-hearted smile. Then she turned and I followed her down the hall into Joanna's room, where she set the figure on the nightstand by the door. She offered me a kind smile and left the room.

I settled into the chair by the bed and watched my wife sleep her medicated sleep. The nurse had evidently shut off the gooseneck lamp. I was thankful for that, because in the shadows it was impossible to see Joanna's terrible bruising. I suspected it was the result of the transformation she had undergone, the trauma that had changed her bones and skin into that of some animal hybrid, some freakish nightmare that Roger Trimble would have said was neither dog nor person but some terrible thing in between. But I could hardly tell this to the good doctor.

I began to worry that the tests would reveal my wife's secret condition. If this were true, I might have to think twice about granting permission for such procedures.

The blonde nurse appeared with the permission forms, forcing the issue.

"I understand Dr. Chalmers spoke to you about these?"

I nodded and she provided a pen and showed me where to sign. I was too tired to think any more. I decided to let them run their tests. Their findings, I suspected, would prove inconclusive.

"Thank you," she said. "We're having a cot set up for you in the office. It'll be ready in fifteen minutes."

"No rush," I said. "I need to go home, feed my dog and get a change of clothes." I had forgotten how dirty and wet I was.

The nurse took the forms and left me with Joanna. I set my jaw on the metal guardrail that surrounded the bed. I took Joanna's hand in mine; her fingers felt cool and terribly lifeless. At that moment the tears I had fought back so valiantly in the car appeared and I wept into my forearm.

Chapter Sixty-Nine

The streets were eerily deserted as I made my way home. It was as if the world had ended between the time I entered Mercy General Hospital and the time I left. The stop lights were still working, however, with annoying regularity, and a few of the homes I passed still had lights burning inside. These, I suppose, could have been nothing but residuals, remnants of a dead world.

I drove through the shadows, detached as if in a dream, incapable of finding peace. I passed empty shops and lighted but seemingly lifeless service stations, past St. Brigid's cemetery with its black wrought-iron gates and shadowy recesses, my headlight beams glinting off the polished marble tombstones.

I turned onto my street, idled slowly past Renko's empty house still lacking the police cruiser and the darkened Trimble residence across from it and turned into my driveway with the regularity of a machine set on automatic pilot. I hit the remote, watched the garage door slowly ascend and the sensor light brighten as I drove into the bay half-expecting to find Tom waiting for me. But he was nowhere in sight; there was only the empty garage. No, that wasn't true, not completely empty; there was Joanna's Honda sitting silently in the other bay. Somehow, empty might have been better.

I sat there long after I killed the engine, not wanting to go inside, watching Joanna's car, waiting for her to climb out and smile at me, then ask me to help her carry in groceries or clothes she'd bought at Macy's or TJ Maxx. These were images of happier times, before the 'night deposits,' before Judd. I wondered if they'd ever return. But thinking along those lines made me feel worse, so I shut the images out.

My insides were churning and I tried to recall the

last time I'd eaten. I remembered Spooky alone in the house and the things I had to gather for my overnight stay at the hospital, so I reluctantly climbed out into the heat, closed the garage bay door by habit and made my way to the back porch.

The yard was as empty as the streets. But the night was a different story entirely; it felt alive and sentient and this was not simply due to the usual sounds of crickets chirping and bats fluttering. There was something else out there in the night, something that made me think of eyes watching from the shadows.

It was only my imagination, I told myself for the umpteenth time since the whole thing began, but I kept cautious vigil as I made my way to the gate nonetheless. As my hand touched the cool metal I smelled burning wood. I wondered if the fire department had gotten the state hospital blaze under control, or if it, like so many other things this night, had gotten away from those who sought to put order to them.

I headed for the patio, conscious of each sound the darkness made. Somewhere a toad croaked. Twigs snapped as if under someone's weight. Each time I spun around, struggling to see into the pitch that surrounded me. But each time I saw nothing and, with a sense of relief, I finally climbed my back stairs and went inside.

Spooky was glad to see me, shuffling over and kissing my outstretched hand as I entered the kitchen. I let her out and she finished her business quickly and came back inside. Then she went to her empty dish and nuzzled it.

I got some dog food from the bag in the corner cabinet and filled her dish. Then I took her water bowl to the refrigerator to freshen it with some water from the spout in the refrigerator door as well as some ice. It filled slowly, reminding me that I needed to replace the water filter under the sink; just one more thing on my 'honey-do' list.

As I stood holding the bowl and waiting for it to fill, listening to the soft hum of the mechanism, my tired brain began to drift. I found myself studying the numerous magnets clinging to the refrigerator door. My favorites included the Brachiosaurus skeleton from the Chicago airport, because, as a boy, I loved dinosaurs. There was the tiny basket of shells from Rockport where Joanna and I went on one of our first dates. My favorite, though, was the Nubble Light replica from York Beach, Maine, where we routinely spend the last days of June and weekends in August.

Nestled among these was a picture of the pair of us standing on Yawkey Way outside Fenway Park, affixed to the door by means of a Boston Red Sox logo magnet. Beside this was the photo of Joanna and Alice Williams taken in the Williams' back yard, each woman toasting the unseen photographer with bottles of beer.

Below the photographs, wrapped in small acid-free plastic sleeves and held in place by a Patriots' football helmet-shaped magnet, was a pair of ticket stubs from a snowy Pat's game Joanna and I attended. The ink had run because I'd kept the tickets in my coat pocket throughout the game, but the print was still legible and the experience, along with the experiences represented by the other magnets and photos, was preserved forever in my mind.

Spooky's nearly overflowing water bowl roused me from my bout of melancholy and I set it down beside her food. Distractions, I suppose, serve a purpose in the great scheme of things. 'Distractions' were just what Joanna and I would need once this whole thing was over. But first we had to get through this night.

I dragged my exhausted body toward the bedroom to pack a small bag. Joanna usually did the packing, but I figured I could manage for one night. The first thing I would need was one of the duffel bags which we kept tucked under the bed.

I found myself standing in the bedroom doorway, my tired mind formulating a mental list of things we would need. My fingers were poised to trip the light when Spooky, who was hovering at my feet, began to growl.

Recollections of the last time she behaved this way lit in my brain and my eyes began scanning the darkness for signs of movement. Immediately they were drawn to a pair of glistening objects glinting at me from the darkened corner of the bedroom. I stood transfixed, my skin crawling, beads of sweat forming along my spine. Could the thing have returned and gotten into my house?

Digging deep, I found a speck of resolve, gritted my teeth, and flicked the light switch.

My breath caught in my throat as the light spilled across the empty bedroom. The glistening specks I'd seen had been the metal clasps to Joanna's jewelry box reflecting a stray bar of light trickling in from the kitchen, nothing more.

"See," I said, more to myself than to Spooky, "there's nothing–"

The window near the foot of the bed exploded in a horrific shower of glass and something the size of a football crashed to the floor.

I shielded my face from the flying glass and Spooky ran for the safety of the living room, yelping.

I uncovered my eyes and stared disbelieving at the thing lying near the foot of the bed. The hot rancid feeling in my gut turned to ice. My terrified eyes told me it was not a stone that had crashed through the window, but something with half-shut eyes and broken teeth, bloody lips and matted dark hair.

I began trembling uncontrollably, my legs growing numb and useless, and my fingers gripping the doorframe for support. An agonizing second passed, during which recognition catapulted my brain to a place well beyond the bounds of reason. The face on the floor was that of

'Gospel' Tom Williams.

Spooky appeared, darting past my feet, growling and yelping and I dropped down and scooped her up.

"No!" I managed, hissing in her ear and clutching her close, nearly crushing her as she frantically clawed at my arms, growling and whimpering. I carried her to the four seasons room and set her down on the floor. I ducked back into the living room before she could follow and closed the French doors, trapping her.

I stood paralyzed, my forehead pressed against the glass, not caring if it shattered and tore into my flesh, my stomach locked in spasms, the sound of Spooky's muffled cries enveloping me. The air fled my lungs and I found myself gasping, struggling to snatch in even the slimmest fragment of breath. I knew I had to call the police, Teschal, if I could reach her. But a terrible confusion had set in and questions were flying through my brain like daggers. What had I really seen? Could Tom be dead? Or was it some sick joke my exhausted mind was playing on me?

I had to find out. I had to know for sure.

Grimly determined, I planted my hands firmly on the doorframe and drew in a ragged breath. But before I could turn and take so much as one step, the light from the kitchen behind me went out and I was plunged into complete darkness.

Chapter Seventy

My head snapped up and I spun around, my heart clawing its way up into my throat. Cautiously I reached into the blackness and felt my way toward the kitchen, using my fingers to search for obstacles. I bumped into something. Reaching down, I felt the arm of a wingback chair. I was in the living room, near the kitchen doorway.

I moved away from the chair until my outstretched hands found the kitchen doorframe. A creaking sound drifted out of the darkness. Had I left the door to the service porch ajar? In the state I was in, I realized I might have left it completely open!

Panicky, I entered the kitchen, feeling my way along the wall, my fingertips finding the cool metal edge of the refrigerator. I drew myself forward, sweeping my hand around the edge of the appliance. But my clumsy fingers bumped into some of the magnets adorning the door and I listened helplessly as they cascaded to the floor.

Cursing, I continued toward the island where I kept a flashlight in one of the drawers. I desperately needed to call the police, but the phone in the kitchen was a cordless one as were the ones in the four seasons room and the bedroom, each useless without power. My mobile phone was still in my car. I would need to use the landline and that was in the cellar with the circuit breakers. I needed a light to navigate the stairs.

Spooky was making a racket in the front room, howling, whining and barking; I could hear her scratching desperately at the French doors. I took a step forward; the fallen magnets crunched beneath my feet. I saw that the magnets were lying in a puddle of moonlight that had seeped in through the windows above the sink.

I was about to take another tentative step when I

noticed something lying among the fallen magnets, something that had no business being there.

The object was a placard, the type found on doors in hospitals and office buildings, though this one looked archaic and dirty. The white letters embedded in its red face were, however, clearly visible in the spill of moonlight. I sensed my lips silently mouthing the words: Aversive Therapy.

I felt suddenly as if I'd been punched in the stomach. It was the placard from the Pelham West building at the old state hospital, the one from the office containing the dead teenager. I didn't bother asking how it had found its way into my house; I already knew.

Something stirred. I scanned the kitchen, my tearing eyes finding the shadowy outline of the kitchen doorway, which the moonlight spilling into the service porch from the screen door revealed to be wide open.

I took a step toward the island and the flashlight, but drew to an abrupt halt as something shifted in the dark space between the door and the stove. My eyes struggled to turn darkness into substance. The movement became a shadow, a shadow which quickly became a lean appendage reaching out for the door. I heard a sound like dead leaves skittering across a cold October street as the tip of the appendage fanned out into elongated fingers and made contact with the old wood. And then the door slowly began to close, its hinges creaking softly until it slipped with a dull thud into the jamb. My eyes traced the appendage to its source and I saw *it* squatting atop the counter in the corner, beside the stove.

It was a jumble of shadows at first, shadows that became arms, legs, and a face of sorts, as my eyes adjusted to the darkness. Glistening eyes watching me from the deep shadows held my gaze. The cold thing that had been living in my stomach for days was everywhere now, in my throat, my lungs, inching its way into my brain. In my haste, I

341

hadn't locked the door, and it had come in after me. But before it had, it had killed the power, plunging the house into darkness by gaining access to the basement through the doghouse, which I'd never bothered locking after fixing the doorknob. Now it was here, crouching less than a dozen feet from me.

"Does she like it?" my visitor whispered, moonlight glinting off the coarse hairs of its arm, penetrating in spots down to the dark sinewy flesh beneath.

"Who are you?" I said, my throat feeling as if it was crammed full of dusty bones.

"Does she like it when you stick it in her?"

Its voice was like razors dragged across a chalkboard and my stomach rolled over.

"I remember when she liked *different* things."

There was something disturbingly familiar about the voice, an inflection, a pause. Something.

"I don't know what you mean," I managed, my thoughts flying around the room like sparrows trapped in a burning barn.

"The little whore!" it growled in a tone laced with such venom that I shrank back against the refrigerator, causing the last of the magnets to tumble to the floor.

A dry cackle gurgled up from my visitor's throat and the room was suddenly awash with the odor of rancid meat.

"I'd let you watch when I tear the little whore open, but you'll be dead by then," it said in an almost sing-song voice.

I swallowed hard, my mind desperately grasping onto a plan of escape. The thing was too close to the back door for me to get out that way. The French doors at the front of the house were closed; I would have to open them, grab Spooky and get out through the front door, which I would need to unlock. It would take too much time. There was only one way out and my visitor knew it as well.

"Who are you?" I asked, sliding my left foot toward the bedroom, hoping the thing wouldn't notice.

A fresh fit of laughter rose up from my visitor's throat. A second cloud of rancid air enveloped me and I felt the urge to gag.

"Don't you know by now?" it asked. "If you still don't know, I'll tell you who to ask," it said, and the thread of familiarity buried in the voice rose closer to the surface, close enough to make me shiver in spite of the heat.

"Who should I ask?" I whispered, and it laughed again. I felt a sensation in my chest like thunder rippling in the distance.

"You should ask Alice," it said in its deep rumbling voice, "while she's small."

I felt the blood drain from my face and my legs went weak. In my mind I saw Alice sitting in the booth at the Fayre, her face hidden beneath the brim of the Red Sox cap. I saw the hint of bruising around her eyes and on the backs of her hands, bruising Alice attributed to her mysterious ailment, bruising I mistakenly attributed to Tom's fists. It was the same bruising I'd seen on Joanna tonight at the hospital. The bruising was part of the syndrome that afflicted Joanna. And Alice.

In that instant I saw the clues that had been in front of me all along, clues I had ignored, clues I had refused to accept. Joanna, Renko, Judd, Tom and me. The thread that held us together was Alice! Tom had been right from the beginning; at some level I had known all along the identity of my stalker.

Alice leaned forward into the moonlight and I saw that her long bony fingers were wrapped around her face as if she was either crying or playing a demented game of peek-a-boo. Slowly those fingers peeled away like the limbs of some terrible spider to reveal what lay beneath and the cold dread moonlight revealed the alien landscape that made up her face. At long last I saw the face of my stalker.

343

There was a deep twisted brow and tiny all-too-bright green eyes, below which hung a crooked snout, wet, wrinkled, like a rotted prune, thick with yellow mucous. And then a wide maw filled with countless teeth, crooked, jagged, brimming with saliva, poking out at horrible angles from grinning lips that had been stretched beyond the point of reason. The face was that of a monster, but a monster with enough of Alice Williams left in it to liken it to a deformed human being, the features swollen, disproportionate, engorged, bulging, as if ready to burst.

"Look at Alice," it hissed, its terrible face fully revealed by the shafts of moonlight, cords of saliva like spider webs dripping from its maw, "now that she's ten feet tall!"

The thing stepped from the counter top to the island, its talons raised, its rancid breath reaching across the room, striking my senses like a fist. Stacks of magazines and sorted mail Joanna kept on the island flew off in all directions, and in that instant of confusion I broke for the only escape route I could conceive; I ran into the bedroom.

I slammed the door behind me and, without considering the shattered glass or Tom's bloody face and dead eyes at my feet I broke for the window and fell forward, through the pane, into the night.

Chapter Seventy-One

I toppled through the ruined window, scraping my back along the side of the frame with its bits of broken glass, before plunging the five feet to the driveway below. I landed hard on my feet and managed to stay that way, fighting off gravity's best attempts to spoil my effort. Ignoring the stinging across my back and the warm trickle of fluid oozing down the side of my face, I bolted for the garage, throwing terrified glances back at the empty window while fumbling through my pockets for my car keys.

I reached the corner of the garage, successfully unhooked the chain link fence section from the latch on my second try, and stumbled through, landing on the asphalt at the foot of the side door with a gut-wrenching thud.

I glanced back at the house in time to watch the screen door at my back porch explode. The remains flew into the night, bouncing off the chain-link fence opposite the porch. Then I watched some terrible shape bounding down the darkened stairs.

Desperately, I reached for the knob to the garage door, twisted it and threw myself against the metal. The door gave way and I rolled into the garage. Spinning around I kicked the door shut and, getting up onto my knees, I flipped the lock in place an instant before something slammed into the door, causing the metal to buckle and dust to rain down from the ceiling.

I got to my feet, ran for my car, tripped over my lawn mower, and went sprawling. The thing collided with the door again and the frame shook. More dust rained down from the loft and there was a loud rattle as the inner doorknob fell away.

I got to my feet, struggled with the key, ripped open the car door and piled inside. Fumbling the key into the

345

ignition, I turned the engine over.

A shadow flitted past the window in the wall beside me, drawing my eyes, and a split second later the window in front of me exploded. Wood fragments and shards of glass rained down on the hood of my car and a dark shape fell to the floor in front of me. Jamming the gearshift into drive, I flipped on the headlights, hoping to temporarily blind the thing; but before I could hit the accelerator and crush it against the back wall of the garage, it clambered up onto the hood and pressed its twisted face against the windshield.

I slipped the car into reverse and stamped on the accelerator.

Tires squealed as I barreled backward. Caught by surprise, the thing fell away, landing between the front of the car and the back wall of the garage. I continued in reverse, crashing into the aluminum garage bay door, tearing it off its moorings. Cables snapped and flew in all directions. Aluminum tracking fell across the windshield and cracks in the glass opened like fissures.

I skidded backward, down the driveway, running over the garage door, clipping the corner of the house as I passed, the tailgate tearing chunks of shingles loose and, probably, killing a taillight in the process. I spun the wheel sharply, backed over the front-most portion of my lawn, and spun out into the street, barely missing the corner of the chain-link fence with my front bumper.

Once in the street, I slammed on the brake with such force that my head collided with the side window. Stunned, I struggled to slip the car into drive as I glimpsed something bearing down on me. Before I could pull away, the passenger side window disintegrated.

Through the torrent of flying glass, the huge claws appeared, swiping at the air. I could hear the thing's hind legs clawing at the door for purchase in its struggle to get inside. The thought of climbing out the driver's side door and running for it had barely lit in my brain when something broke from the darkness and collided with the thing, knocking it off balance.

Alice turned on her attacker and I heard a familiar furious barking. Rufus had come home.

I saw my chance and jammed the accelerator to the floor. I skidded sideways, fishtailing down the street. I heard Rufus yelp and looked into the rearview mirror in time to see Alice hurl the shepherd aside like a sack of grain. Then she was chasing me, springing along, vaulting forward and using her newly acquired limbs to propel her body with more speed than anything human could possibly muster.

I heard myself growling something primordial and turned from the rearview mirror to the road just in time to find a section of the chain-link fence surrounding St. Brigid's Cemetery rushing at me. The fence collapsed around the hood, falling away as I careened through it.

The SUV plowed across the lawn, grinding to a halt just before slamming into a huge black tombstone. My mouth rebounded off the steering wheel and I tasted blood. My teeth had sheared off a slice of flesh from my lower lip, and I spat it into the passenger side.

Dazed, I grabbed the wheel, managed to slip the car into reverse and slammed down on the accelerator. The tires spun on the soft muddy earth and I slid sideways. I slipped the car into drive, turning the wheel full to the left toward the main gate. A fleeting shadow made me glance into the rearview mirror, where I watched a dark shape detach itself from the gloom and scamper up the rear window. Claws clicked loudly against the roof and the sunroof shattered in a hail of glass fragments.

I buried my face in my hands to protect it from the shrapnel, opening my eyes in time to see a gnarled bony talon reaching down through the ruined sun roof. The jagged claws tore at the edge of the dashboard, the ceiling,

347

the visors, leaving deep gouges where ever they struck, as the thing made a sound like a speeding freight train. The claws swung my way and I ducked aside, cracking my head against the side window. The claws found the rear view mirror instead and tore it from the windshield, hurling it aside.

Drawing back farther, pressing my face against the glass, fumbling for the door handle, contemplating a run for my life, I remembered the baseball bat lying on the passenger side floor, but the claw was swiping at the air in front of me, tearing at the shadows. I had to make a try for the bat; it was my only chance.

With my face pressed against the steering wheel, I closed my eyes, let out a primordial scream, and lunged forward. The claw swept past my face, sweeping through my hair and tearing out a fistful of strands. I found myself lying on my side, my face practically on the floor, my hip grinding into the console between the seats. I stole a terrified glance up at the sunroof; the thing was trying to pull itself into the cabin, its face a distorted lump of shadow, its breath as rancid as an old grave.

I twisted my aching body so that my face was pressed against the floor, and I felt something hard and unforgiving bump into my forehead. It was the baseball bat.

Defying the natural alignment of my spine, driving deep gouges into my ribs and hips as I twisted against the console, I grabbed the bat and thrust it upward while contracting my abdominal muscles to lift myself up off the floor. A crack resounded from above as the bat rebounded off the edge of the spent sunroof and a fresh peppering of ruined glass rained down, missing my eyes but finding my mouth. I spat hard and swung the bat. It hit the edge of the sunroof a second time and I heard the dry old wood splinter. I tried to pull back, but Alice caught the other end.

I pulled down on the bat's handle. I heard the wood cracking again, but still it held firm, as did Alice's grip. She wrenched the bat again, pulling it sideways, turning the edge of the sunroof into an unyielding fulcrum, extending the crack that had been opened in the old wood, but I refused to relinquish my only weapon, and I felt myself being lifted off the floor. The side of the bat slammed into the edge of the sunroof and, with a sickening crunch, split in two.

Alice rolled back onto the roof, screeching, and I flopped down onto the passenger seat. The only things filling the sunroof were the branches of a tree and the all-too-familiar face of the Thunder Moon.

I struggled to right myself, pushing back with my elbows and trying to lift my body up over the center console. Alice appeared, glaring down at me with those burning green eyes. She hesitated, her terrible gaze fixed on me, her impossible claws creeping over the edge of the sunroof like a pair of nightmarish spiders searching for prey. I was a deer trapped in the headlights of a car, mesmerized by its own impending doom. Drippings from Alice's maw found my face, hot, foul and thick, like cords of blood, and the spell was broken. I felt the jagged edge of the bat in my hands, closed my eyes and, with as much force as I could muster, I drove the broken tip home.

The old wood sank into something softer than the edge of the sunroof and the night was suddenly filled with a terrible wailing. Then what remained of the bat was torn from my hands and Alice withdrew.

I saw my chance, rolled over onto the driver's seat, slammed the car into reverse, and gunned the accelerator.

I watched Alice roll down the side of the SUV past the ruined passenger window, her thrashing limbs shattering what remained of the glass. I didn't hesitate; I spun the wheel, jammed the car into drive and headed for the main gate, my headlights playing wildly across a forest of tombstones, bits of glass falling away from my hair and body and raining down from the shattered sunroof.

I tore past the big wrought iron gates that marked the cemetery's main entrance, what remained of my vehicle's front end kicking up a shower of sparks as I bounced down from the ramp that led to the street. I veered right, onto a desolate Elm Street, found the accelerator again and raced off into the night with the tires screaming in protest. I glanced back over my shoulder once but saw no sign of Alice. There was no time to lose; I knew where Alice was heading and I knew what she was planning. I had to get there first.

Chapter Seventy-Two

I ran every red light and, for better or worse, never saw one police cruiser, let alone a living soul. It might have been a beautiful, warm summer night or it might have been the dead of winter. That had all become irrelevant. The only reality that existed for me was Joanna and the thing that had once been Alice Williams, the thing that wanted to kill us.

The full Thunder moon was high in the sky, studying the deserted town with macabre fascination, studying *me*. At the same time, I'd never felt so alone. No, not alone, not entirely. Alice was out there, or rather the thing Alice had become was out there. As a woman, she had never tried to hurt me and I could not imagine her hurting Joanna. But that Alice was gone, maybe forever.

How's our girl? It was the question Alice had put to me when I met her at the Fayre, a question she'd asked many times before. Tonight, for the first time, the question took on a sinister tone, a *deadly* tone.

The cold thing living inside me had invaded every inch of my being. I could see its face and it was the face of the thing Alice had become, the twisted half-human face I'd seen watching me from the shadows in my kitchen. She had been hiding in my yard the night I let Spooky out; those had been her eyes I'd seen glistening from the deep shadows beneath the maple tree. She had been in the oak tree and in Renko's garage. And she had killed Renko.

The hospital appeared as if from nowhere, and I veered into the main lot.

Then there was poor Tom, unaware just whose identity he was trying to uncover. Perhaps in the end, he had discovered Alice's secret and Alice had become aware, or maybe she was just tying up loose ends, getting rid of the one person she hated the most, the person she had tolerated in order to be near Joanna. No matter. Whatever had driven Alice into an all-consuming murderous rage remained a mystery.

I considered the hospital on the hill, and the great fiery eye in the sky, the omnipresent moon, hovering above it all, closer to the Earth than it had been in centuries. I wondered if that was what had pushed Alice over the edge. Perhaps Alice's condition was tied into the cycles of the moon as legend insisted. Maybe the urge to change was strongest during the full moon. That urge would be greatly amplified just now with the moon and Mars both so close to the Earth, driving the beast out of its hidden layer, driving it to kill.

I thought of Alice, part animal and part human. This explained Tom's difficulties with the tests he'd tried to run, the idea of cross-contamination that had stumped him. He had been so close to the solution.

I pulled up directly in front of the entrance, killed the motor and climbed out. Ignoring my car's badly dented bumper as well as the odor of anti-freeze, I ran through the automatic doors and into the lobby, but I stopped short when I got inside.

The television perched high in one corner of the room was playing. Some late night talk show I wasn't familiar with was on; the audience was laughing at something. The waiting room was empty and there was no sign of the elderly man who had greeted me earlier.

I crossed the room, the hairs on the back of my neck tingling as if I had stepped on a live wire. I listened intently but the only sound I could detect was that of the television.

I passed the empty information desk. There was no sign of anything odd, no bloodstains, nothing strange other than the fact that the man was not there. I continued down the corridor to the elevators and hit the switch. I turned to study the darkened hallway beyond, but the elevator door opened immediately, startling me, and I stepped inside. I pushed the switch for the ICU but froze when I heard something. A beat passed. Nothing materialized, the door closed and the elevator started its ascent.

As my heart slowed to a reasonable pace, disbelief reared its head. Had I seen Alice crouching in the corner of my kitchen, or had I seen an animal, a bobcat or perhaps one of the coyotes I'd heard so much about lately? I knew that if it all ended here, doubts, like weeds, would sprout in the dark corners of my mind as time passed. It was like seeing a horrible accident, but having the details fall away with time until only nagging feelings of doubt as to what had actually transpired remain. One thing was certain: Joanna was lying in a bed in the ICU and I was determined to see her through this.

The doors opened into the same short, sterile-looking corridor I had visited earlier. In this section of the hospital, at least, things appeared normal.

I started down the corridor, listening to the elevator doors close behind me and my own footfalls. I pushed the automatic pad on the wall and entered the ICU.

The blonde nurse I met earlier looked up from her place at the nurses' station in mild surprise.

"Mr. Graves," she said studying my filthy clothes. "You–"

"I need to see my wife," I said. "Is Dr. Chalmers here?"

"No," the woman said, her gaze following me as I passed. "The doctor is gone for the night."

I spied the police officer sitting in a seat just outside of my wife's room. He was reading a tattered paperback novel. He closed it and set it down as soon as he saw me and stood up.

"Sir," he said.

"I need to see my wife," I said curtly, walking past the man into Joanna's room. I studied her from the foot of the bed. Her condition had not changed.

"She hasn't come around yet," the blonde nurse said from the doorway.

"Sir," the officer said, "are you all right?"

"I need to talk to Detective Teschal," I said. "Immediately."

The officer frowned. A telephone rang and the nurse shook her head.

"Where the hell is Karen?" she said, turning and walking toward the desk. "She's been at that vending machine for fifteen minutes."

I looked to Joanna as the nurse answered the phone.

"Hello," I heard the nurse say. "Hello."

I turned to the officer.

"I want my wife's bed moved to another floor. Right now."

"What?" he said with a frown.

"Hello!" I heard the phone at the nurses' station click heavily into its cradle. "Don't tell me the phones are going to start acting up. Ever since they started working on those elevators...What next?"

"Sir," the officer said, "I can't do that."

"Then who can?"

The nurse appeared in the doorway.

"What seems to be the trouble?"

"This gentleman wants to move his wife to another floor," the officer said, leaning back against the doorjamb and crossing his arms.

The nurse looked suddenly very impatient. "Mr. Graves, she'll be moved out of ICU first thing in the morning, but–"

"Now!" I growled angrily.

The officer pulled away from the doorjamb and stiffened, his hands straying to his belt, his fingers settling on what I presumed to be a Taser holstered there.

"Sir–"

"Mr. Graves," the nurse cut in, "in order to move

your wife we would need to get permission from the doctor, who is gone for the evening, or we can consult with the charge nurse, who is away from the desk just now."

"Can we please locate the charge nurse?" My eyes moved from the officer to the nurse and back again, my patience clearly waning. They must have thought me mad, and they were close to right. I *was* half-mad, desperate, terrified. If they'd seen what I'd seen, they wouldn't be dragging things out like this.

"She should be back any minute," the woman said, glancing back over her shoulder at the desk, as if expecting the charge nurse to materialize.

"Then I'll do it myself," I said and I reached for the IV bottle dangling above the bed.

"No, sir, don't!" the nurse said and the officer pushed her aside and headed for me. Then the lights went out.

"What the...?" I heard the officer say.

"Jesus, first the phones and now the lights," the nurse said. "Everyone stay put, the emergency lights should kick in any second."

I heard her back away and head toward the desk, her footfalls hesitant in the dark. She bumped into something, cursed, then I heard the sound of her fumbling with a phone and saying, "Hello, hello," several times before hanging up.

The officer moved to the window and I saw his face etched in the moonlight streaming in.

"The lights in the east wing are still on," he said. "And I can hear the air conditioning units on the roof below us; they're still working."

"The line is dead," the nurse called out to us.

"What?" the officer said. He moved toward the door. "That's a land line; the electricity shouldn't have any effect on it."

"Since they started working on those elevators," she

said, "it's been one thing after another."

I heard her shuffling about the desk, bumping into things, swearing softly. Then I heard another sound, a sound that reminded me of a piece of metal being dragged along the ground. Something about this new sound chilled me to the bone, and I remembered hearing a similar grinding sound when the third floor stairwell door in the state hospital's Pelham West building opened and closed.

The nurse said, "What the hell? Karen–?"

Then she let out a grunt as if she had accidentally walked into something and had had the wind knocked out of her.

"Hey!" the officer said and I heard him move off into the corridor.

I gripped the curtain behind me and slung it fully open, letting the full tide of moonlight pour through. Pale rays fell across the lower portion of Joanna's bed, but only a muted patch made its way into the corridor, barely illuminating the officer's receding feet. I took a step toward the doorway, banged my shin on the metal chair I had occupied earlier and cursed into the gloom. I turned toward the doorway as the emergency lights above the nursing station came alive. And the world around me ground to a halt.

The vivid antiseptic light ripped through the darkness, spilling across the ICU, stabbing at the nooks and crannies, creating jagged shadows, turning stray IV poles, transport carts, and assorted bits of equipment into twisted bits of scrap in a derelict house. At the heart of it all was Alice, crouching atop the nursing station desk. The long crooked fingers of her left hand were wrapped around the blonde nurse's blood drenched face; the jagged tips were buried in the woman's pale flesh, one grisly digit deeply imbedded in the woman's right eye socket. The nurse's feet were suspended a foot or so from the floor, her legs twitching convulsively. The officer was standing between

Alice and me, surprised, astonished, fumbling for the gun at his hip. But before he could draw his weapon, Alice let out a terrible screech and hurled the nurse's twitching body at him.

What remained of the blonde nurse crashed into the officer and he fell sideways, colliding with a cart full of hospital supplies. A thundering crash filled the ICU as police officer, body and supply cart spilled to the floor. At the same instant, Alice drove her right fist upward into the bank of emergency lights suspended from the ceiling.

The emergency light fixtures exploded in a shower of sparks and metal fragments, and for a few seconds, the ICU was awash in flickering light. Then darkness descended.

Panicking, I lunged for the door, hoping to close it and jam it shut with the chair, but my foot caught on something and I went sprawling.

The chair bounced around and landed on top of me, biting into my throbbing head, opening a fresh wound. I raised my eyes as a series of fresh grunting sounds drifted through the doorway. I grabbed the chair and pushed it aside, but it rebounded off the bed and landed on top of me. Then, from the shadows, there came a muffled cry and the sound of something like cloth being ripped apart. I lay there stunned, staring transfixed into the shadows beyond Joanna's room, my heart tearing a hole in my chest and the dull thrumming of the big air conditioning units perched on the roof below Joanna's window filling the void. Seconds ticked by. Something clattered to the floor in the doorway. My eyes lit on the object; it was the police officer's gun.

Sprawling, I reached for the thing, but a man's hand shot out of the darkness and seized it. The blood-drenched fingers dragged the weapon back into the shadows and a millisecond later an explosion of light and sound filled the night as the weapon discharged. The window above me shattered around the stray bullet as it passed into the night and I was showered with shards of glass.

I laced my fingers across my head and buried my face against my shoulder until the lethal rain ended. Slowly, I raised my head, my eyes focusing on the darkened doorway where something moved. An expanding pool of dark liquid was creeping toward me, mingling with the pool of moonlight that was drifting in from the ruined window. Blood.

My breath hitched in my throat and I gripped the chair lying on top of me with every intention of hurling it aside. But an image materializing in the darkened doorway turned my will to ice.

I watched helplessly, transfixed, the air conditioning units thrumming, as a twisted claw appeared at the edge of the moonlight, setting itself noiselessly down into the pool of blood. I could make out a gash in the forearm just below the elbow as if something had pierced the flesh and torn a small chunk away, perhaps something like the jagged edge of a splintered baseball bat. Dark, crimson fluid was weeping from the wound.

A second claw appeared, curving into a mass of huge bony knuckles, settling into the pool across from its mate. Finally the terrible face with its burning green eyes began to slowly emerge from the darkness, like a horrible ancient beast rising from the blackest depths. A terrible grin split the thing's face open like a volcanic fissure, revealing the forest of crooked teeth. The green eyes found me and the grin intensified, becoming a great crevice, widening until I thought the face might split apart in a bloody avulsion, only to reveal Alice's human face trapped within. Threads of saliva hanging from the twisted maw settled into the bloody pool like drippings of limestone in some forgotten cave. I was alone at the end of the world, staring into the abyss. One slash of its claw was all that remained; one slash of its claw would finish it all.

"See Alice," it said in its terrible half-human voice,

a voice that had grown more alien than ever, now that the thing was in full control of Alice Williams, now that the *moon* was in full control, "now that she's ten feet tall."

It inched closer, the monstrous grin spreading across its face, a crack on the slopes of hell. Its rancid breath enveloped me, and I could see horrific familiarity in its features. I closed my eyes.

In my darkness, a sound found me. It was that of Joanna, moaning from her bed. My eyes snapped open and I watched Alice's murderous expression melt away as her gaze swung from me to where my wife lay. And, to my astonishment, I thought I glimpsed something in that face, some residual trace of the human Alice had once been, some sliver of emotion embedded there that I couldn't decipher.

A second sound followed on the heels of the first, a sound that might have been a door opening or closing. Alice's attention was focused on Joanna lying unconscious in her bed, and there was a delay in her response – but only a short-lived one.

Her elongated ears, like black knives, twitched and she spun toward the darkened corridor beyond. The look of calm had passed from her hellish face as quickly as it had come and murder gleamed there once more, only this time the murderous intent was directed at something other than me, something out in the hall. I wondered briefly if the officer had survived Alice's attack. But she was looking in the opposite direction, toward the small office of Dr. Chalmers and the fire exit I had seen earlier. Before I could shout out a warning to this new intruder, before Alice could spring, there came a deafening report and something exploded in Alice's flank. A crimson shower spattered the doorframe as a wound opened in Alice's side.

Alice whipped around, infuriated, roaring like a jet engine and charging out of view toward some unseen attacker in the hall. Another shot rang out and another and three more and Alice's fearsome roar turned to a terrible wailing that lasted only a second before something unseen hit the floor with a muffled thud. Then a strange silence crept through the ICU, the only sound the undulating thrumming of the air conditioning units on the roof below Joanna's window.

I lay in the moonlight, my pulse pounding, my ears ringing from the deafening roar of the gunfire, awaiting my fate. I heard footsteps approaching; dull, light, stealthy footsteps. I reached for the chair that still lay atop me, gripped its seat, but froze as muddy sneakers appeared at the edge of the bloody, moonlit pool that had gathered in the doorway.

The person wearing the sneakers crouched down in the doorway and pointed a gun barrel directly at me. It was the second time this night that Detective Teschal had trained her weapon on me. I didn't need to speak, to explain; her blanched face told me all I needed to know. I read confusion there, despair and dread so dark and alive it was palpable. Her eyes were huge, not cold anymore, but brimming with some dark, molten liquid. It was as if her brain had been crammed with too much information of a new and frightening sort, and the excess was boiling up into her eyes.

When she realized who she was looking at, she leaned back against the doorjamb and slid to the floor, her arm falling into her lap. Her lips were quivering, her hands trembled. I watched her slide the gun's safety on, then lean her head back against the metal frame and close her eyes.

I pushed the chair lying against me aside. Teschal barely noticed. I managed to sit up, brushing glass fragments away. I heard sirens in the distance, growing louder as the cruisers producing them turned into the hospital parking lot far below. I could smell the remnants of the state hospital fire on the night breeze as it wafted through the ruined window. The last thing I remember seeing was the Buddha figurine Dr. Chalmers had placed on the night stand by the door. It was gazing back at me, its tranquil eyes full of moonlight. I leaned my head back against the wall and closed mine.

Blue Moon: **A second full moon in a calendar month, a rare event, often associated with strange occurrences.**

Chapter Seventy-Three

Once the police arrived, Joanna was moved to the second floor. They found the elderly man who'd been manning the information desk in the ER dead in a bathroom adjacent to the ER waiting room; he'd apparently suffered a fatal heart attack while barricading himself inside. Karen, the charge nurse, had survived; she'd been trapped in an elevator when the power failed. My cuts and bruises were tended to by medical staff and I was given a screening for a possible concussion, which proved to be negative; though my head ached nonetheless.

Teschal set up a series of rooms on the first floor where she and several other detectives questioned hospital staff until dawn. Meanwhile the crime scene division in their antiseptic suits came and went with annoying regularity, trying to piece together what had happened while gathering evidence. The *why* behind it all, I suspected, would prove more elusive to Teschal's logical police brain than the *what*. I, on the other hand, thought I understood; partially, at least.

Teschal met with me briefly after finding me a dry sweat suit to wear, and I explained about Tom and all the bits and pieces that I'd withheld from her. She was not pleased but I firmly believe that she understood my situation. Whether she respected my motives or not remained a mystery.

Teschal arranged to have me shuttled home in a cruiser with the explicit understanding that I would be allowed to gather up Spooky and take her to my sister's house and nothing more. By the time I arrived, two more cruisers and an ambulance were waiting; the police had taken charge of the scene. There was no sign of Rufus, but there was undeniable evidence of my encounter with the thing Alice had become. And of course there was what remained of my friend, Tom. I'd given Teschal his address and she'd dispatched a contingent to take charge of the premises.

I couldn't bring myself to look into the bedroom, let alone enter it, which the police would certainly not have allowed. Instead I collected a shivering Lhasa Apso and took up position on the front stoop to wait for the officer who'd driven me home to get clearance to drive me back to the hospital. Teschal didn't want anyone driving Joanna's car until the forensics' team had had a chance to go over it. What remained of my car had been impounded.

I must have looked like a depression-era hobo, sitting on my front porch with my ill-fitting sweat suit and Spooky lying in my lap. When it came time to leave for the hospital, I found I couldn't bring myself to look at Renko's empty house or the field that stretched out behind mine. There were too many ripe memories festering, too many ghosts.

The police officer took me to my sister's house, where I left Spooky and provided Ellen with a brief explanation as to what had transpired. She insisted on more details, managing to remain calm, as she usually did, and I promised her that I would call her once I'd gotten situated in the hospital, to fill her in on the rest. She reluctantly agreed. The waiting police cruiser probably helped.

I made it back to the hospital around four in the morning. Joanna's new, larger room easily accommodated a cot, and I slept as if I was dead until around eight AM, when Detective Teschal found me. Her face showed traces of fatigue but her suit, a neatly-tailored gray one, did not.

"Mr. Graves," she began, whispering so as not to wake Joanna, gesturing that I should join her in the hallway, "I'd like to show you something."

I nodded, exhausted but realizing that Teschal was not the sort to be put off. I followed her to the elevator, where she pushed the down button. When the doors opened she produced a key which she fit into a slot marked Sub-Level.

"The officers dispatched to Mr. Williams' house discovered his remains in the cellar," she said, as the elevator descended. She paused as if catching her breath. "I'm terribly sorry."

I felt myself nodding slowly, but these words came as little surprise; I'd become accustomed to Alice Williams' handy work.

"I must also advise you that you may have an attorney present for any questioning starting at this moment if you wish." Her words sounded rehearsed, as if she'd uttered them a thousand times before.

I told her that no attorney would be necessary.

"Good," she said drawing a small plastic baggy containing a photograph from the inner pocket of her jacket. "Would you tell me if you recognize anyone?"

I studied the photo, which was of a man and a woman sitting at a campfire. It was dusk and I could make out trees and mountains in the background. At first I failed to recognize either subject. But the longer I stared at the man's lean face and dark eyes the more familiar he became. Then it hit me.

"That's Judd," I said tapping the image. "He's the mechanic from the Fayre."

"His name was Justin Macyzk," Teschal said. "He's from a town in northern California. In and out of trouble. Small time. Moved around a lot. Carnivals and such. Do you recognize the woman?"

The elevator pinged, signaling its arrival, and I shook my head.

"No," I said, offering Teschal the photograph. She didn't take it.

364

"The woman's name is Debra Halston. Ring any bells?"

I shrugged.

"You might know her by the name Alice Jergens, or Alice Williams, since she married."

I scrutinized the photograph more closely. As with Judd's image, the longer I stared at the woman in the photo the more she began to resemble the Alice Williams I'd known. And as my eyes studied the young Alice, a missing piece of the puzzle fell into place with a nearly audible click, and Judd's cryptic warning finally made sense. He had mistaken me for *Alice's* husband. He must have seen me talking with Alice either the night she came to the booth or the day she and Joanna went for a walk. Judd hadn't been warning me about Joanna; Judd had been warning me about *Alice!*

Teschal took the photo and tucked it back into her jacket pocket.

The elevator doors parted and I found myself staring into a long bleak corridor lined with smooth beige cinder blocks, not unlike the sort that lined the corridors of the Pelham West building at the state hospital. They were also the same cinder blocks that lined the late Bob Renko's mud room, at least the mud room that inhabited my dreams.

Teschal led the way, our footfalls echoing in the cool dry air, until we arrived at a large set of swinging metal doors. Set in the wall to the left was a glass partition cordoning off a dimly lit office. A youngish man wearing a pair of light blue scrubs was sitting at a desk, filling out forms. He was wearing a set of earbuds, reminding me of the ones I'd been wearing the night I found the first 'deposit' in my yard. Teschal had to knock twice on the glass to get his attention.

The man raised his eyes, switched the MP3 player off and let the ear buds slip down around his neck. He pushed the paperwork aside, blew a large wad of gum into a bubble, let it pop and came around the desk to meet us.

"Detective," the man said as he joined us in the corridor, "I've been expecting you. I'm Terry. The morgue is this way."

Chapter Seventy-Four

The word 'morgue' echoed in my head like gunshots. Morgues were places where dead bodies were kept. I suppose some part of my brain knew why Teschal had come for me; she wanted me to identify the body of Alice Williams. I thought I had been prepared for this eventuality, but, standing outside the morgue with the chill slowly creeping into my bones, I knew I was not prepared at all. I only hoped I could keep it together long enough to do what was necessary.

Terry pushed open the big doors. A cool stream of air washed past me, reminding me of just how warm I'd felt sleeping on the cot beside Joanna in the makeshift ICU.

I drew in a breath, hoping it would somehow bolster my courage. The air tasted artificial, metallic. I began to rationalize, trying to conjure up reasons for needing to go inside. I told myself I had promised Teschal I would help. I tried to convince myself that it was all for Joanna's sake. But in the end, I think what drove me into the room was a need to see what remained of Alice in order to lay some final questions to rest. Most of all, I hoped that this might somehow set Joanna and me on the road to recovery. Perhaps I was hoping for too much.

Terry led the way with the gait of one who has spent time in the company of death. Teschal followed with much the same demeanor evident in her step, still efficient and neat in spite of all she'd been through. I followed, my step slower, less confident, laced with reluctance. My eyes nervously darted about; my pulse throbbed like a migraine in my temple. I'd never felt so out of place.

The morgue was slightly wider than the corridor but little more than an extension thereof. And it was cold, the sort of cold that gets into your bones and lives there. I felt the night's sweat begin to chill against my body and I shivered.

There were several large metal gurneys, each equipped with a built in sink, situated along the left wall. I grimly surmised that these were for performing autopsies. Beside each was a waist-high tray on wheels, each draped with a green sheet of plastic that, thankfully, hid the morbid-looking utensils I suspected lurked beneath, utensils used to slice through flesh and snip bone. Lining the wall were steel and glass cabinets, looking as cold and antiseptic as the chilled air that surrounded me.

Set into the opposite wall were stainless steel doors, each perhaps two-foot square, each equipped with a large release handle not unlike those found on industrial meat freezers. A small pin attached to a chain further secured each latch.

Terry approached the third door and turned to consider us. It was only then that I saw something in his face, something that might have been reluctance to open the door.

"I've seen a lot of bodies come through here," Terry said. "Most got here by natural causes, but there have been some car crashes, even a few gunshot and stabbing deaths. But this?" Terry shook his head slowly. "Well, I'll be glad when this one's gone."

"Mr. Graves," Teschal prompted, and I dragged my feet toward the door as Terry plucked the pin from its hasp and let it drop. It stopped well before hitting the floor, thanks to its thin chain, and it bounced repeatedly against the door with an annoying pinging sound. Then he pulled the latch, which made a sound far too loud for the relatively small room, and hauled open the door.

A swath of frigid air drifted past me carrying with it the faintest aroma of decay. My stomach began to crawl and the cold thing that had been hiding inside me for the past few days wriggled to life. This was it; there was no turning back.

Terry dragged the contents of the drawer out into the light. A large gray plastic bag, not unlike the one the EMTs had loaded Renko into for his own trip to the morgue, lay atop the drawer. Terry fumbled with the zipper for a moment, swearing once, and commenting that the cold made them tough to work with before I heard the sound of the thing sliding open.

A smell like rotting meat found me; it was the same smell I'd encountered in my kitchen the previous night, it was the odor of Alice's rancid breath, predator stench. My stomach squirmed. Terry drew in a breath and flipped the plastic flaps aside, exposing a horrifically twisted shape that bore little resemblance to anything human. Teschal turned to me and, in spite of my stomach's protests, I stepped forward to get a better look at the thing lying on the gurney. I'd told myself that this would bring me closure. But at that moment, looking at Alice's remains, I realized that closure was something to be found much farther down the line, if ever.

What I saw lying there was a blackened husk that seemed trapped between heaven and hell, struck down in the midst of some ghastly transformation that left it forever in a state of wretchedness. The most obvious feature was the bruising; the skin was a deep shade of purple, tending toward black, giving the impression that the body had been burned in a terrible fire. Clumps of dark, coarse hairs were visible in places and the hair on the head was long and wild. The bones beneath the skin seemed to be bent at odd angles, as if they'd been broken and reset by a demented physician. The joints were swollen as if riddled with the ultimate case of arthritis, the fingers were too long and the knuckles too big and knobby for anything remotely human. The fingernails were thick, jagged and chipped and the feet were long and narrow and horribly misshapen.

Reluctantly I forced my gaze to shift to the face, which was by far the worst part. The eyes were terrible; the whites were the color of dull green mucous, the pupils were vivid green specks and they bulged from the head, swollen to such a size that the lids and cranial orbits could barely contain them. I half-expected those eyes to abruptly turn on me and stop my heart dead.

The ribs poked out in thick bunches like knotted cable and the jaw was that of an ape, thick and twisted. The teeth sprouted from the Neanderthal-like mandible in tangled clumps, and a swollen black length of cable that must once have been a tongue hung, partially severed, like a rotted umbilical cord.

"Mr. Graves?" Teschal prompted.

My mind began to race and I shook my head. No one else on Earth could identify the thing on the gurney as Alice Williams. That is, no one except Joanna.

Teschal nodded, a signal for Terry to seal the bag and put the monster back in its freezer.

"What was that?" I asked, my voice barely a whisper.

"We don't know," Teschal said. "We were hoping you could tell us."

She paused as if waiting for me to recant, but I remained silent, shocked, unprepared for what I had just seen and reluctant to provide Teschal with any missing puzzle pieces.

"The Medical Examiner is working under the impression that Mrs. Williams, if that *is* Mrs. Williams, was suffering from some rare disease," Teschal said as she led me toward the door. "Lion-face Syndrome, Human Wolf Syndrome, many other deforming diseases; these are all real conditions that might explain at least some of what you just saw. The body will be sent to Boston for a complete autopsy. The final answers will have to wait until that's finished. Until such time as DNA comparisons can be made, Mrs. Williams will continue to be listed as a missing person as well as a person of interest in her husband's murder."

The cold thing that had plagued me since Tuesday had gone; it left me about the time I got a good look at what remained of Alice. Perhaps it had been the realization, as Tom had suggested, that I, at some level, had known all along the identity of my stalker. Perhaps it had been nothing more than a nagging premonition, something people try desperately to ignore when they shouldn't. I suspected I would never know for sure.

I glanced back one last time, then Teschal and I left Terry to his gruesome business and walked down the corridor in silence to wait for the elevator, the sound of the drawer sliding back into its dark chamber a faint echo. As my head began to clear, I realized there were still some points I needed to sort out.

"You were in the cemetery," I said, breaking my silence.

"No," Teschal said, her eyes fixed on the elevator doors. "In the neighborhood, though."

"Why?"

"The officer posted at the hospital reported that you were heading home; I decided to monitor your movements, presuming our suspect would do the same. I'd pulled the cruiser from the front of Mr. Renko's house in hopes of our killer returning. I suspected there was something there he wanted and would return to find it. It was a long shot, and I must confess I never imagined it would turn out this way. Not in a million years."

"It took you a while to get there," I said.

Teschal sighed heavily. "I heard the ruckus. I wasn't sure what had happened. I saw the damaged cemetery fence first, then I drove to your house and saw the carnage there. I made a quick search, found Mr. Williams' remains in your bedroom, put in a call to secure the premises and headed off after you. I knew you'd come here."

I felt myself nodding.

"This morning," she continued, "while searching the cemetery, we found a broken baseball bat. Our lab is checking for blood."

It was my turn to sigh as Teschal considered me thoughtfully.

"My conclusion," she continued, "is that whoever that is in the morgue had some sort of psychological breakdown, probably due to an extreme medical condition. Perhaps your wife was kidnapped or persuaded to go along. If that *is* Mrs. Williams, I suspect that she and your wife go back a long way."

Teschal paused to let the possible implications sink in. They did, but I remained silent.

"The details," she continued, "are still sketchy, but I'll figure them out, given time. Judd had been involved with Mrs. Williams back when she was Debra Halston, probably knew both women and somehow got in the middle of it all. Money, drugs, sex. Love. Who can say?"

She considered me coolly, as if expecting me to add some missing information, then turned to study her reflection in the surface of the elevator door when I declined.

"Several people are dead and your wife is at the center of it all," Teschal said. "I suspect that Mr. Macyzk may have been an accomplice."

"An accomplice?" I said. Teschal was speculating.

"The crucial thing," she continued, undaunted, "is identifying that person in the morgue."

Teschal pursed her lips and sighed. "I suppose that a murderous rage like that could be the result of whatever syndrome that person in the morgue was suffering from. Perhaps, if that is Mrs. Williams, she was trying to recapture the past, a lost love, or some demented notion…" Teschal shrugged. "Anyway, that's how my report will read. And I won't be surprised if my captain throws it back in my face."

There was incredulity in her voice. Teschal was all business, and there was no room in her tidy world for unknowns. I must confess that if I had not known the truth, the idea of Alice Williams having killed all those people alone would seem incredible. But I knew otherwise. I had seen Alice when she was ten feet tall.

"Some of these ends may never be sewn up tightly," Teschal said with another sigh, "but I'll do my best."

The elevator arrived and we rode it up to the world of the living in silence. As we neared the lobby, Teschal, who had been staring at her reflection in the metal doors, said, "I shot something in the ICU last night."

She turned to me at this point and I saw something in her face, doubt, worry, I wasn't sure, but it was something that I suspected was completely alien to the face of Detective Teschal.

"If that *is* Mrs. Williams, perhaps you can explain how someone in her condition could not only kill so many people so viciously, but manage not to attract attention when she went out. Unless, of course, she never went out, which brings us back to the accomplice portion of my theory. But if that second person *was* Mr. Maczyk, well, he won't be talking any time soon."

Teschal considered me carefully and I her. What I saw was uncertainty, and I suspected that such a feeling was also something she was experiencing for the first time.

"Can you clarify any of this for me, Mr. Graves?"

There was an unexpected softening in her voice. If she'd been anyone but Teschal, I'd have said she was pleading with me to provide some comfort, some rationalization for what had happened, for what she'd seen. But I couldn't, so I said nothing. It was my turn to study my reflection.

The doors opened with a ping and Teschal lingered in the doorway for a moment, looking at me as if hoping

I'd reconsider my silence, for her sake more than mine. When I didn't, she thanked me for my time, her voice once again locked into its chilly, officious mode.

"And there is the matter of a certain police cruiser's broken window," she said.

I nodded solemnly.

"I'll be in touch," were her final words.

I watched her walk into the glaring early morning sunlight spilling in through the glass doors of the main entrance. Then the elevator doors closed and the elevator carried me back up to Joanna's floor, where I would check on my wife and try to get some more sleep.

Chapter Seventy-Five

A lice was gone. But Joanna had recovered, at least physically. My trip to the morgue had given me some insight into Alice's and Joanna's conditions. Joanna's bruising, which was concentrated around her joints and face, had begun turning green and fading. My time with Alice's corpse in the morgue revealed that her bruising had enveloped her entire body and its hue was much deeper. It was doubtless the result of a longer period of time spent in the guise of her fearsome alter ego.

Joanna's mood had been somber and irritable as of late, a change that, in hindsight, I attributed to the fact that she had become aware of Alice's losing battle with her strange affliction. I'd walked in on at least one phone call I believed to be from Alice where she must have been trying to convince Joanna that this new life wasn't working and it was time to leave it behind. This was doubtless the same tack Alice had used to try to convince Joanna to leave years earlier by means of the strange nocturnal phone calls we'd received. Who knew how many times that scenario had played out between the two of them over the years, each time ending with Joanna setting off with Alice, abandoning the life she'd established, perhaps abandoning those she'd come to love, in a haze of confusion or perhaps even in a pool of blood, depending upon Alice's mood.

I think Joanna had been trying to counsel Alice, trying to convince her not to give up this time, to give this new life a chance. But at some point, I suspect Alice had threatened to kill me and probably Tom as well if Joanna didn't comply, and to save me, Joanna had gone with Alice; she had surrendered to her own addiction and followed her terrible half-sister into the night for my sake.

Alice's inner turmoil had made her a bitter, angry recluse. I imagine that her condition had been poisoning her mind for some time. The damage she'd done to herself by changing might have been irreparable. The structural changes I'd noticed in her bones lingered after death, suggesting that prolonged transformations might eventually become irreversible, rendering her ability to become Alice again impossible.

I doubt Alice and Tom had been very intimate in their relationship toward the end, if ever, and perhaps Alice's enhanced animosity had kept him at arm's length and in the dark as to her true nature. After all, Joanna had managed to keep me in the dark for more than seven years; if not for the events of this past week, I might never have known.

Teschal had been right about one thing; Alice had remained behind closed doors for the most part, blaming ailing health on her seclusion. The few times I'd seen her, at the Fayre for instance, she'd been wearing long sleeves and a baseball cap in an effort to conceal the tell-tale bruising.

I also realized that whatever Alice had become would always have been there if she'd survived, lurking beneath the surface, waiting to be awakened even after she had reverted to her human form, even after the moon's influence had waned. I wondered just how much longer she'd have been able to retain the ability to change back, how many close calls she would have been allowed before the beast took her over entirely. Maybe she had already gone too far; maybe the moon's proximity to the Earth had driven her over the edge of reason once and for all.

Amidst all my theories and questions, I found my thoughts returning to the flicker of emotion I'd seen on Alice's face in the ICU as she turned to look at Joanna one last time. I'd been too terrified to put sense to it then, but since that awful night, I thought I'd deciphered it.

I imagine what I'd seen on Alice's twisted face in that shadowy moonlit room had been longing, or perhaps even sadness, and I found myself feeling pity for the terrible thing, pity for the loneliness that must have hounded its steps, pity for its desolate existence and its impossibly desperate need to keep another like it near. I found myself wondering if Joanna felt the same searing loneliness. I hoped not. I hoped I'd managed to bridge the distance between what she'd been and what she was becoming. I hoped I could continue to bridge the gap between the beast and the human being until the dark thing within her had vanished entirely or at least been relegated to a place so deep within her being that it might never be awakened, not by anger, not by the moon, and certainly not by a desperate friend from her terrible, tragic past.

Tom could never have formed a bridge for Alice; she never really wanted to give up her inner demon as I firmly believe Joanna did; *still* does. And Alice never loved Tom. He was just a means to an end, a way for her to remain close to Joanna. I believe these things; they are the only things that make sense. In the end, Alice lost her fight. Death had put an end to her loneliness, as well as her transformations.

Joanna and I were left to pick up the pieces. But we had one crucial thing that Alice never had; we had each other to hold onto and in the end, that's the only thing that matters.

New Moon: **The first phase of the moon's cycle, often associated with a fresh beginning**

After The Fire

Dr. Chalmers informed us that Joanna's tests were inconclusive and there was no immediate concern. The bruising faded as mysteriously as it had appeared. But Chalmers did say she would stay in touch, just in case, and that Joanna should step up her check-ups with her primary care physician, at least for a time. Joanna agreed, and that was that. The nightmare had ended, at least that phase of it. The rebuilding would, in a sense, be a nightmare of a different sort. Or at least that's how it looked from where I, from where *we*, were standing, having survived the 'fire,' so to speak.

Summing the whole thing up was tragically simple: one summer evening I paused to investigate something in my yard and nothing good came of it. I had refused to let sleeping dogs lie. Everything since has changed. Alice is gone; 'Gospel' Tom as well. And Renko. Reality has shifted as if under some great unseen weight and the world has evolved into some new place where the rules are vague and soft around the edges. I could analyze it all to death, but I am tired, too tired to relive it all in my search for meaning.

The universe continues to turn on its axis, briefly revealing its secrets, astonishing us, surprising us, terrifying us. But it continues to turn nonetheless, as if we were not here, moving along on its mysterious course like some great ship in the night. Tom once said in his irreverent way that some of us were destined to be kissed by the universe, while others were destined to be screwed by the universe, but most of us would have to settle for a polite handshake or a cordial wave. Joanna and I had landed somewhere in the middle.

378

To add to it all, I've been dreaming lately. In my dream, I see a man, Terry, from the morgue, driving an ambulance through the night. He is listening to the radio. Kate Nash. He hears a sound in the service bay of the vehicle, metal clanging against metal. He frowns, kills the radio, silencing the doo wops. The strange noise has stopped, but he pulls over onto the shoulder of the road nonetheless and climbs out into the night.

The man walks around to the ambulance bay doors, glancing warily at the dark trees lining the road as he proceeds, then at the full moon above. He finds one of the bay doors partly open, creaking in the wind; the bay is dark. He frowns at this, realizing that something is terribly wrong. He glances once more at the empty road, then climbs aboard through the open door. He fishes through a compartment in the side panel and produces a flashlight. Switching on the light, he pans the beam around. The gurney is lying on its side; the body bag that had once housed a corpse is torn to shreds. The man cocks his head, frowning. He gingerly lifts a flap of the body bag and, when he does, the flashlight beam swims across the scene behind him, revealing the thing that was once Alice Williams crouching there. Slowly, silently, its teeth glistening before the light, it rises from its crouch, its horrible talons poised to strike. And I awaken.

The image of that thing rising up behind the unsuspecting driver remains fresh in my mind as I struggle to chase the cobwebs of fear away, and I sit there in the late-night darkness, layered in sweat, my heart pounding against my ribs as I hug my knees to my chest. Inevitably my mind begins to revisit recent events. But thinking this way will only lead me into dark places. Perhaps, this time, I should let the past bury the past and start fresh. Perhaps that is best. I don't know if I can do this, being the curious type, the sort who insists on pursuing things to their often-bitter ends. But I'm willing to try, for my sake and Joanna's. In

Joanna's own words, this time, I should let sleeping dogs lie. I only hope that my dreams cooperate.

We've been home two weeks, trying to pick up the pieces, me keeping busy in the yard, replacing the garage door I ruined that fateful night and fixing the section of wood shingles from the corner of the house and those from the garage roof. Joanna is on the mend, but the process is slow. Some scars cannot be seen with the eyes and may take longer to heal, if ever. We are patient.

My questions abound, and perhaps they will all be answered in time, but for now Joanna is my wife, and I love her more than I can say and I will not press the issue. She has explained some things though, about how she'd come to New England, to Wickham, seeking a fresh start, and how she'd thought she'd found one until Alice reappeared.

"You must understand," Joanna began one evening as we sat on the patio admiring the sun-drenched field behind our house, "I was alone for so long, alone in ways no one can understand. Then I met Alice. We were the same. Only as time passed, I realized I wanted a life, a place to call home. I was tired of hiding, of living like a gypsy, keeping everyone at arm's length, moving from town to town, from shadow to shadow. I was tired of fearing the moon, fearing the feelings it evoked in me."

"Alice felt differently," she said after a reflective pause. "Alice *loved* the way the moon made her feel. She loved the power, and she'd use that power to threaten the ones I'd grown to like, those I'd come to love."

Joanna turned to me and I saw tears in her eyes.

"I never knew my parents. I grew up in an orphanage and ran away when I was nearly eighteen. I knew what I was. I found out one stormy night when I was thirteen or fourteen, but I never used it to hurt anyone, I swear."

She lowered her eyes and turned away. "I was ashamed of what I was. Alice wasn't. I was drawn to her, due, I suppose, to some primordial need for companionship, to be with someone like me, a kindred spirit. It seemed right, at first; comfortable, even. By the time I understood what she was capable of, it was too late. I shared her secrets with her, shared the knowledge of the things she'd done. Sometime she'd even show me. And we would run, escape into the night, into the company of our only friend, the moon."

"Are there others like you?" I dared to ask, afraid that Joanna might stop talking, and perhaps more afraid that she wouldn't.

"We found evidence of others along the way, but we never met any."

"And ... the heads?"

A sad grin briefly lit on my wife's face. "Alice knew better than to risk making more of us."

A chip of ice touched my heart when I heard that. It was a phrase that would run through my head like a broken tape loop in the wee hours of many nights to come. I would listen for the crickets chirping to make sure nothing was lurking outside, watch with cold dread for the sudden brightening of the sensor light above my garage and think of what Joanna had said about making *more like her*. And I would think of Teschal's loose ends, of Judd and Renko, of the vagrant in the woods and the teenagers in the West Pelham building, the old man barricaded in the bathroom at the hospital. And I would wonder about Tom's ex, Dale, who had mysteriously vanished, paving the way for Alice.

"She would have killed you," Joanna said, turning to me. "I couldn't let that happen, no matter what."

She reached out and touched my hand. Our fingers intertwined until one hand was almost indistinguishable from the other and we sat there, bathed in the shadow of our house, as the last rays of sunlight washed across the field where, as a boy, I'd played baseball.

I suppose Joanna and I have decisions to make.

Teschal is still lurking about; I see her, occasionally, parked in the cemetery in that big SUV of hers, watching. Twice she even knocked on our door and spoke to me, mostly about Joanna, who declined to speak to her. Finally I asked her to stay off the property as politely as possible, reminding her that the case had been officially closed. I used the word 'lawyer' and, sadly, in today's world, that is a word that accomplishes what many others cannot. She seems to have complied, but I know she is still there, waiting for one of her 'loose ends' to be sewn up. She's the sort who will never be satisfied until she knows the whole story, the sort who will pursue each thread to its bitter end, regardless of the lives that may become unraveled in the process. Much, perhaps, like me. I suppose I knew that about her the first time I saw her climbing out of her SUV in the middle of my street, the night of Renko's murder, with the lights from the surrounding police cruisers catching like flecks of lightning in her steel-blue eyes.

So Joanna and I are faced with options. Moving away from here is one such option. I haven't discussed it with her; she's too busy trying to be normal again. But I don't know if either of us could leave here, no matter what has happened. This is probably because in spite of the bad memories, there are many good ones. And this, then, is life in a nutshell, bits of good and bad, patches of light and dark.

But time passes. Joanna and I spend the evenings sitting on the patio, watching summer sunsets turn weeds into gold in the field behind our house. I can look at it now, that field, and though I can remember playing baseball out there, I have trouble remembering how it *felt* to play baseball out there. I suppose I will, from now on, have trouble remembering that. I don't know if that makes sense. It's as if some parts of me, the parts that feel certain things, have gone numb. I hope it's temporary, because I like remembering those things, things like what each of the

magnets on our refrigerator mean, why they were
purchased and how I felt at the time of each acquisition. I
find myself looking at those magnets, the ones that
survived what I silently refer to as my 'kitchen encounter,'
touching them, trying to feel again, and trying to remember
how to feel. It's like therapy, and I suppose we could both
use some of that. Tossing Teschal's business card in the
trash was a step in the right direction.

But there are the bad memories as well, too many
bad memories to block out entirely. I have to deal with
those if I am to get on with life. Each time the sensor light
above the garage doors brightens, my heart starts to race.
And sometimes, when I look out at the field, I find myself
thinking back to the night when I watched two crooked,
misshapen figures move past what had once been first base
in a child's game of baseball. I remember watching them
pass through the moonlight and shadow as if they had been
born of those parents, and I find myself having to look
away.

The Thunder moon has come and gone and it will
be thousands of years before it is as close to Earth as it was
that fateful week. I'm glad we won't be around for it.

Renko's house stands empty; it probably will for
some time. Rufus has come home, though; he lives with us
now, much to Spooky's displeasure. He probably still feels
like a stranger here, but he's a stranger who saved my life
one dark night and so far as I'm concerned he can leave all
the 'deposits' in my yard he wants; they're not necessarily
good for the lawn, but after all that's happened, all that
Rufus and I have been through together, I couldn't bring
myself to complain.

Joanna is sitting beside me now on the patio,
Spooky lying devotedly at her feet. Rufus is lying at the
base of the maple tree, considering a flock of Canada geese
flying overhead in V formation. My wife's face is still pale.
She isn't free of the specter yet; I can see it in her eyes,

383

especially when a shadow crosses her face, or when the moonlight touches her skin. It may take a long time; worthwhile things usually do. Yet at some level I can't help but feel betrayed. I have been sharing my life with a stranger for seven years, living with a woman concealing secrets I could never have imagined. And the truth was so close, in the guise of the woman married to my best friend, a friend I will miss in ways no words can explain. The hurt is there, like an open wound that will take time to heal. But at the same time, I realize that there was no way she could have told me the truth before I saw it with my own eyes. So in time, the anger will fade and I will survive. Joanna is worth it. *We* are worth it.

Joanna looks to me, streaks of white in her jet-colored hair where no streaks had ever been, her eyes somehow older and perhaps wiser, but no less beautiful, filled with love for me as the final glimmer of daylight fades and she takes my hand and whispers her mantra, "One day at a time."

I squeeze her hand. She saved my life, and I saved hers. We belong to each other in ways no one can understand, and I will grapple with all the moonlight in creation to hold on to her.

"Tell me again," she says, resting her head against my shoulder.

"Tell you what?"

"Tell me how you used to play baseball out there in that field?"

She smiles and with the first glimpse of twilight, I begin my tale again.

About the Author:

I was born in Fall River, Massachusetts in 1961. I have earned a Bachelor of Arts degree in Theater as well as two teaching certificates and a Master's degree in Education. I have worked for more than thirty years in the field of education. My passions include reading, writing, my drums, and the beach. I currently live in the south coast region of Massachusetts with my wife Robin and our Lhasa Apso, Scarlett.

Acknowledgements:

To Anthony Kohler, my editor, many thanks, and all the folks at Solstice for their faith and support. To Nicky Archembault for her advice and encouragement. And to my mother for giving my 7th grade English teacher one of my screenplays when I was twelve years old, which started this whole thing rolling. A special thanks to Kathy O'Riordan for the amazing photograph of me that she took for the back cover.